PRAISE FOR JACKIE FRENCH

'A rollicking plotline, complete with romance, murder, mystery and gold-chasing adventure. The world she's created is utterly immersive. Fans of French are in for a real treat.'
— Better Reading on *The Sea Captain's Wife*

'A work of an exceptional storyteller, crammed full of love and hope for the future.'
— Good Reading on *The Sea Captain's Wife*

'A master storyteller ... [she] gives women a rich, strong, and brutally honest voice.'
— Better Reading on *Clancy of the Overflow*

'The story is equal parts *Downton Abbey* and wartime action, with enough romance and intrigue to make it 100% not-put-down-able.'
— *Australian Women's Weekly* on *Miss Lily's Lovely Ladies*

'Heartwarming, heartbreaking and hard to put down.'
— *Australian Women's Weekly* on *If Blood Should Stain the Wattle*

'Agnes Mulberry changes the lives of everyone she meets in this wonderful, heartfelt story from the inimitable Jackie French.'
— Victoria Purman, bestselling Australian author, on *Becoming Mrs Mulberry*

'This magnificent tale of Agnes Glock, a young Australian woman for whom WWI changes everything, is both sweeping in scope and yet heart-achingly intimate. Set mainly in post-war country NSW and featuring a cast of characters who've been irrevocably altered by the ferocity of global conflict, it's a story about loss, sacrifice and difference; about how compassion and kindness can be the most courageous of acts.'

— Karen Brooks, bestselling Australian author, on *Becoming Mrs Mulberry*

'A captivating masterpiece — insightful, humorous and heart-wrenching. A total delight.'

— Tea Cooper, bestselling Australian author, on *Becoming Mrs Mulberry*

'With her effortless prose and enormous empathy, Jackie French tells a captivating story of personal growth, of generosity in its true sense and ultimately one of courage and hope. Not to be missed.'

— Darry Fraser, bestselling Australian author, on *Becoming Mrs Mulberry*

'Jackie French has created an authentic post-WWI Australia filled with vivid images of a damaged world and broken survivors trying to put themselves back together. This book grabs you from the very first paragraph and doesn't let go till the very last — a story of healing and hope.'

— Robbi Neal, bestselling Australian author, on *Becoming Mrs Mulberry*

JACKIE FRENCH AM is an award-winning author, historian and ecologist. She was the 2014–2015 Australian Children's Laureate and the 2015 Senior Australian of the Year. In 2016 Jackie became a Member of the Order of Australia for her significant contribution to literature and youth literacy. She is regarded as one of Australia's most popular authors with her vast body of work crossing the threshold of genres and reading ages, and ranging from fiction, non-fiction, picture books, ecology, fantasy and sci-fi to her much-beloved historical fiction.
jackiefrench.com
facebook.com/authorjackiefrench

THE WHISPERER'S WAR

JACKIE FRENCH

THE WHISPERER'S WAR
© 2025 by Jackie French
ISBN 9781038903891

First published on Gadigal Country in Australia in 2025
by HQ Fiction
an imprint of HQBooks (ABN 47 001 180 918), a subsidiary of HarperCollins Publishers Australia Pty Limited (ABN 36 009 913 517).

HarperCollins acknowledges the Traditional Custodians of the lands upon which we live and work, and pays respect to Elders past and present.

The moral right of the author has been asserted in accordance with the *Copyright Amendment (Moral Rights) Act 2000*.

This work is copyright. Apart from any use as permitted under the *Copyright Act 1968*, no part may be reproduced, copied, scanned, stored in a retrieval system, recorded, or transmitted, in any form or by any means, without the prior written permission of the publisher. Without limiting the author's and publisher's exclusive rights, any unauthorised use of this publication to train generative artificial intelligence (AI) technologies is expressly prohibited.

This is a work of fiction. Unless otherwise indicated, names, characters, places, and incidents are either the product of the author's imagination or are used fictitiously, and any resemblance to actual persons, living or dead, business establishments, events, or locales is entirely coincidental.

A catalogue record for this book is available from the National Library of Australia
www.librariesaustralia.nla.gov.au

Printed and bound in Australia by McPherson's Printing Group

To Lisa and Julia: thank you for sending me time travelling again to write about royal myths and secrets, so stubbornly kept for over 100 years.

Prologue

Claverton Castle, 30 September 1938

Fish Pie
A delicate dish for an invalid.

INGREDIENTS
Potato Topping
six boiled potatoes
two steamed carrots
eight tablespoons best butter
six tablespoons new cream
six tablespoons finely chopped chives
Fish
one white fish, the length of a man's foot
one cup white wine
four tablespoons cream
three tablespoons chopped parsley
three bay leaves
juice one lemon
tablespoon cornflour

METHOD

Mash the potato topping ingredients together. Simmer fish with wine, cream, parsley and bay leaves for five minutes. Remove the fish skin, head and bones. Mix the lemon juice with the cornflour. Add to the now cool fish and simmer till thickened. More liquid may be needed for a larger fish. Place the fish and its sauce in a dish. Top with potato. Bake till brown on top.

Lady Amelia Claverton, 1892

'A bloody peace treaty?' Deanna could hardly hear the duke's trembling voice over the BBC static. 'The only thing this treaty has won is war with Germany within a year. Chamberlain's a blithering idiot.'

Dusty lifted his shaggy head, startled, the rest of him stretched along the hearth to absorb the warmth of the tiny fire, crouched like a small cat in the giant fireplace of Claverton Castle's kitchen, the only room now occupied despite the shabby vastness beyond. He sniffed hopefully at the fish pie his master had failed to eat.

'Dusty! No!' Deanna woke from her nap in the armchair next to the duke's just as Dusty's tongue reached the potato topping. She removed the tray from her grandfather's lap. He'd moved there weeks earlier, in the only room they could manage to heat.

Dusty sighed. He settled his nose back on the hearthrug as Deanna blinked herself properly awake. Her grandfather's cough had worsened as the cancer tore through his lungs. She'd had little sleep during her vigil the previous night as he sipped morphia and vomited blood on her shoulder, and a long hard day already. 'Only a few days to go, now,' the doctor had said, with the vague helplessness of a man who wished he could do more.

The dream had come again in this afternoon's nap. It was the dream she'd had since childhood: walking between cliffs as a sunlit stream snaked over the stones at her feet. Once through those cliffs there'd be safety, but no matter how often the dream came to her, she could never find her way through.

Maybe that's because there *is* no safety to be found in the world, she thought, even here at Claverton Castle.

Twenty years after the Great War, England was again on the brink of combat as Adolf Hitler invaded country after country to create 'the Greater Germany'.

London's office windows had been sandbagged; air-raid trenches were dug in public parks. Britons queued for hours for ration books and gas masks. Even the keepers at London Zoo had their firearms ready in case bombs freed lions or leopards to terrorise the city.

But she'd had the dream long before the threat of war. The fashionable Freudians would say it had something to do with sex, but then they said that about everything. She couldn't understand the fuss about sex. She'd never felt desire for a man, nor a woman either. Time was better spent cooking a good apple pie, sewing a dress to last a lifetime, or watching an eagle swoop down to grab a rabbit then use the updraft to soar up without a single flap of its wings. *That* was interesting. Yet the limited convolutions of two bodies seemed as fascinating to most people as war and sport.

At least one could dodge football matches. There seemed little chance of avoiding war.

She picked up her needle and returned to sewing what would be the skirt of her new dinner dress, made from the gold satin opera cloak of the second duchess. The wireless muttered on the mantelpiece as the prime minister's plane drew closer to landing. Her grandfather's eyes shuttered and his chin dropped to his chest.

Deanna yawned, despite the nap. She'd dug potatoes most of the morning after helping her grandfather wash and change into clean pyjamas. Then there'd been the fish pie to make, and plum jam expected from her for the Women's Institute sale.

Now she hoped for an hour's quiet sewing before heading out into the estate to add to their store of firewood. This winter would be a cold one. The hawthorn berries in the hedges were already deep red and the squirrels had been hoarding acorns industriously.

Dusty rolled over on the hearth to warm his other side.

Dusty had been born grey, a mixed breed that was all his own: long-legged, hungry and hairy. He had learned early that pretending to be old meant he could spend his days dozing, having his belly scratched, and his dinners served by Deanna. He had already gobbled his own portion of the pie. Dusty, at least, was not worried by the news on the wireless.

Deanna held the skirt up to check its length: the dress design was working out well. No one would guess the age of the glowing fabric, or that it had been stored in the Claverton attics for over a hundred years. She had neither wanted nor could afford a London Season, but old schoolfriends still invited her to dinners and parties. Her grandfather had made her promise not to wear mourning for him, nor to live it, either.

The duke stirred again as sudden cheers echoed from the wireless. 'Sheep following a leader,' he muttered. 'So they can avoid seeing the slaughterhouse ahead.'

Shadows suddenly flickered above the tangled gardens. Deanna peered out the window as three golden eagles soared through the sunlight, the two adults with their massive wings and talons and a new white-patched juvenile, hunting for rabbits in the tangle that had once been the Great Lawn and was now the Monstrous Mess.

'Look! There's an eagle fledgling!' she cried, trying to distract the old man. The duke's love for the almost-extinct birds was as great as hers. His last days should contain joy, not the misery of war to come.

The eagles barely glanced at the castle with its turrets leaning at each corner of the vast structure. Only the rooks that nested in thirty-seven of its thirty-eight chimneys were of any interest to them. The thirty-eighth chimney had crumbled after the last storm, narrowly missing Mr Higgins come to deliver the milk.

Claverton was a classic castle, seemingly nestled in the soil of England, though that was merely because it lacked proper foundations and had been slowly sinking for generations.

Even eagles didn't rouse her grandfather. 'Bombs over Britain,' he muttered. 'A country that can't even feed itself. Saw it in the last war. Now we'll have it here. Starvation, surrender, then slavery ...' He nodded back into a doze.

He had assured her that he wanted no other nurse. It was more likely, Deanna thought, as she tried to make out the BBC announcer's voice through the static of the wireless, that they could not afford one.

She put down her sewing and tried to adjust the static on the wireless. Prime Minister Chamberlain's plane had just touched down.

Was there a remote chance the treaty with Germany would last? Most of England seemed to think it would. The duke claimed that whatever the majority believed was usually wrong. Clavertons were like eagles, he decreed, seeing the earth below with telescopic vision, able to make connections impossible for the sheep below.

Deanna admired her grandfather as well as loved him. He truly was an eagle. She suspected she might be one herself, but she'd seen no evidence that any previous Clavertons had been eagle-eyed, including the one who had been given a dukedom for marrying Charles II's pregnant mistress.

The BBC announcer's voice rose again. 'And there is the prime minister, waving the treaty triumphantly. He *sppt shhhpht*.' The wireless hiccupped into static.

'Turn it off, girl.' The duke opened his eyes. He coughed again. 'Germany has been preparing for war for a decade. We tricked our king into abdicating instead. David would have given us an alliance, not a damn treaty. He admired Hitler, and Hitler knew it.'

Dusty farted, then looked embarrassed. Fish pie didn't agree with him.

The duke sipped the water Deanna held to his lips, then waved it away. 'A treaty isn't worth the paper it's written on. An alliance would let us keep our freedom. That's what David was working towards.' The duke used the private name of the man who had been King Edward VIII before his abdication.

'An alliance with a country sending anyone who disagrees with it to labour camps? Confiscating Jewish property? A leader who is a warmonger?'

'I didn't say I liked the man. Hitler's taken Germany from bankruptcy to domination in five years. You have two choices with a man like that. We either give all we have to beat him, or declare ourselves neutral, like Switzerland and Spain. We're doing neither.'

'There have to be other choices,' Deanna protested.

Another snort, and another fart from Dusty. 'If there are, then no one's found them yet. The history of the world is the history of its wars.'

'Maybe no one's bothered to record the times war was averted.' Deanna would have liked to study history at Oxford, but even though her title meant she would have been granted a degree no matter how poor her work, the cost was prohibitive. Nor could she demean the name of Claverton by taking a scholarship. Besides, by the time she left school her grandfather had needed her, both to run the estate and to care for him.

He managed a smile at her. 'You've got sense, Dee. More than your father ever had. But if the best of the Clavertons is going to survive this war she needs to get ready for it now.'

He lay back, obviously in pain, but he waved away the morphia bottle she held up. 'Had a letter from Chummy last week. You know, my friend in the War Office? Herr Hitler's offered to make David king again once Britain is defeated.'

'Seriously? In the same week Hitler signed the Peace Treaty with Mr Chamberlain? Besides, David was an impossible king. If David *had* arranged an alliance, it would all have been to Hitler's benefit.'

Deanna had known the former King Edward VIII slightly but had not cared to be one of his mistresses. Britain was still ruled by its 'upper 600 families'. Impoverished or not, the Clavertons were one of them. Deanna had heard about the top secret 'red boxes' passed by the king to Germany before he signed its papers, of official events cancelled because the king failed to appear, and an embarrassment of gossip about the notorious divorcee he wished to marry. Mrs Simpson had been the mistress of the German ambassador even when supposedly in love with the king, paid to spy for Germany on top of the money showered on her by the obsessed and none-too-bright monarch.

Dusty rolled over and wagged his shaggy tail to entice the duke to scratch his tummy. The duke obeyed. 'Ha. All politics is show. David is a fool, and his wife a trollop, but she knows that what matters happens behind the scenes. She's the one who leaked the news of their affair to the American papers. The English ones wouldn't touch it with a barge pole. She as good as blackmailed the poor fool into marrying her. But if Simpson had been queen by now, she'd have made sure we had an alliance on decent terms, not war looming at our backs.'

'We can't have a man like Hitler as an ally!'

The duke peered at her from half-shut eyes. 'And we can't win a war against him, not without America and Russia. The last war showed us that. Better England stays free than the whole of Europe be under Hitler's boot. But not with David as king.'

Deanna put another careful stitch into the cloth of gold.

The last time Deanna met him at a cocktail party, King Edward VIII had enthusiastically praised Hitler and his plan to create a master race by getting rid of those not fit to breed — another reason to avoid cocktail parties, and London.

But David was now merely the Duke of Windsor, living in France and married to the woman who had played him for money and information for Germany. He had lost his estates, most of his income, even the right to live in Britain when he signed the abdication papers without even reading them, believing he was being made King Regent for his ten-year-old niece, Elizabeth, and so able to marry whomever he wanted, but with all the power of a king.

When he had discovered the truth the next morning, he had written a speech calling on the people of England to rebel and make him king again. Prime Minister Baldwin had finally convinced the duke to read the speech Baldwin had written for him instead: a romantic claim that the ex-king had given up the throne for the woman he loved. The public was still happier to accept this myth than believe they'd had a traitor king who those in power — including his mother and brother — had agreed must go.

A gullible man, and a stupid one. And yet her grandfather, who was neither, was almost certainly correct. This treaty would be useless, despite the public's cheers. For all his foolishness, David — or his wife — might just have steered Britain into true neutrality, convincing Hitler that his main enemies were the communist Soviets to the north. Instead, Germany and the Soviet Union were allies.

She looked up from the fabric on her lap and found the duke watching her.

'I won't be here to see it,' he wheezed. 'It's you who needs providing for.'

Deanna did not dispute either statement. The title and the estate would be inherited by her second cousin Donald, raised in California by his now-dead banker father, and rich enough to regard a castle with twenty-six bedrooms — not counting staff quarters — and a single bathroom as a useful adjunct to the title. Donnie had adored Claverton as a child. He'd restore it beautifully as its duke. Americans liked titles.

But so did most people. Deanna's own title would hopefully secure her a position at a London fashion house, though the loss to come left her weeping at night.

'I can care for myself,' she assured him.

Her grandfather peered from under shaggy white eyebrows. 'You shouldn't have to care for yourself. Now, if you marry—'

'I won't marry,' she said flatly.

'You can't know that.'

Deanna shrugged, focusing on her sewing. Her blonde beauty and her title had won her two proposals, despite having no dowry and being the daughter of Viscount 'Mad Monty' Claverton, killed in a car race three months before her birth, and an actress who had abandoned her baby daughter to her paternal grandparents, then died in what the newspapers dubbed 'an illegal operation' when Deanna was two years old.

Deanna had accepted neither proposal. She would rather live as a couturier than be an upper-class wife, supervising housekeepers and entertaining to enhance her husband's position. She loved Claverton for its land, not as mistress of its castle. But neither would be hers for long.

'I could marry Donnie,' she suggested, trying to make the old man smile. 'He even proposed to me, you know.'

She and Donnie had both been twelve during his sole visit to the estate he'd inherit, the two of them climbing trees together and exploring the cave under Miss Enid's cottage at Eagle's Rest that they'd pretended was a smuggler's hideout. They'd even written to each other for a year or so, till the correspondence tailed off.

Her grandfather snorted, coughed, then managed a self-satisfied grin. 'No need. You won't have to live on his charity, either. You've inherited Eagle's Rest — the house and land and a tiny income, too.' He waited smugly for her reaction.

The gold skirt dropped to the floor.

'What? How?' She'd loved the house with its crooked chimneys all her life. The house and its land adjoined the estate, about five miles by car or ten minutes on her bicycle from the castle. She'd loved its former owner, too. Miss Enid Constable had been an avid ornithologist, studying and protecting the rare golden eagles that lived on the cliffs and headland of her property and fished in its shallow twist of river wandering down to the sea.

Miss Enid had given the young Deanna seed cake, which she had hated; advice on dressing, which she had mostly ignored ('You cannot go wrong with a good tweed suit, my dear'); and a depth of knowledge of the land around them that surpassed even her grandfather's.

Deanna and Miss Enid had watched badgers spring clean their dens in the twilight as their young tumbled and played. They'd shared binoculars to study the eagles building their precarious twig nests on rock edges. Miss Enid had taught her young neighbour how to trap a rabbit, skin it and simmer it in red wine and herbs, and how to make a napkin when her first period arrived.

But Miss Enid had died of pneumonia two years earlier, after sitting up nights with a young female eagle, the edge of its wing shattered by gunshot, coaxing it to eat and drink. Deanna had released it three months later after placing a blue band on its leg, exulting despite her grief as it flapped three times then soared towards the hills by the sea.

Her grandfather laughed at her shock, then had a coughing fit. Deanna held his medicine to his lips till it subsided. 'Enid made me your trustee.' He paused to take two crackling breaths. 'Wasn't to let you know about it till you turned twenty-five.'

Which would be next week. They both knew he might not live that long.

Indignation mixed with joy and incredulity. 'Why wait two years to tell me?'

'In case loyalty to those blasted eagles stopped you marrying and moving away.'

Deanna shook her head, still trying to take it in. The castle could crumble or Donnie fill it with American bankers for all she cared. She was staying with the land she loved!

'Miss Enid never wanted to be married.'

'She'd have liked to,' the duke said flatly.

'Someone lost in the Great War?' There had been no black-draped photos in the solid old house.

'No. Me. I'd have married her, too.'

Deanna stared at her grandfather in shock. And yet, now she thought about it, a secret love affair explained a lot.

'Your grandmother refused to divorce me. The title meant too much to her.'

Deanna absorbed this. Grandmama was a remote vision who'd dutifully appeared each year for her birthday in the latest Chanel outfit, then vanished to spend the last of the Claverton fortune partying with friends in Cannes, leaving behind inappropriate gifts — a Cubist ivory ashtray, or a teddy bear when Deanna turned ten. Her death a year back had left only the ripple of her funeral in the family chapel.

Miss Enid and her grandfather must have been discreet. Not for Deanna, who'd been away at boarding school often enough for them to meet, but for the village, though there were no houses between here and Eagle's Rest, and it had been seven years since her grandfather could afford servants, except Mrs Thripps, who came twice a week to do the scrubbing.

'You've been the one renovating the house,' Deanna realised. Even Mr Sweetie the postmaster and Doris at the telephone exchange had been unable to find out who paid the workmen who'd been busy at Eagle's Rest on and off since Miss Enid's death.

Mrs Thripps still cleaned Eagle's Rest once a week. Two new glasshouses had been filled with manure beds and potted orange, peach, apricot and lemon trees with coal heaters, Mr Sweetie said — Maggie who did the postal run had peered in. There were also empty beds, presumably for vegetables such as tomatoes and cucumbers that needed more heat than the timid English sun could provide.

But even Maggie couldn't report on the condition of the house. The windows had been covered with newspaper, Mr Sweetie reported regretfully. Mrs Thripps had been smugly silent on the subject. But the woodshed had been stocked, and with a bigger, neater pile than that at the castle. For her, Deanna realised.

She found the duke watching her closely. 'I've had Higgins take stuff down there from the castle while you were out shopping. Furniture. Books ...' he added, still smug, wiping a thread of phlegm from his lips.

Mr Higgins rented the farm next to Eagle's Rest from the estate. He must know too, thought Deanna. 'I thought it all went to Donnie!'

'Not quite all.'

'What's not included?'

He gave a tremulous grin. 'I own Higgins's farm. And anything the solicitors, ahem, haven't bothered to notice over the years, such as the contents of the attics. Higgins will shift the chests down to the Rest tomorrow.'

'*What?*' Those chests of old family clothes, faded curtains, or sheets no one had got round to mending had been her treasure since childhood. Four hundred years of dresses, hats, silk stockings and feathers wrapped in tissue paper she'd used to play dress-ups as Queen Elizabeth or a cavalier and eventually learned to repurpose as the outfits she needed as she grew older.

'I've a few other surprises to help you through the years to come,' the duke said. 'I told you before I'd make provision for you.'

She had taken that as the ramblings of a dying man on morphia. For some reason his mind seemed more focused today.

He paused to catch his breath. 'It's going to be bad, Dee my darling,' he said at last. 'Hitler knows people want to be led. He's good at doing it.'

Deanna sat silent. She couldn't remember the Great War. She knew all too clearly its aftermath — men crippled in mind and body, the destruction of the German economy, paying reparations for a war they hadn't lost.

'I'll probably be conscripted,' she said at last. 'There'll be more women in uniform this time.'

'I'm not having my granddaughter chauffeuring some puffed-up grocer they've made a major. I've provided for you there, too. You'll inherit Higgins's farm from me. Higgins will stay as tenant, in exchange for doing whatever carting and ploughing you need. Put the Eagle's Rest back paddock in potatoes. With the paddock and the farm you'll be classified a farmer, a reserved occupation with no danger of being called up.'

'I don't want to sit out the war growing potatoes—' she began stubbornly.

'I should think not. You're a Claverton! Chummy will contact you after I'm gone. Good man, Chummy. I was at school with him. You'll supply ... information.'

'Information? About potatoes?' A spike of adrenaline as she realised what he meant. 'You expect me to be a spy?' she asked incredulously.

'The preferred term is "intelligence officer". You've got brains and you know people who matter. You'll make a good one.'

'I don't understand. I'm the last person in the world anyone would choose as a spy.'

'Which is why you'd be unlikely to be detected.'

'Grandpa, how on earth could I be a spy? I don't even speak fluent French, much less German.'

'You'll be gathering information here in England, finding the Nazi sympathisers, and those who might do more than just sympathise. The whole damn government is rotten with fascists, and maybe a quarter of "our kind" admire Hitler, too. You mix with the right people. You'll hear things.'

He looked at her keenly, despite his trembling hands. 'Battles don't decide wars, Dee. The people who direct them do that. Germany lost the last war because its army refused to fight any longer, but ours — most of 'em — stayed loyal. Germany was winning in 1918, you know, despite America joining the war.'

Deanna nodded. Even her school friends' parents had accepted this. Patriotism meant proclaiming 'We won the war' instead of

'Germany was tricked into disbanding their army by a ceasefire treaty that France had no intention of obeying'.

'The Germans were better prepared than us then, and they are now too. I'd like to think we'd win this time, but now ...'

The duke shrugged. 'Chamberlain is no leader. Nor is the king. He's a nice chap, but that's not enough. His wife does better, but accepting bouquets doesn't win battles. Once war comes there'll be those who think our best chance is a genuine treaty with Germany, and the man to negotiate that is the king we lost.'

'David's no Bonnie Prince Charlie, a king across the water who men will flock to.'

'Doesn't matter. He'd be a figurehead. People liked the public image the press gave them, the charmer who wept for starving miners. Hitler would keep a tighter rein on him than Baldwin ever did. And that,' he added, 'is the problem. David was a disastrous king two years ago. He'd be a tragedy of a ruler with Hitler as his guide.'

She sat silent, considering it all. 'I have to think about it,' she said at last. 'Spying on my friends ...'

'On new acquaintances — I doubt your friends are fascists. You'll be doing it for your country. You'll do it because you're a Claverton and won't want to knit while others fight!' He snorted again. 'You have your think, my girl, then you'll do what's right. Meanwhile you'll have these.'

He reached slowly into the pocket under his jumper and drew out a small velvet bag. He held it out to her.

The bag was warm from his body. The stones inside were warm too, and glittered in the firelight.

'Diamonds, and good ones.' He coughed, twice. 'I've had Mr Vonderfleet looking out for perfect stones since the day I first held you.' The old man never talked about his son, her father.

Deanna realised her grandfather had assumed he would be her true guardian even before 'Mad Monty' died.

There had to be at least twenty here, or more. 'How could you afford them?' She'd assumed her grandmother, school fees, taxes, and the most essential repairs on the estate had eaten any spare income.

'Ah.' The old face looked undeniably pleased with itself. 'I did what my father did, and his before me, though I only found out after his death. Vonderfleet and Sons have been converting the Claverton jewels into copies for three generations now. My father wanted money for horses. I wanted money for you. Let the American chap think he's getting the Claverton jewels with the estate. Take one of those stones to Vonderfleet whenever you need money. They'll give you a good price on them, and ask no questions, because they know the answers.'

'Grandpa, that's ...'

'Illegal?' The grin was impish this time.

'I was going to say "brilliant". Thank you.'

'You need to meet Chummy,' he said sleepily. He seemed relaxed suddenly, as if he could finally release the reins of life. 'Good chap. Spymaster or not, Chummy's our kind of people ... Sheep, that's what most people are. The Clavertons are the eagles looking down ...'

And picking off the weakest lambs, she thought, just as her grandfather had obviously misled Donnie's father about the jewels. She had no illusions about the birds she loved, or her grandfather. But she said nothing as his head drooped, simply took his cold hand. He began to snore.

One

Eagle's Rest, November 1940

You ask, what is our aim? I can answer that in one word: it is victory, victory at all costs, victory in spite of all terror, victory, however long and hard the road may be; for without victory, there is no survival.

Sir Winston Churchill, May 1940

Her world these days was cow shit, handing out prizes for the biggest, most inedible marrows, and flattering fascists who'd drunk too much port. Deanna shovelled yet another spadeful of fresh manure into the glasshouse's cucumber bed.

In the past week she'd worn draped green silk that clung to her figure while smiling admiringly at a Home Office official who declared Hitler 'a jolly good sport who shows those Jews and communists a thing or two'.

She'd worn blue linen with orange piping and a hat decorated with chrysanthemums to present the awards at Claverton Minor's Harvest Festival. Otherwise she pulled on gardener's overalls each day, stiff with manure, and a pair of green wellington boots, and wrapped her hair in a linen tea towel instead of a

17

silk scarf — something that could be soaked in bleach each night to keep her hair clean.

I bet Mata Hari never shovelled cow shit, she thought as a hunk of muck mixed with hay dropped inside her collar. She fished it out, rubbed ineffectually at the stain on her bra, then picked up her shovel again. The decomposing manure's heat helped grow vegetables like winter cucumbers and tomatoes, luxuries which fetched such high prices from the rich in wartime. Half the potatoes that grew in the field behind the house had to be sold to the government. She gave what she didn't need away.

The people of Claverton Minor — her village and responsibility, even if she no longer lived in the castle — had to be fed. Potatoes and onions weren't rationed, but all food was scarce. A housewife had to queue for hours to feed her family, only to find the shelves empty when she finally reached the counter; and what if she had a war job, or babies, or it was raining?

She stopped to take a swig of tea from her thermos. The manure was delivered by Joe Higgins and his draught horses, who pulled his cart as well as his plough. Those draught horses had undoubtedly been a factor when her grandfather made his preparations for her.

The conversation the night of Chamberlain's return had been their last, though he had lingered, semi-conscious, for another week, until the day after her birthday. She had never had a chance to thank him, in her shock and wonder, when she found out exactly how much he'd 'provided for her' at Eagle's Rest. He had even been correct about her 'intelligence collecting'.

She was good at it. The amount of pro-German sentiment among the influential upper classes, both those born to the aristocracy and the wealthy who had bought their way to influence, had shocked her, even though many of the upper classes — and lower ones — had made no secret of admiring fascism before the war. She couldn't guess how many of those who still admired Hitler would actively support an alliance with Germany, much less spy for them. Others would collate, cross-check and analyse the snippets of intelligence to decide that. Her job was simply to report who said what, and what those already in authority said after three kinds of wine at dinner and madeira afterwards, with a beautiful young woman listening admiringly to every word. Others would decide who should be watched, or removed from positions of authority.

She still felt uncomfortable abusing her friends' hospitality to connive invitations to the houses of pre-war fascists, all now tactfully silent or pompously patriotic in public. She also deeply missed the time she might have spent with real friends instead. But the information she was gathering from Britain's politically tight network of titled or powerful families might prove vital in the months ahead.

Increasingly those influential families were leaning towards 'peace at any price'. The loss of the air force at the ill-fated defence of Denmark, the recent capture and disintegration of the British army at Dunkirk and the thunder of German bombers destroying Britain's port areas and factories had led even those only vaguely fascist before the war to whisper that England should forge an alliance now, before Hitler finally crossed the Channel.

How long before those murmurs became demands?

Better to accept an alliance with Germany while Hitler was still generous enough to offer it than to see their country destroyed, her people enslaved in revenge, Britain's factories given to prominent Nazis to produce whatever was needed to expand the Third Reich's empire across the world.

Deanna made no direct reports; nor had she any direct link to the intelligence agencies. Instead she wrote to 'Uncle Jasper', the 'Chummy' she'd met only once at a Lyons tea shop in London: two pages filled with gossip that contained code words and phrases to cover whatever information she had gathered. Uncle Jasper's replies to her were also seemingly family news — unless you knew the cipher.

But the next dinner party was days away; nor were there any marrows to judge, nor village school plays to applaud. Tonight she could scrub off the manure in the scullery, then take a long deep bath in violet-scented salts — Eagle's Rest had its own water tank and no worries about water rationing, and Miss Enid had either had an inordinate passion for violet bath salts or else she'd hated them and stored every packet she had been given in the linen cupboard.

Miss Enid had not had to spend her days shovelling manure.

After her bath Deanna could pull the blackout curtains, lift the rooster casserole from the oven where it had been not-quite-simmering all day with a dozen potatoes in their jackets she'd added at lunchtime that would last her all week, then put her feet up and share dinner with Dusty, currently asleep in the shade of an apple tree.

Most of Britain's pet dogs, cats and retired but beloved horses had been put down in the first days of the war by government decree. Food must be kept for those who fought. What was left was needed for the children and essential workers. There was no ration for pets, except a few well-connected registered pedigree breeders. But Dusty thrived on leftovers, apart from the usual indigestion of a dog who chewed the leg of a two-week-dead sheep with as much enjoyment as a slice of Deanna's toast and blackberry jelly, unaware of the 'death by vet' fate of the beloved dogs of Britain.

Bees buzzed dutifully, as if also directed by government order, in and out of the glasshouse door, over past the woodland, around the hall. Aircraft buzzed, louder but presumably also dutifully.

Claverton Castle had been requisitioned six months earlier, apart from a few sheds that stored the most valuable furniture the present duke had inherited. The main building was a military hospital and the outbuildings quarters for pilots and ground crew for the new aerodrome, though 'aerodrome' seemed too grand a word for two small huts, a runway, and a hangar that hopefully hid its role under camouflage nets and was too small a target for a German plane to notice.

Deanna had overseen it all in her capacity as agent for the castle estate, yet another duty. Donnie, who might have been expected to run things or employ a manager, had enlisted on the first day he had arrived in England. He'd apparently not had time to visit the estate he'd inherited on his final leave. She hadn't even shared a cup of tea with him. And eight weeks ago now, His Grace Lieutenant Donald Edgar Claverton, Eighth Duke of Claverton, had been declared missing after the evacuation of Dunkirk.

'Missing' was not enough to proclaim the *next* Duke of Claverton, nor was it urgent they find one. At the moment, any new duke's sole inheritance would be the title. Mr Warte of the firm Warte, Finister and Warte handled any legal aspects now, as they had handled the legal affairs of the estate for generations.

The loss of a duke seemed paltry compared to the loss of five thousand men of the British Expeditionary Force, boxed in by the German army at Dunkirk, plus the one thousand civilians of Dunkirk itself bombed in the attack, as well as the shop owners, fishers, weekend sailors and boat owners who had braved shellfire to cross the embattled waters of the Channel so they might take trapped soldiers from the French beaches to the waiting transport ships.

There had been no official announcement or record of the number of civilian lives lost. Perhaps no accurate account could be made. Men and women had simply hoisted sail and rallied across the Channel. Presumably some tally had been made of the number of defence personnel lost, but if so the British public had not been told. Instead the story had been spun as a glorious victory, so many lives saved by 'the people of the little ships'. Deanna suspected the public had also not been told of the true casualties of German bombs raining down nightly on London, and probably elsewhere ...

Loose lips sink ships, the posters said in post offices and beside railway platforms and even on telephone poles. The tightness of officialdom's lips, on the other hand, showed just how close Britain was to total defeat. According to the gossip at the last weekend party (the middle-class term for Saturday and Sunday was slowly edging out the aristocracy's term, 'Friday to Monday') if Luftwaffe Commander Hermann Goering had not overreached in his assurance to Hitler that the German air force could prevent the evacuation, the entire army would have been lost.

She bent to the shovel again, brushing away the flies from her face. Two more barrow loads should do it ...

'Strewth, it's a bloody wedgetail! Coo-ee, mate!'

The words came from outside the glasshouse. None of them made sense. The voice was also a stranger's. She grasped the shovel and strode out. Locals would not steal the ripening fruit beyond the traditional children's scrumping, but there were townies about these days, sleeping in their cars to avoid the nightly bombing raids.

'Hello?' she called, wielding her shovel.

'Sorry, I didn't mean to startle you. Look!' The man pointed to the sky. He was in a blue air force uniform adorned with pilot's wings: broad shouldered but otherwise wiry; tanned skin, brown eyes with laugh lines, early thirties perhaps; and with a broad and decidedly non-English accent. 'I haven't seen a wedgetail eagle since I left home.'

She gazed up as the massive bird soared above them, enjoying sharing the sight. The farmers and villagers of Claverton regarded eagles as lamb thieves and competition for the rabbit meat so badly needed to eke out the tiny meat ration.

'That's a golden eagle, not a wedgetail.' She smiled at her new companion. 'I'm so glad they haven't moved on. It's been ages since I've seen them.' Eagles did not like flying in aircraft-ridden skies, but at least here at Eagle's Rest and in the Claverton woods they were safe from guns and from boys stealing their eggs. 'You're Australian?'

The pilot grinned at her. 'My accent give me away?' He reminded her of someone, but she couldn't work out who.

'You said "wedgetail eagle".' She suddenly realised a lump of straw and cow shit still poked out from between her breasts. She hurriedly plucked it out. 'You only find wedgetails in Australia or southern New Guinea,' she said, trying to cover her embarrassment. 'They're similar to our golden eagles, but not as rare.'

The eagle suddenly dropped, grabbed a frantic hare, then rose in half a dozen massive flaps, queen of the sky and all the squirming creatures below it, till she caught a thermal again and carried her prey back towards the hills by the sea.

'That's the first time I've seen her since the aerodrome started operating,' Deanna said in relief. 'They must be further up the headland.'

'They?'

'A nesting pair. Or I hope they're nesting.'

The pilot met her eyes in the communion of bird lovers. 'We've a pair of wedgetail eagles in the cliffs on our property. Dad wrote they had a fledgling this year. They'll be nesting again soon — lots of bunnies to eat now most of the trappers are in uniform. You're an ornithologist?'

'Amateur. At the moment I'm a manure shoveller.'

Dusty suddenly rose to his feet and gave an abrupt bark, as if realising he'd been deficient as a guard dog. Duty done, he padded over and offered his ears to the stranger. The pilot scratched for a minute. Dusty stretched luxuriously, becoming two yards of nose, shaggy back and tail.

'There's something comforting about a dog, isn't there?' the stranger said eventually. 'I miss ours. Thank you for lending me yours for a few moments. I apologise for bothering you. I knocked on the front door, but there seems to be no one home. I'm looking for Lady Deanna Claverton. I'm Flight Lieutenant Sam Murray.'

'I'm Deanna Claverton.'

'But ...' Flight Lieutenant Sam Murray stared at her.

Deanna laughed. 'You didn't expect a Lady to be covered in cow manure.'

'Well, no.' He grinned at her. 'Not that you're covered. There are at least three clean spots on your face. But the locals down at the pub talked about the old woman who lived here for donkey's years. When they told me up at headquarters that Lady Claverton lived at Eagle's Rest now and was the person I needed to ask about access to the stream, I assumed the two were the same person.'

'Miss Enid Constable died a few years ago. She left the place to me. How can I help you?'

He held his cap in his hands. 'I know it's cheek to ask, but could a few of us from the base fish your river now and then? We'd give you the catch — we've nowhere to cook it, and the kitchen staff would probably turn it into something boiled and bowel stopping. We'd bother you once a week at most.'

'Fish here as often as you like.' It was little enough to do for the empire's air crews who'd come to protect Britain from invasion. Many died in their first weeks of fighting. A few survived for months. All knew there was little chance they'd outlive the war.

'I'd be grateful for a few trout, and you and your friends are welcome to help eat them. It's still a bit hot to get a good catch though,' she added. 'You'd be better off coarse-fishing for pike in the old quarry up past the church.'

His face relaxed. 'We really want a chance to be by a river again.'

She had a moment's longing to join him, to see the water flash over rocks, rippling and singing, and the sunlight glinting on the water as dragonflies hovered over pools. There'd be the scent of floating leaves and tree-dappled earth up there — maybe even a pair of otters ducking as they fished and played. A time to rest, to simply smell and see and be.

He looked at her as if she'd given him the crown jewels. 'Thank you. You've no idea how much it means just getting into the peace and trees for a while. Billo and Graham and I were farmers before we joined up, and where we're from the farms are big, so a lot of us learned to fly. That's why we were recruited, of course.'

'I don't understand.'

'Your RAF came to Australia when war was declared to gather up the best Aussie pilots — Britain had only a handful of pilots back then. Bush pilots can fly anything and go anywhere. Give us the coordinates and we'd land you on Hitler's dinner table. Billo built his ski lodge on a mountain in Tasmania by matching the speed on his craft to the wind so the plane was stationary, and his mate could shove out the materials. Graham's in a Queensland aero club where you have to fly under a bridge to become a member.' He grinned again. 'Strictly illegal.'

'What about you?'

'Oh, I never do anything illegal.' His eyes laughed at her. He *was* familiar, but she was sure she'd never met him before. He certainly wasn't a brother of one of the Australian debutantes who'd come to be presented to the queen before the war. He sounded educated, but not with the BBC accent of the Australian squatter families.

'I won a few races in Europe before the war. About a third of your RAF are colonials. Lots of Canadians, South Africans, plus all the Yanks who joined up even if America won't get into the war, and a fair few Poles and Danes who escaped the invasions too.' He grinned. 'It's hard to find a Pommy accent sometimes, except for the top brass.'

She wanted to ask what kind of plane he flew — a long-range Lancaster bomber or a Spitfire used for close-range fighting off the German planes. Rumour had it that the Claverton aerodrome was used for training in both aircraft. But one did not ask questions like that in wartime.

If possible, one did not ask questions at all. She needed all her tact — and beauty — to elicit information from her targets without an open query.

She smiled at the flyer. 'You're welcome to fish the river any time. Just leave a note on the door to say you're here if I'm not around.' That way she wouldn't need to investigate if she heard voices.

She liked him very much, this flyer from across the world who had come to help save Britain, who loved eagles and rivers and being among trees. How long had it been since she'd actually enjoyed talking to someone about things that mattered, like rivers and eagles?

'Would you like a cup of tea, Flight Lieutenant Murray?' she asked impulsively. 'I made a blackberry and apple pie this morning.'

'I'd love to,' he said, obviously sincere. 'But I need to get back. Thank you, Lady Claverton.'

'It's Lady Deanna, or Lady Deanna Claverton, a courtesy title — sorry, the English title system is very old, very complicated and there's no need for you to understand it. Call me Dee.'

He flushed. 'But you're a member of the aristocracy. They take that seriously over here.'

'I know,' she said wryly. 'But I don't. Or only when I have to.'

'Dee then.' He smiled at her again. 'I'm mostly known as Sam.' He glanced towards the sea as the eagle vanished into the hills above the waves pounding on the cliffs. 'I'm glad to have seen that. Glad England still has eagles, too. My gran used to say that eagles looked out for us — our place is even called Eagle Mountain. Maybe your pair is looking out for you.'

Suddenly she knew exactly who he reminded her of — Grandpa, though the men were totally dissimilar physically, except for the eyes: brown eyes, used to watching distances. The quietness of men who watched, who hunted, not to kill, but to understand. But, of course, it was a pilot's duty to kill, or to train other pilots to kill instead. Kill or be killed, she thought, just as her grandfather must have killed in the Great War. She forced her mind away.

She brushed at the flies hovering around her, the scent obviously delectable to a fly. 'I'd better get back to work. You'll find the best fishing spot just now is a pool by the grove of willows, up towards the hills — you'll need to walk about a mile.'

'We won't mind that.'

'I don't suppose you will.' It was one of her favourite walks, now that the tiny shingle beach and even the steep headlands were covered in rolls of barbed wire and signs declaring that the whole beach and cliffs had been mined.

She doubted the existence of the mines — only a single lorry had passed, loaded with the barbed wire — but it was an effective deterrent, for her, at least. As the signs faced inland and the invaders would come by sea she doubted it would have the same effect on them.

'Feel free to call in with any catch, and I'll cook them for you. Would you mind not climbing up into the hills though? It might disturb the eagles.'

'No worries. The farmers who shoot the eagles back home have rabbits eating every blade of grass they can find. Not on our place — our eagles and goshawks eat the bunnies, and our sheep get to eat the grass. Well, whatever the roos don't eat ...'

'Where is your place?'

'Six thousand acres of cliffs, bush and paddocks, about half an hour out of a town called Budgie Creek. Don't bother looking for it on a map. We know where we are, even if the rest of the world doesn't.'

'What do you farm?'

'Grass, trees, a heck of a lot of roos, snakes as long as a kitchen table, more emus than you can count in a month of Sundays and about a thousand ewes, not counting the lambs and rams. We stock lightly. Too many sheep compact Australian soils so the water can't soak in when it rains, and it washes away. I suppose six thousand acres would make a man Lord Muckity Muck around here, but it's average back home. Sorry,' he added, obviously remembering he was speaking to a member of the aristocracy, even one in overalls and cow shit. 'I didn't mean to be insulting.'

'No insult taken.' She had about a thousand acres herself now, even if most of it was too steep or rocky to be cultivated. Those thousand acres made a barrier between herself and the tenant farmers and villagers almost as strong as her title and her income — small compared to the wealth of those she dined with; riches for a farm worker or grocer. She looked down at the flies on her overalls ruefully. 'I should change my name to Lady Muck.'

'Dee's prettier. Thank you for allowing us to use your river. I hope we'll be able to keep you in fish for a while, anyway. I'd better get back to the base.' He put up his cap so he could tip the brim to her and began to walk over to the motorbike she hadn't heard from the greenhouse, and to which Dusty had entirely failed to react.

Dusty had already retired into the shade. 'You're nothing but a hairy dustbin — the world's most incompetent guard dog,' she told him as the bike's engine whirred.

Dusty shut his eyes again.

Deanna watched as the motorbike rounded the corner. She wished he'd taken up the offer of tea. She'd liked his face, too blunt to be handsome. A man who understood why eagles and men needed refuge from the human insanity of war.

But a woman who smelled of cow shit was not enticing. Nor could she afford a social life, she reminded herself, especially not with an Australian pilot of presumably extreme loyalty to the empire, to have come so far from his own country, and so soon, to protect England. He was not the kind of person to take to dinner parties given by suspected fascists.

And anyway, he was interested in the river, not in her. And was probably married. Or had a girlfriend in the village or working in the castle whom he took to the monthly dances for the airmen and convalescents, and to which she had never been asked.

She returned to her shovelling.

Two

Woolton Pie

INGREDIENTS
Filling
500 grams vegetables on hand: potato, cauliflower, parsnip, carrot
three to four onion tops
one teaspoon vegetable extract
one tablespoon oatmeal
chopped parsley
Pastry
230 grams wheatmeal flour
one level teaspoon baking powder
pinch salt
pinch powdered sage (optional)
570 millilitres cold milk, or milk and water

METHOD
Dice the vegetables. Cook together with the vegetable extract and oatmeal for ten minutes with just enough water to cover. Stir occasionally to prevent the mixture from sticking. Allow to cool. Combine pastry ingredients and

roll out. Place on top of the filling. Bake till light brown. Serve with brown gravy; garnish with parsley.

Recipe from the Ministry of Food
and named for the minister

Two hours later she'd filled each of the garden beds for winter. She looked at her work with pride, waving the flies from her face and blowing the most inquisitive out of her nose. Cow shit wasn't an unpleasant smell, once you'd got used to it. It was even sweetish, with a hint of fermenting summer.

Her cow-shit-fed potted oranges and lemons were thriving, and the neatly staked tomatoes were heavily trussed with ripe fruit. Village-bred hens born to be wary of dogs and foxes pecked under the laden pear and apple trees, also lavished with a mulch of cattle bedding. Autumn's cow- and straw-enriched strawberries and raspberries were ripening too; and out beyond the orchard stretched the potato field.

It too had been fed with cow product, though this time shovelled along the rows from the cart pulled by Mr Higgins's draught horse. She wondered if anyone in the Ministry of Food had ever shovelled cow shit.

Cabbages, carrots, beets, spring onions and Brussels sprouts had replaced the zinnias, penstemons and snapdragons in what was now the front Victory Garden, like other flower beds turned vegetable across the nation. Her spare vegetables went to those in the village without space to grow their own, or the old, the ill, or those crippled in the last war who were not able to tend them. The herb garden flourished, as it had under Miss Enid's care. The glasshouses continuously supplied spinach, winter lettuce, radishes and endives all through the cold months. Two beehives helped pollinate Miss Enid's apple, cherry, plum, medlar, quince, pear, elderberry and mulberry trees, as well as the currant bushes. They also gave honey and wax for candles needed when the village generator turned off early each night to save power, not to mention helping conserve the kerosene they used for lamps. This was almost impossible to find — except in the barrels down in her cellars, which she saw fit to conserve as well.

Her grandfather had indeed provided for her. Deanna was as safe, well fed and comfortable as anyone could be in this war. She and her home should even survive relatively unscathed if — when — Germany invaded. Invaders needed food too, which meant that her crops would be useful to them; neither was she known as an intellectual or, worse, Jewish, Gypsy, blind, disabled, homosexual or a communist, any of which would make her an immediate target. She didn't even have an art collection worth looting.

Fascist sympathisers would vouch for her. 'A good girl, that one. Got her head screwed on straight. Good family, too.'

She owed a lot to the old man, and to the woman she had never known he loved. Not just her life here, but the chance to make a difference for her country ...

'... and it would make a real difference,' said a voice sharp as broken glass behind her, evidently continuing a conversation unheard by Deanna when the speaker had begun to talk outside the glasshouse.

'*Woof,*' muttered Dusty in a half-hearted attempt to do his duty, not even bothering to lift his head this time.

Deanna turned, aware that her overalls were now more soaked than smudged with manure and the cloth she'd wrapped her hair in was disgusting too.

'Mrs Goodword,' she said brightly, trying to look delighted at the sight of the vicar's wife, clad in her usual tweed suit and feathered hat.

Never was a woman less aptly named, she thought, trying not to stare at the fine hair quivering under Mrs Goodword's nose in a moustache that a major general would envy. Mrs Goodword assumed that anything Deanna could do, she would do, from supplying flowers for the church each Saturday afternoon ('You have such beautiful roses, Lady Deanna ...') to providing a basket of glasshouse oranges for the Women's Institute raffle, or allowing the church fete to use the Eagle's Rest garden now the castle grounds were no longer available.

The latter, at least, Deanna had nipped in the bud, before busloads of daytrippers looted her vegetables, orchard and hot houses, peered into her windows to see how the aristocracy lived or stole her teaspoons.

The fete had been given her lower field instead, due to be ploughed up for more potatoes, and Joe Higgins had filled the lane that led to Eagle's Rest with his cows to discourage anyone from wandering up to the house. Even the most honest townies seemed to feel that 'just a few' fruit, veg and teaspoons weren't 'real' theft. A bit like Hitler and Czechoslovakia, she supposed.

The village was proud of its single aristocrat. Some of the older generation still curtseyed or removed their caps as she passed. Deanna was 'their' Lady Dee. They also regarded poaching pheasants, trapping rabbits and stealing wood both from Eagle's Rest's woods and hillside and the Claverton lands as their hereditary prerogative but would be angry at any 'outsider' doing so.

The local poachers could take what they liked from the Claverton estate if they could evade the Home Guard, who patrolled it nightly, but Deanna now rationed 'thefts' from her property as strictly as the government rationed sugar, petrol, bacon and butter. Anyone who wanted to snare rabbits on Eagle's Rest land now had to arrive and leave at the specified time so they didn't encroach on other poachers' allocations — and they had to be gone by early morning, the eagles' favourite hunting time. With so many men away, and so many women doing the jobs previously done by men as well as caring for families, there was less time for poaching, but the wild food on both estates, from bunnies to hazelnuts and elderberries, was a badly needed addition to inadequate diets.

Luckily there were sufficient grandfathers left who knew how to snare a tasty hare or pheasant, and grandmothers who knew the difference between an elderberry and deadly nightshade. Farmers like herself and Joe Higgins managed to siphon some surplus to the village. Here at least no one was seriously in want, even if nettles were added to soup to give it a beefy flavour and hawthorn berries became jam.

Meanwhile Mrs Goodword was still talking. She seemed to take Deanna's manure-soaked overalls for granted, though if she'd commented Deanna hadn't heard. Like everyone in the vicinity Deanna had grown skilled at only tuning in when the vicar's wife got to the point. '... and so I was sure you'd help drive the little darlings to their new — and we must hope — temporary homes. People are so kind to offer their spare beds to those in need, aren't they?'

'Spare beds' sounded all too relevant. 'I beg your pardon? You want my spare beds?'

'We need your *car* to convey some of the new refugees to their new foster homes,' said Mrs Goodword reproachfully, her moustache quivering. 'Another trainload of children is arriving at four pm. The Women's Institute will provide tea and buns. Your presence to welcome the poor little angels would be welcome too.'

The last train of evacuees had been from the poorest part of the East End. Two had thrown stones through the church window, another had been caught shoplifting boiled lollies and several had been lice-ridden. Deanna was not sure 'little angels' was the correct term, nor exactly why they'd find her welcoming. But the village would expect her to be there.

Mrs Goodword shook her head. 'So many parents in London and the ports didn't take the need for evacuation seriously till the bombs began to fall. The wireless news was terrible last night, wasn't it? I said to Arthur ...'

Deanna focused on the important part of Mrs Goodword's message. Her car and farmer's petrol ration were used so often for charitable causes that she made her own deliveries by bicycle. Mrs Goodword was welcome to the small amount left from this month's ration, and the cause was indeed a good one. But she had to make it clear again that was all she would contribute.

'I have enough petrol to drive a single carload of evacuees and foster parents who live too far away to walk, but as I told you last time, I can't take any refugees. I can't work and care for children.'

More importantly, she couldn't attend the parties, the dinners, the croquet matches where she collected information if she was responsible for an evacuee, but she could not use that to make her position clear to Mrs Goodword. Let the vicar's wife think that frivolity in wartime was just what aristocrats did.

'Oh, of course, Your Ladyship,' said Mrs Goodword insincerely. 'I wouldn't dream of asking you to do more. You are always so generous ...'

Which means you are planning to lump me with at least one East End brat before the evening is over, thought Deanna. Mrs Goodword was most effusive when she wanted something. Well, she'd nip that one in the bud too.

Dusty didn't even lift his head as Mrs Goodword returned to her own bicycle, propped up in the lane, ready to cycle the two miles down to the village to coerce another victim into taking a child they did not know, terrified not just of strangers but of the bombing begun a week ago, the debris of buildings, bodies and all they knew crumbling in minutes, the air-raid sirens screaming, the homeless sobbing or sitting dazed. A sudden nightmare sending city children who had not evacuated already on crowded trains and buses into the unknown countryside — over a million of them already, according to *The Times*.

It struck Deanna with a sudden grief that children would probably never be part of her life, not evacuees now or children of her own later, even if by some miracle she met a man with whom she wanted to share a life and a bed. She had not thought of that when she accepted the man she now called Uncle Jasper's offer. A spy could not marry, especially a female spy expected to care for home, husband and neighbours — not even when she was spying in her own country, based in her own home rather than heroically bicycling around France with the Resistance.

Even if the war ended with a German victory soon, which seemed increasingly possible, with the defence force losses surely far greater even than reported, and half London's docklands and East End ports already resembling beaches of driftwood and half-sodden sandcastles, Britain would keep fighting under occupation, and Uncle Jasper would have a role for her.

Even before the war she had accepted that she would never marry, and not just because of her lack of desire. After all, a woman just had to lie there till it was over, then mutter compliments on the man's virility. Few men of her class wanted a wife who wouldn't support their careers, or tend their estates because she loved her own. It wouldn't occur to commoners to court her, except for bounders after her house and land and income. If this war ended like the last, there'd be five women for every man available, and she'd be unlikely to be the lucky one. She would remain single, like her house's former owner, without even a secret lover from the castle.

The memory of the man she'd met this afternoon returned. She'd liked him in a way she'd never liked any man before. He hadn't automatically placed her in the social hierarchy as everyone here did, and no flirting either, which to her surprise she'd rather have liked, though who'd want to flirt with a manure-covered scarecrow? Was that how desire began, with a feeling that you simply ... matched?

But marrying an Australian was impossible. She could never leave Eagle's Rest. A glamorous pilot could have his choice of willing young women, few of whom would do the obvious calculation: that their new husband would be lucky to survive even another year of war. Many a hasty marriage lasted weeks, as new brides become widows. Probably only the pilots captured by the enemy or too severely injured to keep flying had any chance of living till the war's end.

In the meantime, she needed to clean her shovel and wheelbarrow, bathe long enough to remove the stink of cow and, instead of putting her feet up with Dusty, change into the mauve tweed suit she'd made from three men's 1890s shooting jackets, the fabric only slightly faded, to be correctly attired to help meet the evacuees and foster parents at the train station, though her actual 'use' would be limited to spouting variations on, 'Lovely weather,' and 'Jolly good show.' She had finally accepted that Miss Enid was correct: it was hard to go wrong with a tweed suit.

At least now in early autumn there was no need to keep the kitchen stove fire on high to warm the room — just low enough to keep her casserole simmering. The stove ran on wood, replacing the more common coal-fired Aga that her grandfather had obviously seen would have little coal to feed it once war began. The stove gave hot water, too, from its 'wet back', and it took the chill off the bedrooms as its chimney passed through upstairs.

She sighed. It would be a long evening making polite conversation. But she had that beautifully casseroled rooster — everyone who bred hens always had a surplus of roosters — with plentiful vegetables around it and potatoes in their jackets, the apple and blackberry pie, a jug of cream from Joe Higgins's cows and a bed warmed by a large, hairy dog to come home to.

She lifted her head to gaze at her estate, and its beauty. She lived well, dutifully and usefully. She was also lonely. Fulfilling her duty meant she would continue to be lonely, till she became the village recluse like Miss Enid. She picked up the shovel and a handful of straw to clean it.

Three

Better Pot-Luck with Churchill today than Humble Pie under Hitler tomorrow.

World War II slogan

Two hours later, smelling slightly of mothballs and violet-scented bath salts, she emerged from her grandfather's old Morris Minor — a disappointment to the village, who would have preferred a Daimler or Rolls-Royce, though the old man claimed he'd done a hundred miles an hour on the stretch along the cliff road, confident that the local bobby would not book him.

She made her way through the crowd in the waiting room, nodding greetings, asking about children's progress and great aunts' gout with practised interest. Women balanced their knitting under their arms as they held the cups of weak tea and fish-paste sandwiches that had been provided for those hosting the evacuees — generous women indeed, given that the village of Claverton Minor had taken nearly two dozen children in the first evacuation.

'It's been a perfect autumn day, hasn't it, Your Ladyship?'

'It has indeed, Mr Pockley. How is your father's rheumatism?'

'Better in this warm weather. I'll tell him Your Ladyship asked after him.'

The children would be given cocoa made with powdered milk, and buns sweetened with the dried fruit Deanna had donated to the Women's Institute for the cause, though made with the grey 'wholemeal flour' that rumour said contained anything from sawdust to rat droppings, which was all that was in the shops now, as well as being the chief ingredient of the despised 'National Loaf'.

The crowd parted as Deanna made her way to the official table. Two women dropped curtseys, still knitting. Any woman not knitting these days was regarded with suspicion: socks or belly bands or balaclavas, or jumpers or cardigans made from the wool unthreaded from old garments. Even Queen Elizabeth and the princesses were rarely photographed without knitting in their hands.

Deanna herself carried four needles supporting half a khaki sock, begun for her by Mrs Thripps. Somehow her own knitting always tangled. She hoped no one noticed that the sock grew no longer before the train arrived.

Mrs Goodword rushed forwards — her knitting was pale puce, possibly a muffler for her husband to wear as he cycled around his parish.

'Lady Deanna, how kind of you to come! And what a splendid sock!' The gleam in her eye showed she was quite aware it was no work of Deanna's. 'I did want a quick word with you. The jam-making efforts of the Women's Institute have been simply splendid, but could you possibly spare more apples? They have a most superior setting quality, and possibly more plums ...'

'Yes, of course, Mrs Goodword. Please tell them to pick what they like.' People, people everywhere, she thought, and no one I want to talk to ...

Deanna had not attended Claverton Minor's village school — it had been boarding school for her from the time she was seven years old. The castle was too distant from the village for her to have accidentally met other children at the pond or river and become friends with them. She'd spent her holidays helping Miss Enid, just as, she now realised, Miss Enid had been helping her, a girl who was motherless, auntless and grandmotherless. Deanna smiled as she glanced down at her tweed suit, adorned with the small necklace of pearls from her grandfather. She wished Miss Enid could see her and approve.

She'd had no chance to make local friends as a child and all the years since had been spent caring for the estate and her grandfather. He would have been smug at the accuracy of his predictions, she thought, Britain's armies so nearly obliterated so quickly.

The months after his death had been frenetic. She'd had the funeral to arrange and her own personal items to pack to move from the castle to Eagle's Rest. Cataloguing the remainder of the castle's contents for the lawyers, corresponding with Donnie about arrangements, establishing a new routine with her own land to care for and learning the needs of potato plants, not to mention meeting 'Uncle Jasper' and the informal training that followed, had eaten the uneasy year of truce while Germany's ambitions loomed ever darker on the horizon. And then had come Poland, and the real war, and soon enough Donnie calling to say casually in his American accent, 'Hello, old thing, how are you? Can you believe the government wants to commandeer Claverton? Would you mind keeping on with the business for a while? I only reached England last night and enlisted this morning,' as if he was asking her to mind his cat instead of what turned out to be a whirlwind of practical and legal arrangements with the tenants, completing the paperwork of requisitioning, and constantly inking signatures and submitting power of attorney papers et cetera.

As well as working her new farm, she'd spent weeks exploring the treasures placed for her to discover upstairs as well as the extraordinary secret bounty of the cellars: the Louis XV writing desk snuck into her new library, possibly priceless; the damask curtains that had hung in the castle study; the abundance of books, the chests in the attic, not only transported but dusted and de-spidered. She'd spent a week or two crying over the care and love that had provided it all. She had perhaps been happiest when she cried and remembered.

'Lovely weather, Your Ladyship.'

Sunlight like butter at midday and gold velvet twilights, but she couldn't say that to Mrs Tartley. 'Yes, simply splendid.' Mrs Tartley, a nice woman with two grandchildren and a passion for crocheted hats, ran the paper shop now that her husband and sons were in the infantry. Today's hat was pink, purple and orange.

But Mrs Tartley was not a friend. No one in the village seemed capable of making the leap between their class and hers. Like Joe and Agnes Higgins, the villagers remained friendly but deferential — a cup of tea was offered in the parlour, not the kitchen, and served with the best china, an interruption to their busy day and hers.

Mrs Thripps was friendly, and an invaluable source of gossip, but perhaps twenty years and the interests of two quite different generations as well as class habit separated them.

'Hasn't the weather been perfect, Lady Deanna?'

'Excellent for the tomatoes, Mrs Tuffet. Mrs Harrington, how lovely to see you. How is your mother's gouty foot?'

'Much better. I'll tell her you asked.'

'Wonderful June weather, Lady Deanna.'

Too lovely, Deanna thought. War had made a sunlit month a danger. More clouds would mean fewer air raids, hindering the enemy's ability to see the target below. 'Yes, beautiful, Mrs Billings. You can almost see the grass growing!'

Mrs Billings's son had been evacuated with a chest injury from Dunkirk, but one did not ask about matters like that, at least not in a crowded railway station where tears could not be hidden and information that might be useful to the enemy possibly overheard.

'I bet your roses look a treat, Lady Deanna.'

'They badly need pruning and manuring.' Roses would be in as short supply as stockings and sugar soon, as gardeners 'dug for victory', trying to supply the sixty per cent of food Britain had imported before the German blockade.

'Such a lovely day, isn't it, Mrs Johnson?'

The cobbler's wife gave a pleased simper. 'Just beautiful, Lady Deanna.'

Deanna's exclusive girls' school should have taught a thousand and one remarks about the weather, she thought, instead of how to curtsey when presented to the queen, how to sit with one's back not quite touching the chair, or walk elegantly with a book balanced on one's head …

'I bet your pears are fattening nicely, Lady Deanna.'

'It's been an excellent year for pears, Mrs Porter.'

And your Billy will be sneaking over to fill a bag with them, she thought. But a certain amount of theft for personal use was traditional.

Mrs Porter lowered her voice. 'I hope we don't get none of them black evacuees this time.'

'I beg your pardon?'

'The poor folks at Buttermere! Two of their evacuees were black as the ace of spades. I heard from Mrs Sweetie that their pa's a sailor, and I bet their ma's no better than she should be. But what could the Buttermere folks do? They'd put their names down and had to take them. It wasn't right, not givin' them any warning like that.'

'I'm sure the colour of their skin makes no difference, Mrs Porter.' She smiled. 'I danced with a charming Indian Maharaja once.'

Mrs Porter gave her a look that plainly said, *Easy for you to say, dancing with Indian princes and your big house with empty bedrooms and your vegetables, and no worry your spare bed would hold a kiddie with dark skin tonight, nor what you'd give your family for tea tomorrow.*

Suddenly, in the crowded room, fuggy from the tea urn, Deanna felt desperately isolated. It wasn't that none of these women were her friends. None *could* be her friends: she would always be Lady Deanna to the older villagers. The younger ones, her age and less prone to sudden curtseying, had jobs, and only weekends off.

In the last eighteen months Deanna's true 'work' had been confined to 'Friday to Monday' visits, limiting her social life to contacts who might be useful, whose dinners and luncheons of estate pheasant or venison, wine from well-stocked cellars, quail eggs and black-market butter would bring new acquaintances who might be even more useful.

Not friends. The schoolfriends she was still in contact with after four years of caring for her grandfather were driving ambulances each night in London or had joined one of the women's services or vanished to other war jobs; nor could she implicate them in her own investigations and betrayals by asking them to visit Eagle's Rest for a few days. But they had given her letters of introduction to potential fascist sympathisers among the aristocracy and not asked questions, guessing perhaps at the reason they knew never to discuss.

Even the vicar and his wife had not asked her to share a meal after her grandfather's death, assuming perhaps that anyone endowed with a title was equally endowed with friends, or even subconsciously believing that Eagle's Rest, having housed a hermit-like bird lover for thirty-five years, now housed another woman who wished for equal privacy. Except, of course, when Lady Deanna was needed to do her duty.

'Tea, Your Ladyship? I wish you could see my crop of peas this year. Splendid, they are, not a drop of mildew.' Mrs Filmer the butcher's wife lowered her voice, emitting a faint scent of lamb chop. 'It's Septimus's secret spray: ten buckets water to a cup of powdered milk, with a half bucket of fresh wee added — it has to be right fresh, not even an hour old, if you'll excuse my coarseness.'

'It's good to know that even, er, wee, is helping the war effort, Mrs Filmer.' Deanna accepted a cup of hot water that had been briefly acquainted with rationed tea leaves and tucked her knitting under her arm. 'Yes, a beautiful day ...'

Couldn't someone nudge her and whisper with a grin, 'Our Bert's been scrounging firewood on the estate. Your grandpa wouldn't have minded.'

At least Mrs Thripps passed on the news that everyone else was too polite to mention: how Boggins's best cow had exploded from what Boggins said was lightning, so the ministry would compensate him, but what was surely just the bloat; that Elsie McMurtry was in the family way and her young man not free to marry her till he came back from the Middle East; and that Mr Sweetie the postmaster had been delivering letters personally — *if* you know what I mean, Lady Dee — to the widow Scrump, and her husband not dead two months yet after the defeat in Denmark.

Four o'clock arrived. The train did not.

Five o'clock. Women muttered about getting Dad's tea. Deanna noticed that Mrs Filmer had finished an entire khaki sock and was casting on a second. The crowd thinned as those who lived close enough to hear the train arrive hurried home to feed their families.

Younger women replaced them, some still wearing the headscarves and overalls of the workers at the new coffin factory outside the village, meant to be a secret but once known to Mr Sweetie the postmaster (Corporal Sweetie in the Home Guard) was known to everyone within a week, for if you couldn't trust those you'd known your whole life with the news of a coffin factory, what were we fighting for?

These women knitted more slowly, hands tired from carpentry but still dutifully clicking their needles.

Six o'clock.

Seven. The newcomers went home to eat their dinners. The four pm crowd reappeared to take their places, weary now. Mrs Goodword had sent a message up to the vicarage to bring down the garden party chairs. Women sat with sighs of relief, knitting, darning, a few shelling peas, and knitting, knitting, knitting. Chatting became muttering.

'... probably been cancelled and they haven't bothered ...'

'Yes, dark as the bottom of a coal cellar they were ...'

'... there's been a cow on the line, most like ...'

'... what if the train's been —' That voice stopped, as if its owner could not say 'bombed' about a train full of children. A phone call by Mrs Button, who'd served at the ticket counter before the war but now was stationmaster, gave the news that the train was delayed, and no one knew why or for how long: in other words, no news at all.

At nine pm the station's blackout curtains closed and shadows began to grow, despite the long late autumn light. The name of the station had been removed, to confuse invaders, though as this was the end of the line any pre-war map would show an enemy army their location.

Finally, the familiar *chugga-chugga* sounded in the distance. The unified sigh of relief could almost have lifted the roof. Mrs Button briefly turned on the electric light that might make the platform a target if it were to stay on all evening.

'Ahem.' Mrs Goodword gathered her forces. 'If you kind people will wait here, I will meet the supervisors and shepherd the children indoors ...'

It would be impossible to fit anyone else in the waiting room, even if they were small, thought Deanna. But it was equally impossible these days to light the platform brightly enough to match children with foster parents. Bright lights drew enemy bombers.

Deanna had underestimated Mrs Goodword. Not only were the children squeezed in, but the first arrivals were allotted within seconds and left the waiting room with their foster parents, thus making more room.

This was especially impressive as no child had been allocated a billet. This second evacuation was more chaotic than the first. Until their parents had taken them to the station today it was impossible to know how many children there would be.

Within half an hour about forty scared and wide-eyed children, too hot in the overcoats officialdom had decreed they must wear, hung with their gas masks and labels giving their names and parents' names and, presumably, with the required spare underclothes, night clothes, slippers or plimsolls, socks, toothbrushes, combs, towels, soaps and face cloths, and each now clutching a bun and sporting lips daubed with cocoa, had been matched with volunteers.

And they would be good matches, thought Deanna wearily, hungry for her dinner. Mrs Goodword would make sure the boys didn't go to farmers who just wanted cheap labour, or any child to a woman who'd demand a London slum kid hand over their ration card to feed her own family, then expect them to scrub her floors, to take the place of a servant who'd chosen higher pay and a day-and-a-half off a week working in a factory.

Mrs Goodword was formidable. As, indeed, were all the women and the few men who had been here, even Mrs Porter with her unthinking bigotry, but still taking strangers into her home to parent for an indefinite time, possibly for years. As self-sacrificing, perhaps, as any sailor in the small boats that had sailed to Dunkirk.

Deanna pasted on another smile, silently lamenting her aching feet in their kitten heels, and prepared to join the small group, presumably in need of transport, that had gathered around Mrs Goodword.

The group parted like the Red Sea, leaving a gap around three girls, small, medium and slightly larger, dressed identically in blue gingham, bare-legged and in shabby black shoes. None had an overcoat or bag of belongings or clutched a teddy bear. None had any label around her neck. Their heads had been recently shaved, presumably to rid them of nits — Deanna could see small razor nicks in the bare flesh. All three were so thin a wind might have snapped them.

How could children starve like this in England?

They were also filthy, with brown smudges on the arms of their too-short dresses and on their bare legs. The smallest one stank. A brown smear of presumably faeces stained the back of her gingham skirt. It was dried, so it had been there a while.

The girls stared at the floor expressionlessly. None held a bun, and their clean lips indicated they had not been offered cocoa. For the first time Deanna saw Mrs Goodword appear helpless.

Deanna looked at her enquiringly. Mrs Goodword shook her head. 'We've three more children than are on the list for this train. One of the carers noticed a collection of children from an orphanage on the station platform in London — that might explain the gingham. But the orphanage children went in quite another direction. These three must have hidden till this train reached here. No one seems to know their names, or even where they've come from.'

Deanna smiled at the girls, trying to ignore her aching feet. 'That's easily solved. What are your names, and where do you come from?'

The girls did not look up at her. Their bare heads shone in the electric light. One was possibly fourteen, the next maybe ten. The other could have been a skinny three, or an even thinner five. Their faces had been wiped clean of all expression, though not of the accumulation of smut and grit from the steam train.

'I ... I don't know what to do,' said Mrs Goodword helplessly. 'We can't take more at the vicarage. One perhaps, but not three ...'

The girls immediately held hands, as if to emphasise they would not be parted. They still did not look up at the adults surrounding them.

'I can't take no more, either ...' The words could have come from any of the women in the group, now clutching their own evacuees as impeccable reasons why they could not possibly take more.

'Lady Deanna, I know it is an imposition, but you do have spare bedrooms. Just tonight, till we can make other arrangements. The girls need sleep, and food and ...' Mrs Goodword's voice broke on the word 'cleaning'. She suddenly looked exhausted, physically, emotionally, and almost about to cry.

Which would not do.

A Lady Deanna might be the symbol of a village. The Mrs Goodwords of the world organised it — the better parts, at least.

Deanna handed the vicar's wife the car keys. 'Will you drive,' she dug into her tired mind for names, 'Mrs Suggs, Miss Peacock, Mrs Torrence and Mrs Graham and their new young friends home, and then come back for me and the girls? There's not room in the car for all of us. Yes, I do have spare bedrooms, but it can only be for tonight. As you know, I'm not always home.'

And the vicar's wife assumed that those absences were for mere social reasons. 'Temporary' could easily become permanent. Deanna would need to see that it did not.

Mrs Goodword vanished with her posse and a screech of gears.

Deanna turned to the girls. 'Have you had dinner?'

Three shaved heads shook. The oldest girl met Deanna's eyes for the first time. Her face had the blank look of a child who had cried so long they no longer believed tears could help.

Deanna reached into her handbag for a block of chocolate — almost impossible to obtain for months — and blessed her grandfather once again for his forethought in making sure she had plenty. She broke it into three and handed a chunk to each girl. They took it automatically, the youngest looking queryingly at her older sisters, apparently not sure what a block of chocolate was for. The oldest girl gave her a slight nod as if to say, *It's safe to eat.*

'This will stop you starving till we get home,' said Deanna brightly, puzzled at the lack of delight, as well as the girls' silence.

She manufactured a smile again. 'My house is a bit far away, but there's chicken stew and potatoes in their jackets in the oven,' which she had hoped would last her and Dusty all week, 'and an apple and blackberry pie. I've even got some cream!'

She held out her hand to the smallest child. 'Come on. Let's get you cleaned up first. You two wait here and eat your chocolate.'

'No.' The oldest girl's voice was quiet but stubborn. 'We go together.' Her accent was educated, clear and precise, very different from the East End slum voices of the other children on the train.

'Very well. It'll be cold out in the lavatory though.'

Deanna led the way to the ladies', then matter-of-factly stripped off the child's soiled dress — faeces had no horrors for someone who had cared for a dying old man — and the girl's underpants, also gingham, the elastic sagging, and clearly secondhand — then lifted the child into the wash basin.

'I'm sorry, the water will be cold.' She quickly scrubbed, using her hands and her handkerchief. She draped her tweed jacket over the naked child, then took off her blouse to use as a towel, leaving herself in her chemise and brassiere. She put the jacket back on the child, so it hung coat-like on her thin frame. It looked odd, but sufficiently dress-like to get them home. She wriggled back into her wet blouse and tucked it into her skirt, then picked up the child again. Her wrists were like chicken bones.

'You still won't tell me your names?'

Silence.

'I'm Deanna Claverton. You'll hear me called Lady Deanna too. You can call me ...' She hesitated, trying for something child-friendly. 'Aunt Dee. My grandfather called me Dee. And by the sound of the gears groaning here comes Mrs Goodword with my car.'

The girls moved closer together as they followed Deanna out of the waiting room, shivering in the evening air despite the lingering summer daylight. Mrs Goodword stepped out of the car, presenting Deanna with a professional smile. 'So kind of you to take the girls.'

'Until tomorrow,' said Deanna firmly.

'Yes, of course. Just as soon as I can find a suitable place.'

The oldest girl showed a flicker of weary contempt. They are used to being shunted like parcels, thought Deanna. But this was not the time to bicker with the vicar's wife. She had made her position clear. She would repeat it tomorrow — but not in front of the girls.

'Who wants the front seat with me?' she said brightly, thankful that daylight saving meant there was just enough light to get home on the familiar road without dimmed headlights.

No one answered. The oldest girl opened the rear door and all three climbed into the back seat together. Mrs Goodword waved at them with tired gaiety as the car left the station yard.

Thankfully for Deanna's diminished petrol ration, it was only ten minutes to Eagle's Rest — and even less to the castle, for the train route had been chosen for his lordship's convenience last century, though only the edge of the estate and not the castle itself was visible from the road.

The girls stared at the house with neither curiosity nor approval as Deanna turned into the driveway. The house had no architectural features worthy of the name: a two-storey rectangle topped with chimneys, its bricks yellowed with age, a small wooden porch at the front and a larger one at the back. Ivy competed with late roses up the walls; more roses tangled along the fences.

The front garden beds might now hold cabbages and Brussels sprouts instead of snapdragons and lupins, and most of the lawn and rose beds had been dug up for potatoes, but Deanna had left the rosebushes around the house. Smoke trickled from the rear chimney; the air smelled of ripe apples and strawberries; and the flicker of leaves and almost imperceptible murmur of the river met them when Deanna parked in the shed and opened her passengers' door.

The girls merely looked wary.

'Come on. We'll go in the back way,' said Deanna in what she realised was a falsely bright tone as the girls cautiously slid out of the car. 'I mostly live in the kitchen these days, to save fuel.' Kitchens seem to be my destiny, she thought grimly, then smiled at herself. She was no Cinderella. She preferred a good kitchen to a cocktail party anyway. Much less a ball.

And it's a good kitchen, she thought with satisfaction as she unlocked the back door, locking up being a precaution never needed till the war brought strangers to the district. The house had been built by a prosperous grocer for his retirement in the

1890s, demolishing the decayed small Elizabethan manor that had stood there but retaining its cellars.

The grocer had obviously ensured sound walls, good drainage, and even a bathroom before his death a decade later, as well as excellent comfort for the servants, his wife possibly having been in service in her youth.

The kitchen had a stone fireplace at one end, surrounded by two wide sofas and two armchairs; a long scrubbed wooden table stood in the middle both for eating and for cooking; and an enclosed wood-fired stove between cupboards and benches at the other end of the room still warmed the rooster stew. The few shelves held only the most commonly used condiments and pots and pans. The rest were housed in the commodious scullery next door.

Gently faded Persian carpets softened the flagged floor. Paintings from the castle hung on the walls furthest from any smoke from either fire. Deanna suspected one was a Monet waterlilies, sitting incongruously with Miss Enid's own efficient portraits of her eagles in flight or on the nest, but loved it too much to have it evaluated and become a possible target for thieves.

She looked back at the children hovering by the door, glad she had pulled the blackout curtains before she left. 'Come in! I can't put on the light till I've pulled the curtains over the door. The electricity will go off soon so we need to make the most of it. I think they must be keeping the generators on for longer than usual to welcome you evacuees.'

The girls took perhaps three steps into the room. The middle one turned and pulled the blackout curtains across.

'*Woof?*' The world's most unenthusiastic guard dog wandered over to them. He sniffed their shoes, and then the smallest one's bottom with more attention. The child moved tactfully away, while the middle girl rubbed Dusty's ears to distract him. Dusty gave her a toothy grin of appreciation.

'Dusty! Sit!' Deanna ordered, glad at least that the girls showed no fear of dogs.

Dusty ignored her. He leaped up onto the sofa and regarded the newcomers with interest.

Deanna flicked on the light, wondering what to do with her charges. Should she get them clean after their journey and find nightwear for them? She looked at their white, thin faces as they stared around the unfamiliar kitchen, arms clutching each other, the older girl trying not to show her terror, the younger ones almost in tears at the unknown to come.

No, food first. And warmth. They were shivering despite the heat of the day and the warmth from the slow combustion stove. She grabbed a pile of Miss Enid's silk shawls from the hooks by the back door.

'Sit,' she said, just as she had to Dusty. The girls moved towards the table. 'No, not at the table, over on the sofa that doesn't have Dusty on it. I'll put a match to the fire.'

They sat obediently, backs straight, hands in laps, then found Dusty abandoning his own sofa and sprawling across the three of them, tail wagging, grinning up at them, delighted to have found new human cushions.

Suddenly they became children again, not quite smiling but no longer concrete-faced, rubbing his ears, neck, back, whichever bit was in reach. Dusty glanced at Deanna reproachfully, as if to say, '*This* is how a dog should be treated,' and gave himself up to being hugged.

Deanna draped the shawls around the girls' shoulders, then placed a wooden tray on the bench — the tray that had taken afternoon tea outside so many times while she and Miss Enid sat at the garden table sharing binoculars, gazing at a pair of eagles inspecting the headland for rabbits, rodents or carrion, or watching seagulls pierce the blue of the sky.

The casserole from the oven went onto the tray. She took the lid off, exposing the elderly rooster that had been slowly cooking since breakfast, the rest of the casserole filled with sauteed carrots, celery, onions, garlic and parsley. She quickly cut the bird into chunks, filled a big bowl with potatoes in their jackets, and grabbed the butter dish and a loaf of homemade white bread. She hoped the children didn't know the mechanics of rationing and wonder where the meal's ingredients came from, especially the pure white flour.

A bowl for each child next; cutlery and a pair of serving spoons; butter knives; a plate of sliced bread already buttered; and three glasses of milk.

'Dusty, down!' she ordered.

He clambered off the sofa, deciding to give her a starving-dog look instead of reproach. Her grandfather had trained him not to beg from the table or sofa, but leftovers were his prerogative. He settled himself on the hearthrug where he could continue reminding the eaters that a hungry hound waited for their crumbs.

Deanna put the tray on a coffee table by the sofa and placed a ladle into the casserole. 'Use your fingers for the bones,' she told them. 'I do.'

She helped herself to a bowlful of stew and a potato and sat on the armchair opposite. It wasn't till she had eaten two hungry spoonfuls that she noticed none of them was eating.

'You don't like chicken?' It would not have been tactful to say the bird had been a rooster and she'd been the one to chop off its head. Townies were squeamish about home-killed meat.

The youngest looked bewildered at the word 'chicken'. The other two looked longingly at the food. She realised that chicken would not have been offered at an orphanage, and almost certainly not butter either, though possibly a smear of dripping. But surely the older two remembered eating food like this with their parents? Were they waiting to say grace, or for some other ritual?

Perhaps they could not believe this bounty was real, or that she really intended them to eat it.

'Eat,' she ordered quietly.

They began to spoon up the stew, slowly at first, then ravenously, chewing the crusty bread and its rich covering of butter with such wonder that Deanna stopped eating just to watch the pleasure on their faces.

'More?' she asked when the bowls were empty, and the plate of bread and butter too, and only a single potato remained in the bowl. 'There's apple and blackberry pie too, remember. I get my cream from the farm next door. Maybe you can meet Jessie tomorrow. She's a jersey cow. She likes apples.'

They could fit in a visit to Jessie before going to whatever home Mrs Goodword had found for them, she told herself. Deanna would make sure they had a good breakfast too. And clothes — children's fashion changed more slowly than adults'. Her old school and holiday clothes up in the attic would be suitable; she'd go up in the morning to sort that out. Though the girls would need new underthings. Mrs Goodword must see to that.

It didn't occur to her that they might be ill after so much unaccustomed food until they were eating the pie, slowly now, savouring each mouthful. But they had colour in their faces. The trembling small fingers were steady; their eyes no longer darted this way and that to find the next danger.

'*Gruff*,' Dusty reminded her, rising from the hearthrug and stretching, an almost straight line from nose to tail. She scraped out the remnants of the casserole for him, making sure there were no small bones in it, added the chopped potato and some cold porridge — she always made extra for him — and put it on the floor.

The girls had finished the pie. Thankfully, none of them looked vomitously green. They leaned against each other, exhausted and sated but still too wary to relax entirely.

'Bath time,' she told them. 'We've got our own hot-water supply, so there's no need to skimp like people in town. You can bathe while I make up your beds.'

Three heads shook. Why refuse to bathe? And why wouldn't they speak?

'You need to wash before you go to bed,' she reminded them firmly but gently. The train journey had left them grimy, and they probably hadn't been clean to start with. At least the shaved heads meant they wouldn't still have lice.

'There's violet-scented bath salts,' she added temptingly. 'And I'll warm your towels in the oven.' Nanny had done that for her, so many years back. Which reminded her she owed the old woman a letter, up in Scotland now with her sister, and there was the letter for Uncle Jasper to write too, even if this one contained no vital information.

There had been no objection to the bathing before. All at once she realised. 'You all want to sleep in the same room?'

Three nods.

'One of the bedrooms has a double bed. Could you share that?'

Emphatic nods and looks of relief. That was understandable. In a world with no parents, home, clothes or even their previous shelter, they needed to stay close to each other.

'One room then. I'll fill the bath for you then find you some nightclothes.' She left them cuddling Dusty again, his whiskers faintly stained with stewed carrot.

Four

CARELESS TALK COSTS LIVES ... Be like Dad. Keep Mum.
                                World War II propaganda poster

Two of her cotton blouses would work as nightdresses for the smaller girls, she decided, and a petticoat for the older girl, with a shawl each. The attics had no blackout curtains, so she couldn't go up there to forage for children's nighties and clothes from her own childhood tonight.

Thankfully Miss Enid had loved shawls of all kinds, from soft Shetland wool to crocheted ones from the village fete to fringed thick China silk. Most of her clothing had been given to charity on her death, but the shawls remained hanging by almost every door.

Eagle's Rest's bed linen, quilts and blankets must have been supplemented from the castle during her grandfather's renovations. She doubted Donnie would regret or even notice the loss of two dozen patched sheets, or chests of faded quilts and blankets with their stitched ends slightly frayed. He, or his heir, certainly had no need of them.

The bathroom was next to the scullery — inconvenient for trips to the loo at two am but presumably it had been easier to install the plumbing there. The bath was enormous, easily big enough for three, with mahogany surrounds and bronze eagle taps, and there was a toilet on a mahogany platform with matching wooden seat and cover.

The girls sniffed the soap, passing it to each other, felt the thickness and warmth of the towels, gazed at the plenitude of steaming water, and the new toothbrushes Deanna fetched from the linen cupboard. She left them to it.

She hauled last week's sheets off the drying rack in the airing cupboard then made up the largest bed.

The next priority was to get them in bed and asleep, partly to ease their shock and weariness, but also so she could write that letter to Uncle Jasper, which must be posted tomorrow, with a second letter with the same information couched in different gossip the next day. The mail was unreliable when postal vans, trains or entire streets might vanish in the nightly bombing.

She hurried downstairs and into the bathroom.

The unexpectedly empty bathroom. The kitchen was deserted too. Even Dusty had vanished.

'Hello?' she called.

No answer. Of course they wouldn't answer. Were they hiding? Had they run away? Were they trying to run back to their home — their real home, not the orphanage? Surely not tonight, now darkness had fallen, with no torch, no streetlamps, even the moon hidden under the cloud walled sky.

She peered into the dining room, unused for years, then the sitting room with its furniture under dust sheets — some of the pieces that had come from the castle were valuable, possibly priceless, and needed protecting from sunlight, moths, silverfish and dust until the land was finally at peace again and she could invite friends to stay — real friends, people she liked, instead of those seduced by a dream of fascist superiority.

One day I *will* have a life of my own, she thought. The lights will come on again across Europe, and I will use my dining room, filling it with laughter and good food.

She crossed the hall to the library ...

And there they were, the three of them wrapped in shawls and makeshift towel nightdresses sitting cross-legged on the floor of the shelf-lined room — no! Four of them — Dusty had wound himself around the smallest child, or she had wound herself around him. All of them were completely, obliviously absorbed in books they must have chosen from the shelves. The smallest child pointed out a picture to Dusty.

Thank goodness. And thank goodness too that she kept the blackout curtains drawn in this room, opening them only when she needed a book in daylight.

Had they been exploring or did they find this room by instinct? Because, as she glanced at the titles the girls had chosen, she realised something else too. These girls were educated readers.

The smallest clutched Kenneth Grahame's *The Wind in the Willows*: enchanting, but not easy for a child her age; the middle girl was rapidly turning the pages of Ethel Turner's *The Secret of the Sea*; and the oldest — Heaven help us, Deanna thought — was engrossed in Charles Darwin's *On the Origin of Species*, absorbing each page as hungrily as she had eaten the stew, as if she had been starved of books as well as food. These girls are intelligent, Deanna thought. There were plenty of shelves of children's books here: picture books, Beatrix Potter and Enid Blyton with entrancing illustrations, yet even the youngest had moved on to a more complex book.

She also saw clearly quite how badly these girls had been treated. Much of what she had taken for smudges from the train's soot were in fact bruises — variously coloured, so not the result of a single accident — bruises like bracelets on wrists and arms and even ankles, where they'd been grabbed and held hard, or even tied up, and what looked like the marks of a cane on their shoulders, one that had been wielded so hard it had left scars. The older two girls were as thin as the youngest, their shoulders sharp as angels' wings.

The electric light flickered, a sign the power would go off in ten minutes. Deanna lit two of the lamps she kept in the hallway, then slipped back to the library.

'Time for bed,' she said. 'The electricity is going off in a few minutes. Take the books with you if you like. You can read by lamplight till you feel sleepy.'

The girls stood, clutching their books. Dusty looked affronted at the interruption. He made his way out the door, presumably back to the warmth by the stove, leaving a rooster-smelling fart behind him.

'Come on. The bedrooms are upstairs. You must be exhausted. Sleep as late as you like tomorrow.' She smiled at them. 'You can take the books with you when Mrs Goodword finds you a new home.'

The oldest girl took the youngest's hand and began to move to the door. The middle child stayed exactly where she was.

'I like this room,' she said. Her voice was clear, with what newspapers referred to as the 'Oxford accent' of the educated, mixed with some other slight accent too. The girl gestured to the floor-to-ceiling books, the rolling ladder to get to the higher shelves, the desk in the corner, possibly used by Louis XV or one of his mistresses, but now with the inkwell, blotting paper and pen wiper for her letters to Uncle Jasper.

There was no reason for anyone to be suspicious if they found Deanna writing a letter, but she still didn't feel comfortable composing them where someone might knock on the back door, or even knock then come in like Mrs Thripps, who still came twice a week to 'do the rough', and who collected Deanna's rations too, which saved her queuing up.

'We had a room like this at home,' said the girl, 'but not as big.'

The older girl hissed, 'Shhh!'

'No.' She met her sister's eyes. 'It is important we say something. If we don't say anything at all the moustache woman back at the station who gives orders will send us to another orphanage, or to families who'll only take one of us each, and we may lose each other.'

The youngest gave a cry at her words.

'Silence won't save us,' the middle girl told her sisters. 'It helped us escape, but if we don't speak it will all have been for nothing.'

The youngest girl hid her face in her sister's shawl. The older girl bit her lip, then nodded reluctantly.

'My name is Rosa,' the middle girl told Deanna stubbornly. 'I'm ten years old. My older sister is Magda. She's fourteen. Anna is five.' She pointed to each, meeting her older sister's eyes as if daring her to contradict. Were these really their names? Deanna wondered.

'What's your surname?'

No answer.

'What are your parents' names?' Deanna asked carefully.

'They are dead,' said Rosa, as if that closed that matter. 'Not from the war. A car accident, before the war began.'

And still no name. 'You have other relatives?'

'No.'

The older girl, whose name was possibly Magda, said quietly, 'We have been in an orphanage since our parents died.'

How long had that been? A year? Two years? Three? An orphanage explained the gingham, but not the lack of labels or, for that matter, why there hadn't been any other orphans on the train with them. 'Which orphanage?'

'It doesn't matter,' said Magda, with clipped upper-class vowels like her sister's, and Dee's too. 'The orphanage has been closed because of the bombing, but we are not going to the one they are sending us all to. Ever. We removed our labels and slipped into another train that was about to leave. We climbed up onto the luggage racks under the bundles.' She shrugged. 'I don't think the orphanage authorities will look hard for us. They may not even know we're gone.'

Probably not, thought Deanna. The confusion of moving over a million children across Britain meant that few records were kept at departure, relying on the children themselves to arrange contact with their parents.

Rosa stared at Deanna with desperate eagerness. 'May we stay here? Please? We'll work hard. We know how to scrub, to polish floors. We did that at the orphanage. We grew vegetables too. We can do all that for you.'

The older girl, Magda, nodded. 'I promise we'll be no trouble. Anna needs to be shown how to do things sometimes.'

'No, I don't!' said a small voice from the folds of her sister's nightclothes.

'Yes, you do. But Rosa and I will show her, and make sure she doesn't bother you. We'll be so quiet you won't know we're here, except for our cleaning and polishing.'

'You all need to go to school,' said Deanna helplessly.

'We only went sometimes at the orphanage. I'm old enough to leave school, anyway. I've done my eleven-plus. I'll work harder than any servant. We all will. We ... we won't eat as much as tonight either. We just hadn't eaten anything since yesterday.'

A girl as intelligent as this had to stay at school. They all did! But not till they had clothes. Ration books. Not till they had bodies to match their spirit from good food, and their eyes had lost their shadows; and Mrs Goodword almost certainly would not be able to find a household willing to take three girls, not with so many evacuees already placed. She might not even try. These girls knew it.

Dormitories were being set up for groups from boarding schools, and presumably from orphanages too. Mrs Goodword would have to send the girls to one of those, if they insisted on staying together.

Deanna's only knowledge of orphanages came from Dickens. Surely conditions were better now? But the girls looked as if their flesh had melted away, leaving their eyes enormous in their thin faces. They'd had no overcoats. Gas masks, but nothing else, not even a teddy bear. The hard blankness of their faces had slowly melted into pleasure when they cuddled Dusty, when they closed their eyes in wonder at the flavours of bread and butter, of rooster cooked with vegetables, of fruit pie with thick jersey cream.

She couldn't keep them here. It was impossible. Even if she didn't have the letters to Uncle Jasper and the other matters she must keep secret, she had no idea how to care for children.

Except, she thought, as Magda's arm automatically held little Anna to her, these children had already been taking care of each other, and protecting each other too. She had shelter to offer them, even clothes, and good food, not to mention a library, Dusty, the gardens and orchards and woodland she had loved to roam in as a child too, the lap of the waves and the lullaby of the river and the rustling songs of trees to ease their terrors.

It was unthinkable. But, looking at the flickers of hope on the girls' faces, there was only one answer she could give. 'Of course,' she said gently. 'You can stay here as long as you want to.'

Five

There'll be bluebirds over
The white cliffs of Dover
Tomorrow, just you wait and see
There'll be love and laughter
And peace ever after
Tomorrow, when the world is free

Lyrics from 'The White Cliffs of Dover'
by Nat Burton,
a song of World War II

Finally they were in the double bed in the second guest room and, when she glanced in, asleep, curled together like puppies, books still in their hands, with Dusty lying snoring across their feet like a shaggy quilt.

She removed the books to the side table, then noticed that the youngest, Anna, held something, her small fingers still tight about it. Deanna looked closer. It was a slice of tonight's bread, wrapped in a handkerchief. Emergency rations, she thought, for when there is no food again.

A wave of anger and protectiveness swept through her. She turned off the lamp. The girls didn't stir, even when Dusty slid off the bed and padded after Deanna.

She made her way back to the library, put on thin leather gloves, took out notepaper and ink. She had already worked out how to hide the information the letter must contain. If it hadn't been for her grandfather's introduction, she might assume this was a game.

Dear Uncle Jasper,
  I hope you are well. All is the same here, but oh, the queues for the rationing! I am sure that Mr Filmer is adding sawdust to the sausages. It's silly, but I miss marmalade the most!

She had, in fact, made twelve jars of it from the fruit in the glasshouses. The marmalade complaint was just another distraction.

  But the real news is that Sandra and her husband [the names a previously agreed code word] *are so looking forward to Johnny coming back! He was on one of the last ships from Dunkirk and has wangled some leave ...*

She wrote on, nonsense now, a reminiscence of playing hockey with Cousin Mary, Uncle Jasper's imaginary daughter, two pages to disguise one fact that might possibly be useful.

Four nights earlier she had caught the train to Scotland, ignoring the signs demanding, *Is your journey really necessary?* to spend a couple of days at a shooting party, glad that in these days of staff shortages no one would think it strange she had no maid. She was, in fact, an excellent shot — she'd learned to shoot for food, not sport — but the men would not like to be shown up by a woman, men ostensibly in charge of defending Britain but who had the time, so soon after Dunkirk, to come to Scotland for a few days' entertainment.

She had spent the days changing clothes, playing bridge, eating excellently cooked game from the estate and the black market and drinking sparingly from the excellent pre-war cellar, while her target, the daughter of an honourable, married to another honourable who was now 'something in the Home Office', drank glass after glass of Château Lafite champagne. She boasted about her pre-war renovations to their country home and, with a little encouragement, the importance of her husband's job, and the humiliation of the forced evacuation of Dunkirk.

'I mean, darling, we need to stop pretending it was a victory to get so many home, don't we? Germany could have *crushed* us, but they didn't.' She lit another cigarette, fitting it into its holder, and politely offered one to Deanna. 'Bippy says Germany had us *totally* over a *barrel*, but spared us in hopes we might come to our senses and form an alliance or at least announce neutrality. Poland and France will do *much* better now under German rule, if they only had the sense to know it.'

She carefully blew a smoke ring. 'Have you ever been to Germany, darling? Bippy and I went over in '38. Everything *so* efficient, and Herr Hitler certainly knows how to put the Jews in their place. It's the Jewish bankers who are behind this war, *everyone* knows that, just to make money from selling armaments. Why should we quarrel with Germany? Our own royal house is German, despite their change of name.'

'I couldn't agree more.' Deanna, having taken the cigarette and lit it, was holding it away from her rather than inhaling. 'I've heard,' she added casually, 'that the Duke of Windsor was working on a draft alliance with the Germans before Churchill shipped him off to the Bahamas. That was why he was sent off so quickly.'

Deanna stubbed out the cigarette. 'Poor old David. If it hadn't been for that wretched abdication, we wouldn't be at war now. David said as much last year in that interview the BBC refused to broadcast.'

'I know. Bippy told me all about it. David had *style*. Yes, Simpson is an oik and can be a bitch at times, but at least she knows how to dress — not like the dowd we have now, all good works and *knitting*. Darling, I refuse to knit. Can you imagine the Duchess of Windsor knitting?'

Deanna grinned at her. 'Plots, maybe. Not socks. I've heard David might even return to England to continue the negotiations,' she added carefully. 'That he's even arranged the treaty terms.'

Her companion looked at her in surprise then took another swig of bubbles. 'I didn't know you moved in those circles. It's all got to stay *very* hush-hush, so hardly anyone knows the plan, Bippy says. It's too bad of him not to come up for the shooting with me. Oh, it's all so *boring*. The war and politics, not even being able to go to Paris for a decent dress. Tell me, where did you find that *divine* silk thing you wore last night?'

It had been a very vague hint indeed, and from a semi-drunk and not very bright woman — who was, however, exactly the kind of person who might overhear more than she was meant to, then let information slip.

She might also have totally misunderstood anything she had heard, but thankfully Uncle Jasper must have many correspondents like Deanna. A jigsaw of lost and damaged pieces might possibly be put together so the true picture could be seen.

So many innocents in English history had died when exiled kings tried to regain their thrones and failed. But the former King Edward VIII would have German forces to support him. He might just succeed.

Deanna signed the letter, addressed the envelope, then left it in a drawer of the desk. She'd post it tomorrow, along with a letter to Vivian, a schoolfriend now in uniform, and a note to Mrs Thripps' nephew, who was recuperating from an amputation sustained after the evacuation. Deanna had met him only twice, once as a schoolboy, the second time when he arrived to show 'Lady Deanna' the splendour of his uniform on his final leave.

Tomorrow ...

What on earth had she let herself in for?

The girls would need feeding as well as clothing. She wasn't worried about not having enough food for them, either tomorrow or in the future. The garden, hens and Higgins's dairy would provide much of it. But the food must be cooked, and cooked well, because just now they needed the kind of nourishment that would show them life could be safe, and good — to remind them, perhaps, of what it was like to have a home and security. Her grandfather had given her that when neither of her parents had been interested enough to care for her. In some strange way, this felt like repaying him.

She needed more sugar than her fortnightly ration if she was going to cook home-like food for the girls; nor did they have ration cards of their own yet. She needed flour, too, of a quality not obtainable anymore, even if she had had a spare hour to queue for it.

But she'd had a grandfather who had foreseen just this need, having lived through the rationing of the Great War, and seen the starvation in countries that had been conquered, too.

Deanna crossed the library and lifted the carved eagle at the end of the mantelpiece, then pushed. A section of shelves slid away, leading to the not-so-secret passage, a short landing and then the stairs down to the natural caves the original manor house had undoubtedly been deliberately built over, in the days when hiding or escaping might mean life or death, with a conventional cellar under the scullery as a decoy.

This end of the caves had been fitted with shelves to make a secret cellar, far larger and deeper than the one under the scullery, and the corner she had furnished as an air-raid shelter in the unlikely event that this area was bombed.

She didn't know how many knew the 'secret'. She'd been about ten when Miss Enid had first shown her the caves; nor had she objected when Deanna showed them to Donnie. Mrs Thripps, who had 'done' for Miss Enid as she still did for Deanna now, certainly knew about them, as did Mr Higgins, who helped carry the provisions the old duke had arranged for his granddaughter. Gossip spread like march flies around the village.

Possibly everyone from Mr Septimus Filmer the butcher to 'Three Fingers' Harrison the carpenter knows of the cellar under Eagle's Rest, she thought, lighting the candle lantern just inside, then carefully pulling the door closed behind her. She didn't think the girls would wake, but neither did she want them finding a gaping hole in the wall.

Those who knew about the cellars would guess they contained Miss Enid's wine. Mrs Thripps knew the cellar contained several sacks of white flour, white and brown sugar in oilcloth-lined chests, and a chest of tea, for she shared in the bounty, taking a little each week. Hoarding was illegal in wartime, but this had been stored a good year before the war and so had not contributed to the shortages.

Mrs Thripps did not know, however, that if one removed some of the bricks at the end wall of the cellar, a pair of twelve-year-olds could wriggle through the gap and follow the cave down to its opening on the cliff overlooking the sea a good quarter mile away. Possibly neither Miss Enid nor her grandfather had known what she and Donnie had discovered, as the brick wall had obviously been put there to stop just that access. The cave ended in an abrupt and dangerous drop to rocks below. The cave itself would only be accessible by boat at high tide, and even then only with an expert skipper and crew to stop the craft crashing against the cliffs.

Nor did Mrs Thripps know about the second door, again a set of sliding shelves that had walled off part of the existing cellar. This was where her grandfather had stored true treasure for her: provisions enough to see her through a decade of war, or even longer. They were the kind of foods that the Army and Navy Stores sent to colonial administrators, or that travellers bought when heading to India or the Middle East: extremely hard chocolate; sugar and flour in metal barrels; packet after packet of tea sewn in oilcloth to keep its freshness; coffee beans; dried fruit, by itself or packed in brandy; cans of corned beef and sardines as well as pâté de foie gras and truffled goose breast, presumably for Christmases; tins of olive oil and lard; and assorted other cans including vegetables and fruit.

The cans and tins would easily last a decade down here in the cool, well-drained and ventilated dryness. The sugars and white flour would keep indefinitely, as would the tea, even if its flavour faded. The dried fruit in brandy would last forever as well, if growing a little more solid over time. The medicine chest was well stocked, including with prescription painkillers, presumably obtained during the duke's illness.

A tall cupboard held shotguns, rifles and pistols, as well as boxes of ammunition, for hunting food or possibly defence. Either way, the old man had surely had fun planning it all and executing it without either village or granddaughter knowing, though it must have taken the last of his strength to move it all with Mr Higgins. Deanna remembered days he had come in, white and exhausted. She had thought he had been hunting, or even simply walking his estate, not wrestling sacks and chests downstairs and across a rocky floor. It must have taken a year at least, or even two ...

Tonight, however, she only needed flour and sugar, taken from the first cellar. In fact she hadn't yet needed anything from the next. She might in a year or so, though, with three more mouths to feed. She ladled flour and sugar into old biscuit tins kept for this purpose and brought back when empty — no one would query someone carrying a biscuit tin in a library, where one might easily need a snack — then stopped, goosebumps rising on her skin.

Something was scraping beyond the wall.

Six

The men that worked for England
They have their graves at home:
And bees and birds of England
About the cross can roam.

But they that fought for England,
Following a falling star,
Alas, alas for England
They have their graves afar.

And they that rule in England,
In stately conclave met,
Alas, alas for England
They have no graves as yet.
    'Elegy in a Country Churchyard' by GK Chesterton

She pulled most of the shutters across the lamp and kneeled by the bricks at the end of the cellar. She managed to push a few more out of the way, the mortar crumbling, catching them as they fell to muffle the sound, then listened.

The air smelled of rotting seaweed, and the sand that washed halfway up the cave each high tide, leaving more salt behind each time. The scraping she'd heard had been far off, towards the murmur and crash of the sea, but another sound was clear now — footsteps, walking softly, but the sand squeaking slightly with each step. Only one person's footsteps, she thought, but whoever was in the cave must have come by boat, so there might be more following.

Should she call the police? The land between here and the sea was hers, so anyone in the cave was trespassing. But calling the police would mean giving away the secret of the cave. The police might even search the cellar and find the one beyond and convict her for hoarding. She had no way to prove the purchases had not been hers. Legally, she should have handed much of the food in when she found it.

Did whoever was behind the wall know about the entrance to the house, or had they found the cave by accident?

Not in wartime, she thought. No boat would roam the coast at night now, and nor would fishers risk the waves that smashed just below the cave's entrance at high tide, the only time it could be accessed, just to explore what looked like a crumple far up in the cliffs.

She took the key from under a chest, unlocked the arms cabinet, took out a small pistol and loaded it, but kept the safety catch on, then slid it into a cup of her brassiere, hoping the tweed jacket would cover any bulge and that the safety catch held ...

She squeezed through the gap in the brickwork — her good tweed skirt would be ruined — then stood up, catching the sea scent that had sunk into the old bricks that reinforced the roof. This part of the cave, at least, had either been deliberately dug or at least enlarged, perhaps back in the days of religious persecution when priests had to arrive or escape in secret, or during the war between the Cavaliers and the Roundheads, long before the merchant's substantial house had replaced the original manor.

She no longer needed light. She pulled all the shutters on the lamp, making her invisible. Her feet and her sense of smell could find the way, and her skin too, heading directly into the breeze on her face from the sea.

She rounded a corner, and there it was, a torch, undimmed, bobbing up and down. 'Stop right where you are,' she said calmly. 'Put your hands in the air, and drop any weapons.'

The light halted.

'Dee honey?' said a man's voice weakly, incredulously. 'I'm really here? This is Eagle's Rest?'

It was unmistakably an American accent. She un-shuttered the lamp just as a shape sagged against the cave wall. She ran to him, but he managed to straighten and limp towards her.

'*Donnie*. You're supposed to be dead! I mean, how …?!'

He was dressed in a moth-eaten jumper that stank of fish and patched trousers and was barefoot; there was a trickle of sandy blood where he must have stubbed his toe. A wound on his forehead had been roughly stitched. His hand was wrapped in a bloody cloth. A strangely shaped hand …

And yet he looked the same, despite it all. The unusually high forehead he'd claimed was a mark of superior intelligence. His brown hair hadn't darkened. His teeth shone with the electric whiteness of every wealthy American. His face had merely gained maturity, his jaw stronger, his nose no longer that of a sunny boy, his eyes … Wary eyes, she thought. Eyes that had seen too much pain. Eyes with a touch of desperation.

He laughed tremulously. 'Not quite dead, though it looked like I might be for a while. A French fisherwoman found me in the water and hid me under a pile of fishing nets. They came for me at night — the French I mean. Sheltered me in a cellar, found me a doctor ... well he was really a vet, but he seemed to know what he was doing.'

'They brought you here?'

He nodded. 'I showed them vaguely where I needed to go — I didn't want to mark the exact location on a map in case we were caught. I didn't even tell the fishermen where the cave was till we were past the beach.' He swayed, then took a shuddered breath. 'It's further than I thought. Would ... would you help me?'

She slipped her shoulder under his arm and managed to get him to the brick wall hiding the cellars. He sat, slumped, as she pulled away more bricks, then slid in first to help pull him through. 'Can you make it upstairs?'

He snorted, just like the twelve-year-old boy had snorted. 'I've made it all the way from Dunkirk. I can get a bit further.' He hesitated. 'Is anyone upstairs? Miss Enid?'

'She died, four years ago. She left the house to me. But I had evacuees foisted on me this afternoon. They're exhausted so I don't think they'll wake.'

'Good. I ... I need to get the exchange to phone someone in my regiment. I ... I'm out of uniform.'

'I doubt the army will court-martial you,' she said drily. 'Here, let me help you again.'

They reached the top of the stairs. She pulled the door across, then closed it behind him, and helped him across the library to the armchair next to the telephone.

Dusty gazed at them from the sofa he was not supposed to lie on, as if to say, *Rules do not apply so late, when we should be in bed.*

'*Woof?*' he enquired. He sniffed vaguely towards Donnie's jumper, then decided it was more smell than substance. He seemed totally uninterested in the newcomer, unlike the girls.

'You are the worst watchdog in England,' Deanna informed him.

'Dusty old boy? Remember me? You were just a puppy! But you were grey then, too.'

Dusty lowered his head. None of the words referred to food, and nor was the newcomer offering to scratch his neck.

Deanna picked up the telephone receiver. 'I'd better speak to the exchange for you and give a message or Doris will gossip all over the village. What number do you need?'

'My unit's. Here, I'll write it for you. Ask to speak to Captain Mark Hayward. Tell him I'm here, and add "Mermaid", but don't mention the caves. They should remain secret.'

'I certainly hope so,' said Deanna wryly.

'God, it's good to be back. I never realised I thought of England as home till the war. England and Claverton — I felt safe as soon as I scrambled from the boat into the cave. I hope the French fishermen get back safely. They risked a lot to get me here.'

She nodded as he lay back in the armchair and shut his eyes. This was a man who had enlisted as soon as war was declared, to fight for a country where he was not yet even a conventional citizen, despite his title. She wished her grandfather had known his heir was a good one.

His face was pale under the dirt. She felt his forehead briefly as the phone rang. No fever, thank goodness. 'Doris? It's Lady Deanna. I'm sorry to disturb you so late. I need …'

She asked Doris to find the number and put her through. She put the phone in its cradle again, waiting for Doris to call back, hoping it wouldn't be long.

Tring … She grabbed it at the first ring. 'May I speak to Captain Mark Hayward? No? Could I speak to whoever is in charge then … My business?'

Suddenly the entire day became too much. 'Could you please tell whoever is in charge that my name is Lady Deanna Claverton. I have the Duke of Claverton with me. He's not dead but escaped from France badly wounded. The word he's asked me to use is "Mermaid" ... Yes, I'll hold.' She waited perhaps twenty seconds till another voice spoke, a male one this time, then handed the phone to the man in the chair. 'He wants to speak to you.'

And their conversation would probably need to be private, though they would both know that Doris would be listening, wide-eyed. Doris would not phone the newspapers, but the news of Donnie's return would be all over the village by tomorrow, though Doris could be depended upon to keep secrets too. Dee slipped out to the kitchen. Dusty followed her, correctly assuming she was going to prepare food. She heated the cocoa she had left for herself while the girls had drunk theirs, then scrambled three eggs and buttered a slice of bread. Remembering Donnie's injured hand she cut the bread into small pieces next to the eggs. She carried the lot in on a tray just as he put the receiver down, Dusty trotting behind in case of leftovers.

'Food. Honey, you are an angel.'

'Anything but. Angels don't smell of cow manure after working in the glasshouse. Just be glad I've bathed. A few hours ago you'd have smelled me from the other end of the cave.' She watched him eat hungrily and slightly clumsily with one hand. 'Donnie, I'm more glad than I can say that you're back.'

'No gladder than I am. I used to dream of Claverton after I got back to America, the ancient woods covered in moss and the crumbling towers we weren't supposed to climb. I can't believe America won't join the war. "Too proud to fight!" What rubbish! I dreamed of Claverton over in France too. I wished I'd come here just once before I left, but there was so little time.' He smiled at her. 'It's the same scent, even now. Woodsmoke — it must be the kind of wood — and old books, and Persian rugs just like up at the castle.'

They *were* the rugs from the castle. She said hurriedly, 'I'll make you up a bed.'

'No need. A car is coming to pick me up.' His lips twisted. 'It seems the Duke of Claverton is about to return to his ancestral castle, but this time as a patient. Dee, honey, come and see me tomorrow?'

'Yes, of course. What do you need?' The chests upstairs had no men's pyjamas, and she doubted he'd like an old-fashioned nightshirt; nor would he have coupons yet.

'The army will supply everything. Or the hospital.' He ate hungrily, but as if his face hurt. 'How is Claverton?'

'The castle itself isn't in bad shape — the army has done a lot of renovating, but they've changed a lot too. The ballroom is divided into four wards and the yellow sitting room is an operating theatre. But they've done some work on the foundations and erected scaffolding around the towers and mended the front steps and cut the grass. Only the hospital staff and patients live in the castle itself. They've put Nissen huts on the old croquet court and up the walk to the hermit's cave for ... everyone else.'

'I was so disappointed there was no hermit,' he remembered. 'It was the best holiday I'd had, thinking one day this would be mine ... I'm sorry, that was tactless.' He smiled at her ruefully. 'You loved it as much as I did. More, probably.'

She shook her head. 'I grew up glad it's yours, not someone else's. Or will be when the war is over.'

'Did we get most of our men back from Dunkirk? I heard nothing in France. It doesn't help that I don't *parle* the *français*.'

'Things aren't going well,' she said briefly. 'But don't think about that tonight.'

'I'll focus on a hospital bed with clean sheets, hopefully some morphia and a proper surgeon tomorrow.'

She wanted to ask how badly his hand was hurt. Presumably he had lost fingers. An engine growled outside and she ran to the door before the knocking could wake the girls. Four men stood there in uniform, two with the red bands of military police. Of course, she thought, they must make sure Donnie is who he says he is. The other two men carried a stretcher.

She led them inside. Donnie let them lift him onto the stretcher. He must have kept going before from sheer force of will. He held her hand tightly as they carried him to the ambulance, as if unwilling to lose the connection with home.

'I'll see you tomorrow afternoon at visiting hours,' she promised, then realised she'd have three children to care for. Thank goodness Mrs Thripps was due to come in. She could watch them.

She waved the ambulance out of sight, though she knew he could not see her.

He was her past, suddenly become her present: the only boy she'd ever fancied herself in love with, or at least walking down the aisle towards while she wore white satin trimmed with a hundred white silk roses, and another hundred as a train behind her.

This was a man, not a boy, but he was one she admired, one who would be at least her neighbour and friend when he regained the castle, a man with the courage and integrity to fight Hitler and to defend the country his heritage connected him to.

To think that only that morning she had been lonely.

A grey nose poked around the door. 'Watchdogs usually turn up when people arrive, not when they leave,' she informed him.

Dusty stretched, looking at her reproachfully as if to say, *Watching is your duty, not mine. How can a dog get a good night's rest around here?*

He followed her upstairs to his cushion in her room. She briefly peered into the girls' room again. They were huddled together, breathing deeply, faces almost as pale as Donnie's had been.

Donnie. Something saved, at least, from the wreckage of this war. She found she was smiling as she changed for bed.

Seven

Uncle Jim never threw anything away. He died ten seconds after they gave him the hand grenade.

            World War II joke

She slept late the next morning, past rooster crow and lark song. She peered at the clock on her bedside table in the dimness of the blackout. Ten o'clock!

Had last night really happened? Was yesterday real? And if so, what was happening now? She threw on fresh overalls, tied her hair up in a scarf and hurried down the hall.

The door to the girls' bedroom was open, the bed bare, the blanket and quilt neatly folded — no sign that anyone had been there at all. Nor could she hear voices below.

Had they vanished? They had escaped from one orphanage. Had they run from her too? She automatically pulled back the blackout curtain from the window halfway down the staircase, then stared. A sheet that had not been there yesterday flapped on the clothesline, and two towels too.

Anna had wet the bed, she deduced. Anna probably often wet the bed, which was why there was no damp patch on the newly bare mattress. The two towels on the line had presumably been placed under her to soak up the night's urine. The girls must have silently stripped the bed, so as not to wake Deanna, washed the linen and hung it up. Where were they now?

And how was Donnie? She hoped they were able to operate on his hand — it had looked bad.

She opened the kitchen door to find the girls sitting neatly and silently at the table, still in the makeshift nightclothes she had given them, their bare heads slightly fuzzed with what looked like dark hair, their gas masks tied around their waists as they read — different books from last night. Could they have already devoured their first choices? She noticed the ashes had been swept from last night's fire and a new fire laid but not lit. The girls were keeping their promise to be silent and to clean for her. She wondered if they had scrubbed the bathroom, too.

They looked up at her, apprehensive.

She smiled. 'Thank you for washing the sheet.'

Anna stood up. 'It was me. Don't give the others the cane too.'

'What?' Deanna exclaimed, about to express disbelief, but then remembered that girls who had wet the bed had been caned at her own expensive boarding school. Discipline would be as hard, or worse, in an orphanage.

'No one gets the cane here, even if you drop my Dresden vase! It was my fault giving you cocoa at bedtime. But we'll put a waterproof cloth under your sheet tonight, and a couple of towels so you don't have to sleep on a wet patch, just in case. Now, breakfast. I'm so sorry I slept so late! You must be starved. Scrambled eggs? Boiled eggs? Real ones, not powdered — you can help me feed the hens later. Or pancakes?'

No answer. Then Rosa said slowly, 'Mama used to make us apple pancakes.'

'I can do that, though they may not be exactly like your mama's. You'll have to tell me how to make them like hers. Did she grate the apple and add cinnamon?'

Rosa nodded.

'Then I can probably make some almost as good. I even have some cinnamon.' Deanna opened the fridge. 'Milk?'

Three cautious nods.

'We got milk at school,' said Anna cautiously. 'I liked it. I never had it with chocolate in it before like last night. Magda said chocolate was good, but I didn't know it was so good.'

'Cocoa for breakfast too then? After breakfast I'll show you the attics. There's a chest there with all my old clothes — ones I outgrew when I was young — as well as things from lots of my ancestors, and old curtains and feathered headbands, even crinolines and the silk beaded evening slippers my great-grandmother wore — all kinds of things. We'll look through them another day, maybe when it's raining. Today we'll just choose modern clothes you like. I can alter any that don't fit you.'

More nods. They are used to secondhand charity clothes, she thought. Hopefully they might find something pretty today.

The first priority was to make the girls smile. To make them look at the world with joy, and see it was beautiful. To watch eagles survey the valleys, or squirrels scamper down tree trunks, and the wind stroke the trees ...

'Do you like walking in the woods? We've a stream here too, and a tiny beach. It's barricaded off, but we can see the sea once we cross the bridge.'

'We walk often,' said Magda stiffly. 'Matron made us walk around the block for an hour each afternoon for exercise. There were no trees there. But before ... I mean, long ago ...' Her voice faded.

'I remember walking among trees,' said Anna. 'Papa threw sticks for Woofer ... Mama explained how each tree has its own music ...'

'Your mother sounds like a very wise woman.' And if they've been taught to hear the music of the trees, the woods might heal them, thought Deanna. 'Dusty won't run after sticks though. I think he only really loves us for the food.'

Anna shook her head firmly. 'He loves you. He looked to see you were all right when you came in. And he cuddled us when we needed it. He is the most loving dog in the world! He just likes food too.' She hesitated. 'Papa said a dog's duty was to be loved.'

'*Huff*,' agreed Dusty, under the table, already waiting for crumbs and having found Anna's feet an acceptable headrest.

Deanna grinned. 'Your papa sounds wise too. Dusty will come today if we carry a picnic basket. We'll walk through the orchard first so I can show you the garden and beehives — don't get too close to the hives — then through the wood and over the stream. There's a tiny bridge just wide enough for one person.'

The room seemed lighter, as if hope was a colour and had seeped through the kitchen window.

'We can make sandwiches from yesterday's bread.' Deanna lowered her voice to a whisper as she poured the first mix into the frying pan. 'I might even have a bottle of pre-war lemonade.'

'That would be very nice, Lady Deanna,' said Magda politely, as if she didn't quite believe in picnics or lemonade and expected to be handed a broom after breakfast instead. Her sisters however had tentative smiles.

'Call me Aunt Dee. Here we are — the first pancake! Cut it into four — I'm hungry too — and I'll make the next. After lunch I have to go and visit my cousin in the hospital at the castle next door.'

'There's a castle?' Anna looked up from buttering her pancake quarter.

'You didn't see it last night?'

'The blinds were down in the train and then it was nearly dark,' said Rosa. 'Truly a castle?'

'A classic castle. Queen Elizabeth even slept there once — the bed is still in the same room. I used to live there, but it's a hospital now.'

'Does it have a dragon?' breathed Anna.

'Only Matron.'

'Or a ghost with a head under its arm?'

'Definitely no ghosts. My ancestors were too boring.' Except for her parents, but as everyone pretended they had never existed to sully the name of Claverton, it was hard to remember they were actually her ancestors too.

'I'll show you some of it another time — the army is pretty good at giving me access. The cousin I'm visiting today is actually the duke, so he might be able to wangle something. Mrs Thripps will be here this afternoon though — she comes twice a week to help clean. You'll like her. You can read or explore the house — just don't go beyond the garden unless I'm with you. You don't need to carry your gas masks indoors,' she added gently. 'Hang them on the back door for when we go out.'

'What if there's an air raid, Aunt Dee?' asked Magda, in that voice almost devoid of emotion.

'I don't think we're in any danger here.' Other than from bombs aimed at the aerodrome, she thought, but even that was a good ten miles away. 'You can hear the village siren from here, though only just. And we have an excellent shelter — the best. It's just, well, it's a secret one. Mrs Thripps knows, but don't tell anyone else. Come on, I'll show you. We'll make more pancakes afterwards.'

They followed her, holding each other's hands again, Anna in the middle, as Deanna led them into the library, still dim from the blackout curtains, then pushed at the shelves. She turned on the light — the village generator must be running again. 'See? Just go down the stairs. I've put cushions down there, but we must take more for you, too.'

'Is that all food?' asked Magda, staring at the unmissable sacks and tins and chests labelled *Sugar* or *Tea* in wonder.

'Yes. And bottles of wine and pop — I'm not a hoarder,' said Deanna apologetically. 'My grandfather put it all down here for me, long before the war. But it ... it might be a good idea not to mention it's here.'

'Why did he put all the food here?' asked Anna.

'He guessed there'd be shortages, and wanted me to be safe when he couldn't look after me.'

'Why couldn't he look after you anymore?'

'Shh,' said Rosa quickly. 'Adults don't like stupid questions.'

'How can you understand the world if you don't in...ves...tigate?'

'My grandfather died just before the war began,' said Deanna.

'I'm sorry,' said Rosa.

'He'd been ill a long time. I miss him.' She would not cry in front of the girls — they looked as if they might begin to cry too. 'If you hear the air-raid siren, come down here. There are torches and lamps if the electricity goes out. Choose some books to leave here too, just in case. But I don't think we are in danger of air raids here.'

Just invasion, she thought. Almost certain invasion. It was a wonder Hitler hadn't already given the order while Britain's forces were in so much disarray. But why waste bombs on a single house or a crumbling castle?

I must repair the hole to the cave before the girls notice it, she realised. And make very sure they are asleep or at school each time I go into the second cellar. It would probably be weeks before they were settled enough to face attending the village school. Hopefully by then their hair would not look too strange under a beret.

By then, too, they might have remembered how to smile, and Anna might not feel the need to hide morsels of pancake in her pocket.

Two hours later an extraordinary number of pancakes, well buttered, had been consumed, with several passed under the table to Dusty, which she let the girls think she hadn't noticed. A dog was comforting, as that man, Sam, had said yesterday. Anna certainly thought so. Deanna reflected that her days of supplying excess eggs to the Women's Institute were probably over.

Magda and Rosa had simply stared at the trunks in the attic: to them old clothes must be all rejects. Anna had been impassive too at first, until Deanna had dragged out an orange organdie party dress with a full skirt and puffed sleeves edged in lace.

Thankfully the skirt was lined, hiding the lack of underpants, as the small girl refused to be parted from it. She wore it now as the four of them passed through the edge of the woodland, crossed the bridge over the river and began the climb up the headland's rocky knobs, bare except for a few gorse bushes, and passing through suspended valleys with strips of trees sculpted by the wind, poking crooked arms above soil enriched by thousands of years of autumn leaves.

The girls' silk scarves flapped around their shorn heads. Magda wore a slightly too long navy pinafore over a white blouse. Rosa had chosen a kilt, with a blouse topped by a lacy cravat. They all wore socks from Deanna's own dressing table, showing above the worn black shoes they had arrived in. Dusty followed them with the resignation of a dog who knows there will be a steep climb and hopes the leftovers from the picnic will make up for it.

The breeze from the sea stung their faces, but the climb was worth it for the view, despite the barbed wire below them.

Trees stood at their backs, leafy sentinels. A green sea and white-frothed waves slapped at the cliff face. The vast circle of the horizon was marred by the distant grey of what might be a destroyer or the merchant navy, bringing food, but apart from that it was a world free from war — seagulls yelling and circling, eyeing Miss Enid's old wicker picnic basket, a familiar container of crusts from thousands of meals up here.

'I didn't know there was so much green in the world,' Anna whispered.

'I remember —' began Rosa, then stopped at a warning glance from her sister. If the girls didn't trust her enough to give her their surname, they wouldn't mention where they had lived.

Deanna spread the blanket and laid out the vacuum flask of chocolate milk, the metal cups that went with it, sandwiches — cheese and tomato made with Mrs Higgins's cheese and Deanna's glasshouse tomatoes, a rare luxury in wartime — strawberry jam, and quickly made Welsh cakes rich with currants, sugar and butter, well beyond the weekly rations, but hopefully the girls would not realise that.

'Look at the castle from here,' breathed Anna. 'It's got those pointy things ...'

'Turrets,' said Magda.

Anna nodded. 'It's got *everything.*'

Except decent plumbing and proper foundations, thought Deanna, amused. But that was the army's concern and then Donnie's. She was surprised how little she missed it.

It might have been different if she'd had memories of grand dinners, of playing hide and seek with friends. But her life with her grandfather had been restricted to a few rooms even before the final descent into the kitchen. The happiest memories of her childhood were at Eagle's Rest. The castle's decrepitude had been a nagging responsibility as long as she could remember: the main banister crashing down, repaired with the cheapest wood possible and a handful of nails by Watson and Sons, the village's 'a couple of nails and she'll be right' carpenters; the dead rat in the drawing room, with a stink that had pervaded the entire castle till Dusty triumphantly retrieved it and left it under the kitchen table, gazing hopefully at Dee in case she might like to swap it for a biscuit.

'I always liked Eagle's Rest better than the castle,' she said, undoing her scarf and letting the wind run its salty fingers through her hair.

'Why is it called that?' asked Magda, in her precise tone.

Deanna pointed to the hills beyond them. 'A pair of golden eagles nests on a ledge through there — one of the last pairs in England, though there are still some up in Scotland.'

'Only one pair?'

Deanna nodded. 'The young have to find their own territory, at least ten square miles of it. Miss Enid lived here before me,' she added. 'She left me the house and the land that goes with it.' She smiled. Such a small phrase to encompass so much beauty.

She bit into a sandwich, blessing her grandfather, Miss Enid, who had protected this headland from bungalows or caravans, her ancestors, who had built a most unimaginative castle but had had the sense — or desire for good hunting — to leave the woods around them alone, and the God who created all this beauty, even if humanity was focused on its destruction.

Magda and Rosa ate their cheese and tomato sandwiches slowly, with appreciation, and perhaps replaying memories of eating similar food with their parents. Anna went straight for the jam, somehow getting it on face, fingers and dress, still staring at the castle. 'It's like in the fairy stories.'

Deanna smiled. 'Not exactly.'

Magda shook her head. 'I suppose you would know … Lady Deanna.'

'Lady Deanna Claverton. I'd have to have a title in my own right to be just "Lady Deanna". A distant cousin has recently inherited the duchy.'

'Why didn't you? You'd be a duchess!' said Rosa.

'Because girls can't inherit titles.'

'Why?' asked Anna.

'I don't know. Maybe because the men who built the castle thought a woman couldn't fight to protect it.'

'I can fight,' said Anna. 'I kicked Jamie Prothero when he said —'

'Shh.' Magda put her hand quickly on Anna's arm. 'You were on bread and water all the next day because of it.'

'I'd kick him again too,' said Anna stubbornly.

'Look, see that hole over there?' said Deanna quickly. 'It's a badger's den. If we come out at dusk we might see her hunting for her dinner.'

'Badgers eat earthworms,' stated Rosa. 'They can eat hundreds of earthworms a night. I've read about them. How do you know it's a female?'

'She had babies last year. This year too, I hope.'

'Will we see the eagles today?' asked Rosa, as a plane suddenly erupted from beyond the woods, then turned in a circle to fly over them then back over the castle.

'Not after that,' said Deanna drily. 'Eagles don't like aeroplanes.'

'Will they fly away?' asked Anna anxiously.

'I hope not. Eagles need a lot of land to feed and if they fly too far from here farmers might shoot them because they think they take the lambs.'

'Do they?' asked Magda.

'Sometimes, I'm afraid, if the lambs are weak or sickly. But mostly eagles eat rabbits. The hill is alive with bunnies at night. And I've even seen an eagle catch a fish in the river.'

'Can we see the rabbits?' demanded Anna.

'Definitely. Maybe a fox too. There's a pair of squirrels in the oak tree by the house as well — they're storing acorns and hazelnuts for winter. We can watch for them tomorrow if you like.'

Anna ate another sandwich thoughtfully, rubbing Dusty's ears as he consumed his tenth bread crust and looked hopefully at the Welsh cakes.

'I think I'm happy,' Rosa said suddenly. 'I didn't think I would ever be happy again.'

'I'm glad.' Deanna impulsively bent over and kissed the scarf over the bare head. 'I'm happy, too.' To her surprise she meant it.

'Can we really stay here?' asked Rosa in a small voice.

Deanna found three pairs of eyes staring at her. 'I said you could last night,' she reminded them.

'You said we could stay as long as we wanted to,' said Magda. She looked at Deanna almost defiantly. 'That's not the same as always.'

It was indeed different. Suddenly she had a strange feeling of connection, as if some vast hand had tangled them in wool. She would need to wield scissors to cut it, but she had no wish to.

'Yes,' she said, quickly, before she could think of implications that would make her hesitate, a hesitation these girls would see. 'Yes, you can stay with me. Always, if that's what you choose.'

'Like a family?' Anna's eyes challenged her. So young, she thought, and fierce too. They couldn't beat that out of her at the orphanage.

'Like a family. You three and me, and Dusty. I don't have any other relatives, except Donnie, who inherited the castle.'

Anna's small hand crept into hers. 'We don't have anyone else either.' She hugged Dusty, who endured it. 'You're my woof brother now,' she informed him.

I've crossed the Rubicon, Deanna thought, staring at the girls, the dog licking Anna's face again, either in affection or for jam. They are my responsibility now.

Which meant she couldn't go to the Beamishes' house party next Friday-to-Monday. She would need to tell Uncle Jasper. He would not be pleased.

She would also need to telephone Mrs Beamish and explain, and hope she would say, 'But, my dear Lady Deanna, you must come for at least a day! Bring your new girls — Nanny can keep an eye on them — and Stanley can meet you at the station …'

Tongues were looser after dinner, after wine, liqueur or port, but she might still find out where the Beamishes stood politically. Henry Beamish was a colonel in the Home Guard, but private views these days were not the same as public ones. He had been a close friend of Mosley's before the war, though never a member of Mosley's fascist Blackshirts.

Somehow she would need to combine caring for the girls with gathering intelligence.

My problem, she thought, and possibly my joy too.

Somehow, unexpectedly, she might have found a family. 'Yes,' she said more definitely. 'Eagle's Rest is your home. I am, well, let's say your aunt, for now. It won't be all picnics though. You'll need to help in the garden.'

'Can I milk a cow?' asked Rosa.

'I want to milk the badger,' said Anna.

'Silly, you can't milk badgers.'

'But Aunt Dee said they have babies.'

'You still can't milk a badger, can you, Aunt Dee?' queried Rosa.

Magda said nothing, as if uncertain whether to believe Deanna's promise. She, at least, was old enough to realise the magnitude of the impulsive words. Words, like Hitler's treaties, could easily be forgotten.

'I've never tried to milk a badger,' said Deanna. 'Badgers bite.'

Dusty rolled over, as if he had understood the word 'bite'. He nudged Anna hopefully, with the look of a dog who deserved a snack.

'May I?' asked Anna, holding up her crusts.

'Yes,' said Deanna resignedly. It was too late to teach Dusty manners now. The small girl buried her face in his fur as he munched the bread then licked her cheeks in case there was still some flavour to be found. Dusty had obviously decided these new humans were desirable providers of scraps of scrambled egg and jammy crusts.

She realised they had still not told her their surname.

Eight

Brown Betty

INGREDIENTS

60 grams margarine
eight to ten slices stale bread, crumbed
two large apples
three tablespoons golden syrup
a quarter teaspoon ground or grated nutmeg
one teaspoon cinnamon
one lemon if possible
small teacup water

METHOD

Brush a pie dish or tin with a little of the melted margarine and put a layer of stale breadcrumbs in the bottom. Cover with a layer of grated apples. Drizzle half the golden syrup over the apples, dot with margarine and sprinkle with the spices mixed together and the grated rind of half the lemon. Repeat the layers and then add a final layer of stale breadcrumbs on top, dotted with margarine. Mix the juice of the lemon with the small teacup of water and pour over the pudding. Sprinkle with a few teaspoons of sugar if available. Cook in a medium oven for forty-five to sixty minutes. Serves six.

A wartime recipe to use stale bread.
Substitute butter and it will be delicious.

Mrs Thripps was beating the dust from the kitchen carpets when they returned, her brown and grey hair in its usual scarf, and the usual stub of an unlit cigarette in the corner of her mouth.

'You're in the papers, Lady Dee! You and the duke!' she called out as they approached. 'It's a miracle!'

She looked curiously at the girls as Deanna introduced them. 'Mrs Goodword gave me a parcel for you,' she told them. 'A big one. Shoes and underthings and school uniforms. She said to phone her with the girls' names and previous address and she'll register them for their ration books.'

Which meant Mrs Goodword expected Deanna to keep the girls and hadn't appeared today to avoid an argument. Which was fair enough, given she had the bedrooms, and her only specific job — other than farming — was a secret one. But she did need the girls' surname and address. She glanced at them and saw by their discomfort that they had realised this too.

'I've left the newspaper on the table for you,' Mrs Thripps continued. 'I bought two copies so you could have one to keep. Our new duke coming home again! I can't wait to meet him again — he was no higher than a broomstick when I saw him last. I picked up your butter ration too,' she added to Deanna.

Mrs Thripps kept some of Deanna's ration for herself, a bonus for working here. Deanna had all the butter she needed from Mrs Higgins. 'I changed the sheets on the beds and made up the other bedrooms too. Be a love, girls, and take these mats inside for me. I got that much dog hair out of them I could knit another dog. I need to be going — my Arnold will be wanting his breakfast or his dinner. He doesn't care which it is, as long as it's a good one.' Mrs Thripps' husband was at least a decade older than his wife, a volunteer fire warden at night, and a professional fireman by day, though past retirement age, if there had been such a thing as 'retirement' in this war. 'I'll be back later to put the washing in the airing cupboard.'

'Thank you, Mrs Thripps. Would you mind staying a little later this afternoon to keep the girls company? I'd like to visit my cousin in hospital.'

Mrs Thripps moved her cigarette stub to the other corner of her mouth. 'I'd say all of England would like to visit His Grace.' She winked at Deanna. 'Handsome, ain't he? You should see the photo in the *Daily Clarion*. He could be one o' them 'ollywood film stars.'

What on earth had the newspaper said? Deanna left the girls to pull the rugs down and hurried into the kitchen. Donnie's photograph was on the front page. He did indeed look handsome. *Duke Rescued*, yelled the headline, and a subheading: *Comes ashore near his own castle*.

Deanna scanned the next lines anxiously. Had he mentioned the cave?

> *Donald, Eighth Duke of Claverton, listed as 'Missing Presumed Dead' at Dunkirk, arrived exhausted at the home of his cousin Lady Deanna Claverton last night. Men continue to return all along the coast ...*

The rest of the article said nothing more about Donnie or Claverton — both the hospital and the aerodrome were classified information — or herself, she read with relief, apart from a small photo of her with a glass of champagne and a low-necked dress ... the one she had made from the fifth viscount's second wife's court dress, which made this occasion the reception at the German embassy, where she had first met, and disliked, Mrs Simpson, now the Duchess of Windsor.

Donnie's photo however took up a third of the front page. The propaganda merchants must have been briefed as soon as he had called his commanding officer to say he had returned for the news to make the morning edition. The editors would have loved a good-news story to try to balance the bombing raids, the armies of children seeking refuge away from cities that might be a target, which meant any city at all, the rationing and the shortages of everything, including hope.

Donnie looked younger as well as considerably cleaner in the photo, presumably taken when he'd enlisted as he was in uniform, with a cap that covered his high forehead so that his whole face lost its usual proportions.

The face in that photo had an innocent gaiety, despite heading into battle. The Donnie she had met last night was thinner, his eyes sunken, with a harder look that Dee thought was not just exhaustion and pain. What has Donnie been through since then? Deanna wondered. He would probably never say. Men hadn't after the last war, nor those who had escaped the failed Danish campaign at the beginning of this war, like Mrs Thripps' nephew who had lost a foot and who spent his days in a dark corner of the pub, nursing a single beer for hours, for beer was in short supply too.

Surely Donnie would want the cave kept secret even from the authorities. It had been *their* cave, and they believed no one had been along it for maybe hundreds of years. She suddenly realised Miss Enid and her grandfather must have known about it, for small portions of the wall had been reinforced with concrete.

Miss Enid would also have heard their voices echoing with excitement down there — she had almost certainly kept a closer eye on them than they had realised, a woman who saw much and said little, and was most capable of keeping secrets.

I need a bath, she decided. And a pretty dress. Not a respectable going-to-church dress, or a dutiful opening-the-fete dress, but something flowery, and a hat — she had only three, hats being something that didn't fare well locked in trunks for generations, and nor did she have millinery skills. But she did have a choice of silk scarves and late roses to decorate one. A pink and yellow floral scarf on a straw hat, she decided, to match a gold and green linen dress with a wide skirt, and daisies embroidered around the neckline.

I have just had a picnic, she thought, and I am making a visit to someone I want to see, not out of duty, nor to warn him to be discreet, but simply because I want to see him, talk to him, laugh with him, remember with him. She would be pretty for him: a young woman spending time with a young man.

She smiled as she went to have her bath, with an extra helping of violet bath salts.

I need to plan tonight's dinner too, she thought. Plan every meal, instead of cooking up a pot of something to last for days or snacking on an apple and cheese.

Omelettes would be quick, and boiled new potatoes; the girls could pod some peas. Then apple crumble, which would only take two minutes to put together as she had stewed apple left from the batch she'd made for the pie.

So much can happen in twenty-four hours! she thought. Poland could be invaded, a king be tricked into abdicating.

And Dee Claverton might have found a family — not just the girls and Dusty, but Donnie too.

Nine

Why couldn't Hitler find his moustache?
It was right under his nose all the time.

World War II joke

It had been months since she had been on the Claverton estate. Only two years earlier she had spent months without leaving it. The rhododendron hedges had been trimmed and the shaggy grass turned back to lawn, but more for access than aesthetics. The driveway had also been freshly gravelled, and the crumbling front steps repaired.

Once inside, the differences were more profound. A line of trucks and ambulances filled the back courtyard. The Great Hall was now a Minor Space, divided by a blank white wall. The tiny area held a reception desk, a bell and Mrs Haddock in Red Cross uniform smiling at her brightly.

'Lady Deanna! I knew you'd be here as soon as it was visiting hours. You did look ever so lovely in that photo. Your cousin is sitting up and had a good luncheon. Cook made it special! We had to welcome our duke home somehow. Now if you would just sign the visitors book …'

Deanna suppressed rebellion at having to sign in to what had been her home for twenty-five years, accepted directions to Ward Six, which were not difficult as only one hallway led to what had been the ballroom. It was divided by the same blank white material into numbered rooms. Number six was at the far end, the door open, showing six neatly made beds, with only one occupied. A bored Donnie read the *Daily Clarion*. He looked clean, in striped pyjamas, his hand freshly bandaged, and not at all as if he'd had to undergo further surgery.

He put the newspaper down. 'Dee! Honey bun, am I glad to see you. I'm out of my mind here.' He looked at her appreciatively. 'Boy, do you look swell. Your hair is like sunlight and that dress would cheer up a regiment.'

She twirled on impulse, so the wide skirt — a silhouette that had so briefly appeared again in the late 1930s — swirled around her. 'No gorgeous nurses giving you bed baths?'

'The Duke of Claverton is treated far too reverently. Matron attended me. She's at least eighty-four and apologised for the lack of bathrooms when she handed me my bedpan. I apologised to her for not having had them installed.'

Deanna laughed. 'I'm glad you're looking well! You were exhausted last night.'

'So well that I have already been visited by officialdom. I'm being drummed out of the regiment for the crime of lacking two fingers, but in return am to be given a Home Office job suitable for my social position. I did explain I know almost nothing about England, not even whether sitting in the House of Lords means you get assigned a seat on first-come-first-served, but it seems that ignorance is irrelevant.'

'But intelligence isn't.' She sat on the only available chair. This man had managed not just to survive but to escape. That in itself was formidable. She hoped he would be given a real job, not just carted around to look handsome and help with recruiting.'

He lowered his voice. 'Dee, I said I'd climbed a path up the cliff I found as a boy, but it crumbled as I came up so it can't be used again, then I staggered to your front door. Once anyone knows about the cave there'll be Home Guard swarming your cellar with rolls of barbed wire.'

'I was worried about that. Thank you.'

He grinned at her. 'It's not as if the Nazi invasion is going to begin via your cellar. Have you told anyone else about the passage? No? Then now we are the only two people in the world who know about it. I didn't even tell the fishermen who brought me across — they thought I was headed for a shallow sea cave and then a path up the cliffs.'

'It will stay our secret. Mrs Thripps — my cleaning lady — knows about the cellar, and I've shown it to the girls as they will need to know how to use it in case we need a bomb shelter. But none know about the cave. I'll block the entrance off tonight after they're in bed.'

'Good. You do realise a burglar could use it if anyone knew about it.'

'They'd need the help of someone very good with a boat. Anyway, I've nothing worth stealing.' She felt vaguely guilty about the lie, but the increasingly valuable contents of the second cellar, the diamonds sewn into the hem of one of her old bras, the antique desk in the library, the Monet, needed to stay secret.

She found Donnie still smiling at her. 'I've even been found a serviced flat, as Claverton House is now also a hospital, as well as a car and driver. I must say, they do seem appreciative of my providing two hospitals — and of course my title.'

'It makes you excellent propaganda value,' she said lightly.

'I am, aren't I?' He looked at her speculatively. 'So are you.' He nodded at the newspaper.

'You'll get used to it,' she said wryly.

He laughed. 'Dee, honey, I'm already used to it. Being rich in America gets you almost as much attention as a duke in England. We just avoid titles to seem democratic. I must admit I prefer "His Lordship" instead of "Mr Donald E Claverton".'

'You could have stayed out of the war in America till it's all over. If the Germans win they'd be equally impressed by your title and your money, and probably even let you have the estate.'

'I think it might be a matter of "when" the Germans win,' he said quietly, all laughter vanishing. 'You didn't see them turning our army into hamburger at Dunkirk.'

'I think you might be right. Don't go around saying it though. We must all be bright and optimistic. Practise saying "Jolly good show" twenty times a day — it's your ducal duty.'

'Jolly good show,' he said enthusiastically, wiggling his eyebrows at her. 'How are your evacuees?'

'They're orphans and need a home, and I can give them one,' she said, a touch defiantly. 'But I need to find out who they are — they haven't given me their surname yet. Probably afraid that once they are identified they'll be sent back to wherever the orphanage is being relocated.'

He looked at her in concern. 'That's rash. They could be anyone.'

'They are intelligent, love books, are resourceful, hard-working, and loyal to each other. That's enough.'

'I may be able to use my Home Office contacts to find out who they are — once I actually gain some contacts. Would you possibly invite me down for a weekend once I'm settled in London?'

'Of course. You're family!'

It would be another weekend when she could gather no information. But she felt no guilt. The publicity about Donnie's arrival might mean even more invitations. And *I am finally getting a life of my own*, she thought.

Ten

A Scotsman, an Irishman, a Welshman and an Englishman are captured. The German officer says, 'You get a final wish before you are shot.'
The Scotsman says, 'Play "Scots Wha Hae" on the bagpipes.'
The Irishman says, 'Have a soprano sing "Danny Boy" to the accompaniment of the Irish pipes.'
The Welshman says, 'I'd like to hear "Men of Harlech" once again, sung by a male choir.'
The German turned to the Englishman. 'What do you wish?'
'Can I be shot first?'

World War II joke

It was later than she'd expected as she wheeled her bicycle into the garage at Eagle's Rest. It had been so good to talk to someone without subtly manoeuvring the conversation to subjects Uncle Jasper would find interesting, to share stories of Grandpa, and of Donnie's own parents, whom she had never met. His mother had died of pneumonia the year before he spent the summer at Claverton, leaving his father free for an affair with the woman who briefly became his second wife.

There was just enough light for Mrs Thripps to cycle home without bothering with her war-dimmed bicycle light. Children needed an early dinner, too, didn't they? She had failed her first day of parenting.

Deanna hurriedly opened the back door, then stopped.

Her normally empty kitchen was full of people. Mrs Thripps sat at the table for the first time Deanna could remember — she normally carried a cup of tea and a biscuit around as she worked.

Now she leaned back, puffing at a fresh cigarette — she had never actually smoked one of the dangling butts before — laughing, while Dusty lay on his back on the girls' laps, all three absentmindedly scratching his chest while listening to a man in a pilot's uniform, his back to her as he fried something on her stove ... her stove, and frying, in wartime, and in almost unobtainable lard too.

Whatever it was smelled wonderful.

He kept talking, his back towards her. '... and we just sat there as the goanna marched off down the hallway, the leg of lamb in its mouth — believe me, you don't want to argue with a goanna that big. Then Mum stood up and said calmly, "Sausages for lunch, everyone?"'

The laughter subsided as everyone registered Deanna's presence. The man turned and became the pilot from yesterday ... Sam, yes, that was his name, and those four extremely large fried trout must have been caught in her stream.

'Lady Dee! I hope you don't mind. I called in to give you the fish and a can of dripping my sister sent me, the silly ass; she heard England had no dripping but I don't know what she thought I'd do with it, so I was going to give it to you.'

'And I said it'd been an age since I'd had a bit of fried fish and chips,' said Mrs Thripps, 'which gave him the idea to start dinner for you and the girls, so I'd better be going.' Though she made no move towards her handbag, much less the door.

'I love fish and chips,' said Anna persuasively, a totally different child from the terrified waif of yesterday, comforted by the smell of chips, the laughter, and the story from a distant land where no bombs fell.

'Mr Murray said chips should be cooked twice,' explained Magda. 'Once to cook and the second time to swell up and crisp. That's what his mother taught him.'

'He showed us how to clean fish, too,' said Rosa eagerly. 'I never thought about the anatomy of a fish before. One of them had a half-digested dragonfly inside. It was so interesting! Fish must have digestive juices just like people ...'

'I've dusted the fish with flour, ready to cook,' said Sam, interrupting the anatomy speculations and untying the apron — her best apron, a lovely floral — from around his waist. 'Reheat the chips in the hot fat for about five minutes for them to brown ...'

'*Woof*,' added Dusty, reminding his human cushions to keep scratching ...

Both Mrs Thripps and the pilot stayed for dinner, of course, with only a moment's persuasion. There were clearly enough fish and chips for six, plus dog.

'And Arnold's on nights down at the station, so he'll have his supper there,' explained Mrs Thripps. 'Mr Higgins dropped in a can of cream if you want me to fetch some of them apricots we bottled last month,' she added in an unsubtle hint, and it seemed that Sam wasn't on duty till ten o'clock, taking trainees up into the darkness that bombers called home ...

Deanna sat and let Sam cook, a luxury she hadn't known in her own home for over ten years, while the girls set the table as if they had been doing it forever instead of only watching her take out plates and cutlery for two meals. Mrs Thripps stubbed out her cigarette and gave a sigh of pleasure as she took off her shoes under the table.

Twenty minutes later the table held a platter of perfectly cooked fish, and crisp and light brown chips, as well as a salad of lettuce leaves picked by the girls and lemon quarters Deanna had ducked out to grab from the glasshouse. She usually gave the lemons to the Women's Institute for war effort marmalade, but fish and chips — and a new family — deserved to be celebrated.

They passed the platters round, helping themselves, while Dusty's nose under the table followed the direction of the chip platter.

'Do goannas bite people often?' asked Rosa, resting her knife and fork while she asked the question — the girls' manners were impeccable, Deanna noticed, and almost certainly not learned at the orphanage.

'Never known anyone to be bit,' said Sam, whose mum had also obviously taught him table etiquette as well as how to cook chips. 'Everyone's got more sense than to argue with a goanna. I did know a shearer who was bitten by a wombat — they're like your badgers but more determined. If a wombat digs a burrow under the road, you move the road, because you won't move the wombat.'

'They're savage?' asked Magda, helping herself to more fried fish, then slipping a chip to a drooling Dusty.

'Mother wombats can be savage when they have young. But one was dozing outside this bloke's caravan, and he tripped over it, so it bit him then marched off. The bloke had to have six stitches.'

Deanna felt it might be time to slip in a question of her own. 'That reminds me, girls: Mrs Goodword needs your surname so she can register you for ration books.'

Three faces — the smallest slightly greasy — turned on her with perfect innocence. 'Our surname is Smith,' said Magda.

'Anna, Rosa and Magda Smith,' said Rosa, as if to make it completely clear.

'The orphanage was called St Cuthbert's,' Magda added helpfully.

'It was a very small orphanage,' recited Rosa carefully. 'There were only twenty orphans. And the nuns.'

'Lots of nuns,' said Anna very seriously.

'Only *five* nuns,' corrected Rosa.

'Really? What denomination?' Deanna took more chips as Sam offered her the bowl. They really were excellent chips, as soft inside as they were crispy outside, almost making up for all the work growing the potatoes.

'I ... don't understand,' said Magda, losing her certainty.

'Roman Catholic nuns, or Anglican?'

'Oh, Anglican, definitely,' said Magda, staring at her chips.

Deanna carefully didn't look at Sam or Mrs Thripps. 'Good. I'll let Mrs Goodword know. How long did it take to catch these monsters?' she asked Sam, peeling back another fish from its bones.

The girls relaxed.

'A couple of hours. They were really biting today.' He'd caught the need to talk about something else too. 'Your eagles hovered above for a while to have a look at me, then decided I was too big to eat.'

Anna giggled, as much in relief that their lie had been accepted as at the joke, thought Deanna. For it was most definitely a lie.

A well-thought-out one, though. These girls were no fools. Smith was an acceptable name, and with a million child evacuees, lost records and many areas with no records at all, no one was going to quibble about giving ration books and identity cards to three more Smiths, not when so many people were already not just homeless but without any form of identification, all blown away by German bombs.

Nor would anyone want details about St Cuthbert's orphanage. After the loss of so many men in the Great War, later to influenza or polio, and with many of the working poor unable to care for their children, almost every district or suburb in England had a small orphanage, run by a religious group or the local council or charity, usually with little supervision or even records.

One day they'll tell me, she thought. In a few weeks, maybe, when they're settled and know they can trust me not to send them away, no matter what their secret. She hoped they really were orphans, and not escaping abusive parents or relatives who might claim them. Rosa, Anna and Magda — or whatever their real names were — seemed to fit, not just at Eagle's Rest, but into her life. Loneliness and solitude had exploded into laughter and firelight. Even Dusty wore a grin. He had adopted Sam, resting his head on his lap all through dinner, and not entirely because Sam had been the provider of food.

'I'll go get them apricots.' Mrs Thripps crumpled her napkin and headed for the library and the secret door to the cellar, shutting the kitchen door in case Sam heard the panel open.

Sam fits too, Deanna thought, sitting here talking about the ways of animals, absentmindedly rubbing Dusty's ears just like Miss Enid used to, with eyes like her grandfather's. His hands clearly had worked the land, just like her hands now.

'I'll get the cream,' she said as the girls began to clear the table — family manners, not visitors' — as comfortably as if this was their own home.

Which it is, thought Deanna stubbornly, no matter who they are.

Eleven

Eggless and Sugar-Free Cake

INGREDIENTS
two cups self-raising flour
half a cup grated apples
half a cup chopped dates stewed in enough water to cover till soft

METHOD
Mix gently. Bake in a moderate oven till brown. Serve while still warm, with butter, cream or mock cream if available.

Life became routine remarkably quickly, partially due to the sterling efforts of Mrs Goodword and her lists. Within a week Magda, Rosa and Anna had ration cards and new school shoes without holes, and were enrolled in the Claverton Minor village school with all the other evacuees, thus doubling the number that the school's teacher, Miss Hannaford, had to cope with. Like the other newly arrived children, they were asked to stand up in church on Sunday and be welcomed by the village vicar before the congregation rose to sing 'Abide with Me'.

Anna's, Rosa's and Magda's bald heads were not even especially conspicuous. Many of this second corps of evacuees had industriously scratched all the way to their new homes. Their new foster parents had shaved their heads 'just in case' and given them a thorough scrub in outdoor wash houses before allowing them inside.

'Several of the poor dears had never seen a bathtub,' Mrs Goodword confided to Deanna after church. 'Slum children, all of them. Such a shame! Most don't even know how to use a knife and fork! One little boy insisted he had always had black rings around his neck, elbows, knees and toes. It took half an hour of scrubbing with carbolic soap to prove him wrong! Ah, there is Mr Cliffard, the photographer for the *Daily Express*. We thought a photo of you and your three little darlings standing on the church steps together would be such an encouragement for more foster parents to volunteer.'

She shook her head. 'They say the railway stations are simply full of the homeless every night. Children living underground! Now if you stand here, Lady Deanna—'

'No!' Anna hid her face in Deanna's skirt. Rosa lowered her scarf over her face.

Magda smiled apologetically at the photographer. 'Please excuse us. Our family never takes photographs.' She deftly melted into the crowd, who were drinking weak tea brewed from last week's leaves, dried and used again, and eating Mrs Palmer's experiment with sugarless, butterless biscuits sweetened with prunes: not entirely a success.

It seemed the photograph was not going to succeed either.

'Really!' Mrs Goodword huffed through her moustache. 'What kind of people don't have photographs taken?'

Ones who don't want to be recognised, thought Deanna. The photographer had wandered over to take artistic impressions of the lichen-covered headstones. 'I'm so sorry.'

'They have been through a lot,' Mrs Goodword admitted. She lowered her voice. 'Did you hear there was a German invasion at Southend last week?'

Deanna shook her head. 'I'm sure it's just another rumour.' If the Germans invaded, they'd have kept on going, she thought.

By the end of the second week the girls' bottom sheet no longer had to be washed each morning. The weekends and the daily hour spent outdoors before dinner exhausted them physically: collecting eggs; weeding the vegetable gardens; bagging potatoes pulled to the surface by the new potato digger on the even-newer tractor. This was the delight of Mr Higgins's life, a gift just before the old duke's death to complement the draught horses, an integral part of the arrangement to manage Deanna's farm, as well as supply her with whatever the Ministry of Food's regulations allowed. Or whatever the Ministry of Food didn't know about.

The peace of Eagle's Rest had soaked into them. They had already lost the fragility of almost starvation, and a dark fuzz of hair made an extraordinary difference to their former waiflike look, as did the loss of tension in their faces. Apart from the buzz of planes and the postman's whistle, the outside world might not exist. The air smelled of ripening apples and the tang of salt air, hazed by the dust of the wheat harvest on farms further inland. Cucumbers and tomatoes ripened fragrantly in the hot house. Half the tomatoes were kept for Women's Institute chutney. Deanna and the girls bottled the rest for winter.

There were apples and pears to pick, too, to store in sawdust in the shed; and blackberries from thorny clumps to turn into jam on sticky evenings; plums to bottle; and elderberries for winter syrup; and runner beans to pickle. Deanna supervised mushroom collection in the dewy grass every morning in the cow paddocks. Anna made it her job to gather the eggs, while Rosa bicycled to the Higginses' farm for the milk each morning before breakfast and Magda learned the secret of hard kneading to give a good crusty loaf of bread.

The plenitude seemed to settle the children too, as did the security of the cellar, both as shelter and for the safekeeping of food. They adored the romance of the secret door, visiting the cellar at least three times a day for the novelty of sliding back the panel and slipping inside, giggling, and coming out again.

As Deanna had hoped, the hostesses for her next two social engagements sympathetically accepted the excuse of housing evacuees. 'How tiresome for you, darling! I do hope they don't have lice or steal the silverware. Oh dear — you didn't get a mixed-race one, did you, or an East End Jew? You hear such terrible stories.'

Deanna assured both Mrs Sloane-Weebs and the Honourable Patricia Worthington her evacuees were well-spoken, white-skinned, well-mannered and clean.

'Can't you at least come for lunch, darling? Dickie will pick you all up from the train,' suggested Mrs Sloane-Weebs. 'The children can eat in the kitchen. I'm sure Cook will find something for them.'

'The children' did go, having armed themselves with two books apiece. They headed for the kitchen door while Deanna sat in an Art Deco dining room and ate clear salmon soup, salmon mousse, undoubtedly black-market roast beef in pastry, though lacking the pâté de foie gras that would have made it Beef Wellington, cheese souffle and chocolate mousse — black market too, unless, as was probable, the cellars here had also been well stocked with goods likely to be scarce.

Later, as her hostess took a cocktail shaker into the gardens and drank glass after glass — extremely bad form — with Deanna, her social 'lion', a true aristocrat, she drunkenly confessed her husband's fears.

'They'll be here within weeks, Dickie says!' she exclaimed, as they sat on the stone benches overlooking the fountain, still dappling into its circle of water despite official pleas for the public to use as little electricity as possible. 'And won't they make us pay for defying them? It will be just like France — the Nazis will confiscate Dickie's steelworks. They take whatever they like, you see — and we'll be broke, homeless. That fool Churchill — I'd like to see *him* fighting on the beaches! Dickie says he's positively senile, for all his blather. Someone has to do something, or we'll lose everything! Oh come on, let's walk. I can't bear this sitting still.'

'What does Dickie think the prime minister should do?' asked Deanna sympathetically.

'Make an alliance with Germany, of course. Dickie says everyone in his club is saying the same thing. Hitler is being remarkably generous. Everyone knows the real enemies are the communists. Make peace now, while we still have a chance of decent terms. But Dickie says Churchill will never do it, no matter how much he is urged.'

'People are urging him?'

'Well, they must be, surely … Deanna, darling, are those your urchins?' She peered at the girls sitting neatly on a stone seat across from them beyond the rose gardens. 'They look quite presentable.'

'Oh, they are,' Deanna assured her, winking at Magda.

Donnie arrived at Eagle's Rest for a single night, dropped off by his chauffeur, who was staying in the village. This was a disgruntled Donnie. As Deanna had feared, he was being toured across Britain to give speeches to encourage enlistment. Eligible men had all been conscripted by now, but many in 'reserved occupations' could still be spared and were his target.

He sat at the kitchen table describing the Colonel Blimps and Home Guard Majors who escorted him, with an uncanny mimicry, which made Deanna laugh, but which the girls ignored, knitting socks as they played cards or chess on the sofa with Dusty while Donnie and Deanna spoke together.

Were they intimidated by Donnie's title? Or perhaps, she thought, just wary of a stranger.

Dinner was formal. Mrs Thripps stayed late to set the table: crystal wine glasses, silver cutlery, with the worn Claverton crest. Mrs Thripps also volunteered to serve the meal, mostly so she could get a good look at the new duke; she was dressed in what Deanna suspected was a maid's costume from her years on the variety stage before her marriage, with a short black skirt over her varicosed legs and a white cap. They ate clear beetroot soup with dill and sour cream. The girls drank theirs without slurping, spoons facing outwards. Rabbit fricassee was served with potato souffle, glazed carrots and green salad; a chocolate mousse followed from her hidden store, with anchovies on toast as a savoury.

The girls ate silently, impeccably, then helped Mrs Thripps before vanishing without being asked for bath, bed and book reading. Even Dusty managed to impersonate a well-mannered dog, sleeping by the fire and following the girls outside.

'Are you happy, Dee?' Donnie asked, sitting on the sofa by the fire with her as she sipped cocoa, and he tried one of the old duke's bottles of port.

'Yes,' she said, surprised at her answer. She took up her sewing again, glad she had a good store of needles, for they had just been made 'luxury goods', like toilet ballcocks, kettles, pencils, toys and prams, and would no longer be produced. The girls were going to need warm petticoats for winter, and the ration allowance wouldn't provide nearly enough cloth.

He glanced at the sleeve she was shortening on a child's dress. 'Despite all the work, and the three youngsters?'

'The girls actually do a great deal of work here. I'd be happier if they did less. Their orphanage had them working night and day "for the good of their souls" and to teach them to be good servants, the only job orphans are supposed to be given.'

She had noticed the scullery floor had been scrubbed right to the corners every week since the girls arrived. Tonight the banisters were polished and shining, as was the dressing table in Donnie's room, which even had a small vase of fresh rosemary on the dresser.

'The orphanage seems to have sent their charges to school about once a week — just enough not to be reported to the authorities,' she added. 'But the girls managed not just to keep up their schoolwork, but to scavenge the school library for everything they could read.'

He stared at the gleam of his port in the firelight. 'It must be hard for you, seeing strangers at the castle.'

'Not really. We only lived in a few rooms. Grandpa was always worried a tower would tumble on the butcher. I loved the nights he let me sleep here.'

'Dear old Miss Enid.'

Deanna laughed. 'I loved her, but I'd never call her a dear. She gave the postman a tongue lashing once for calling her "lovie" instead of "Miss Constable".'

'She made good ginger snaps though.'

'I'll make them for you tomorrow before you leave,' she promised.

He took her hand and gave it a quick kiss. 'You really are a darling.'

She flushed but didn't draw her hand away.

Autumn deepened with gaudy foliage and purple shadows. The oak trees in the garden turned gold and crimson; the nights were suddenly cooler. Sam turned up with his fishing mates to borrow her axe and they replenished the house's wood supply. There were rarely the same faces fishing or wood-chopping for more than a week or two. Deanna didn't ask if the men she'd met had been reassigned or killed in action. Eagle's Rest was so clearly their 'no war' zone, a refuge where the men could eat apple tarts around a kitchen table, ask schoolgirls about their homework, and scratch the ears of the dog nosing under the table for dropped crust.

Donnie rang her every few nights to moan about his day and ask about hers. International calls were difficult these days — he must have little chance to talk with friends in America. She supposed he had no one else to talk to in England. His former comrades-in-arms, it seemed, had been lost at Dunkirk or sent to the Middle East. He was unlikely to run into even a vague acquaintance on his recruiting drives.

So she was surprised to see him at Patricia Worthington's, where once again she arrived merely for Saturday lunch, leaving Magda, Rosa and Anna learning fly-fishing with Sam and his mates, Mrs Thripps guarding the picnic basket from Dusty and refusing payment for the time spent.

'It's a day in the sun for me, Lady Dee,' she insisted. 'Otherwise, I'd be doing the ironing on me ownsome, what with Arnold on nights again and snoring his head off.'

There had been about two hundred at the railway station that morning, many of them young men going off to basic training, with loved ones saying goodbye. The boys looked more lost than resolute; the girls and women were thin-lipped, trying not to cry, or managing tears and a smile of farewell at the same time.

She had met every man in the railway carriage at village functions. They stood back politely to give her a choice of seat. She let them, guiltily, for she was giving up nothing and they were giving up so much; she muttered, 'Good luck,' and, 'We'll all be thinking of you,' as she passed them, shaking hands quickly so they could spend their last moments with those they loved, not social ritual.

A car met the train, its chauffeur too old to be conscripted, and took her past gardens of chrysanthemums and red and orange autumn leaves dappling well-mown lawns, with nary a sign of Victory Gardens of cabbages or turnips.

'Dee, honey!' Donnie left a group drinking champagne on the terrace and came to meet her, kissing her cheek. 'Patricia said you'd be here.' He smiled charmingly at his hostess. 'Pattycake's kindly put me up for the weekend.' He offered Deanna his arm. She took it.

'We couldn't possibly have you stay at a hotel!' pressed Mrs Worthington, sixty going on forty and reputed to have had two facelifts in Switzerland. 'How lovely to have you both here. Tell me, Lady Deanna, how *is* the dear castle? Have they damaged it terribly? You hear terrible stories of drunken soldiers throwing darts at family portraits or painting priceless frescos khaki.'

'They've probably stopped the castle falling down before Donnie could claim it,' Deanna said frankly. 'There aren't any frescos to ruin. They've added nothing that can't be easily removed.'

'Let's hope that's soon then. You must tell me, where did you get that fabulous dress?'

'It's an old one, a Doucet of my mother's,' Deanna prevaricated, not mentioning that she had shortened the hem and added a collar to the square neckline.

'It is simply *too* gorgeous.'

'But not as beautiful as the woman wearing it.' Donnie smiled at her.

Their hostess waved over some other guests. 'Jimpy, Bobo, Bussy, you know Lady Deanna Claverton, don't you? Deanna, this …'

Deanna let the talk flow over her. There would be little chance for accidental talk with her host or hostess today, not with

Donnie claiming her. Nor did anyone seem to be talking about the war, despite the increased bombardment of major ports and cities and the decrease of the food and clothing ration. She hoped the conversation would be more substantial at lunch.

At least she had a pleasant half hour with Donnie before the meal, as they walked the gardens and he described his home, a sun-drenched hillside mansion in California with a swimming pool.

'Do you have any wild animals?'

He gave a shout of laughter. 'The same old Dee — not impressed by my magnificent residence. Yes, we have coyotes, and wild cats, and a friend even has a few buffalo and you can surf with the sea otters down in the bay. You haven't asked about movie stars.'

'I'm not really interested,' she admitted.

He looked at her seriously. 'You are a woman in a million: one who doesn't give her life to frivolity, but duty to home, and family and country. Now, let us hint that you be chauffeured home after afternoon tea, so you can enjoy your family.'

'You are family,' she pointed out.

He kissed her hand, to her surprise. 'But I have had you for a whole afternoon.'

She arrived home to a kitchen smelling even more triumphantly than before of fish and chips.

'You have to eat that one, Auntie Dee!' Anna pointed to the largest trout. 'I catched it!'

'Caught it,' corrected Rosa.

'That's what I said! Dusty tried to eat it but only took one bite. Good dog, Dusty.'

Dusty wagged his tail with the assurance of a dog who preferred his fish fried, and with chips, with people who didn't seem to mind his flatulence, inevitable after eating potato.

Sam's friend stood up politely to be introduced.

'It's Flight Lieutenant Carruthers, isn't it?' Deanna offered him her hand. 'Call me Deanna. Thank you for taking on my ragamuffins for the day.'

'What are ragamuffins?' Anna asked. Deanna looked at the child's bright red satin skirt embroidered with golden peacocks: though it was worn under a sensible jersey, the garment was totally unsuitable for a weekend of fishing, but the child had fallen in love with the fabric. It had taken Deanna five minutes to run up the skirt on the treadle sewing machine — one seam and elastic at the top and it was ready.

Magda and Rosa had chosen a selection of sensible corduroy skirts to wear with jumpers or blouses, each skirt trimmed with different colours and designs of braid that they sewed on by themselves as the family listened to the radio during the week, or while Deanna read to them.

'I hope you had half as good a day as we did.' Sam held out her chair for her as she sat. Mrs Thripps was once again smoking a fresh cigarette — Deanna realised that Sam probably gave her his tobacco allowance.

'No, to be honest.' She had learned nothing. Mr Worthington was in banking, as Donnie's father had been, and Deanna supposed Donnie still was, technically, even if the bank his grandfather had started was managed by others now. They had talked about Bolivian mines at luncheon.

The women had indulged in a spirited comparison of French fashion designers, now sadly beyond their reach, then bewailed rationing and the servant problem, with so many women signing up for jobs in factories at five times the money and with two days off a week, as well as regular hours. As Deanna's only servant, if she could be called such, was currently entertaining the other end of the table with a story about how she had once danced the Charleston with film star Leslie Howard, at the beginning of his career when he was starring in *Charley's Aunt* and Mrs Thripps still on the variety stage — details of that side of her life Mrs Thripps had never permitted her employer to see before. Deanna considered herself blessed in that department and was glad she had said so this afternoon — though her answer had implied a staff of possibly ten instead of two sevenths of one.

'I was bored to the back teeth,' she admitted. 'I usually am at these affairs.'

'Then why go?' Sam asked with genuine curiosity.

She could not say, 'Because I'm employed — though not paid — to supply information.' She shrugged instead. 'It's hard to say no, sometimes. I hope the girls weren't a nuisance?'

'It was the best fun I've had since I enlisted,' he said frankly. 'Anna fell in four times — she carefully hung her skirt up to dry on a branch and wore Rosa's overcoat, while Rosa demanded to know every detail about how kangaroos reproduce. Thankfully I had to do a project on biology on them at high school or I'd have been stumped.'

'And Magda?'

'She found out her fellow fisherman is a chemist in civvy street, and had him drawing equations in the sand. Don't worry — he enjoyed it too. You should have heard the screams when they caught a fish!'

'They really did catch them?'

'Let's just say the fish were caught on their rods,' Sam said tactfully. He glanced at his watch.

'Need to be getting back?'

'Not yet. I told Magda I'd beat her in chess, and Johnny admitted to being a champion tiddlywinks player.'

'My money is on Magda, and I bet we can win at tiddlywinks.'

'Magda's a bright kid,' Sam said. 'They all are.' He lowered his voice. 'Have you found out any more about their background?'

So he had noticed their continued evasions too. 'Not a thing. They didn't mention anything from their past today?'

'Only that Magda learned chess from her mother, who is the one person who has ever beaten her in a match. They also had a dog — Anna was staring at nothing for a moment, then Dusty jumped up and licked her face. She hugged him and said, "I miss Woofer."'

'They were certainly well educated before they were sent to the orphanage. Miss Hannaford says they are far advanced for their ages in every subject, but that Anna has rarely if ever been to school before. She'd never used a slate, though she can write in paragraphs. The orphanage probably never bothered to enrol her. She says they don't really mix with the other children,' she admitted.

'They're fine kids, whoever they are,' he declared. 'Hey, not fair! I want more of those chips before they go to the dog.'

Dusty looked resigned.

Twelve

They have sown the wind, they shall reap the whirlwind.
　　　　　　　　　Sir Winston Churchill quoting Hosea 8:7
　　　　　　　　　　on visiting Coventry after the bombing

Life continued — peaceful and ordered at Eagle's Rest, even as bombs rained on Coventry from night till early morning. The first bombers dropped high explosive bombs on the town's factories and military bases, but equally in civilian areas, destroying a third of the homes completely and damaging many more. The Nazi propagandists coined a new word: *coventrieren*, to raze a city to rubble.

Coventry Cathedral was burned to the ground. The entire city centre was destroyed as well as its hospitals; surgeons and nurses removing legs or trimming shattered arms or trying to lessen the agony of the inevitable last hours as they worked behind walls of sandbags or in canvas tents, till they too were blown up.

Only six hundred civilian lives lost and a thousand injured, the headlines proclaimed, trying to make tragedy into a triumph of stoicism. Many of those who lived in the town left to sleep in the countryside each night, and 'nearly all' the air-raid shelters had survived the bombing. The newspapers didn't specify which air-raid shelters became coffins instead of safe nests.

Deanna had loved Coventry Cathedral, the silent arches that seemed eternal, the smell of stone that had known incense for hundreds of years.

It was easier to mourn the cathedral than imagine the dead: women who spent their final seconds hunting for children still playing in the yard, to herd them into Anderson shelters so carefully dug in beneath the cabbage patches; the elderly, who almost made it down the road to the shelter before death swooped down on them; the deaf, reaching for a cup of tea, unaware of the hell unfolding around them; the hopeless, who sat back in their chairs and simply waited. Death would come from the sky one day. Why not tonight?

The RAF bombed Berlin, Hamburg, Bremen and other cities in retaliation the next night. Bombs were not just a weapon now but murderous revenge.

Johnny Carruthers did not visit again. Anna asked Sam just once if he would come fishing again but didn't question it when Sam said briefly, 'No. He's been transferred,' his face so carefully blank that the little girl glanced at Deanna to confirm what they must all suspect.

Johnny Carruthers was dead.

'I'm sorry Anna asked about Johnny,' Deanna said quietly, as she and Sam drank their now customary cocoa when the girls had gone up to bed after one of their trout suppers.

Sam nodded. He managed to smile at her. 'Tell me something that isn't about the war.'

'There's a new sign at the grocer's taking up all the window that isn't sandbagged:

NO EGGS

NO LEMONS

NO ONIONS
NO LEEKS
NO MANGLES
NO PAPER BAGS.'

'No mangles?'

'Mangelwurzels — like overgrown beetroot. They used to be cattle food. All food is scarce now, rationed or not.'

'But you feed us all.'

She flushed. 'Most is home grown, but ... I've got a guilty secret.'

'Only one?'

She gave him a light kick under the table. 'Any more comments like that, Flight Lieutenant Murray, and you won't get apple tart. My grandfather predicted this war. He knew he was dying. He spent the last two years of his life inconspicuously accumulating stores for me — sugar, white flour, golden syrup — things that would last for years, as well as tea and the kind of chocolate they send out to India that stays edible for decades, too. I've even got a small amount of coffee if you'd like a change from cocoa.'

'Cocoa will do me. To tell the truth, I've only ever had coffee once and didn't like it much. We Aussies are tea drinkers.'

She glanced at him curiously. She had met Australians before: young women who came to England to 'do their season' and be presented at court, and couples invited to pheasant shoots or deer hunts.

They had drunk coffee, and their accents had been almost English upper class. It seemed the Australian social structure was as complex as that of Britain. Sam's family was obviously well off. He was educated too, even if he hadn't gone to Oxford or Cambridge, as many rich colonials did automatically, even if they had no academic inclinations and could hardly finish a degree. Many didn't even try.

He was also unlikely to survive the war, though at least as a trainer he was safer than most. At times Deanna wondered if she should have stopped him becoming so much a part of their lives. The girls had known far too much loss already.

But she liked him enormously. And he really did fit into the family they had created, which now increasingly included Mrs Thripps, who 'just happened to be passing' several times a week, and not just to enjoy a cup of truly strong tea with sugar, but to help sew hems of dresses foraged from material in the trunks and to mend school uniforms — somehow Anna's hem was ripped at least twice a week, and Rosa's often needed lengthening as she began what seemed to be a never-ending growth spurt. All three girls had grown taller since they'd arrived, which Deanna attributed to good food and the security of what seemed a haven from the war. Their skins had a bloom from fresh air and work in the garden had given them muscles that the orphanage scrubbing hadn't produced.

Mrs Thripps even spent hours guiding Anna's fingers to learn an unexpectedly curved and swerved copperplate longhand, or telling the stories of a youth Deanna had never suspected.

'Me and Mum and Dad had a vaudeville act, the Amazing Dancing Andersons. That's how I met my Arnold — he was a stage-door Johnny. Oh, he was so romantic! He used to bring me flowers after every show and followed us around the country every weekend for six months, and then he showed up with an engagement ring. Mum said I better snap him up quick, him having a steady job and a cottage he'd inherited from his aunt, despite him bein' a bit older than me. I'm his second wife, you know.'

'But you have to clean now,' said Magda, sipping milk as Mrs Thripps poured her second cup of tea and briefly removed her cigarette to drink it.

'Well, I don't exactly *have* to work, lovie, but I was bored,' said Mrs Thripps frankly. 'And there was this great big blinkin' castle, and let's face it, dear, no duke was going to invite me and Arnold to supper. So when Mrs Peterson — she was the last cook at the castle — said His Grace needed a char I put myself forward so I could have a look-see, and it was the duke himself who recommended me to Miss Enid. It made a nice change from the village, goin' up to the castle. The stories I could tell you —' She stopped, suddenly remembering the age of her audience.

'My grandfather was in love with Miss Enid,' said Deanna tactfully.

'Yes, that was it,' said Mrs Thripps, relieved there was one secret she need no longer keep. 'Used to sit hand in hand in the garden looking at them blasted eagles — not when they knew I was watching, of course.'

'People in love marry,' stated Anna.

'Well, they couldn't, 'cause His Grace was married to Lady Dee's gran, but, well, sometimes marriages go sour and sometimes they stick. Me and Arnold have had the sticking kind, but His Grace weren't so lucky.'

Mrs Thripps met Deanna's eyes. 'He and Miss Enid were happy, never doubt that, and Miss Enid had Lady Dee down here most days in the school holidays. This was always a happy house.'

It is again, thought Deanna. And if they lost Sam — if every time she heard a plane or the few times they had felt the vibrations of a flaming crash she wondered if he was the pilot — she and the girls would find other ways to create happiness in their lives, as people must when there was war, whether it was between nations or between two people ...

'How did you meet Leslie Howard?' breathed Magda. 'He looks so handsome in the magazine article about the movie he's making.'

Dee made a private note to take the girls when *Gone with the Wind* finally arrived at the picture theatre in Claverton Major, the bigger town one railway stop from the village.

'Well,' said Mrs Thripps, stubbing out her cigarette and placing it back in her mouth again, 'it were like this. I'd just done me big dance number — four back somersaults in a red silk dress that swirled like a tornado, and red satin underpants, ending with the splits, then up on me feet to take a bow. And there he was in the box above the stage, standing and applauding. He sent this note with the biggest bunch of orchids you ever saw. We had supper at the Ritz, oysters and lobster and champagne and a giant steak — if it weren't for Mr Hitler I'd have steak twice a week — and then we danced to the jazz orchestra and he whispered in me ear, "So, shall we make beautiful music in my room?"'

'What did you say?' asked Magda, agog.

'I said, "No thanks, but ta for the supper. Me dad's waiting outside to take me back to our lodging." But oh, that man was a fine dancer. Not even out of breath.'

The price of toilet paper had gone up from sixpence to eleven pence a roll, Mrs Thripps informed them one morning. '*If* you can find any on the shelves. It's all these ships being sunk.'

Exact numbers of these losses were never given but they could be deduced by the lists of 'dead' or 'wounded'. All of Claverton Minor knew the British armed merchant cruiser *Forfar* had sunk because the Filmers' son had been on it, and was listed as 'missing, presumed dead'.

'Our duke was missing and turned up all right,' said Mr Septimus Filmer, defiantly confident. 'Our Ted will be back.'

Mrs Filmer nodded but said nothing.

Thirteen

God gave us memory so that we might have roses in December.
JM Barrie quote that became
a popular saying of World War II

The air smelled of woodsmoke and autumn leaves. Anna held Sam's hand as she pointed up at the oak branches. 'See! You can tell it's a squirrel's nest because the twigs and leaves are woven together. Magpies weave their nests, but not like squirrels do. Anyhow, I've seen a squirrel in it!'

Sam smiled at her. 'What was it like?'

'Its tail was *ginormous*! But you can tell if you have squirrels from gnawed pinecones under the tree or scratch marks in bark.' She lowered her voice. 'Our squirrel has buried thousands of nuts and acorns under this tree! Auntie Dee says squirrels have been using the tree for hundreds of years.'

Sam squinted up at the nest. 'It doesn't look a very comfy place to spend all of winter.'

'Aunt Dee says it's *in*sulated. The inside is all soft and mossy so the squirrels can snuggle up and eat hazelnuts and acorns all winter.' She turned to find Dee watching them. 'I was just telling

Sam that's why the squirrels don't have to share our bedroom,' she explained.

'Or the library,' she said drily. 'Do wombats make nests?'

'They live in deep burrows, the rooms lined with dried tussocks and bracken. We had one once who picked Mum's lavender to make a scented bed for herself.'

Anna giggled. That is a wonderful sound, thought Deanna. 'I just came in to say the scones are ready.'

'Scones!' Anna raced inside.

'You've done wonders,' said Sam, watching Anna scatter her wellies and slam the door in her haste to get the last of the strawberry jam before her sisters ate it.

'They're happy, I think. Still scared of something, but I don't know what. Have you noticed they don't play?'

'They play chess and tiddlywinks.'

'I mean ball games, or rounders. They don't stay at the school for afternoon games either. If it's raining, they read and knit, and Rosa loves to sew. They assume that any spare time must be spent on work. I came in this morning to find Magda cleaning the fridge. They'll weed and pick vegetables till they nearly drop with exhaustion, or I call them for dinner.'

'That was probably what they were taught in the orphanage.'

'Or they are trying to make me think they are indispensable, no matter what I find out about them.'

'It can't be anything too terrible. Dee, I was wondering ... would the four of you like to take the train to Claverton Major next Saturday? I have the day off. We could have lunch — maybe compare real fish and chips to mine — and go to the movies.'

'I'd love to, but I can't,' she said regretfully. 'The girls and I have agreed to Mrs Goodword's "suggestion" to serve at the tables at the Bring and Buy sale for the Polish Orphans Fund. But another day? As soon as we can?'

The gossip would fly faster than a Spitfire. Claverton Minor and Claverton Major would know Lady Deanna was Walking Out with a pilot from the base — an Australian at that.

Let them gossip, she thought. Because I will be doing exactly that.

Fourteen

Welsh Cakes — the World War II Version

INGREDIENTS

110 grams margarine, butter or dripping
170 grams plain flour with three teaspoons baking powder added (or use self-raising flour)
a quarter teaspoon ground nutmeg
60 grams sugar
one small carrot, grated
60 grams currants (or mixed dried fruit)
one fresh egg or one reconstituted dried egg
one tablespoon milk

METHOD

Rub fat into the flour and baking powder mix until it resembles breadcrumbs. Stir in nutmeg, sugar, carrot and dried fruit. Mix the egg and milk together and add to dry mix to form a stiff dough (add more liquid or more flour as needed). Treat mixture as pastry and roll out on floured surface to a centimetre thick. Use six-centimetre rounds to cut out discs. Pre-heat and grease griddle or heavy frying pan. Put in Welsh cakes and cook until golden brown on both sides over a moderate heat (about four minutes).

Donnie's phone calls continued, making her laugh with wry comments about his new acquaintances, colleagues and hosts, but she had no idea he planned to arrive till a black car flying the Union Jack drew up one afternoon. Deanna peered out of the glasshouse as the driver saluted after he'd opened the limousine's back door.

Donnie was still in uniform, Deanna realised, even though he had been invalided out: probably necessary for propaganda.

The chauffeur handed him a large suitcase, saluted again, and started the motor. He was halfway up the lane before Deanna emerged from the glasshouse.

'Dee, honey? Can I stay the night?' He grinned. 'You can't say no. The car has left.'

'I could say, "Borrow my bicycle and stay at the pub."'

'But you won't.'

She grinned back at him. 'It depends on your manners. We have high standards here. I hope you brought your evening clothes.'

'As a matter of fact, I did.' His glance took in her manure-stained overalls, the tea towel over her hair. 'Dee, you're really working, aren't you? I thought all your talk of potato fields was a way of getting around petrol rationing. I had no idea you were doing the work yourself. I should have offered you an allowance straight away!'

'I don't need one. I've enough to get by.'

'Shovelling manure in a glasshouse! You should get a man to do that.'

'I doubt there is a man spare,' she said drily. 'Don't you know there's a war on?'

'But you are—'

'The cousin of a duke and so shouldn't get my hands dirty? Donnie, most of the women in England have jobs now, in factories, if not in uniform. This happens to be my job. I enjoy growing things, too.'

'I still think I should make you an allowance.'

'No, thank you, but I appreciate the offer.'

He grinned at her. 'I don't need your permission to do it.'

'Try it, and I'll put soap in your soup and nettles in your bed. Do you remember how you did that to me when we quarrelled over who should be the Normans and who should be the Saxons?'

He laughed. 'I apologise profusely. We'll talk about an allowance some other time.'

'We will not. Come on. I'll show you to your room. I'll even change into a dinner dress if you make your own bed.'

'My own bed! You're joking.' He looked appalled.

She laughed. 'Donnie, surely you had to make your bed in the army!'

'I certainly did not. I had a batman. And then for a while I didn't have a bed to make. I do know how to make a bed — we had to make our own at school — but it's been years since I had to do it.'

'Then this will be a pleasant refresher course.'

She led him to the warmest spare room — the three girls still shared the largest bedroom — showed him the linen closet, then bathed and changed, not into a dress but flared fuchsia silk trousers with a matching embroidered tunic that she suspected had been her mother's, and a tasselled shawl to wear over it that could have been from any period in the last two hundred years, for only the kitchen fire was lit.

He was downstairs before her. He'd also changed out of his uniform, into flannel trousers and a thick, plain blue jumper. He smiled at her. 'Now that's much better.'

'You didn't put on your evening clothes.'

'I thought your evacuees might feel uncomfortable with too much finery.'

'On the contrary, we've spent every rainy Sunday afternoon making the most magnificent dresses out of taffeta and damask and beaded velvet — all old stuff I've been collecting for years,' she added hurriedly, carefully not mentioning that they might have been part of the estate he'd inherited.

She put the kettle on to change the subject quickly as he sat at the table, exactly where he had perched all those years earlier with Miss Enid at the head of the table and Deanna on the other side. 'You're in luck. I've been culling the roosters, so you have coq au vin without the vin tonight, instead of parsnip pie.'

'No wine? Dee, my sweet, I saw the racks in that cellar of yours quite clearly.'

'And you may drink from them, and so will I, but the girls will not, which is why I don't put wine in the coq a not-vin. Here — I even made Welsh cakes yesterday.' She passed him the plate. He took one carelessly, as if he had no idea how precious the butter and currants in them had become.

'Miss Enid used to make Welsh cakes,' he remembered. 'And toffees too — real tooth-breakers.'

'I think she only made toffees for you and me. I never saw her eat one. But she did like Welsh cakes. I love them too.'

'As did your grandfather. I remember him scoffing a whole plate of them.' Donnie took another.

She blinked. Her grandfather had been allergic to dried currants. Miss Enid always had ginger biscuits for him instead, and avoided chutney that might contain currants. Americans didn't eat Welsh cakes, she supposed. They even called biscuits 'cookies' and scones 'biscuits'.

He probably thought gingerbread was a form of Welsh cake.

'He used to feed Welsh cakes to Wolf too, the old bulldog you had as well as Dusty that year.'

What bulldog? thought Deanna, puzzled. But Donnie had spent only one summer here. He must have confused that holiday with one somewhere else.

He glanced at his watch. 'I'd better get this over before your evacuees come back from school. Dee, I wanted to tell you in person. I've found out who those three are.'

'What? How? Who are they?' she asked eagerly.

'I've managed to make some contacts in the Home Office. It really wasn't hard to trace three orphans who are sisters.'

It had probably taken some official's secretary days of leafing through records, but she didn't correct him. 'Go on.'

'Their Christian names are correct — that made it easier too. But their surname is Fleishman.'

'German!'

He looked at her with sympathy. 'And Jewish into the bargain. That's why they didn't tell you, of course, though the orphanage would have their names. Their father ran the English side of the family wine business. When he and his wife were killed in a car accident four years ago the children were taken in by their paternal aunt and uncle.'

'Here in England?' she asked, dazed.

'Yes. Herr von Fleishman took over his brother's position in the business. He and his wife are childless. When it became likely that the Fleishmans would be sent to an internment camp they decided the girls would be better off in an orphanage, but they are anxious about them. I arranged a phone call with Herr von Fleishman in the camp he's in. I was able to reassure him the girls are in a happy home, but Herr von Fleishman has changed his mind. The camp has a good school and a playground, and all kinds of activities. He would like the girls to join him and his wife.'

She stared at him, cold to her bones. 'No.'

'Don't worry. The girls are certainly better off here for the time being than behind barbed wire. But it's possible the authorities will decide they should be with their uncle and aunt. Even if they don't, you must know that after the war ...'

'They will go back to their family,' said Deanna dully. She sat entirely still. 'Don't tell them,' she said at last. 'They'd hate me to know they're German. They'd worry about it being known in the village, too.'

And they are happy here, she thought. It's not just the comfort of Eagle's Rest, and having a library of their own, and animals to watch. We are family. I'm not imagining it.

'I won't tell anyone,' Donnie assured her. 'But you needed to know.'

'Yes,' she said. I had a family this morning, and now I don't, she thought. But what if the girls decide they want to stay with me? It must be over a year at least since they've seen this aunt and uncle: a long time for children that age.

Outside, a swish of tyres meant the girls were returning. They'd want hot cocoa, and Welsh cakes ...

Could you really think a ginger biscuit was a Welsh cake? Grandpa hadn't even let Dusty eat Welsh cakes in case he licked him afterwards. He'd made a fuss when Donnie gave him half of his. Donnie couldn't have forgotten it.

She said quickly, 'I forgot to tell you — the painting you asked me to sell for you, the one that hung in the Blue Room that we thought might be a Turner? It turned out to be genuine. The money has finally come through. I donated it to the Red Cross, just as you asked me to do in our phone call before you left.'

She waited for him to frown, to say he didn't remember asking her to sell a painting, and certainly not a Turner.

Instead he smiled at her. 'Thank you. I hope you got a good price for it.'

What on earth was a Turner worth? 'Five thousand pounds, for which the Red Cross is grateful.'

'Really?' Donnie frowned. 'The market must be down. But it's better the money goes to a good cause now than the painting staying in storage. Thank you again.' He smiled at her. 'You have done so much for me.'

'Just as you have for me. Hello, ragamuffins! How was school?'

Dinner was once more formal and polite. The girls ate silently while Deanna and Donnie discussed people he had met in England, acquaintances they might have in common. He wanted to know more about the role he would need to play when he sat in the House of Lords. 'I don't even have an ermine cloak, Dee, honey. I'm not even sure what an ermine is.'

'It's an animal, like a weasel, with a fluffy coat in winter. They are bred in cages now,' said Rosa.

He smiled at her. 'Thank you.'

Rosa nodded and bent to her meal. Do they suspect he is in a position to find out who they really are, Deanna wondered, and are trying to be inconspicuous? No: he'd made no attempt to include them in the conversation. Perhaps they guessed he preferred to talk to Deanna and were being polite.

The girls did their homework at the kitchen table after dinner. Deanna dutifully brought up a bottle of port — she didn't care for it, but Mrs Thripps could have the rest of the bottle. There was, in fact, little wine in the cellar — her grandfather had preferred scotch whisky. She had offered Sam port once, but he had explained he couldn't drink when he might be on call.

She was glad Sam hadn't called in tonight. He and Donnie had never met, and when they did — if they did — they would have nothing in common. Sam was so obviously not 'our kind of people', even apart from being Australian.

She also needed to consider whether she should tell Sam about the girls' true heritage. He was fond of them. But though he might vanish from their lives anyway when he returned to Australia, assuming he survived, he certainly thought of Magda, Rosa and Anna as at least temporary family. He thought of her as family too, but whether as sister or, potentially, lover she couldn't tell — nor was she sure which she wanted it to be. Both of them were bound to their own lands, but the love of land was part of the bond between them.

But the difficulty of the Welsh cakes could not wait. They were such a small thing, but a Turner was not a minor item, and nor was it from long ago. No matter what Donnie had been through he should remember asking her to sell the painting, or, if not, just come out and say so. 'Sorry, honey, I can't remember that at all. But I'm glad it went to a good cause ...'

There was only one reason she could think of for him to *pretend* to remember.

She excused herself when the girls went to bed and went to her bedroom, but she didn't change into her nightgown. Instead, she waited till she was sure Donnie slept, then slipped down to the library and the telephone.

She had a phone number memorised, an emergency phone number only, for things that could not wait for a letter, or that could not be explained in code.

'Doris?' she asked when the telephonist at the village exchange answered. 'It's Lady Dee. I'm sorry to have got you out of bed. I need to tell my uncle I'm coming up to London tomorrow and can call in.'

'Urgent business, Lady Deanna? It would need to be to go up there now, with all these raids. I'll put the call through for you now. No, no trouble at all.'

Deanna put the phone back in its receiver. It rang again only thirty seconds later — the exchange at the other end must have many phone lines and many people manning them. 'Uncle Jasper?' Thankfully no one in the village, or the circles in which she and her grandfather moved, knew anything about her long dead mother's family, though if she had a real maternal uncle, Dee had yet to hear from him. 'It's me, Dee. I have to come up to London tomorrow afternoon.' She assumed Donnie would have left by then. 'Is there any chance of a cup of tea and a bun? I do hope Auntie is over the influenza. The Ritz at two o'clock? How lovely! Yes, toodle pip to you too, and love to Aunt Florence.'

The Ritz at two o'clock meant the same Lyons tea house at four pm — she could catch the last train home but it would be midnight before she reached Claverton, and so best to ask Mrs Thripps to stay the night.

She put the phone down and stared at the secret panel, wishing that opening it might tell her secrets too. Because the man sleeping upstairs in her spare room was not Donald, Eighth Duke of Claverton, and she had no idea who he might be.

Fifteen

'Are you in the army, mister?' asked the little girl on the train.
'Yes,' he replied.
'And have you ever killed anyone?'
'Probably,' he said.
'With a machine gun? Or a hand grenade?'
'No,' he answered. 'I'm the regimental cook.'

World War II joke

It was all so easy, she thought, as she sat in the second-class carriage as the train clacked on its rails. She hadn't seen Donnie since he was twelve years old. As soon as he had called her 'Dee' in an American accent, this dark-haired man stumbling towards her, she had assumed that was who he was.

Who else could even have known about the cave? It was almost impossible to see if you didn't know it was there, and only a skilled boatman could reach it, at the right tide.

And now? The Eighth Duke of Claverton had been publicly welcomed and acknowledged by his second cousin, his childhood friend. That was enough to establish him in the eyes of authority.

What of his fellow soldiers from his short time in the English army? Presumably, none had returned yet, either because they were dead or imprisoned or serving elsewhere, but still, he must look ridiculously like Donnie, or someone would have noticed he didn't resemble the photograph taken just after he was commissioned. Or had he been an imposter all along? Was that why he had never come to meet her?

No, that wouldn't work; he could have established himself as Donnie Claverton with her just as easily then, but there was too great a chance of meeting someone from America — or even another country — who had met the real Donnie, or that publicity around him enlisting would reach the States, where the real Donnie might have something to say about it all. The imposture was much more likely to have taken place in France: her cousin could have vanished into any Nazi hospital or POW camp with no one to say an 'escapee' wasn't really him.

Nor could it be a long-term con job, even if Donnie was already dead and buried in an anonymous grave. One day, inevitably, someone in America would point at a photo of the duke in his ermine robe and say, 'That is not the man I was at college with/played golf with/who dated my sister ...'

Even if the resemblance *was* very close, one day the man who had stayed in her house last night must meet someone who had known the real Donnie. And the real Donnie might still turn up, mightn't he?

Surely this man must have met the real Donnie to know so much. Except, she suddenly realised, this stranger thought he knew things which were not true. He had thought his predecessor had loved Welsh cakes when that was the one cake he never ate. He'd been casually sure they'd had a dog called Wolf.

Someone — Donnie? — had fed this man or his superiors obviously false information, as well as real. Was it a message from her true cousin to her? Who else, after all, would know about Grandpa's allergies? Dee shivered. What had they put Donnie through to give so much detailed information?

Or was she building a house of cards that would tumble down? Perhaps the man she now knew *was* the real Donnie, but he'd had that head injury — he still had the rough stitches. His memory could have been affected. He had played with a dog called Wolf with another family, been mistaken about the Welsh cakes. He might even know his memory was faulty and so had pretended to remember a request about a painting.

What was true, and what was not? And if the man she had called Donnie himself was a lie, what about Herr von Fleishman and the girls she was beginning to think of as her daughters, who were still in her care, whoever they were, and would be cared for, no matter what. Which was why she had a diamond in her brassiere today, where it would be safe even if someone stole her handbag.

Vonderfleet and Sons was still standing, even if much of the East End was rubble topped by permanent choking dust, twisted metal, and peopled by grey faces with tight lips and eyes that gazed down, both to make sure they didn't step on unexploded bombs, broken glass, or body parts missed by the ambulances, and to avoid seeing the extent of each night's new chaos. The street stank of sewage and, worryingly, gas. Vonderfleet and Sons' small front windows were barred, taped and sandbagged to halfway up.

Deanna had tactfully removed the diamond from her brassiere in the ladies' at the train station, waiting three quarters of an hour just to get into a cubicle, then keeping a firm grip on her handbag as she made her way down the street, a far emptier street, both of people and vehicles, than the last time she had been in London, only a year before.

The shop's exterior was unimpressive. It would have looked like a low-class jeweller's even without tape and sandbags. The interior was no better — a narrow shop with room enough for a glass-topped counter, showing a small selection of jewellery and wristwatches, with price tags ranging from five pounds to fifty, and room for possibly four customers, if they wanted to know each other well. A girl in a dustcoat looked up from an account book. 'How can I help you?'

'I have an appointment with Mr Vonderfleet.'

'Ah yes, of course. Come with me.' She didn't ask Deanna's name. The girl opened the counter flap and took keys from her pocket. What Deanna had assumed was a wall became a door, but with no handle. The girl pushed and slipped inside. Deanna followed her and the girl quickly shut the door behind then.

'Dad! Lady Deanna to see you.'

The girl slipped out the door again. Deanna heard the snick of the lock.

'Lady Deanna, a pleasure. Please accept my condolences on the death of your grandfather. Under the, ahem, circumstances, it did not seem tactful to send a card from the firm or myself.'

Mr Vonderfleet was sixty perhaps, round-shouldered, balding, stubby-fingered and snub-nosed. 'Please take a seat, Lady Deanna. May I offer you coffee? Chicory coffee,' he added with a smile. 'Not black market or rationed. My wife grows and bakes the root herself and adds a touch of beetroot for sweetness.'

'I would like a cup. Thank you.'

The room must have taken in the area behind several shopfronts. A large metal safe stood in one corner, with smaller ones around the walls. A long table stretched almost the entire length of the room, littered with tools and little machines Deanna didn't recognise. A small refrigerator stood by the far wall next to a gas hotplate and a table already laid with salt, pepper, a jar of pickled cucumbers, and plates and cutlery for four neatly piled at one end.

'I hope you don't mind it black.' Mr Vonderfleet placed the kettle on the hotplate. 'I presume you have something for me?'

She presented him with the crumple of brown paper as he slid on a pair of gloves.

He opened the crumple and smiled. 'Ah, I sold your grandfather this, perhaps ten years ago. I do not even have to examine it to recognise it. It is a good time to sell, and not just because of the De Beers advertising. Americans are buying diamonds for security, and diamond mining has all but ceased due to the war. All those out there,' he waved towards the shop, 'are artificial diamonds. Of course, industrial diamonds are in demand too, but a jewel like this,' he gazed back at the diamond with the smile of a lover, 'is worth far more than its size might warrant. It is flawless — a rarity among jewels. Two diamonds of the same weight and cut can vastly differ in value. Clarity and colour are what matter. Most diamonds that seem clear have some small shading, and clarity can't be measured by an amateur, who may only notice that one diamond gleams like a star in the electric light in a woman's tiara, while other similar stones are relatively dull.'

'You said this is flawless?'

'Not just flawless — I, myself, would not sell a client such as the duke a flawed stone. It is of the first clarity.' His smiled turned to her, paternal.

Grandpa told him about me, she thought. Maybe the two men sat and drank coffee many times, talking about their grandchildren. Grandpa said that I could trust him.

'You have most politely not asked me how much it is worth, because of course I will give you what it is worth, and not take commission, for that is what I promised your grandfather.'

'But you can't take no commission!'

He shrugged. 'What else are friends for if not to help their friends' families? Besides, it will help my reputation to have this stone to sell again, so I will profit, just not from you. Now, a good cut diamond is perhaps six hundred pounds a carat. A carat is the size of the diamond. You have here a four-point-eight-carat diamond.'

'Nearly three thousand pounds!'

The smile became a laugh. 'The larger the stone, the larger the price, if the quality is the same. A four-carat stone is worth far more than four one-carat stones. This has also been cut by a master, me, and possesses a clarity seen once, perhaps, in a decade.'

The kettle whistled. He took it off the hotplate and poured water into a tin coffee pot. She realised he was deliberately building up the tension: part of his profession perhaps, to increase expectation and desire, even though in this case neither were necessary.

'Here.' He handed her a porcelain teacup and saucer.

She sipped, then sipped again. 'It's good. Would your wife give me her recipe?'

'I have watched her many times. You slow-bake the chicory root till it is dry, and the grated beetroot too, then grind them together. Hilda makes it fresh each week, for it does not keep its flavour like true coffee. Now, your diamond …'

'Yes?'

'Twenty-five thousand pounds,' he said calmly, watching for her reaction.

'Twenty-five *thousand*?' A good house cost perhaps a thousand pounds, a bungalow less than a hundred. The average man's wage was about five pounds a week, a woman in a good job made maybe two pounds. Twenty-five thousand pounds would pay for school fees for all three girls, and for them to attend university too. She could buy new clothes for herself and the girls if they ever became available, every book she fancied. She tried to think of what else she might want to use money for, and failed. She couldn't give most of it away to charity, or not all at once, without raising questions about how she came by the money, and demands for income tax as well as inheritance tax. And this was just one of her diamonds ...

I am rich, she thought, trying to take it in, when I thought I would spend my life relatively poor. Her income from Miss Enid and the farm had already been enough to keep her in modest comfort. But this!

'How could my grandfather have possibly afforded to buy a stone like this?'

Mr Vonderfleet's eyes lit with amusement. 'He paid nothing. He traded it for a far larger ruby, for which I gave him an excellent artificial replacement, and set for him in a most ugly tiara.'

She knew the piece, totally hideous as well as pretentious, and her grandmother had never worn it. It had three large rubies at the front, and smaller ones at the sides — or what had once been rubies.

'Are ... are the other diamonds you found for him as valuable?'

'Three of them are worth far more, the others a little less than this, but diamonds increase in value, or, at least, rarely lose it compared to the cost of other items. No diamond producer will want to flood the market and see the price of diamonds fall.' He obviously enjoyed her shock.

Was she guilty of receiving stolen property? No, she thought. The jewellery had belonged to her grandfather ever since entailed property was made illegal back in 1925, even if the earlier substitutions had broken the law.

She didn't want to be rich; not luxuriously rich. But she did want security, for herself, the girls, and the eagles and other animals on her land. It seemed she had it, and far more.

'Thank you, Mr Vonderfleet.'

He gave a small bow, then kissed her cheek. 'It has been a delight, always, to know your family. I will give you some of the money now, and then others will deliver the notes to you over the next few months. You will not want the money in a bank,' he added warningly. 'Governments have long noses and empty pockets.'

She left with nearly three thousand pounds in her handbag, which she held tighter than ever.

Sixteen

It's a long way to Tipperary,
It's a long way to go.
It's a long way to Tipperary,
To the sweetest girl I know!

Lyrics from 'It's a Long Way to Tipperary' by
Jack Judge and Harry Williams,
a popular song from World War II, though
sung for decades before

The Lyons tea shop smelled of dust and damp clothes. Four years ago there'd been the scent of hot buttered teacakes.

'Teacakes are off, love,' said the chippie, an elderly woman with tired eyes. Almost everyone in London seemed strangely blank, as if the explosions had caused all but the strongest emotion to seep away. 'I can do you a scone or mixed sandwiches.'

'Sandwiches, please, and tea.'

The bread was fresh, even if it was a 'standard loaf' — leaden grey. The mixed sandwiches contained 'cheese', like lumpy margarine, more pickle than corned beef, and lettuce with beetroot, as 'salad', as well as fish paste — more paste than fish, if indeed it had ever had fins.

She ate. She drank. Uncle Jasper didn't come. I am going to miss the last train, she thought, deeply grateful for Mrs Thripps. I need to find a telephone.

The crowd around her ate and drank too, weary and incurious, never guessing they sat near a woman with nearly three thousand pounds stuffed into her handbag in a brown paper bag.

'Darling, I'm so sorry I'm late!' A young woman she had never seen before bent and kissed her cheek. 'Uncle is waiting for us.' Her accent was middle class, her reddish hair short and curly under a slip of a hat that matched the unobtrusive navy blue of her coat.

Deanna smiled back. 'Perfectly timed. I've just finished my tea.' She gathered her own coat and hat, and the handbag that had rested on the floor with her foot between its handles so it was impossible to steal.

She followed her new companion onto a bus; she copied her and asked for a threepenny fare, but, like her, abruptly alighted after only two stops and began to walk, presumably confusing anyone who followed them. They seemed to turn corners for hours, but it was probably only twenty minutes. The area was familiar: sedate townhouses, three storeys and a basement, and blocks of modern serviced flats.

They slipped into the doorway of a block built perhaps fifteen years before, with Art Deco pillars. The reception area was small and unattended. Her companion did not turn to the lift but unlocked what looked like a cupboard door, but which led to yet another reception area, perhaps in the building next door.

This time they did take the lift. The woman spoke for the first time. 'You did that like a professional! Well done.'

'A professional what?'

The woman looked puzzled, then nodded understanding. 'Uncle said you were new to the cloak and dagger stuff, without any proper training.' She offered her gloved hand. 'I'm Robyn.'

Deanna didn't ask for a surname. 'You know who I am?'

'Yes.' The lift shuddered to a stop and Robyn pulled open the doors. The area before them was small, bare and carpeted, with only one door. Robyn knocked.

The door opened. A middle-aged woman in a tweed suit and eyeglasses nodded at them. 'Uncle is expecting you,' she said to Deanna.

Deanna entered the study — leather-topped desk, leather armchairs, two wooden chairs and a small bookcase below a map of the world.

A man she had never met stood up politely from behind the desk. 'I expected someone else,' she said calmly.

'The man who said he was your grandfather's friend Chummy, who recruited you at the tea shop? We can phone him if you are uncertain. He never met your grandfather. I didn't want anyone seeing us together and making a connection.'

'This seems ... discreet.'

'I'm glad you think so,' he said drily.

'What do I call you?'

'Uncle Jasper will do. Definitely not Chummy. No one has called me that for years, thank goodness, except your grandfather, and he only did it to annoy. Please do sit.'

She sat, trying not to stare. 'Excuse me, but there is a small grass snake peering out of your top pocket.'

'Oh, that's George. Ignore him.' The man called Uncle Jasper clasped his hands on the desk. 'Let me guess. You have hurried here to tell me that the man you took to be your second cousin is a fraud.'

She stared in earnest now, more startled than by the snake. (She was quite fond of grass snakes, though not of adders.) 'You knew?'

'We suspected.'

'Why didn't you tell me?'

'Surely that is obvious.'

Was this a test? 'Because I identified him as the Duke of Claverton.'

'Exactly. From that moment all the information that came from you was suspect.'

'I had never met Donnie as an adult,' she explained. 'We had one summer together when we were twelve. He had no time to come down to Claverton when he arrived in England last year — or, at least, he had other priorities.'

'Ah. I had presumed you had frequent visits. Luckily one of his ... priorities ... soon after he arrived in England was the daughter of a friend of a friend, who is married, so the affair was kept discreet. But when he didn't contact her on his return we arranged for them to meet. He didn't recognise her. She says that physically they are very alike, especially the most obvious features like height — he is not quite as tall as your cousin, but army measurements can be inaccurate in wartime — that high forehead, hair colour and American capped teeth. Even certain gestures and phrases are the same, but she is sure it's not the same man. His reappearance was also far too convenient. Any man who makes it over the Channel in times like this has to be investigated as a possible collaborator. Or — something else.'

'But you haven't arrested him.'

'We are curious,' Uncle Jasper said quietly. 'He is under various forms of surveillance at all times. It has been ... interesting ... to see the houses where he has chosen to stay. Their inhabitants seem to all be of much the same political views as those you have been investigating.'

Dee swallowed and raised another concern. 'Uncle Jasper, this man gave me information about the three young evacuees, the ones I've mentioned in my letters.' Anyone intercepting them would have found it strange if she had not. 'He said a friend in the Home Office identified them.'

'He has no friend or contact in the Home Office,' said Uncle Jasper shortly. 'We have been careful about that. Ironically, the most difficult time to have him watched is when he is with you.'

'A visitor in one of the houses where he has been a guest couldn't have helped him find out?'

'No.' Uncle Jasper smiled. The snake peered out of his pocket again, then returned into the warmth. 'His chauffeur is experienced at picking up downstairs gossip, and we invariably have a guest list. The guests too are under surveillance.'

Yikes, thought Deanna. The whole bloody country must be watching each other. Which, now she considered it, was probably the case.

'Whatever you've been told about your evacuees by the man who claims to be the Duke of Claverton will be fabrication. He presumably expected to find the house occupied only by yourself and is trying to find someone who will claim them. Do you wish to know more about these girls?'

'Yes. Not just because I ... I love them. I accepted Donnie — the man who claims to be Donnie — too readily.'

'You think you may have been equally hasty about your protegees?'

'No,' said Deanna with certainty. 'But I need to know why they are hiding who their parents were, and possibly their true surname.'

He stared at her silently for a moment. 'You did not tell us they are hiding their origins,' he reminded her quietly. 'It is, perhaps, something we should have known.'

She flushed. 'I kept hoping they'd trust me enough to let me know their secret. And they *are* only children, though I know it's naive to think that children can't pass on information. But I am sure these girls are not.' She met his eyes. 'What should I do about this man who claims to be my second cousin? He phones me nearly every night and has visited my home, and obviously plans to again. I thought it was because he knew no one else in England but now ... surely every time we speak together there's a greater risk I'll guess he's an imposter. Why keep seeing me?'

Uncle Jasper shrugged elegantly. 'His pursuit is interesting. It might just be that you are an attractive woman, but I suspect he would not waste time on romance or flirtation, not when he may be exposed at any moment, including by making the kind of mistakes with you that must have aroused your suspicions. If he is here as a common German spy, he'd assume that as Lady Deanna you'd be an excellent source of information and introduction, but simply having the title of Duke of Claverton will give him entrance to any house he wished.'

He sat back and looked at her thoughtfully. 'The man may, of course, simply be an American conman who knew your cousin and is trying to take advantage of Donald Claverton's death and his own resemblance to him. He'll claim what money and valuables he can, then vanish. That would make it a police matter, of no interest to us.'

'Who is "us"?' she asked. Her not-uncle chuckled indulgently.

'Not important, my dear. That is exactly why I choose to operate from a flat in Mayfair, and not a government office. Though to be honest, it is my secretary who makes the important decisions — and now you truly know something of more importance than the name of the organisation you work for.'

'Do you think he is a spy?'

'Possibly. I think it more likely that his attraction to Eagle's Rest is not yourself — attractive as you undoubtedly are — nor your connections, but your cellar, and the passage leading from it to the sea. It would be ... convenient ... for any other person wishing to enter England unnoticed.'

He smiled at her look of shock. 'The information about the passage came from your grandfather, shortly before he died. The old duke was concerned the passage might be used for exactly the purpose to which it has been put. Unfortunately, England has a long history of the successful smuggling of alcohol, tobacco and Catholic priests via caves and secret passages. It was also almost de rigueur at one time to have at least a priest-hole.'

She held her hands in her lap. She felt almost as violated as if this man had intimate knowledge of her body. 'How many people know about the cave?'

He looked almost sympathetic. 'Seven from this agency, though each may have told another two people. In these days we must not assume we will survive any given week. Knowledge must be shared, however discreetly. But I assure you that it will stay discreet. You need not worry that one afternoon a daytripper will attempt to dangle off the cliff to find the cave. There is no file that mentions it.'

'I see. Thank you.' She had no choice but to accept his assurances. 'What do I do now?'

'Robyn will drive you home tonight. She'll stay with you, telling anyone who asks that she has an emergency fill-in job in the area and is staying with you because she used to be the secretary of one of your schoolfriends. I'd make her a schoolfriend, but it would be too easy to check the school roll.'

Nor does her middle-class accent fit, thought Deanna. Robyn's manner also lacked entitlement — she hadn't taken the empty seat on the bus — and the other side of that coin, the carefully taught graciousness to smile at the overworked conductress.

'What will she be doing?'

'Filling in for the manager of a nearby factory.'

'The coffin factory down the lane from the Scout Hut?'

'Botheration. Is its present use that well known?'

'I don't think anything can be kept a secret in a village like ours.' Except, she thought, the identity of their duke and the existence of her cave.

'At least the factory hasn't got into the newspapers.'

'But why should it be secret?'

'Because any week now we may be invaded, and every night we are bombed, and there are deaths, and will be more deaths, and deaths mean coffins; and we do not push our dead into communal pits in the ground. Or we do not *yet*,' he added grimly. 'But the public does not need to know that aspect of our operations.'

'I see,' she said slowly. 'Do you think invasion is inevitable?'

He smiled reassuringly. 'If I thought that I'd be setting up a clandestine BBC radio in a cave in Wales and re-banding our most effective armed forces units into resistance cells.'

'What will save us then?'

'The grit and determination of the British people, of course, just as it says every night on the wireless.' He gave a short laugh. 'And several other factors, none of which it is advisable for you to know. Will you accept Robyn into your household?'

'To spy on us?'

'Partly,' he said frankly. 'She can pass on information and assess it in ways you cannot. But mostly because she is an excellent shot.'

'So am I,' Deanna said automatically.

'Of pheasants and grouse perhaps. Could you shoot a man?'

'Yes.'

'Perhaps you should have hesitated before giving that answer.'

'I don't need to. If that man — if any person — threatens my daughters or my country, I will shoot without hesitation.'

Uncle Jasper did not need to know she had peppered Jason Weatherby with buckshot when she had found him poaching without an appointment on her land, which had led to the healthy respect the villagers now had for her determination to control who snared rabbits when at Eagle's Rest.

Uncle Jasper opened a drawer in his desk and handed her a small oilcloth bag. A pistol less than half the size of her hand sat within it.

'Keep that on you at all times. It's short range only, about two yards accuracy, but will kill at that distance. It's already loaded.'

'I can't carry a loaded firearm with me the whole time!' Making soup with the girls, weeding in the glasshouse …

'If you need it, I doubt you will have time to load it. Don't worry, the safety catch is secure. It has six bullets. Robyn has more ammunition for target practice. If anyone is about to take it from you, shoot quickly six times, even if you have no target. The pistol will then be useless and can't be used against you. If you do need it, count how many bullets you have left.'

Suddenly she found herself almost trembling with the weight of fury. She had not truly believed till now. The man who claimed to be Donnie had lied about her daughters, had made himself at home at Eagle's Rest.

And she had liked him. She had thought of him as her cousin. That was the worst of all.

Uncle Jasper seemed to think that was all the instruction she needed, or perhaps it was all he had time to give. His snake had become a small lump at the base of his pocket, invisible unless you knew it was there.

He stood. 'Ask Robyn if you have any further questions. She may not answer them, of course, but don't hesitate to ask.

I presume you would like to use the phone in the outer office to tell Mrs Thripps you will be late?'

'Yes. Thank you.' So Uncle Jasper even knew that Mrs Thripps was babysitting the girls. Or, more likely, he had deduced it.

He stood. 'Thank you, Lady Deanna. Your work has been invaluable. I think, however, that you need accept no more invitations from fascist sympathisers for a while. You can use the need to supervise your evacuees as an excuse, nannies sadly being in short supply these days. You'll learn more for us keeping watch at home. Robyn will give you a new telephone number to memorise for an emergency. Be assured that if you phone, help will arrive within ten minutes.'

Home, she thought. *My* home, Miss Enid's, the refuge not just for her but for her daughters, for Sam and his friends, who had volunteered to cross the world and probably die for it, home for the badgers on the headland, for the hares, the field mice, the voles, for the eagles, even the water rats. Suddenly Eagle's Rest was not a refuge, but a field of war.

If it was to be a battleground, then she must win.

Seventeen

A lieutenant says to a soldier on target practice, 'That recruit is pretty good.'
'Yes, though maybe we should check his background.'
'Why?'
'After every shot he wipes his fingerprints off the rifle.'
World War II joke

They were silent as Robyn dodged her Morris Eight through traffic, around sandbags and away from blocked roads and craters or waves of broken pavement. Deanna waited till they were well clear of London, and the road was almost free of traffic, thanks to petrol rationing, before asking, 'How should I introduce you? What name should I give, I mean?'

'Call me Robyn McCallister, known as Rob. I'm actually Roberta.'

'And not McCallister?'

'Andrews.'

'That's very forthcoming. Uncle Jasper said I might ask you questions but not necessarily get a reply.'

Rob grinned. 'I gave you an answer. It might not be the truth.'

'Who do you work for?'

'Military intelligence.'

'You're in the army!'

'No. Neither are you. You haven't signed an oath yet, though you might be expected to later.'

'Why not now?'

Rob stared at the road. 'To keep you secret, so you can stay effective. Half our intelligence service got the job because they were at school with Jimbo, half are senile or alcoholics, and possibly a third are fascist sympathisers. Once you sign the oath you're officially on the books, and so can be found, and then officially expelled, framed for a crime or even shot by any of the public school fascists who assume they are superior, supported by the fascist grocers' boys who know they are superior and blame the system because they were still grocers' boys till the war made them majors. You need to stay off the books as long as possible.'

'That adds up to more than one whole. Plus, I was also offered this job through, er, family connections.'

'The groups aren't mutually exclusive,' said Rob. 'The old school chums can be senile, drunks and fascist at the same time. For that matter, any of them may be also useful — Churchill drinks like a fish and drops off to sleep in the middle of a conversation, but he's made a surprisingly effective leader, even if half his decisions are stupidity. Thankfully, Hitler's choices are often insane.'

She darted a glance at Deanna. 'I have never said this, of course. You were offered the job because Uncle Jasper was at school with your grandfather, but you actually proved to be surprisingly good at it.'

'You mean some of that gossip I sent was useful?'

'Extremely. A man who expresses total loyalty and confidence in the office but has a wife expecting imminent invasion … Let's just say it's a good idea if certain information doesn't pass his desk.'

'So who exactly am I working for?'

Rob laughed. 'There are intelligence groups popping up like balloons at a birthday party these days. Most of us are under the umbrella of military intelligence but neither they nor we are in that department except by name.'

'I suppose there can't very well be a department of intelligence.'

'It would end up being staffed by chums from Harrow or Eton,' said Rob, 'or chinless honourables without a brain cell between them. I say, I'm sorry, I didn't mean to imply ...'

Deanna grinned. 'That I'm mentally deficient because I have a title? Don't worry — I have noticed that the upper classes rarely provide true achievers.'

'There was Lord Byron.'

'Who was also mad, bad and dangerous to know,' Deanna pointed out.

'True. Lady Deanna, this is in strict confidence. The main reason you are not on the books is so that anything you see can be denied. The British public is rarely told the truth, and certainly not about ...' she took a breath, in the manner of someone making a decision '... the Duke of Windsor. Nor would they want to believe it. Baldwin himself could admit publicly he wrote the abdication speech, and tricked the duke into reading it, and only a handful would abandon the romance of the king who gave up his throne for love.'

'So I'm of sufficient rank to overhear information, but not important or male, so won't be believed if you need me discredited.'

'Pretty much. That's one of the reasons they rely on women so much in intelligence — it's not just that we're good at it, and less conspicuous. They can shut us up more easily.'

'I see,' said Deanna slowly.

'Still want to keep going?'

'Yes. I need to know what happened to the real Donnie. But mostly I began this work because it's worth doing. I still feel that way.'

'Thought so,' said Rob. 'Look, I'm sorry to foist myself on your home like this. I'll pull my weight — I do know a weed from a turnip even if I can't grill either.'

'It's easy to add another potato to the pot. Do you enjoy chess or tiddlywinks?'

Rob laughed. 'I adore tiddlywinks. I play it with my niece — she's six. We're reading *The Wind in the Willows* together just now. I miss her,' she added.

'I think you might fit in quite well,' said Deanna.

Within a week, Rob's presence seemed almost as inevitable as Mrs Thripps'. Magda and Rosa were wary at first, politely calling her 'Miss McCallister'. Anna dragged her into a game of tiddlywinks after dinner the first evening and decided she was 'Auntie Rob' after winning three matches.

Rob also helped sew costumes for the Christmas play. ('I know you'll make them superbly,' Mrs Goodword had blithely informed Deanna, when she had bestowed this new duty on her.) This year's play was Queen Elizabeth and Sir Francis Drake defeating the Armada, helmets on loan from the Home Guard, but with papier-mâché swords in case of accidents.

The autumn leaves turned from red and gold to brown. Deanna took the girls mushrooming, racing from tree to tree, yelling in triumph when they found a giant horse mushroom, or spiny hedgehog mushrooms or clumps of oyster mushrooms on the beech trees. There were dandelion and watercress leaves to collect for salads or to replace lettuce in sandwiches, and even some rosehips left to make rosehip syrup for winter.

Rob drove off to the coffin factory in her little Morris every morning, picking up several workers who lived uncomfortably far away for bicycling on the way. Deanna wondered how those factory workers would cope once Rob and her car left, especially if it snowed, making it impossible to bicycle till it melted.

Because surely the mystery of Donnie's identity would be solved soon. It was possible that there was even a simple explanation, as Uncle Jasper had suggested: but if a fellow American had taken Donnie's place in England, he must have been devastated to find debts instead of bank bonds. He could, however, presumably fake Donnie's signature and order possessions in America be sold, and the money sent to him.

Meanwhile, village life went on. It was rumoured that Mrs Murtagh's son had lost his sight, with major burns as well. She vanished from the grocer's shop to nurse him. Donnie rang each night but didn't drop in unannounced again.

The house — and its secret cave — could not be left unguarded now. Rob slept in the library after the girls had gone to bed. The cellar door was kept open, too, though any noise far down the cave was unlikely to be heard in the house. Deanna worked close to the house.

For some reason Sam called in less often now, only once or twice a week, taking the girls fishing with him, though he didn't invite Deanna the one time Rob was home from the factory when he called by and she was therefore free to leave.

Somehow, things had changed between her and Sam in the past weeks. He usually fished alone now, leaving the catch wrapped in newspaper on the shelf by the back door, out of Dusty's reach. Nor had he asked her to go to the cinema again. He hadn't even cooked up another trout feast. She would have asked if she had offended him, but he seemed to carefully make sure they had no opportunity for confidential conversation. She missed him. She hadn't realised how much he'd been part of the household.

The labour shortage cut deep now. The only men to be seen in the village out of uniform were the old fellows who spent the few sunlit hours on the bench in front of the pub. Queues grew longer outside the butcher, the baker, the fishmonger, the ham and cheese shop, and the grocer. Women carried letters in their pockets to read as they waited, sharing any piece of news or funny anecdote, but were more often silent, intent, crying, even when there was no bad news, for the good news they wanted was so rarely there. *I am safe. I am coming home.* Other women carefully ignored their tears, or hugged them, without needing to give the reason why.

A new factory was being erected with extraordinary swiftness on the other side of the village. Rumours said it would be making Spitfires, or ammunition, torpedoes, or a secret weapon that would devastate the enemy. Already women were being recruited, with men, mostly invalided veterans, as foremen.

At least with Rob in residence Deanna had another adult to talk to in the evenings, exchanging gossip about the factory — Deanna knew most of the workers there, by reputation at least — or anecdotes about their very different childhoods, Rob's as the daughter of a prosperous grocer.

'I won a scholarship to Oxford,' Rob admitted. 'They'll keep it for me till after the war — Uncle Jasper has pulled some strings. I'm going to study chemistry.'

'No wonder Magda adores you.'

'I'd love to know more about their parents, and not just for Uncle Jasper.'

'Surely they can't be a security risk.'

'Not knowingly. But they might innocently give information about the layout of the house, or when it could be empty.'

'Not these three. They give out less information than a broken clock. Besides, how could anyone be sure they'd end up here?' She thought back to the dirtied child, the three defiant faces. She had taken them on impulse ...

What if someone knew her well enough to guess she would take three bald-headed, smelly children, abandoned by everyone else, and that she was lonely enough to keep them, too? No, it was too possible that someone else might have volunteered, or even that Mrs Goodword would have insisted on the three being sent to different homes, none of them Eagle's Rest.

She tried to put the thought from her mind. 'I've enrolled Magda at Hawthorne Grammar, beginning next term. Rosa and Anna can stay at the village school a little longer, so they can make friends here.' Something she had badly lacked herself. None of the girls were making any connections with local children either, she had to admit, or trying to, though nor were they being picked on. The school was a precarious balance of villagers and evacuees these days, and the girls didn't seem to have much in common with either group. 'Hawthorne is only three stations away on the train, so they'll be day girls.'

'Good. Boarding school sounds horrid.'

'It was, though I made some good friends. They're mostly in the services now, or married straight after their London Season and scattered around the country, with their hands full managing their husband's estates while the men are in the armed forces. None of them have the kinds of views that would interest Uncle Jasper.'

'Why did you …?' Rob hesitated.

'Agree to inform on my own kind? I'm not sure,' Deanna admitted. 'Partly because it was the last thing my grandfather wanted. He took me in, provided for me. He was a bit of a fascist in his own way. I suppose I am too …'

'What?!'

'Oh, not like Hitler, or Mosley and his Blackshirts. I'm more Darwinian. I like intelligent people who think for themselves, but I don't assume those traits run in certain classes or races. The

English fascists assume they are superior but every one of them I've met has been a gullible idiot.' Deanna shrugged. 'I was gullible myself with Donnie.' They had agreed to keep calling him that in case they were overheard.

'Not your fault. It's an uncanny likeness, or a very carefully crafted one.'

Deanna once again thought of what the real Donnie must have endured. 'Entirely my fault. I was so glad to have family, to know the estate would be loved. He knew exactly what I wanted to hear.'

Rob looked at her watch. 'The girls should be asleep by now. Time for some practice.'

'What kind of practice?'

'Pistol,' said Rob shortly.

'I can shoot,' said Deanna. 'Quite well in fact.'

'Huntin', shootin', fishin' and fox hunts, the traditional toff recreations,' said Rob unemotionally, before repeating Uncle Jasper's question: 'Can you shoot a man?'

'If I need to.'

'Where?'

'I don't understand.'

'That's why we need to practise.'

Moonlight shone like a silver tide down the headland. Treetop shadows shook their heads. Rob pinned a cardboard outline of a man on a tree outside the library window. 'Pass me your pistol.'

Deanna pulled it out of the gap between the cups of her brassiere and held it out. 'What are you doing?'

'Fitting a silencer. It's too bulky to carry ordinarily but right now we don't want to wake the girls or attract attention. Right, where do you shoot to kill a man?'

'The stomach? His heart?'

'Not the stomach. Might take him minutes to die and he'll be screaming. Heart first, to stop him, then you have a chance to aim at the forehead or kidneys as fast as you can, or the back of the head if he's turned away from you. Go!'

Deanna shot. The pistol made a whooshing sound, a little like an eagle when it dived.

'Not bad,' said Rob a little too casually as holes appeared in the heart and forehead of the figure. She's impressed, thought Deanna smugly.

'Don't shoot to kill unless you have to. Better leave them incapacitated for questioning.'

'Like this?' Deanna's pistol left a bullet hole in the wrist.

'Might bleed to death. Try a knee, if you don't mind them making a noise.'

'How do I stop them making a noise?'

'No easy way, I'm afraid. A shot to the chin can work — they may not be able to talk afterwards, but they can write — but it must be a perfect shot, side on, or you'll get the carotid artery and they'll be dead.'

'That's in the neck, isn't it? Grouse are smaller than a man's neck. I can shoot grouse.'

Rob nodded. 'You'll do. Now a bit of self-defence. We'll try that in the library where we won't be disturbed. Better put down some cushions first.'

It was two am before they finished, and the library fire was almost out. Deanna felt bruised, especially her hip — apparently the best place to fall on. But she could disable an unsuspecting man from behind, slip from the grasp of one who grabbed *her* from behind, or — hopefully — duck, twist and bend, throwing him over the top of her and down, but that was not to be relied on.

'We'll train again tomorrow night.'

'You'll fall asleep at the factory.'

She gave Deanna a wry smile. 'I have a comfortable sofa in my office, a telephone in case anyone needs to contact me, and an under-manager who does the real work. You should try to get a decent nap today too.'

'The potatoes ...'

'I forgot to tell you — Uncle Jasper has arranged for a couple of land girls.'

'Rob, what do you expect me to do if it comes to a confrontation?'

'I don't know,' said Rob frankly. 'We don't even know what kind of situation to suspect — Donnie slipping out carrying a set of submarine plans, or a single German spy slipping in unnoticed, or even an advance group sent to do last-minute reconnaissance before the main landing. If one or two spies come in, it's best to follow them to see who they contact and hope more follow the same route.'

Rob halted as a shadow moved uphill under the bare orchard trees. She ran outside. Deanna followed her.

'Jamie Watson!' called Deanna softly. 'I know it's you!'

'Your Ladyship.' The shadow removed his cap. 'I know it's old Clyde's night for the snares but he's down with the gout.'

'Good luck then. Rob hasn't tasted my pheasant and apple pie yet. Rob, this is Jamie Watson, carpenter and part-time poacher. We have an arrangement — I get half of whatever he poaches. It used to be one out of four, but I have growing girls to feed now.'

'*Woof*,' muttered Dusty from somewhere indoors.

'Mr Watson and I have met at the factory,' said Rob, smiling. 'See you tomorrow.'

'Yes, ma'am, Your Ladyship.' Jamie tipped his cap again and strode up the hill.

'Do you think he saw or heard us shooting?' asked Rob, concerned.

'Wouldn't matter. There's a war on. He'll think it's exactly what it was — one woman showing another how to defend herself. The Women's Institute is demonstrating how to make bayonets from broomsticks and carving knives on Wednesday; the next week it will be how to fill garbage bins with rocks to roll in front of tanks. And did you know that the vicar will give a lecture on Hannibal crossing the Alps to attack Rome on Friday night? He has even promised a slide show, though presumably not of Hannibal or those specific elephants.'

'How will that help against an invading army?'

'Hannibal heated limestone rocks then blew them up with acid wine. We're on limestone here. The vicar has had the Scouts piling old wooden furniture around part of the vicarage stone garden wall. He plans to set the piles alight then squirt the wall with vinegar. Onlookers are advised to dress warmly and carry a garbage-bin-lid shield.'

'Really?'

'Really and truly. Let's hope it doesn't work or there won't be a stick of firewood left in the county. Come on. I could sleep for a week.'

Eighteen

Hitler inspects the army parade and stops by a good-looking soldier. Hitler says, 'You are an example to Germany! Tell me what you wish for when you are in the front line under artillery fire, and I will try to grant it.' The soldier says, 'My greatest wish, mein Führer, is that you will stand next to me!'

World War II joke

Sam remained distant. Donnie continued to telephone, so often that Doris on the exchange began saying, 'It's the duke again, Lady Deanna,' in a knowing voice hinting at wedding bells.

There would not have been bells, even if he had been who he claimed to be, she thought that Saturday as she dug parsnips and carrots to store in the scullery cellar. If she ever married her husband must seem ... inevitable, as it had been when she met Magda, Rosa and Anna. Her mind and spirit had said, 'They are family,' just as she had felt with Sam.

She stopped digging, the garden fork motionless in her hand.

If was as if she suddenly truly saw him now he was absent. For the first time she understood not just love but that phrase in the wedding vows: 'With my body I thee worship.'

Her body warmed, as if every hair anticipated being touched. Her bosom was more than a bouncing nuisance, and there was a strange ache just above the join in her legs.

It is just the war, she told herself. People have hasty love affairs all the time in war, as if sex could defeat death.

She did not want a hasty affair with Sam. She wanted to watch the eagles with him, laugh at dinner with him and the girls, and yes, feel his hands on her body ...

All at once she heard his voice, real, not imagined, talking to Rob. Rob appeared a moment later, a string of fish in her hand.

'I've been fishing with that nice Australian airman — thought I should check him out, but he seems exactly who he says he is. He said to thank you again for the use of the stream.'

'He's not coming in?'

'No. Did you expect him to?'

'Yes.' Deanna thrust the garden fork at Rob. 'Would you mind finishing these? The girls are in the kitchen cooking a surprise dinner for us, one that needs many eggs ...'

She ran between the beds of Brussels sprouts, beets and cabbages, cursing her wellies, too clumsy for speed. Sam was nearly at the woods at the beginning of the estate.

'Sam!' she yelled.

He turned and stared at her. She was suddenly conscious of her filthy hands and probably smudged face, and her filthy overalls, but then she had been covered in manure when they first met.

'Sam,' she panted. 'Will you stay for dinner?'

'That's kind of you, but I need to get back,' he said politely.

'Why?'

'Your cousin had a word with me,' he said flatly. 'I gather nothing is to be made public yet, so I haven't given you my congratulations. I apologise if my attentions were awkward for you.'

'What on earth are you talking about?'

'Your engagement to the Duke of Claverton,' Sam said stiffly.

'Engaged to … Donnie? Are you crazy?'

'But he said …'

It made sense. Of course, it made sense. The man who was not Donnie would not want an airman and his friends hanging around Eagle's Rest and its cellar.

'Sam,' she said carefully. 'There are things I can't tell you. Please don't ask — I'll tell you what I can as soon as I can. But I am not engaged to Donnie, never have been, never will be, never could be …'

'He said he'd asked you ages ago, and you'd said yes.'

'He didn't, and I didn't.' She began to laugh. 'Well, actually we did think of it when we were twelve, but we changed our minds a year later. I didn't even meet him again till a couple of months ago.'

She grabbed his hand, hoping he didn't mind the dirt. He didn't pull away. 'I don't love him, you idiot.'

'Then why did he tell me that you're engaged?'

'That's part of the … stuff … I can't talk about. But if Donnie tells you anything, not just about me but about the war, or the girls or anything, don't believe him. Just pretend you do and tell me.'

He looked at her thoughtfully. 'The Duke of Claverton arrives from America, is almost immediately sent overseas and declared missing at Dunkirk, then turns up again late at night and his cousin identifies him?'

Sam was no fool. Eagle-eyed, as her grandfather would say, and making all too many connections.

'Sam, would you mind awfully not thinking about this, or speaking to anyone about it either?'

His face relaxed into a smile as he looked down at her. 'What *can* I do then?'

'Come to dinner. You've met Rob; she'll be there too. But in a few weeks …' She took a deep breath.

'You'll tell me what's happening?'

'I don't know when I'll be able to do that. But there is a truly ghastly dance at the church hall for the Widows and Orphans Fund. The vicar plays the oboe and his wife mutilates "The Blue Danube" on the piano; everyone will stare at us and gossip but the Ladies' Guild will do a good supper — well, the best they can — and there will be at least one waltz where we'll be cheek to cheek.'

'Dee …' he said slowly.

'Please come.'

'Of course I'll come with you. And I am going to knock your cousin's block off.'

'No, you're not. You'll pretend you and I are just friends even if one day we might be more …'

His hand tightened. He pulled her to him and kissed her very gently on the lips. She thought, clinically, toes really do tingle, then she just thought about his body as he pressed it closer to hers, and then more urgently, his fingers in her hair as the kiss deepened.

'Aunt Dee! Sam! It's ready! We asked Mrs Thripps too, to show her we can really cook.' Anna stood nearby, arms on her hips. 'It's a special dinner. We spent *hours*. Why were you kissing Aunt Dee?' she added curiously.

Sam laughed, keeping hold of Deanna's hand. 'Because she's nice to kiss.'

'Why haven't you kissed her before then?'

'Stupidity,' said Sam. 'Don't worry, we're coming now, though I need soap to get rid of the smell of fish, and your aunt needs to remove a ton or so of grime.'

Romantic, aren't we? thought Deanna. That, too, seemed entirely inevitable.

Nineteen

The need is great, the time is short. URGENCY must be the watchword. It's a full time job to win.

British World War II poster

The girls had set the table not just with cloth, plates and cutlery but with a small vase of holly and winter roses, as well as Deanna's largest platter.

'Do you like them?' asked Magda apprehensively.

'Mama showed us how to make them,' added Rosa.

'Mama said they are full of vitamins. What's a vitamin? We didn't put any in.' Anna looked anxiously at Magda.

'Silly, the vitamins are in the eggs and the spinach,' said Rosa. 'I've told you what vitamins are.'

'No you haven't. You said I wouldn't understand.'

'I'm not sure anyone knows what a vitamin is,' said Rob. 'They are one of those things that need more investigation.'

'The real question,' said Deanna, now clean, in a green wool dress with mauve flowers embroidered on the bodice, and with Sam having reclaimed her hand, 'is whether those pancakes are as delicious as they look.'

They were: thin delicate French crepes with lacy edges, not solid English pancakes — no wonder the girls had needed so many eggs — with layers of chopped buttered spinach in between, lavishly covered with creamy cheese sauce. Thank goodness for Mrs Higgins's dairy and mild fiddling with the record books, and the cheeses in the cellar. Few others in England would eat a meal like this tonight.

Deanna took a mouthful. 'Wonderful!'

'*Woof,*' agreed Dusty, who had discovered that cheese sauce often dripped onto the floor.

'The best in England,' said Mrs Thripps. She winked at Deanna. 'As long as someone else does the washing up.'

'We'll clean,' said Magda quickly. Dee smiled. The sink was piled with what looked like every bowl and saucepan from her cupboards, now splattered with drips of pancake mix.

'I've never had savoury pancakes,' admitted Sam. 'We have them with honey or strawberry sauce and ice cream at home.' He grinned at the girls. 'This is the best meal I've had since I came to England. No offence,' he added to Deanna, briefly taking her hand under the table again.

'None taken. Rob, have another one.'

'I've already had three. Don't you know there's a war on? I'll need a barrage balloon to carry me to work.'

Dusty slunk between their legs, licking up more sauce.

'Dusty! That tickles!' reproved Deanna as he licked her ankle. She stood and picked up the platter. 'Come on, woofy one. I'll scrape the leftovers off for your dinner.'

The door opened suddenly behind her. She turned.

'How wonderfully domestic!' Donnie's dark shape filled the doorway, light spilling out into the garden.

'The blackout!' cried Deanna.

'Don't panic, honey. I'm sure no air-raid warden is patrolling around here, nor any German bombers.'

Donnie pulled the curtain back behind him. No, there haven't been German bombers, Deanna realised. This area had been surprisingly free of bombing, despite the aerodrome, though she sometimes saw planes flying in formation in the distance. 'Donnie! I wasn't expecting you.'

'I'm sorry,' he said ruefully. 'I tried to phone but the only call box we passed was out of order. Tomorrow's recruitment rally has been called off — some Home Guard colonel has the grippe — so I have a weekend free. Do you mind putting up with me again?'

'Of course not! I'm delighted.' She managed to smile, and he bent and kissed her cheek. She wondered if anyone else had caught the slip — the German 'grippe' instead of the English and American cold or flu. The man who was not Donnie stared at Sam, his expression hard to read. 'You must be Flight Lieutenant Murray. Dee has told me about you.'

'We've already met down at the pub,' said Sam evenly. 'I'm sure you remember.'

'Ah yes, I remember now.' Donnie looked curiously at Rob.

'Rob, this is Donnie, who is also the Eighth Duke of Claverton. Donnie, this is my friend Rob. I invited her to stay here for a few weeks.'

'Ha,' said Rob. 'Poor Dee was conned into it by her old friend Dodo Northbridge. I used to be her secretary. Should I call you "Your Grace" or something?'

'No need,' said Donnie easily. 'This looks like you've had a feast!'

'We have!' Deanna smiled at the girls. 'Magda and Anna and Rosa prepared it as a surprise. Crepes with spinach and cheese sauce. Dusty's even licked the saucepan.'

'I've eaten. My last hostess also loaded me up with cans from Fortnum and Mason, so I can make a contribution to the weekend's rations.'

'There is fruit salad for dessert,' said Anna. 'There's enough for you too. I sliced it *perfectly*.'

Deanna found Mrs Thripps looking at Donnie thoughtfully from her seat at the other end of the table. 'How lovely to meet you again, Your Grace.'

Her accent! thought Deanna. Suddenly Mrs Thripps was speaking in the perfect tone of a peer of the realm.

But of course, she had been in the theatre, and had worked for the duke and Miss Enid for decades. Nor was she dressed like a char tonight. She'd changed into her Sunday best for 'dinner with Lady Deanna', a dress and matching jacket Deanna had made for her last Christmas from a pale pink tweed.

'I'm sorry.' Donnie gave her a slight apologetic bow. 'Where did we meet?'

'No matter,' said Mrs Thripps airily. She stood, bent and kissed Deanna's cheek, then gave each of the girls a hug. 'I'd best tootle off. Look after yourself, Deanna dear. Good evening, Your Grace.'

'Good evening.' He obviously forgot her as soon as the door closed: an elderly woman of no importance.

Mrs Thripps suspects, thought Deanna. Mrs Thripps hadn't even married Arnold when the real Donnie had visited Claverton. The girls didn't seem to notice the change in accent, nor realise that a char lady did not kiss her employer, even if she'd had dinner with her. Sam glanced at her but kept his expression carefully blank. Rob and Magda began to collect the plates.

The man who was not a duke smiled at Deanna again. 'May I use your phone, Dee, honey? There are some calls I need to make.'

'Of course.'

He vanished, smiling at Magda too, her arms full of dishes, then at Rosa and Anna. 'A good meal but it would be better with some bacon, eh?' he said as he passed. 'Luckily I've brought some.'

'We don't eat bacon,' said Anna.

'Don't be silly,' said Magda quickly. 'You just don't remember it because they didn't give us bacon at the orphanage. Bacon is delicious. We used to have bacon and eggs for breakfast at home.'

'Mama never—' began Anna.

'You need to put out the dessert bowls,' said Rosa.

The man — I must think of him as Donnie, thought Deanna, or I may slip up — vanished towards the library. The fruit salad had just been served when the phone rang. He reappeared. 'This call is for you, Flight Lieutenant.'

'Me?' Sam shrugged. 'Someone must have guessed I'd be here if not back at the base. Excuse me.'

He returned a minute later. 'I'm wanted on duty, and as soon as possible.' He glanced at Donnie, then back at Deanna. 'I'll be back tomorrow, if I can.'

He, too, kissed Deanna's cheek, then slid behind the first of the two blackout curtains before pulling back the second to slip out the door.

Rob looked at Donnie and Deanna. 'I think the girls and I need an early night. I'll do the washing up since the girls cooked. You relax for once.'

'You're a darling,' said Deanna casually. She moved to one of the sofas. Donnie took the one opposite as the girls vanished to the bathroom, and Rob washed and dried. They talked of inconsequentials until — remarkably quickly — the kitchen was orderly and empty, Rob shepherding the girls to bed with the promise that Dee would give them an extra-long story.

The girls were still crammed in the one double bed, a bit like puppies in a basket, as she read them *Biggles in Spain*. At least they had their own nightdresses now: good thick flannel from perhaps the 1890s. Deanna was glad nightwear had changed little over the centuries.

She came down to find Donnie had poured two glasses of cognac. He handed her one, then leaned back, his legs stretched out towards the fire. 'Rob has gone to bed, too? Excellent. Peace at last.' He grinned at her. 'Shall we drink to peace?'

'To peace!' She raised her glass, then sipped. He must have brought the cognac with him, for there was none in the cellar.

'Who was that peculiar old lady?'

'Mrs Thripps, the char. The girls invited her to dinner to prove they could cook.'

'Your char! Like a maid of all work back home? Well, what do you know.' The white teeth gleamed as he grinned at her again. 'How does a "char" afford a dress like that?'

'I gave it to her for Christmas last year.'

'High fashion for a servant?'

Deanna shrugged. 'I made it myself.'

'*You* made it?'

'I'm an excellent seamstress. I had to learn to be, if I was to have some acceptable clothes.'

He looked at her sharply. 'Your grandmother was holidaying on the Riviera the year I was over here and giving parties at Claverton House.'

'The parties stopped the year I turned fourteen. Claverton House in London was let, and the servants dismissed,' she said briefly.

'Dee, I had no idea! I'm so sorry. It is time we sorted out that allowance.'

'I told you I don't want one!' The last thing she needed was the complication of an allowance put in motion by a man who didn't have any such authority. 'Miss Enid left me enough for all I need.' She gave him a rueful smile. 'All the money in the world won't let me buy haute couture now, anyway, and I love sewing. Mrs Thripps does enjoy clothes, so I've made her something wonderfully unsuitable for the last three years.'

He shook his head. 'Poor Dee — you've been landed with a houseful, haven't you? And now this Robyn woman too. You're a close friend of her last employer?'

'She and I were at school together. She's in the WAAC now. Any luck getting a position that doesn't involve you shaking hands and smiling sedately?'

'*Wanted, a suitable position for a useless duke.* They will have me extolling the virtues of parsnip pie soon.'

'You're not serious?'

'Very. I am under suspicion, my darling Dee, and so are you.'

The shock on her face was real enough to convince him, she hoped. 'Under suspicion of what?'

'Fascist sympathies.'

'What on earth? But that's ridiculous! You're in the army! We're *Clavertons*!'

He sipped his cognac and looked at her speculatively. 'You don't have to pretend with me, you know.'

I must be careful, she thought. 'What do you mean?' she asked cautiously.

'I mean we have both been noticed at the homes of people who have the sense to recognise that since the Dunkirk disaster Britain cannot win the war. Within weeks Germany will invade these islands and occupy them faster and even more ruthlessly than France.'

'That doesn't make me fascist,' she said flatly. 'Just intelligent.' She couldn't overplay this.

'What would you think about an alliance with Germany, allowing us to stay neutral?'

She managed a scoffing laugh. 'That would be our only hope, wouldn't it? But Churchill will never allow it,' she said, making her voice bitter. 'And the newspapers are full of propaganda. If they didn't keep printing Churchill's speeches and actually showed more of what is really happening, the deaths and the damage and how close the country is to running out of food, much less ammunition, I think the British public would demand we begin negotiations, at least. But Churchill and the press barons have them under a spell.'

'Your former king would have arranged an alliance.' He looked seriously at her over his glass. 'He could have convinced the public, too. Everyone adored him when he was Prince of Wales. I met him, you know, in Paris just before the war, when I was there on business.'

'You should have visited us if you were so close!'

'Your grandfather was ill. I was afraid it would look as if I was evaluating my inheritance.' He shrugged. 'The Duke of Windsor, as he was by then, isn't particularly bright, but he's got more vision than the military intelligence. They assigned him to evaluate the Maginot Line, and he actually made a good job of it. He told British intelligence that it was useless unless it went through the Ardennes Forest. He told me they assured him that the Ardennes Forest was impregnable, and the French could hold it easily. The duke doubted anyone had even read his report. He was pretty fed up with the British government by then.'

'Did you like him?'

Another shrug. 'I neither liked nor disliked him. There's not much to him — it's his wife who is the real force. But I told him I was going to be a British duke, which amused him, and we spent some time together. I was curious, that was all. Did you know the Germans tried to convince him to return to England from Spain earlier this year to broker an alliance with Hitler in return for restoring him to the throne?'

'What? He turned them down, of course.'

'How do you know?'

'Because the Duke of Windsor is now Governor of the Bahamas,' Deanna said patiently. 'It was on the news. Donnie, how do you know about the Germans trying to get him to come back to England? Surely David isn't still writing to you.'

'I doubt he can write openly to anyone. All his mail would be checked or withheld. I have it from a man I met at the Folton-Smythes'. In fact, I think he had been asked especially to meet me. He knew I'd met David, knew I felt invasion was inevitable. Did you ever think it a coincidence that the London bombing began the day David sailed for the Bahamas?'

A chill. 'I don't understand.' Had the real Donnie met David in France, or was this all lies? She realised it probably didn't matter.

'Hitler held off the invasion while he thought the duke might agree to return, and an alliance with Britain might be possible. Do you know why David refused to return to England?'

She shook her head. 'I didn't know he had refused. I thought he was just offered the governorship and took it.'

'He wanted to come back here — he's a simple man at heart, and loves this country, for all he seems a playboy. Churchill ordered him to come back here.'

'Then why didn't he come?'

'His single condition was that Queen Elizabeth or the Princess Elizabeth meet his wife for at least ten minutes. They refused! David thought the people would stand by him after the abdication, that there'd be a popular uprising demanding he be king again. But then of course the newspapers began to print stories about his escapades.'

'People sympathised,' Dee said slowly. 'But it would take far more than that to make the British people rebel.'

'So he went to Germany, where Hitler gave his wife full royal honours. Hitler has always made it very clear that he regards David as the true king of Britain.'

She swallowed. 'But ... he isn't.'

'Why not? If a king can simply sign a bit of paper and no longer be His Majesty, why can't another piece of paper be signed to give him the throne again?'

'Because Churchill wouldn't allow it. The present king would never sign it.'

'But what about the people of Britain? They do have reason to demand David's return now. What would they choose — continued bombing and the certainty of invasion, or an alliance that would make Britain neutral, with no bombing, no food shortages with the blockade lifted, leaving Hitler free to establish his Third Reich across the rest of Europe?'

Instead of answering, she asked a question of her own. 'You asked if it was a coincidence that the bombing began the day the duke sailed for the Bahamas? Was it a coincidence?'

'No. It was the duke's idea. He sent a telegram to Hitler suggesting England be bombed into submitting to an alliance, and then another after a few weeks suggesting that the bombing increase. It was read by British intelligence of course, but then sent on to Sweden then Germany, to see how Hitler would react.' He shrugged. 'We've seen how Hitler reacted.'

She had no name for what she felt. Rage? Horror? No words either. David actually urging the destruction of the people he once ruled! She forced herself not to show her disgust but give noncommittal disapproval instead. 'That's terrible!'

'War is terrible. But the moment David is crowned king the bombing will stop. There'll be bananas in the shops again and no sugar and tea rationing. Dee, honey, I visited Germany for business just after I went to France. David gave me introductions to some high-up people there. Hitler doesn't want war with England like the Kaiser did. Hitler hates France for what France did to them after the last war, and he is deeply afraid of Soviet communism, but England? England can stay neutral, like Spain or Switzerland.'

He began to whistle. It took Deanna a minute to recognise the tune — 'The Skye Boat Song', supposedly sung by the sailors taking Bonnie Prince Charlie from Scotland after his supporters had been slaughtered when they lost the battle at Culloden to restore him to the throne. 'Donnie,' she said slowly, 'are you saying the Duke of Windsor might return to broker an alliance? He could do it, you know.' She allowed eagerness to seep into her voice. 'They'd offer the throne to the man who stopped the war.'

His smile was like a teacher's when approving of a pupil. 'Exactly.'

'But surely it's impossible to get him into England now — much less for people to know what he's offering ...'

And all at once she realised why it was not impossible at all. So this was why Donnie was here. Not as a spy, other than to find influential people who would support a peace treaty. No, not a spy. A scout.

'The king over the water,' she said quietly. 'But it's an awful lot of water between here and the Bahamas, Donnie. Bonnie Prince Charlie failed, and he had an army of supporters.'

'So this king will come as the Prince of Wales, which is the title the people most fondly remember him having.'

'You ... you don't mean he has agreed?' She stared at him, trying to look concerned and yet entranced by this new possibility. 'Donnie, how do you know all this?'

He waved a hand, as if the question was irrelevant. 'I'm a patriot. Someone who thinks war is the most vicious of human inventions. I'm also a businessman. You've always thought of me as the heir to the dukedom, but my true work is banking. When I was taken prisoner in Dunkirk, I managed to have a message sent to some of the Germans I'd met. And here I am.'

'So you didn't escape,' she said slowly. Even now he isn't admitting his masquerade, she thought. But of course, he needed her to trust him.

'I escaped, but not in a stolen fishing boat. I convinced the Germans I could help bring about peace between our two countries. It's possible, Dee! So many of the well born and wealthy in this country want exactly that.'

'The Duke of Windsor will actually leave the Bahamas and come to Britain?'

'He has conditions. He will come on a friend's Swedish yacht, and he will send for his wife later. I don't know all the details —'

I bet you do, thought Deanna.

'— but he will be taken to the home of a prominent and most reputable supporter, for a live interview with the BBC.'

'Churchill will stop it!'

'It will be a live broadcast. The BBC won't know who is going to speak till the last moment — they'll think they'll be covering a quite different event. The duke — or Prince of Wales, which is how he'll be addressed — will be accompanied by several peers sympathetic to the German cause. Again, I don't know the details. The plan is impeccable, Dee!'

She nodded thoughtfully. 'There is no way the newspapers can keep the offer secret after a broadcast.'

'Exactly. The prince will be driven straight from the BBC to the East End, with cameras to record him comforting those who have been bombed out, just as he was so sympathetic to the starving miners. He'll do it beautifully. Then the cameras will follow him to Buckingham Palace. They can hardly turn him away.'

'They can keep him there to silence him.'

'Not once he's announced he brings an offer of peace. Not if there is no more bombing from the moment he speaks to the

BBC. There really would be a rebellion if they imprisoned him after that, or if he was inconveniently assassinated.'

Deanna stared. 'They wouldn't kill him?'

'While he's alive he's a threat. England will have a week to agree to the terms of the treaty — not a military alliance, just neutrality. Why should British soldiers die for France? Why should the country starve for Poland?'

She sipped her cognac, trying to look relieved, hopeful. This was it! 'I can't believe David agreed.'

Suddenly his expression was hard to read. 'That's the problem. He almost fled to the German embassy in Spain at the start of the war to take up Hitler's offer. At the last minute, he ran for Portugal instead. He is loyal to this country despite everything. He needs to be convinced that England won't reject him a second time — and that he'll be safe. He's not ... courageous ... physically or mentally.'

'I'm amazed he'll risk this.'

'He was furious that his Maginot Line report was dismissed — he knows the Dunkirk debacle would never have happened if anyone had paid attention to it. He abhors being surrounded by "black faces" in authority. Mental or physical defectives, dark skins, Jews, gypsies — Hitler wants to improve the race by getting rid of the subraces, but the duke goes further. He's a eugenics enthusiast — only the best physically and mentally should be allowed to breed.'

'I did know that,' she said slowly. She smiled wryly. 'He led me to understand I'd be acceptable.'

'I should hope so! He's also afraid British intelligence wants to assassinate him, and that they took him a thousand miles away to be able to do it without Scotland Yard watching. While he lives, there will always be another claimant to the throne. But I think, at heart, he truly wants peace.'

'And to be king again?'

'Of course. He abdicated thinking he'd be regent. I imagine he may get what he wanted in the first place — a king regency that will continue for life, even after Elizabeth is twenty-one. She is female, after all. By then he'll be firmly established as "the king who saved us from Churchill's war".'

Female. Subraces. She felt ill. 'It ... it's hard to accept it might really happen,' she said. 'I've heard hints, of course. But I thought it was just people like me, wishing for an end to the destruction, not a plan to actually bring that about.'

He met her eyes, then took her hands in his. 'There is a plan. It's all in place. It can happen in a week, or two at most. We need to move fast before the duke can lose his nerve.' His hands tightened on hers. 'Will you be part of this, Dee? How much will you risk for peace?'

'Anything. But I don't know what I *can* do.'

'Will you give your promise to help the plan tonight?'

'I just have.'

'Help others, not just me.' He looked at his watch. 'There's a practice run-through tonight. In ten minutes two men will arrive in the cave to assure themselves the Duke of Windsor can land there safely and easily.'

She sat back in shock. Ten minutes! So that was why Donnie had been so tense when he discovered a houseful of people, not just the three girls he had been unable to shift, but an Australian pilot and Rob too, a clearly capable woman, both almost certainly loyal to the present king and government.

He is going to use my cave, and my house, where my family is sleeping, she thought, contriving to look slightly excited, subduing her fury to glance at him admiringly.

'We Clavertons serve our country as it best needs,' he said, with apparent deep sincerity.

We Clavertons! She wanted to beat him with her fists. What have you done with my cousin?! Instead she gave a faint nod, and lifted her chin in simulated pride.

'Come down to the cave with me now. Convince the men who are coming that Eagle's Rest will provide a safe entry for the prince. David may well be nervous.'

'I should think so.'

'A yacht is too slow and too visible. He'll have been transferred to a German submarine. So you need to convince the men tonight that you can reassure him, that David knows you, and that you'll welcome him to your house as your king.'

He gave a brief smile, a quite different smile from any she had seen earlier. It was the first hint of ruthlessness or deception she'd seen in him, beyond his imposture as duke. 'Actually, he believes he is coming to Claverton Castle. He'll see the castle as they near the shore. He won't find out till he reaches the library here. He doesn't know there'll be a car waiting here to take him immediately to another location to make his broadcast. The authorities will be looking for him as soon as they discover he's left the Bahamas,' he added grimly. 'His wife can cover for him for a few days, saying he's ill and wishes to see no one. That might just work for long enough to get him here, but we need to assume they may already be on the lookout for him.'

The man who was not Donnie was speaking quickly and efficiently now he felt secure in her support. 'We'll have to move him, away from the coast, and fast. But he doesn't need to know that either. Once he leaves the Bahamas, of his own free will, he is committed.' He stood and held out his hand. 'So. Will you come?'

Twenty

A man was arrested for calling Winston Churchill a fool. His political opponents made a meal of it. 'Are we living in a police state, where we cannot call the PM a fool?'

Churchill raised his eyebrows. 'The man was not arrested for calling the prime minister a fool,' he said, 'but for letting out a state secret at a time of war.'

An anecdote from World War II, possibly not apocryphal

The house creaked, as if reproaching them. 'I was built for middle-class comfort, not royal escapades and rebellions.' Deanna tried to think of a way to alert Rob. Calling her now would give away the whole pretence. Hopefully she had eavesdropped, but Donnie had spoken softly, and blackout curtains soaked up sound as well as light.

An owl hooted dismally outside as Deanna led the way to the library, or possibly ecstatically, having gobbled a mouse. It was hard to tell with owls, even harder than calculating the plans of enemy agents.

This is not how it was meant to go! Deanna thought desperately, moving as slowly as she could. Any German agents were supposed to come up the cave and sneak through the house so they could be followed and then captured away from Eagle's Rest, not examine the passage then sail away again.

What if they found the cave unsuitable? What if they simply vanished without giving any clue to their plans or identity?

'Are you coming?' Donnie was obviously trying not to show impatience.

She had to think. She didn't have time to think. 'Shouldn't I change? I can't meet David like this! I should at least have my pearls on, some lipstick.'

'I told you, he's not coming tonight. The men you'll meet will expect exactly who you are: a woman in wartime who has only just been told about the plan.'

'I'm sorry — it's all been so sudden.' And was meant to be, she thought, for there must be a hundred objections to the plan as he'd explained it to her tonight, as well as details of what would happen once David assumed power again or stormtroopers marched through Piccadilly Circus.

Instead he dangled two choices she must make tonight — continued war and death, or the return of King Edward VIII.

'Donnie, this won't put the girls in danger, will it?'

'Tell the children that old friends have dropped in, and to go back to bed. I had hoped the children would have been interned with their aunt and uncle by now. Having that factory woman foisted on you is bad luck too.'

'But what if they do suspect something?'

'Don't worry.' He patted his pocket. 'Drops of nux vomica in their breakfasts and the children and woman come down with a week of stomach flu so they can't mention anything they've seen or heard.'

He used the correct word, 'flu', this time, and accidentally gave her more information. David would arrive within the next week: before the girls and Rob got over 'stomach flu'.

'They'll just have to be housebound for a few days,' he added, confirming her suspicions. 'They shouldn't suspect a thing — David will be through the cave and into the car within minutes.'

He glanced at her ruefully. 'I had to tell that pilot friend of yours we were engaged. I apologise for that. I wanted him out of the way as well. I gather from his expression tonight you have informed him we're not.'

'I had to! I had no idea what he was talking about and he could see it. Donnie, you might have warned me. Trusted me! At the very least asked me to pretend to be engaged to you.'

'No chance to get you alone, and it's not the kind of thing you say on the telephone, with half a dozen operators listening in at every exchange. One of them was sure to ring up the newspaper for a *Duke of Claverton to Wed His Cousin* story and we'd have the gossips of the nation staring at us. Dee, we need to hurry.'

Through the library, into the cellar. Donnie pulled the bookcase firmly shut after them, pulled out a torch, then clattered down the stairs. He strode over to the bricks and started pulling the loosened ones away from the gap in the wall.

The gap grew into a rough-edged hole, big enough to bend and step through rather than squeeze. He must have come down here the night he stayed at Eagle's Rest. He clambered through. She followed him, down the passage, towards a corner.

The corner moved, becoming two shadows shaped like men, in sailor jeans and pullovers, not uniform.

'Ah, Your Grace. Thank you for welcoming us to your estate.' This voice was English, and aristocratic, even vaguely familiar, but whoever stood there had turned off their torch, and Donnie did not shine his in their direction.

'It's a pleasure, but this particular passage belongs to my cousin, Lady Deanna Claverton.' The man who was not Donnie shone the torch at her. 'Dee, honey, these are the friends I was telling you about.'

'Delighted to meet you. Welcome to Claverton,' said Deanna, feeling absurdly like someone saying lines in a play. She heard rather than saw at least two other figures move.

She reached into her pocket for her own torch as soon as he turned his away from her and then wriggled her fingers into her brassiere for the pistol, knowing she might not get another chance. She shoved her hands, clutching torch and pistol, into her pockets.

The man who'd spoken shook his head apologetically. 'Claverton, old chap, I'm sorry, but that wild entrance simply isn't suitable for David. We need to try option B.'

'It is entirely suitable!' snapped the man who wasn't Donnie. 'The castle will reassure him more than any of us can.'

'What if he slips climbing off the boat into the cave? You didn't say it was so rough.' This voice was English too, and also aristocratic. Once again she almost recognised it.

'That keeps fishermen away. We can secure a rope from the top. Even if he falls he'll be safe.'

'He'll shit himself,' said the first Englishman. 'He'll be good for nothing for days.'

'Then you must make sure he does not slip. You must calm him down!' The third man's voice was accented — German. 'Tell him it is romantic, your Bonnie Prince Charlie. He is a valiant hero, a Siegfried!'

'You obviously don't know David,' said the first English voice wryly.

'Then drug him,' said the German voice matter-of-factly. 'As soon as he is asleep we lift him into the cave on ropes, bundled up, so he isn't bruised, and carry him upstairs and into the car. When he wakes up he'll have no choice but to play the part he agreed to.'

'Nonsense!' The first voice was emphatic. 'David will claim the Germans kidnapped him, and if you try drugging him, it wouldn't be far from the truth. I don't know what they'll charge us with, but I do know that we'll be shot. I'm heading back. I want no part of this, or plan B either. When Claverton said he had an almost invisible cave where you could enter at high tide I didn't envisage waves crashing us against a cliff.'

'I'm sorry, old boy,' said the second Englishman. 'But he's right.'

The foreigner spoke quickly, and in German, arguing or ordering.

'No!' The first Englishman spoke more firmly. 'I'm not risking any more for this. There's too much that can go wrong.'

His torch splintered light back through the cave, showing the path towards the sea.

'But His Royal Highness has promised he is committed to this ...' said the German quickly. 'He has given his word.'

The second Englishman paused briefly. 'If David's promises were pigeons England would be covered in pigeon shit. He changes his mind in the blink of an eyelash. There's no chance of this succeeding unless everything is perfect.'

He glanced back, so Deanna had a brief glimpse of his face, high cheekbones, thin mouth, receding hairline. 'I apologise, Your Grace, Lady Deanna. I know you are doing your best. But sadly it will not be enough.' He turned away and began to walk again.

'Plan B then!' called the German.

'No.' This time he didn't even turn. 'I'm sorry. I'm out of it. Too cloak and dagger, and too slapdash too. I should never have agreed to a plan with David at its core. Come on, Henry. Let's get out of here.'

Once they were gone there would be no way to identify them, to stop the Germans from finding a more suitable landing site for their 'plan B'. And other more determined English collaborators.

She had to stop them. At least if they could be identified and questioned, something might come of this. The whole plot, perhaps, would collapse.

And the Duke of Windsor would get off scot-free. But better that than taking back the kingdom, or worse, civil war in Britain, Culloden all over again, with Germany marching in to pick up the debris.

Memory slashed briefly ... the paper silhouette of a man tacked to a tree ... disable them. Don't kill them, because then they'll take their secrets with them.

She lifted the pistol out of her pocket, clicked off the safety catch, raised it with both hands. Two loud shots. One. Two.

The two men dropped, screaming, clutching their legs.

She tried to find the German in the darkness, then heard a huff. Pain blinded her for a second, a force that thrust her back against the wall. Her left arm wouldn't work ... had to work ... she forced it up again as the Donnie imposter grabbed her, wrenched the pistol from her, then exclaimed something in German.

Another torch suddenly shone behind her, so bright it blinded her. Five shots, not loud, but puffing like a panting dog: a silencer ...

The Englishmen stopped screaming. The German fell, silent, clutching his leg. The man who was not Donnie ducked away, so abruptly that Deanna slid down the wall, trying to staunch the blood streaming from somewhere high on her left side. It was hard to breathe, harder to think ...

'Dee!' Rob's voice. 'Press on this. Hard.'

Vaguely, Deanna felt Rob's right hand move and press down on a pad of some sort. Agony flashed even harder, but she knew it must be done. Slow down the bleeding ...

Rob and the torchlight flashed away, back towards the house and the escaping Donnie. She heard a thud, a body fall and, impossibly, Mrs Thripps saying, 'A duke my bloody arse. Give me that clothes line, girls. Don't worry, I learned knots from the Great Majesto himself; he could get out of a suitcase in twenty seconds. There, young fella me lad, you won't get out of that in a hurry.'

'The girls!' Deanna managed to gasp. 'Don't let them in here!'

It was too late. Three girls, three torches. Magda carried blankets, Rosa the first-aid kit from the cellar — Deanna had shown them everything that might be needed in an air raid.

Anna shone a torch at the Englishmen who'd been walking away. 'They're dead,' she said emotionlessly. 'Their heads have holes in them. They are very neat holes.' She looked down at the German. 'He is still alive.'

Mrs Thripps appeared, carrying a cast iron frying pan. 'You move an inch, Jerry, and you'll get this on your noggin too. Lady Dee, we need to get you rolled over onto a blanket so we can carry you out of here.'

Hands strong from scrubbing and beating blankets helped her. 'Keep your eyes on the Jerry, girls. Tell me if he moves. I'm going to have a look at this wound.'

'We have seen injured people before,' said Rosa, her voice not quite steady. 'We saw a man with his legs blown off after the bombing in London. He was dead, of course.'

'We saw Mama and Papa,' said Anna, tremulous now. 'Mama was still alive for a little while, lying on top of me in the car, because I could hear her breathing, then she was dead and still on top of me and not breathing at all. Will you stay alive, Auntie Dee?'

'Of course,' Deanna managed, trying to sound certain. 'You shouldn't be here. You ... you should be in bed!' Such a mundane reproach after all this.

'We listened to you talk,' said Magda, her voice still steady. 'We always listen, after you think we are asleep.'

'We need to know if you are going to let us stay,' said Anna. 'In case you tell that man we just tied up in the cellar, or Sam, or Rob, "I think I can no longer put up with three children." I'm glad the man in the cellar is not your cousin,' she added. 'He never said anything to you, but I could tell he knew about us.'

'Knew what?' asked Deanna faintly. The world was beginning to feel cold and black, even colder and blacker than a cave should be. The waves sounded closer. For a moment she thought an extra high tide was washing in, then realised the sound came from herself, a violent hush that made it hard to hear what was happening around her.

Mrs Thripps' hands unbuttoned what was left of the top of Deanna's dress. 'The bullet's gone right through just below your shoulder,' she said. 'Seen something just like this when we was treading the boards with Wild William's Western Gunmen. Can you move your fingers, love? That's right.' More pressure on both sides now. 'She's goin' to be fine. You go and tell Auntie Rob to help carry her out of here, then make your Auntie Dee a cuppa tea. In fact, make all of us a cuppa tea, nice and strong now ...'

'No,' said Rosa. 'We will stay. Auntie Dee, our surname is Grunberg. Mama and Papa were German, and Jewish. Shh, Magda. Auntie Dee must know. She may not want Germans and Jews living in her house.'

'I ... I want three daughters living in my house, called Magda, Rosa and Anna, or whatever your real names are. But ... but I do want a cup of tea. Please.'

She forced herself to stay conscious. She had to get the girls out of here. More men might come up the cave from the waiting boat, and even if they didn't, her daughters had seen too much, far too much, and not just here ... 'Make yourselves cocoa, with lots of sugar.'

She suddenly heard the sound of a new man's voice, authoritative. The next moment the chauffeur appeared, carrying a blanket. Rob was there too, kneeling beside her as the girls moved away. 'Dee, we are going to carry you now. Don't worry. All is secured.'

Her country was smashed by bombs, an enemy was preparing to invade, and aircraft buzzed like bees. She could hear bees now. The whole world seemed to buzz: even the voices turned to bees.

Twenty-One

Change and decay in all around I see;
Oh Thou who changest not
Abide with me.

Lyrics from 'Abide with Me' by Henry Francis Lyte,
a hymn popular in World War II

The world was white when she awoke. For a moment she thought of clouds and angels, then realised she was staring at the ceiling. She turned her head, which hurt, and found three girls sitting on chairs by her bed, in her own bedroom.

'Anna, go and tell Auntie Rob that Auntie Dee is awake,' said Magda.

'No! I want to stay! Auntie Dee, did you mean we can really be your daughters?'

'Yes,' Deanna managed.

'Will we be called Ladies too?' demanded Anna eagerly.

'Not even honourables, I'm afraid.' Her voice sounded ridiculously weak.

'There's tea,' said Rosa, 'but it's cold now. Should we make you some more?'

Deanna began to shake her head, then stopped. The room whirled.

'People who don't eat or drink die,' said Anna, bending over her, so Deanna could see the white face and shadowed eyes.

'Then I'd like tea. Sandwiches.'

'What kind?' asked Rosa.

'Any ...'

'Not fish paste,' said Anna, her voice stronger now as she went out. 'Auntie Dee doesn't like fish paste. Can we call her Mummy now? Tomatoes are full of vitamins ... She's awake now, Auntie Rob,' she added, as a figure appeared illuminated at the door.

No lights, thought Deanna. It must be daytime.

'We're going to make *Mummy* tea and sandwiches.'

'Good. No need to hurry. She has to drink this first and take her medicine.'

Rob sat on the chair beside her. 'How do you feel?'

Deanna waited till the girls had left. 'You killed the two Englishmen deliberately,' she said. 'You could have just disabled them.'

'There was every need to kill them. This is war, Dee. People die in war, though I don't think those men expected to. Last night never happened. You have to remember that. The girls need to understand it, too. Both men died in a car accident. They knew little anyway, and now can tell nothing. The Duke of Windsor is a loyal member of the royal family, doing his duty in the Bahamas.'

'You left the German man and the man who pretended to be Donnie alive.'

'They have information. They will be questioned. Discreetly. The girls and Mrs Thripps have been told that they were spies, and that the man who pretended to be your cousin is a spy too but they know not to speak of it or tell anyone about the cave.'

'What was Mrs Thripps doing here?'

'Doris at the exchange rang her. She heard Donnie give some unfamiliar man orders to ring and tell Sam he was wanted at the base. Then Mrs Thripps looked out her window and saw Frederick — Donnie's chauffeur, but actually put there by Uncle Jasper — get into his car at the pub. She was already suspicious of the man who pretended to be Donnie, so Mrs Thripps followed on her bicycle. She found the chauffeur with me, listening in the cellar. She nearly donged both of us, thinking we were spies too. Thank goodness no one heard her — she had the sense to be quiet.' Rob grinned. 'But she and her frying pan got the imposter duke before we could disable him. We're lucky he hasn't a cracked skull. Here, drink this.'

Deanna took the spoonful, blinking at the bitterness. 'What is it?'

'Morphia. The doctor prescribed it this morning while you were still under. Reserved for the armed services, but Frederick — that's the chauffeur — flashed his ID. He's regular army, some kind of special unit. Everyone will be in a special unit by this time next year.'

'No peace alliance,' whispered Deanna.

'You can't make an alliance with wasps and expect them not to sting you. I'm going to prop you up now so you can drink this cocoa. You've lost a lot of blood, so you need fluids, but the doctor says there's no damage to the bone, though you won't be using your arm for a few months. The bullet went in and out just under your shoulder bone.' Rob held the cup up for her. The pain was dulling already from the morphia. Deanna just felt sleepy.

'I'll tell the girls you'll drink their tea after you've had a nap,' said Rob, standing up with the cup. 'That was excellent work, Dee, nipped in the bud. I doubt the Germans will try luring the Duke of Windsor a third time, especially not after he has been told — discreetly — that the authorities know he agreed to come to Britain. He will deny it, of course. The Duke of Windsor is very good at denying what he doesn't want the world to know. He is even good at denying things to himself. Sleep well, Dee. It was a jolly good show.'

Like a hockey match, thought Deanna, her eyes closed, her mind blurring but unable to rest. Jolly good show, girls. You've won the day. But we haven't won. We've only scored a goal, and the other side are leading by a long, long way ...

Had she done the right thing? Two men had died. Hundreds of thousands of men, women and children would die because the hope of an alliance with Germany had died today.

Her grandfather would have been proud, but every bomb that fell on Britain now would be her fault. Every death, each loss, every child who screamed at the night, every forest cut for telegraph poles or pit props ...

I will ask Sam, she thought blearily. I don't care who else I can't tell — I'm going to tell Sam. Sam will know. I will ask Sam ...

Twenty-Two

What do you call a crocodile who fights for Britain?
An allied gator

World War II joke

He sat next to her when she woke from a doze that afternoon, a small posy of golden winter aconite flowers from the castle gardens next to the bed.

Someone had arranged them in a vase for him, just as through the day they had made her tea and toast, scrambled eggs, orange juice, poached eggs.

Rob had helped her to the bathroom and given her morphia twice more. She had slept twice and woken each time to find three faces watching her, despite the books in their laps, in case she died.

She supposed she should have been taken to hospital. She vaguely remembered a doctor, sometime in the shadows of the past eighteen hours. Hospitals meant questions, to which answers could never be given.

Sam kissed her lips gently, then drew back. 'Anna told me you've been battling spies.' He took her hand. His was warm and callused, the kind of calluses that didn't vanish in two years of being a Flight Lieutenant. 'She said Mrs Thripps hit the man who wasn't your cousin over the head with a frying pan, and that people died but you'd promised that you wouldn't. I hope the last bit is true.' He smiled at her gently. 'Explanations can wait till you're stronger.'

'It's all pretty much true.' She had been ordered not to tell anyone. It did not seem to have occurred to anyone to wait till she agreed, much less signed the Official Secrets Act. Possibly what had happened in the cave was too secret even to trust to any intelligence service records.

She trusted Sam more than she trusted any agency, even one run by a man named Chummy, who'd been at school with Grandpa.

She told him everything. He sat, nodding but not speaking, till she had finished, then held a glass of water for her to drink, for the effort had made her right hand tremble. Her left was disabled by the sling.

'So, did I do right? Men died last night, Sam. The war is going to continue because of what I did and didn't do.'

'Of course you did right. If I thought otherwise I wouldn't be in the RAF.' His brown eyes met hers, so like her grandfather's, and hers too. 'It would have been easy for me not to fight. Farming is a reserved occupation in Australia too.'

'But you came.'

'Yes. Though I've done precious little fighting, except vicariously, showing others how to kill. I was with Bomber Command for the Denmark campaign.' He gave a bitter shrug. 'Our whole invasion lasted six hours. I was briefly in Bomber Command in France, too, till I was wounded — a shoulder wound, just like yours. I have killed people, Dee. I don't know how many — nor have I seen their faces, except sometimes in nightmares.'

She'd had nightmares last night. But dreadful dreams flew the night air for everyone these days.

He managed a smile. 'They put me on training as temporary light work till I was fully recovered, and I turned out to be good at it, so I train men to kill people rather than do it myself. So yes, I think what you did was right — was bloody marvellous. I think we're going to win, too, though things will get worse before it's over.'

'How can you be sure we'll win?'

'Because blokes like me are staying. Because Mrs Thripps bashed a Nazi over the head with a frying pan and a dear little old lady waved a staff car down last week and asked if they could spare her a cup of petrol because she'd read a recipe for a Molotov cocktail and wanted to make some ready for the invasion.'

She laughed, then stopped when it hurt.

He stroked her cheek. 'You know, I don't think I've ever felt skin as soft as yours. Winning isn't the point. Evil has to be fought, and the things Hitler is doing are turning Europe evil too. Evil is contagious. We have to stop him before anyone who has dark skin, or is Jewish like your wonderful daughters, or is communist, or mutters the wrong word about the Führer will be in labour camps until they die.'

Some hard knot inside her vanished. Last night had been right. Sam said so.

'Tell me about your home,' she said sleepily. 'Has it changed much since the war?'

'I haven't seen it in two years, remember. Dad's in charge of it now — Mum died when I was seven, of polio — but his heart is none too good.'

'Is it good land?'

He laughed. 'Not what you'd call good, but not bad for Budgie Creek. The river flats are in lucerne. The rest is rough grazing, or cliffs and gullies. Excellent eagle country, and more wombats than you can poke a stick at.'

'A river?'

'Wider than yours but not much deeper, flowing over sand, but roaring like a horde of stampeding elephants in a flood. There always seems to be a mob of kids swimming in the river in summer — me and my sister and our cousins when we were younger, and their kids now.'

'Any of your family in the air force too?'

'Army. I'm the black sheep of the family, taking the lazy way out, letting an aeroplane do the work. Two cousins, and my sister Deb's husband is in Malaya.'

'Deb sends the dripping?'

'And Anzac biscuits sometimes — I'll bring you some of the next lot.'

'What's an Anzac biscuit?'

'Hard enough to last the war and good enough to keep fighting it.'

She felt her eyes begin to close again. 'I seem to keep sleeping.'

'I'll be here when you wake up.'

She let sleep take her, knowing he would be.

Twenty-Three

How to Make Soap Last Longer

Wet yourself before the bath and rub the soap foam all over your body. Put the bar of soap out of direct sunlight to dry. Remember — every lick of soap you save is a lick against Hitler!

Household advice from
World War II

Rob left a fortnight later, so it wouldn't look like she vanished immediately after cars had been glimpsed at Eagle's Rest that night. Mrs Thripps had informed Doris who had told everybody that Lady Dee had fallen off a ladder, and that Donnie had left with the chauffeur. Mrs Thripps came daily now, partly to help but mostly so she didn't miss anything. Deanna was glad of the bundle of banknotes, topped all the way up now by Mr Vonderfleet's couriers, that allowed her to pay daily wages.

'What now?' Deanna asked Rob the night before she left, having made sure the girls were in bed and had promised to stay there. 'No more letters to Uncle Jasper?'

'I suspect your cover has been blown. Someone must have known those men were coming to your cave. They've vanished, but you haven't. British fascists won't trust you — or invite you.'

'Especially with three Jewish daughters. Rob, now we know their surname, could you ask Uncle Jasper if they have relatives who'll claim them? I may need some influence as a single woman to adopt them.'

'It won't even occur to the authorities to object,' said Rob drily. 'There'll be a good many orphans needing homes before this is all over. I think any adoption will go through easily once their identity has been officially established.'

'I'll need to change their ration cards.'

'Wait till they can take the name Claverton. The girls were right, you know — the next few years will be hard for anyone with a German background.'

Deanna nodded.

'Who is the Duke of Claverton now?' Rob asked.

'You mean if Donnie — the real Donnie — is dead?' Deanna felt no guilt for her actions in the cave. She did feel guilt at her betrayal, which was stupid, for that man had not been her cousin. But she had felt, for a while, that she did have a family.

It had been illusion, all of it.

'Someone even more distant, assuming there is anything to come back to. The title may even lapse if Donnie is dead.'

I don't even know who I worked for, she thought. Just a man called Uncle Jasper who had a snake in his pocket. How much of what has seemed like Rob's friendship has been surveillance too?

She gave herself a mental shake. She had daughters; she had Mrs Thripps, who had somehow graduated to calling her 'dearie', with 'Lady Dee' only in public. She had Sam, and the eagles, the squirrels, and the badger on the hill.

'Has the pretender said anything about Donnie, the real one, my cousin?'

Rob shrugged. 'Above my pay grade and "need to know". I'm sorry I'm running out on you.'

'I'm fine. What will you do now, or is that classified?'

'Definitely classified. But I'm moving to a new unit after Christmas.' Rob hesitated. 'Probably overseas. It's top secret. Don't worry if you don't hear anything for months.'

That sounded like something a real friend would say. 'Of course I'll worry. But we are all fully occupied with worrying anyway. Should I still write to Uncle Jasper?'

'Yes. You still have a cave that the Nazis know about. They may suspect its usefulness is over, but you never know. Frederick's rigged up an alarm, by the way. If you hear bells ringing, you know someone has tripped the wire.'

'Thank you. I don't fancy a German invasion coming through my cellar. I wish the traitors had held off till after Christmas so you could have joined us.'

'I promised Mum I'd be home for Christmas dinner.' She grinned. 'Mum doesn't have your secret cellar of goodies though.'

'I'll pack you a hamper of farm produce — honey, farm cheese, cream, half a dozen oranges and tangerines. I'll even throw in a rooster.'

'You're a darling.' Rob hugged her, careful of Deanna's arm.

Deanna smiled, trying not to look bereft. Of course — Rob had a family and friends to return to.

But Deanna had Sam.

A Christmas card arrived among others from friends, ostensibly from Uncle Jasper, written by some secretary, almost certainly not the impressive one who had opened the door in the Mayfair flat.

'That nice man o' yours coming for Christmas?' Mrs Thripps asked casually a week before as they polished the silver together. Deanna was able to use both hands for light activity. 'Posh places have Christmas house parties, don't they?' Mrs Thripps added, even more casually. 'Always wanted to go to a Christmas house party.' She carefully didn't look at Deanna as she added, 'O' course a respectable married couple staying here would be chaperones, like, wouldn't they, if a single man was to stay here over Christmas ...?'

Sam had four days off and would occupy the third spare room. Deanna had wanted to invite him but had been afraid gossip might hinder her campaign to adopt the girls. With such unexceptionable chaperones Sam no longer had to spend four chilly days playing cards in a Nissen hut.

Mrs Thripps dedicated herself to her vision of a 'posh' Christmas party. They cut the tree in the Eagle's Rest woods, a small one that could be chopped up for next year's firewood. The castle Christmas ornaments had ended up in Deanna's attic: a whole box of silver baubles and glass peacocks with bobbing green glass tails, and wooden animals in once bright colours.

The traditional crib and manger were hand-carved wood, too, possibly a hundred years old or more, the figures stark and serious, the paint faded, the child in the crib, and the ox, the ass and the watching sheep, and Joseph and Mary, carved as one, arm in arm.

Mrs Thripps hung mistletoe on every convenient beam, and in a few unexpected places. Deanna had never seen mistletoe hung above a loo before. The celebrations defied those who'd strip joy from the world.

Santa Claus filled stockings for everyone, including Deanna, Sam and the Thrippses, with the usual tangerine orange at the toe, as well as new books for the girls from the limited range still being printed, and a tin of homemade toffee in each stocking.

Santa also presented Arnold Thripps with newly hemmed handkerchiefs cut from an old sheet; Mrs Thripps had a 'new' nightdress; Sam had freshly knitted socks; and to Deanna's delight her Santa Claus tangerine and toffees were supplemented by a homemade necklace of salt clay figures, painted to represent her and all present this Christmas, including Dusty.

Dusty's stocking held home-baked carrot dog biscuits, though he had already munched the plate of biscuits left for Santa Claus, leaving three hairs and a dribble.

Morning church was sedate, and cold around the knees and ankles for every woman who had irrevocably laddered her last pair of nylons and refused to wear woollen ones, with prayers for peace that somehow included destroying the enemy on every battlefront, and a collection to aid the homeless.

Deanna had tactfully asked the girls what service they had attended with their parents.

It seemed that 'Jewish' had been Hitler's ethnic description, not a religious one. They had irregularly attended an Anglican Sunday service at Oxford. 'Papa loved the singing,' Magda said wistfully.

Their clothes for Christmas Day were sedate too. (You cannot go wrong with a tweed suit.) Deanna wore one of Miss Enid's she had renovated, in shades of green, and also altered another for Mrs Thripps, extremely proud in shades of pink and purple.

Deanna had found the girls boarding school overcoats she had grown out of, with the school braid and emblem removed, and different braid added to each one. Even if she had been prepared to spend money conspicuously, it was impossible to find good quality coats anywhere.

Sam wore his uniform and sat between Deanna and Anna, and the entire congregation pretended not to keep glancing at them in case they missed him holding her hand, with a small breeze of whispering every time he spoke to her.

Conventions and restraint vanished once they reached home.

Mrs Thripps wore the latest creation Deanna had made for her, based on a silver sheath from 1920 with a matching coat trimmed in purple feathers.

Anna had a multicoloured tulle fairy costume from Deanna's youth, complete with silk wings, and refused to wear anything else for the whole four days. Magda and Rosa wore their party dresses, and Deanna the prettiest frocks in her wardrobe, with her great-grandmother's velvet cloak to keep her warm outside the kitchen, where both stove and fireplace were well stocked with wood.

Sam stayed in the pre-war civilian suit he had presumably worn when he came to England, while Mrs Thripps insisted her Arnold wear the old duke's dinner jacket.

Mr Thripps did not object. He said little the whole visit but grinned often, showing the gaps in his teeth, ate hugely, drank bottle after bottle of cider, and mostly snored the sleep of a man who has worked all day and watched the skies for enemy aircraft all night, despite the noise of Christmas carols sung frequently, loudly and out of tune, the shrieks and laughter of dunking for apples, and the boisterous games of charades, Animal Vegetable or Mineral, and Sheep Sheep Come Home.

The cellar was raided. Roast wild goose, gravy, roast potatoes, roast parsnips with brown sugar, glazed carrots, buttered Brussels sprouts, a mountainous Christmas pudding, trifle made from bottled peaches, mulberry jelly, creamy custard and sponge cake dipped in orange juice instead of sherry. Orange juice was scarcer than sherry now, but the oranges in the glasshouses were giving their first good crop.

Deanna gave Sam a jumper she had knitted and a book, *Birds of Northern England*, from Miss Enid's library — there had been no bird identification books available in any of the London bookshops she had rung. The girls presented everyone with a knitted face washer (Anna), and embroidered, hand-hemmed handkerchiefs made from another old linen sheet (Rosa and Magda).

Sam apologised for his lack of gifts in return — he had asked his sister to send them but they hadn't arrived.

Deanna had pondered over her own gifts for the girls. She finally decided on the traditional old-fashioned pearls, courtesy of Mr Vonderfleet, small but good, four each on a silver chain, to be added to each Christmas until, finally, each girl had an entire necklace, exactly as Deanna's grandfather had done for her, and the parents of her schoolfriends had done for them.

The girls received them quietly, with none of the screams and giggles that had greeted the filled stockings.

'You do like them?' Deanna said anxiously.

'You really are making us your daughters,' said Magda quietly.

Rosa was crying but smiling too. 'Mama and Papa began a necklace for Magda when she turned ten. Someone must have taken it from our things at the hospital. They were going to begin one for me, and Anna too.'

'My necklace is going to be bigger than yours, now,' said Anna with great satisfaction, 'because I've started earlier.'

She alone did not regard the necklace as anything but jewellery, possibly because she had been too young when her parents died to know its significance.

'No, it won't,' stated Rosa. 'They will all be the same size, won't they, Auntie Dee?'

'Exactly the same size,' said Deanna. 'And just like mine.'

'All the gentry wear pearls,' said Mrs Thripps, with great satisfaction. She shook her head. 'I don't think it right though that the girls don't get titles when they get adopted. A Lady and three Honourables — wouldn't that be something?'

Not really, thought Deanna. Her title had brought her only intrigue, and a glimpse into the lies and betrayals of government.

All I have that I value, she thought, did not come from a title. Except, of course, the diamonds, and the banknotes in the cellar.

If only it could always be like this, Deanna thought, as everyone (except Mr Thripps) gathered around the vast homemade jigsaw puzzle that had been Mrs Thripps' gift to the household, as well as knitted gloves and socks for everyone, Sam and her husband included. Mrs Thripps looked over at the gramophone. 'What we need now is a good tango. Come on, Arnold, love. Put a record on the Victrola, wind her up and let's dance.'

Deanna stared. A tango? She had only seen it danced at the less respectable London dance clubs. Mrs Thripps must have brought the gramophone record with her.

Arnold obediently cranked the handle. Dusty stopped pretending to be a hairy hearthrug and stared as Mr and Mrs Thripps progressed across the room, Mrs Thripps' varicose-streaked leg lifting higher than her head at every turn.

'She's incredible,' muttered Sam.

'Well, she was a professional! But I never thought I'd see Arnold Thripps tango!'

'A waltz!' declared Mrs Thripps, slightly out of breath. 'Come on, girls — your mum and I will show you how.'

Somehow Deanna was in Sam's arms. Mrs Thripps danced with Magda and Mr Thripps guided Rosa's and Anna's steps and kept the gramophone wound.

Slowly Sam's body moved closer to hers, till her head was on his shoulder, which was exactly the right height, and she wished she could place this moment in a glass terrarium, where she could watch it whenever she needed comfort, with children laughing and a dog snoring, and, somewhere, eagles nesting.

Twenty-Four

January 1941

BOMBERS DESTROY CITY CENTRE
OVER 1,400 FIRES IN LONDON
IN TWO HOURS GERMAN INCENDIARY BOMBS GUT THE ENTIRE HISTORIC COMMERCIAL CENTRE OF LONDON

Claverton Major Gazette
30 December 1940

It was time for the girls to go back to school, which for Magda meant beginning her first year at Hawthorne Grammar. Deanna tentatively suggested that the girls use the name Claverton from now on.

Magda and Rosa agreed immediately. Deanna suspected they had already discussed the possibility. Their own name had brought threats and exclusion. Both girls must know that as the war progressed the hatred of anything German would only increase.

Anna merely looked curious. 'Why?'

'So people don't go to the toilet in your schoolbag,' said Rosa bluntly.

Deanna looked at her sharply. 'Has that happened?'

'Not here,' said Magda expressionlessly.

'Miss Hannaford already calls us the Claverton girls,' said Rosa. 'She has since we first arrived.'

Miss Hannaford is no fool, thought Deanna, even if she was not proficient in the mathematics or Latin Magda would need. 'I'd like you to have my name because we are a family, and yes, it's a useful name. But you should keep your parents' name too. Maybe hyphenate them after the war.'

Possibly, by then, hatred and prejudice might start to fade a little. One day even racism might sleep forever.

'Would I be Lady Anna?' The prospective possible lady bounced on her tiptoes.

'No, I explained before. Not even an honourable, I'm afraid.'

'I'd rather be a princess.' Anna looked enquiringly at Deanna, as if the provider of this small Eden should surely also be able to provide such a title.

'You'd have to marry a prince. England doesn't have any just now, except Prince Edward of Kent, and anyway he'll only be a duke when the present king dies.'

'Why?'

'That's just the way it is. I think you'd find him boring, too.'

'There are other kinds of titles. Daddy was Professor and Mama a doctor.' Anna considered.

Mrs Thripps poked her head out of the extremely cold larder, where she'd been wiping down the shelves, wearing a floral pinnie over two pullovers of different shades of mauve and a pair of her Arnold's trousers, from the top of which poked long knitted underwear. 'I got a title you can have. I had it, and me mum and dad had it, and so did me sister Mavis afore she died, so now I can give it to you.'

'What is it?' asked Anna eagerly.

'"The Amazing". We was "The Amazing Andersons". You can be "The Amazing Anna".'

'I like it,' Anna decided. 'Thank you, Mrs Thripps,' she added politely. She grinned at her sisters. 'I'm *Amazing*!'

School began for three days, then stopped as snow fell, fat flakes drifting with that peculiar, white silence; they remained on the ground for five days' worth of asserting that the drifts were far too thick for bicycling to school.

'Not safe for man nor beast,' Mrs Thripps declared, gazing out the window. She had arrived as the first flakes fell that morning, carrying a suspiciously well-filled string bag, and took up residence once again for the snow's duration. Arnold joined her each evening, dropped off by the village fire truck, which seemed to have no trouble forging through the snow. No enemy planes could fly or see where to drop their bombs in weather like this, nor an invasion force find its way through fog in the channel, so he reckoned his air warden duties were suspended.

Sam's superiors echoed the sentiment. He arrived with a suitcase which contained not just his civilian flannel trousers, shirts, vests and pullovers but the tin of dripping, and the famous Anzac biscuits his sister Deb had sent him for Christmas with hand-knitted socks and knitted underwear, but which had only just arrived.

Deb had also sent gifts for Deanna and the girls, some from her and some from Sam's father, though Deanna suspected that if Sam's father was like her grandfather, his gift-giving was delegated to the nearest available female.

Deanna wondered exactly what Sam had told them about the inhabitants of Eagle's Rest. But her new soap was rose-scented, just like the girls' bath salts, already unobtainable, even if not rationed, and the extra can of dripping was welcome. Home-churned butter and the olive oil in the cellar had enriched their table, but once the Christmas goose fat had been used up she did miss the dripping, for rabbits had little fat on them, especially now in winter.

'This is from me,' Sam told her, Arnold and Mrs Thripps tactfully retiring early for the night with the girls to give the two of them time alone. Deanna had lit logs in the fireplace again to help warm the rooms upstairs. The village electricity was turned off at eight pm these days, leaving them with candlelight and red snickerings as the flames laughed their way towards the chimney.

She opened a small, flat parcel, then carefully unwrapped the cardboard. It was a framed painting on canvas, the colours startlingly bright in the dim light, as if sunlight was enclosed by the frame.

Bright blue mountains and an even richer sky, olive-green tree-covered hills with a field in the foreground, though no fence or hedge could be seen, just three sheep below the nearest hill and an animal that was not a badger walking nose down with evident determination.

She stared unbelieving, and then suddenly did believe, believe utterly, because behind it all were the cliffs she had dreamed of ever since she was a child, the cliffs she had to walk between to find ...

What? She still had no idea. She stared, unable to believe that her dream was real, at least on canvas.

Sam seemed worried by her silence. 'Do you like it?' He might have been speaking of the painting or its subject.

'It's beautiful. Thank you — I love it. Is it a real place?' she asked tentatively, desperately hoping the cliffs weren't a dream the artist had shared.

'Yes. The eagles nest just through those cliffs, or they did the year I left home.'

'Who painted it?'

He relaxed. 'My second cousin, Three — his real name is Andy but there are two older cousins also called Andy, and a younger one. The family likes the name. Three even makes a good living, to Uncle John's amazement.'

'It that land near your home?' She tried to keep her voice casual.

'Behind the homestead. The stream flows even in a drought — the house was built there to use the fresh water.'

She wished the painting had shown his home, too. He had never brought out a photo of it, or of his family, and she didn't like to ask. She pointed to the animal in the foreground. 'That's a wombat?'

'Yes. It wouldn't be out during the day, but I asked Three to put one in for you, so you could see it isn't badger-like.'

'You still need to meet a badger.' She gazed at the painting, realising that if she married Sam — and a man and a woman surely did not spend so much time together without the possibility arising — she would need to love his country as much as she loved hers.

She put the idea away. It was too large to think of now. Even visiting Australia was impossible till the war was over, if it ever was. And if England lost ...

She would not think of that tonight. 'I've dreamed of something like those cliffs.' She tried to make her voice casual.

'They're the heart of the place, for me anyway. Dee ...' He seemed about to say something, then stopped. 'Cocoa?' he asked.

Dee wondered if he, too, saw that the love of their respective homelands might have helped bring them together, but it was also potentially a problem.

The war has given us time, thought Deanna, as she poured milk into the saucepan and took a cover plate off the stove. Decisions made quickly, in passion, so often came to the wrong answers.

The seven of them made a snowman the next day, with a carrot nose, Mrs Thripps firmly deflecting her husband's suggestion of a snowwoman, anatomically correct about the bosom.

They made snow barricades and had a snowball fight, Sam and the girls against Deanna and the Thrippses, while Dusty snored by the fire when he wasn't snoring by the stove.

Mrs Thripps taught them the can-can, the rhumba and various 'belly dances' to the music on the wind-up gramophone and staticky music on the BBC. Deanna danced with Sam. 'I wish this never had to end,' he whispered, and drew her into the corridor to kiss her while everyone pretended not to notice.

The snow melted. The Thrippses left. So did Sam. She felt the warmth of his lips for days.

An hour later the planes began to fly above again, black flies buzzing against the steel-grey clouds.

Maggie the postwoman arrived for the first time since the snow began, her head covered in a moth-eaten balaclava and her hands in three pairs of mittens as protection against the wind, which still had icy teeth, and brought her a letter.

She served her steaming cocoa and a homemade apple bun, heated up too. She waited till she had left before she opened the letter.

Uncle Jasper was asking her to tea. His letter informed her that Cousin Mary would fetch her on her way back from a Red Cross meeting up in Scotland. Which meant Deanna would instead go to London by train.

Suddenly she thought of Sam, the brevity of life, and of her own body, no longer merely useful for shovelling cow shit. She called a number on impulse and was told Amy was out with the ambulance but would call when she got back.

The phone rang three hours later.

'A call from the Honourable Amy Lloyd for you, Lady Deanna,' said Doris at the exchange, with her usual slight excitement at being able to listen in to conversations between the aristocracy.

She's going to be shocked at this one, thought Deanna, amused.

'Amy, thank you for calling back. How are you?'

'Tired, grubby and engaged. His name is Hugh, he's a captain in the navy and his family has an estate in the Highlands with endless sheep and no central heating. I wear three sets of long johns when I'm up there but he's worth it. How are you?'

'I've adopted three orphan daughters, developed muscles from digging potatoes, and I met a man. Or I think I have.'

'You're not sure if you've met him?'

Deanna could almost see the grin. 'I'm sure he's real. I'm not sure if or when ... Amy, darling, could I have the name of the doctor who fitted you for your diaphragm?'

Doris gave an audible gasp at the exchange.

'Of course! And thank goodness — I was afraid you'd miss out forever. Sex is the only pleasure that isn't rationed these days. Except of course it is for me, with Hugh at sea ... Her name is Dr Hilyard and she's still practising, because I had another fitting three weeks ago, in case diaphragms are unobtainable up in the hills of Scotland. Who is he? Where's his family from?'

'He's Australian and a pilot ...'

Deanna could feel the reaction down the phone. A sea captain had a better chance of survival than a pilot these days.

'Gather ye rosebuds while ye may, Dee darling,' Amy said at last. 'Did you hear Pongo's flying planes too? Not fighters or bombers of course — they don't let women have weapons — but transporting planes from one airfield to another. Pinkie is driving this horrible colonel who's a bum pincher. She had to borrow her grandmother's corset so there's nothing soft to pinch ... Oh, and Marj caught it in a raid four months ago. They saved her leg but she'll always need a stick.'

'Oh, poor Marjory. I hope she'll still be able to ride.' Deanna realised how far the war and work for Uncle Jasper had separated her from her friends. 'Give her my love.'

'I will. Darling, you've simply disappeared for the past two years ...'

'Too busy with potatoes and daughters,' Deanna equivocated. 'Not to mention supplying the Women's Institute with fruit for their jams and opening flower shows in aid of Polish orphans.'

'You make that appointment with Dr Hilyard, darling.' The voice on the other end of the phone grew sombre. 'There are precious few rosebuds to gather these days. Don't waste a single one of them.'

Twenty-Five

Make your shoes last longer! Save shoe leather by lining your shoes with fresh newspaper every week. Your toes will be warm and your shoes will last longer!

Helpful Hints from World War II

Dear Dee,

I feel I know you already from Sam's letters. I am so glad he has met you! I'm glad the dripping is useful too; we are dripping in dripping, so to speak, boiling down the fat every time Dad kills a sheep. I'm glad it's not rancid by the time it gets to you. I seal it well before posting it.

I just had a letter from Ron from somewhere the censor wouldn't let me mention but you can guess! Ron weighed the envelope with pennies and threw it from the train window as they were embarking and someone picked it up and sent it on to me! There is kindness everywhere. Ron says he is alive and would be kicking but they're too crammed in to wiggle a toe, which could mean he's in a train, a barracks or a trench, but who knows with this war? If it IS any of those the censor will probably blot it out!

Do you know about bowerbirds? The males make nests with lots of blue things to attract females, or to beat other males in the best-dressed bower stakes. Anyway, I found an old bower yesterday — and inside it were my very best blue lace French knickers, which are no longer lacy or fancy. But I wore them on Ron's last day so they shall stay — washed — in my underwear drawer as a talisman that he will return.

I went over to Eagle Mountain from our place in town yesterday to help Dad dip the sheep. The land girls learned quite quickly. It was 108° in the shade and my bra strap broke, which is a calamity as there is no elastic to be had!

Love from Deb and Misty (A Border Collie unfortunately attracted to male dingoes. But she is a good companion, especially with Ron away.)

PS Dad says to give you his best wishes too.

First Class to London was crowded but a young lieutenant stood so she had a corner seat.

When the train line passed close to the castle she was startled to see how much estate woodland had been cleared of its timber, the stumps standing forlorn among what had once been grass and glades where bluebells had grown in spring. She doubted they would grow there now.

So much was known yet unfamiliar: the railway stations' gaudy flower gardens now green with cabbages and leeks, the windows taped in case of blasts, hastily dug Anderson air-raid shelters, and patriotic signs. Bare ground or frosted mangelwurzels glared brown after the snow, where once deer had grazed and badgers dug their setts.

The steam locomotive rattled and hiccupped because of poor quality coal, and seemed to halt every hour to let a troop train take the line.

She had provisioned herself with a thermos and a plentiful supply of egg and cress sandwiches and cheese and lettuce ones, as well as the obligatory gas mask, correctly assuming there would be no dining car. English social reserve thawed as she opened the sandwiches, and she ended up sharing them with the only other woman in the carriage, a WAAC, and the four men in uniform.

She was buffeted by the crowd on the station platform, but as she passed the gates and reached the road, a black car pulled up exactly opposite, the young woman driver in her khaki uniform swiftly exiting and opening the back door for her. She didn't speak. Deanna murmured her thanks as the car pulled out into the traffic.

They drove, stopped, and drove again repeatedly as men and overalled women in headscarves, all with rough, work- and cold-reddened hands, pushed rubble or broken glass out of the roadway, or carried sandbags from one side of the road to the other. Evidently the car was not headed to the Mayfair flat.

Deanna suddenly became aware she had been hearing vague popping sounds, like many champagne corks, becoming louder and clearer, and then the unmistakable boom of an explosion.

The driver muttered something and pulled over to the kerb. 'Follow me,' she ordered.

Deanna looked, but all she could see was cloud. The air suddenly shuddered with the wail of an air-raid siren — the raid in broad daylight must have taken the authorities by surprise. Screams seemed almost orchestrated with the drum-like pounding as Deanna and her companion were pushed with the crowd to the nearest air-aid shelter.

Something spat behind her. She instinctively swerved as bullets shattered the pavement. Each spun up a small spray of debris. A man dropped, then a woman.

A building exploded upwards behind them. Its debris rained down, along with a woman's arm that fell on Deanna's foot. Deanna stared at it as the driver pulled her onwards, refusing to let her stop to help.

If the driver were killed or even badly hurt, she had no idea where she was supposed to be going. She would have to go home, and await another letter ...

Another house rose in the air, curiously intact until it descended, its impact muffled by the far greater noise all around. Deanna glanced up again. The cloud was darker now. Not cloud. A sky filled with planes, so low she could make out the swastikas.

More bullets spat.

The shelter was a concrete box, already crowded. A woman's brawny arms pulled Deanna and the driver inside, then shut the door. It was almost impossible to breathe.

What had been air was dust and sweat, the stink of fear. More screams outside.

People pushed at the door, trying to get in, but no matter how desperately they pleaded the shelter was full.

'Bastards are strafing,' muttered someone.

'Language!' said a man primly. 'Ladies present.'

'I'd use worse language than that if I could get hold o' them bastards,' said the woman who had dragged them in. 'Listen! Our lads have 'em on the run!'

The noise hadn't changed, as far as Deanna could tell, but her informant was obviously experienced, for the sound of gunfire grew more distant, and the explosions stopped. Another siren blared.

'All clear,' said the brawny woman. She elbowed her way out. 'Ladies first. I want to see if I've got a home left. Thank God the kiddies are up in Wales.'

She hurried out. Deanna and the driver followed almost as fast, the crowd behind them eager to leave.

Bodies too shattered to be alive lay pressed against the wall of the shelter. The buildings around had crumbled, except for the two Deanna had seen destroyed. Small fires burned among the debris.

Already an ambulance had drawn up, with others making their way through the rubble. Figures had been covered in blankets. Even the arm had been removed, possibly to be reunited in a coffin with its owner. The air-raid wardens and firemen and ambulance drivers had kept working through the bombing, Deanna thought. Seeing it made the daily heroism real.

The footpath was dust grey, except for pools of blood, and half a teddy bear.

Miraculously their car still stood where they had left it, grey with dust instead of black, its windows shattered.

'Bugger,' said the driver. She pulled out thick gloves and began to punch the glass free.

Deanna took off a shoe to help, standing one legged like an ostrich. She put the shoe back on as the driver swept the back seat free of shards. The car started.

The driver swore again, this time with relief. She carefully drove between the ambulances, around women with faces of dust and blood. The brawny woman sat in the gutter, her face blank, her body rocking with sobs. Had her home gone, or a friend or loved one? Deanna knew the driver wouldn't stop to ask.

This happens every night, she thought, and sometimes the day too. Life would stop entirely if everyone paused to help or try to make order from the debris. You did your assigned job, and you got used to it.

And that was the true horror, she realised. You got used to things. These East Enders got used to flying houses spitting rubble that killed or maimed. She had become used to secrecy — she hadn't even asked the name of the driver who shared this danger with her.

Sheep? thought Deanna. Then I am one of them. But when your country is fighting for its existence, and the time to prevent it had long past, what could you do?

Be vigilant for the rest of your life, to see the crossroads where one road might lead to war, and another peace, or justice or simply co-existence, for as long as possible.

The car finally emerged into an area that seemed free of bomb damage, apart from taped or boarded-up windows. Sandbags lined the roads; anti-aircraft guns occupied a park which had perhaps held swings.

They stopped opposite the steps down to a basement flat. Deanna smelled Irish stew when the driver opened the front door. The living room looked like a living room — the sofa held a sleeping bag, two gas masks, and a large cardboard box containing cartons of cigarettes. The driver ushered her into the bedroom, which was not a bedroom but an office, with a desk, more cardboard boxes, a telephone, and a man.

Uncle Jasper. If his snake was in his pocket it didn't appear.

He stood politely. 'Thank you for coming, Lady Deanna. Any trouble on the way?' he asked the driver.

'Just busted windows and windscreen.'

'Good. Thank you.'

The driver closed the door behind her.

Uncle Jasper passed Deanna a wet handkerchief. She supposed he must keep a supply in his desk drawer. She wiped her face and saw a small streak of blood, but when she dabbed her face again no more appeared.

'A nip of brandy?'

'No, thank you. It's not ... not the same as reading about it in the newspapers.'

'No. First of all, Lady Deanna, thank you for your service.'

'I wish I could say it was a pleasure, but I'm glad to have been of use. Would you like the pistol back?'

'No. You may need it again.' He lifted a hand as she opened her mouth to question him. 'I see no particular reason why you should. The enemy know that the people guarding your cellar will stop any incursion. Ah, before I forget.' He passed her a sealed envelope.

She stared at it, hoping he didn't think she expected to be paid.

'Petrol coupons,' he said. 'For the petrol you have expended for a good cause and will undoubtedly do again.' He smiled faintly. 'You do not use the black market.'

'Thank you.' She put it in her handbag, still clean inside thanks to a tight clasp. Did he know about the diamonds? Probably not, for there'd been no reason to spy on her grandfather. 'What will the public be told about the duke's disappearance?'

'Nothing. No announcement is made when a man is sent back to active service. There will be a small notice in a few months saying he is missing in action again. If your cousin is alive at the end of the war, he will return. If not ...' Uncle Jasper shrugged. 'There's another reason for your presence. The man who is not your cousin has told us nothing, not even his name. You'll understand what we want to know, of course — details of the plan, the people involved ...'

'Whether the Duke of Windsor truly fancied himself Bonnie Prince Charlie, coming over the sea, this time successfully? I can tell you that, at least. Donnie ... or whatever his name is ... told me that they expected full cooperation.' She repeated the details he had given her.

Uncle Jasper stared at her, expressionless. 'You realise, of course, that this never happened? I'm glad the others involved believe you were simply capturing German spies. You can never speak of the Duke of Windsor's role. Not even to Robyn, nor to your husband if you marry. It must never be known that a king of England was prepared to betray his country, to bomb it into submission so he could regain the throne.'

'Very well.' Let David Windsor wither into insignificance. It was, after all, his most appropriate role. She saw no reason to tell Uncle Jasper that she had already told Sam.

'The prisoner has said he wishes to speak to you. We have no reason to grant him a favour, except it is possible he may say something of use. He's asked for a private meeting, but we will be listening, and he will expect that.'

'I understand. Where is he?'

'Down the hall.' He rang a small bell on the table. Deanna almost expected a parlourmaid to respond.

Instead, two young men in army fatigues appeared. One carried a battery lamp. He unlocked the door opposite. It led to a corridor, blank, dark and concrete, with no pretence of habitation. The doors were metal. They passed four before the men halted, unlocked the fifth, then stood back.

The room was windowless and dark, except for the light from their lamp, and cold. She wished she still had her overcoat. The soldier turned up the lamp, exploding the room with too much light for its barrenness. She saw a small solid table, and two plain wooden chairs, a concrete floor, walls and ceiling, all unmarked.

The man who was not Donnie sat on the one chair facing the door, blinking in the sudden light, his manacled hands resting on the table. His ankles were chained too. He looked thinner, and his hair was longer, and lighter at the roots, with a pale fuzz at the front where he must have shaved it to achieve Donnie's high forehead.

'We'll be just outside the door, miss,' said one of the soldiers, placing the lamp on the floor near the door so the room's shadows danced.

Miss, she thought. They don't know who I am.

'Dee,' said the man who was not Donnie. 'I'm glad you came.'

She didn't say she had been given neither choice nor notice of the visit.

She sat opposite him. 'I'd like explanations.'

'Not an apology?'

She considered. 'No. You acted for your country in wartime, and you had reason to think I'd be sympathetic. I suspect at times you even told me the truth. I'd like more truth, please. What to call you, to start with.'

'Kurt.'

'So you really are German?'

'Most definitely.' He smiled grimly at her. 'I studied in the USA, however, and later worked in the German embassy there. I assume that whoever is listening to us will now eventually find out who I am, or was, which is good, as one day my family will learn I died honourably. You know your people will shoot me? Soon, I expect.'

'I was told they'd hang you.'

'The English are so short of ammunition then?' The American accent was tinged with a German one too, now.

'What about Donnie?' she asked urgently. 'Is he alive?'

'No. We didn't execute him — he was badly wounded, but he lived for another two weeks after he was captured. I'm not sure who came up with the plot for me to impersonate him. It was sheer luck that we looked so similar. I would never have passed with anyone who knew him well so I had to be careful not to meet anyone he served with once he arrived in England.'

'How did you find out so much about him?'

'He believed he was in a French hospital, under German control, which was in fact the truth. He wanted to talk — quite badly — to someone he thought was a fellow American. I was given appropriate wounds. The stitching made them seem like a major injury.'

'But the lost fingers were real.'

'I had to be safely beyond combat again. Your cousin and I shared a room, two Yanks who had volunteered. He told me all about the castle he'd inherited. He loved the place. I gather you and he had a magic summer playing there. He would have returned but the old duke didn't invite him again, possibly because of his illness. Your Donnie was full of plans for the place after the war. He was not a banker like his father, and I think not a soldier either. He cried when he knew he was dying and would not see Claverton again.'

She bit back tears herself. She didn't know why it mattered but it did. The man who had inherited Claverton had loved it. She hoped the next duke would too, but it did not seem likely.

'He'd recently broken up with a girl he'd expected to marry, then been involved with a married woman who simply wanted an affair. I think he hoped you'd resume your childhood friendship.' The wry smile appeared again. 'That made it very easy for *me* to resume it.'

'He didn't know you planned to impersonate him?'

'Of course not.'

And yet Donnie had given him at least three pieces of misinformation, presumably hoping she'd notice. She suspected this was only part of the truth. But which part?

'How did he die?'

'Gangrene. We truly did all we could to keep him alive.' He shrugged. 'Alive, he could give us information.'

A hideous, painful death. Deanna forced herself not to cry. 'If you give names of British sympathisers, they will probably let you live.'

'I know. Nothing I have told you this afternoon will be of any use to them.'

'This is goodbye then.' She didn't know what she felt, and then she did. Regret, and a deep sadness — for yes, she had liked him, and he would not have offered the information about Donnie's love for Claverton if he had not liked her. Two patriots, working undercover for their countries.

He had not betrayed her — though he would have, if he'd known she was anti-fascist — but she had betrayed him.

'I'm sorry, Kurt. After the war — which we will win, because we will not surrender — I'll find your family and tell them of your bravery.'

'When we win — because you are outnumbered and blockaded and America will never enter the war — tell them I had happy days picnicking by a river, and a final Christmas with laughter and a kiss under the mistletoe.'

'But you had neither.'

He smiled. 'They do not need to know that.'

She stood, walked around the table, and kissed his cheek. He lifted his finger then wrote an address on the table, lifting his eyebrows to make sure she understood. This was something the listeners could not hear, nor could they read.

She nodded to show she did understand, then knocked on the door. It opened. She left, while behind her the soldier took the lantern, leaving the prisoner once again in darkness.

Twenty-Six

Rhubarb Blancmange

INGREDIENTS
one sachet gelatine
one cup water
two cups chopped rhubarb, stewed in a little water
one tablespoon flour
one tablespoon powdered milk
two tablespoons honey or sugar if available

METHOD
Heat the gelatine till dissolved in the water. Add the other ingredients and mix well. Leave in a cool place until half set, then beat thoroughly till it is light and airy. You will find it deliciously creamy!

Recipe from the
Claverton Major Gazette 1941

Uncle Jasper waited with a pot of tea. The electricity must be back on again. An unlimited tea ration seemed to go with the job. He stood politely.

This time she poured them both tea as soon as she sat down, added milk and sugared her cup well, and didn't speak till she had drunk. She put the cup in its saucer, took a sandwich — it was either mock cheese or fish paste. It seemed that unrationed departmental luxury only stretched as far as tea.

'Well,' she said curtly. 'You heard all that? Is there anything further you wish to ask me?'

'No. I need to warn you though that anything he told you may not be true. Your cousin, in particular, may still be alive if the Germans can use him, possibly in a prisoner exchange. Lady Deanna, the three girls you are fostering ...'

'Are German, and Jewish. Yes. They told me, and they say they don't have an aunt and uncle. I believe them. I think of them as my daughters.'

'The girls are telling you the truth. The man who called himself Kurt did not.'

A little of her guilt and sorrow seeped away. 'Go on.'

'There are no aunt and uncle. As far as we can tell the girls have no relatives who might claim them. They were taken straight to a council orphanage in London when they were released from hospital.'

Her poor daughters! 'Surely there were some relatives or friends of their parents who would have taken the girls after the accident? Families of their schoolfriends?'

'If there are relatives no one remembers them visiting England; nor did the family ever leave England on holiday. Their parents had friends, certainly, but the accident happened when the Grunbergs were holidaying in Devon just before war was declared. The girls were severely injured and hospitalised for months too. They didn't tell you this?'

She had seen scars but assumed they were from beatings at the orphanage. 'They've told me almost nothing beyond their names, and that they are German, and Jewish, as Hitler defines it, not by religion, and lived in Oxford for a time. I haven't asked for more.' Her daughters needed time to put their former lives behind them.

'Possibly — probably — someone at the orphanage used the threat of being interned if they misbehaved. They may even have been told they could be sent back to Germany and shipped to a labour camp for Jewish prisoners. That might be why they escaped to a different train from the other orphanage children. Certainly they'd have suffered because of their name, both because it is German and due to antisemitism.'

'They said their parents were killed in a car crash.'

'Yes. Their father was a professor of German literature, and their mother had completed her PhD in chemistry. All three girls were born in England, and there is no record that they ever visited Germany. The girls were still hospitalised in Devon when their parents were buried in Oxford. I've had enquiries made. Their colleagues and neighbours liked the family, but quickly became vague when asked what had happened to the children, assuring us that family or friends must have taken them.'

'None of them tried to make sure?'

'Lady Deanna, I suspect they were very careful not to make sure. Few families would want to take on three children, especially those with German–Jewish names. At the very least they'd be risking their own families facing the anti-German prejudice of the last war. They might even have their loyalty questioned, if they had been so close to a German family.' He shrugged again. 'They'd also be aware the girls might be interned when the war began.'

'But they won't be?' Deanna asked anxiously.

'No. The girls are British citizens by birth, and, even if they were not, I doubt they could ever be seen as a security risk. You wish to adopt them?'

'Yes.'

'Then there is one gift we can offer you, at least.' He passed another envelope over to her. 'The approvals have all been signed. All that is lacking is your own signature. If and when you wish, your lawyer can finalise the adoption.'

She stared, not quite believing, then tore open the envelope, scanned the papers, scrawled her signature in five places, dated the pages, and passed them to him to witness.

He rang the bell and handed the papers to the soldier who entered. 'Could you please co-witness our guest's signature?' He waited till the man had signed and left.

'Thank you,' she said again.

Uncle Jasper smiled. 'It's a convenient gift when others do all the work. I think it prudent if I remain your Uncle Jasper for the duration,' he added. 'Keep writing to me, though not necessarily as often, and I'll arrange for appropriate replies. If you do hear anything it will probably be misinformation, given to you deliberately. Do pass it on, with the details of whoever gave it to you and those they mixed with. You have the phone number and address if you need to contact me again outside of that, but hopefully you won't. The Germans know the main agents in this affair have vanished, and will presume them killed. I doubt they will try to use your cave again.'

'I'm glad.'

'Your best use to Britain now is to grow potatoes.' He smiled. 'It's been a pleasure to work with you, Lady Deanna. After the war perhaps we can meet under different circumstances. Your grandfather and I were close friends from childhood.'

'I don't remember meeting you. You didn't even visit him towards the end. No one visited him.'

He looked at her, perhaps surprised she needed this explained. 'He was a proud man, and wished to be remembered as he was before his illness. I'd have come anyway, but by then he had suggested your employment. If I had come to Claverton you'd have known my name, and others might have connected you with me. I have gone to some trouble to keep my position discreet.'

She raised an eyebrow. 'It would only take a phone call or two to find the true name of a student called Chummy at Harrow.'

'And you won't make those calls. Your grandfather said you had a good eye, and a way of drawing people out, but loved the land too much to go to university or consider a position that might take you away from Claverton for long.'

'He provided for me well,' said Deanna lightly.

'Another sandwich?'

She took one, aware her body needed fuel, and wondering if she would be in time for the last train.

'Lady Deanna, there is one thing more. I say this both as Uncle Jasper and your grandfather's friend. Do not continue your friendship with Flight Lieutenant Murray.'

She looked at him sharply. 'You can't believe Sam is a spy!'

'No. But it is possible that soon his sympathies may be … divided.'

'You will need to give me more than that,' she said coldly.

He spread his hands. 'I can't. Nor can I forbid you to see him. I am merely warning you in my official capacity, and as your grandfather's friend, to limit the time you spend with him, and certainly any intimacy with him.'

She considered for a moment. 'Thank you for your warning.'

'Will you take it?'

'To some extent. I won't share anything with him that might be useful to the enemy, but then from now on I am unlikely to have any information of use. Flight Lieutenant Murray is far better situated to be an informant than me. Why do you let him continue in his position if you don't trust him?'

'He is a superb instructor; nor do we have any evidence his sympathies are divided yet.' He glanced at his wristwatch. 'The car will take you home.'

'Thank you.' She stood, holding the papers to her chest. 'Thank you too for these. I'll send them to my lawyer tomorrow.'

'I could arrange it ... No? Then by all means, give them to your lawyer.'

He knows I don't trust him, either, thought Deanna. She suspected lies came to him as easily as they did to the man who called himself Kurt.

Had Uncle Jasper really been a friend of her grandfather's? Was this really the 'Chummy' Grandpa had spoken of? An adoption of three daughters that had not quite passed its final stage would be an excellent way to persuade Lady Deanna Claverton to take on ... almost anything, if the powers that be thought she, or her title, might be useful again.

I have daughters, she thought, exultation rising as she realised what had happened. I have a family, and a home. I have a friend to share this with — no, two friends, for Mrs Thripps had passed into the realm of 'friend' now, and yes, I trust Sam far more than anyone in this intelligence tangle.

Sam is my friend, and more ...

And the man in the room next door?

I do not know him, she thought. I do not know how much of what he said was true or false. I do not even know if his name is Kurt, or if Donnie is dead, or even if Donnie's last thoughts were of Claverton. That is what I would have liked, and that man guessed it. I will allow myself a small amount of grief for him, but only that. He gave his life for his country.

Or had he? Country was a nebulous word. Had Kurt been fighting for the right of German Nazis to rule the world? She loved the land itself, not a nation. War was not good for eagles, or woodland. The land itself suffered because humans made war.

War encompassed them. But she would see Dr Hilyard before she left London, even if it meant Uncle Jasper would guess why she had asked her driver to take a detour on their way to her home. She would find a bookshop for gifts for her daughters, too. This was a time to focus on the living.

Twenty-Seven

Let no tears add to their hardships
As the soldiers pass along,
And although your heart is breaking
Make it sing this cheery song:
Keep the Home Fires Burning,
While your hearts are yearning ...
Lyrics from 'Keep the Home Fires Burning'
by Ivor Novello with words
by Lena Guilbert Ford

War soared above them: English Spitfires, Dutch Fokkers or German Focke-Wulfs and Messerschmitts. War meant ploughed land that had belonged to field mice and butterflies, grass snakes and beetles. War stole the icing from wedding cakes, the toys from shops, the clang of church bells on Sunday. War snatched people loved, or those who had been an integral part of a loved community, valued only when they disappeared.

War gave telegram boys nightmares reliving the anguish on the faces of those they had handed yellow envelopes of *dead, missing in action* or *believed captured*.

War brought men in expensive suits and bowler hats to discussions around polished tables — where a president's wife dared to change the fortunes of the world: Mrs Roosevelt's campaign finally succeeded when Congress passed the Lend-Lease Act in March 1941, authorising the president to lend war supplies to nations whose defence he deemed vital to American security. Roosevelt quietly provided limited military support as well.

War, however, did not have the power to halt spring at Claverton. Bright green leaves wriggled out of fattened buds, flowers dappled the early crabapple trees, and the brown leaves of a certain dell turned into a bluebell carpet, its shades changing with the breeze.

And, this dusk, war did not stop a mother badger completing her spring cleaning.

Five faces — one sticky with jam — peered through the bracken in the twilight as the family lay on their stomachs on the hill. 'Look! There she is,' Anna whispered to Deanna.

'Her cubs are coming out. Three of them!' Sam was as excited as the girls, as exultant as Deanna.

The badger nosed back into her hole to emerge with a ball of bracken, which she pushed away; she then repeated the process.

'The babies are playing!' The Amazing Anna looked entranced as the cubs bit each other, twisted and rolled. 'They're doing Roll Me Over in the Clover and Do it Again.'

'Anna! Where did you hear that?' Deanna kept her whisper stern as Sam didn't quite manage to smother a laugh.

'Billie at school sings it.'

'Billie shouldn't. It's rude.'

'Why?'

'Shhh,' hissed Magda. 'They'll hear you.'

They watched in silence as darkness thickened across the hill. It was almost midnight, but daylight saving had stretched the dusk.

By the time the mother badger had her sett cleaned to her satisfaction, the Amazing Anna was already asleep, curled in the grass like a dormouse. Sam quietly picked her up and carried her when they went back to the house.

'Thank you,' he said, once the girls were in bed. 'That was wonderful. I thought badgers would be like wombats, but they're totally different.'

'How?'

'I'm not sure, apart from the shape of course. I'd say more intelligent, but if a wombat wants to it can solve almost any problem, like how to use a lever to move the stone you've put in the hole it made to get to the vegetable garden.'

'Do you shoot them?' she asked, with slight trepidation.

'No. Dad puts in wombat gates — heavy bits of wire and metal that wombats can push through but lambs can't. My great-grandmother used to say grass seeds lasted in wombat and kangaroo dung in a drought even when the ground is bare. It might be true — our paddocks come back with grass when most of the neighbours' are weeds.'

'It's hard to imagine a time so dry all the grass dies,' she said slowly.

He smiled at her. 'You can see the bones of the land then. After all, the grass dies in winter here and all the leaves fall — English winters are more barren than Australian droughts. The land just has different ways of resting.'

'True. But we can have fireplaces to keep us warm in winter.'

'We have the river to swim in — it melts from the mountains so it's always cold and never completely runs dry — and verandas to keep the sun from the windows and to catch the breeze so you can put your boots up with a cold beer in your hand and yarn the afternoon away till it cools down enough for the dogs to wake up and it's time to check the sheep. Speaking of dogs, where's Dusty?'

'He's taken to sleeping next to Anna, now they sleep in their own rooms. But if you'd like a biscuit, he might suddenly appear.'

Sam laughed. 'Let him sleep, but yes, I'd like a biscuit. How old is he?'

'You know, I never asked?' She opened the biscuit tin, kept full now with a house of daughters. They were oat and cob nut crunchies today. 'He arrived when I was at boarding school, a long-legged puppy when I first met him, chewing up my school shoes. I suppose he's fifteen or so, maybe more.'

'Thank you for sharing your dog with me. And your family and home and tonight. I think,' he added lightly, 'you may even have saved my life.'

'I don't understand.'

He looked at the window, not at her, even though the darkness was covered by the blackout curtain. 'I spend my days, or nights, training boys to charge the enemy as if the war were a football match, and if I train them well, they win a dozen matches, and then they die. Somewhere in Germany there's a man much like me, thinking just the same way.

'We are killing people night after night and it will make no difference at all to the progress of the war. Each killing just makes the other side more determined to get revenge ...'

That fit with what her grandfather had said about the Great War: millions killed in order to win a few yards of space, but to no purpose. The war had ended because German troops refused to fight but went home to help feed their families.

'Why do we keep spending so many lives and so much money on bombs then?'

'Because the fool who is Commander-in-Chief of Bomber Command, Arthur Harris, is wedded to an outdated strategy that has been shown to be useless. I doubt he has the imagination to see that war might be fought in any other way. Sorry, he's probably your cousin or something.'

'No relation, but it wouldn't matter if he was.'

'Sometime, a year or so ago, we became our own enemy,' he said softly. 'And we do not even know it.'

She remembered Uncle Jasper warning her that Sam's alliances might change. Was this what he meant? That Sam might become a pacifist? But what if he did? Pacifists grew potatoes or worked as medical orderlies. They were no danger to the defence of the realm. They simply did not kill.

'You don't think we should be fighting?' she asked.

'Ask me an easy one, like how to make water boil without a kettle. No, I don't think we should be fighting, but once we began to fight, or, rather, once the men who do the deciding agreed that we should fight, then we have to keep fighting it because losing would be worse.'

She looked at him with trepidation. The thought that haunted her sometimes returned — only sometimes, because in this war and with three daughters her body was too tired to wake too often at two am. What if she had made that bargain with Kurt? Had told him, 'I know you're not my cousin, but if you and I can help stop this war with a treaty you may use my house, my name and all my contacts. I will even persuade David if he baulks at the last minute.'

Perhaps, possibly, even probably, the deaths would have stopped, at least in Britain. But not in Russia, Poland, France, or across the world as Hitler stamped out his Third Reich.

'Do you really think we shouldn't try to stop Hitler?'

He looked surprised. 'Of course! But the time to do that was in 1919, when the French tricked the Germans into a treaty that wasn't what they'd agreed to at the ceasefire. Or maybe we could have stopped him in 1925 when Germany was starving, trying to pay French reparations, or in 1933 when he grabbed power, or the League of Nations stepped in to stop him re-arming. Even a drover's dog could see that Germany meant war. By 1938 it was far too late.'

'Why didn't we?'

'Dee, love, you're the one with second cousins in the House of Lords. You tell me. But I'll tell you one thing — men who've fought a bushfire together back home tend to patch up their feuds.'

'Work for good together?' He just called me 'love', she thought.

He frowned. 'I dunno. It's not as simple as that. But governments have got used to solving problems by going "bang" at each other or hacking with swords. What if they asked, "How can we stop evil?" Because once you've fired the first shot, you've lost the war. No one will truly win this, Dee. This war is just continuing the Great War and that was just following Crimea and Waterloo. This war will lead to other wars.'

'You studied history?' she said, surprised by how deeply he had theorised.

He grinned tiredly at her. 'I studied sheep. I plan to study them again. But I had some good teachers. I doubt the boys at Harrow or Eton get as good a schooling as I got at Budgie Central. In fact, I know they didn't, or we'd not be in this mess now. Miss Lee came to us from the history department at a university because she'd never have got a wage as good, being a woman, anywhere else. She told us you can't know where you are if you don't know where you've been, and if you don't know where you are you'll end up going in the wrong direction. Which is what we're doing now.'

She sat silent, bending automatically to rub Dusty's ears. He had indeed heard the biscuit tin open and knew Sam would indulge him.

Grandpa believed we were eagles, she thought, able to look down and see what was right even if the majority disagreed. Maybe she and Sam could see this war more clearly than the field marshals. But eagle vision didn't necessarily show you how to run the world, nor even how to survive, she realised. If it did, then golden eagles wouldn't nearly be extinct while humanity crowded the planet, despite war after war. 'How do we turn round?'

'Just now? I don't think we can. Just hope that when a bushfire strikes the whole world, we work together to put it out and end with handshakes instead of enemies.'

How could Uncle Jasper doubt this man? Deanna thought. Sam had more integrity, a greater sense of duty, than anyone she'd met.

Sam stood. 'And now I'd better get back to showing lads who don't even have to shave every day how to land in a parachute in the dark when their plane's on fire, and hope they get a chance to use the knowledge.'

He hesitated, then kissed her hand. 'You really have saved my life.'

She dimmed the lamp so he could slip between the blackout curtains without showing a glimpse of light an enemy pilot might use to coordinate his position.

Twenty-Eight

Butter rationing getting you down? Try this clever trick! Butter the underside of the bread instead, so the butter rests on your tongue. It will seem twice as thick and just as moist!

Helpful Hints from the Ministry of Food, 1941

Pig manure was as good for potatoes as cow manure. It just stinks more, Deanna thought ruefully, as one of the land girls drove the tractor down the furrows while she shovelled last year's pig shit, composted with sawdust, on either side.

Skylarks laughed above them, rising and falling through the sunlit air as if amazed that humans would put themselves to so much effort.

A rhythmic undercurrent followed by infrequent crashes indicated the Women's Land Army were cutting down more trees in the Claverton woods.

Two of the female forestry workers had stayed at Eagle's Rest for a few days till the local Women's Hostel had been completed, among so many other efficiency huts springing up within days beside cottages and hedges that had taken years to build and would last hundreds more. But England didn't have time to build structures with endurance or beauty now. The land girls had assured Deanna that the only wood taken was straight, tall trees, not the ancient ones with twisted branches and deep hollows where owls and squirrels nested.

But every tree lost meant trampling bluebells or snowdrops, potentially disturbing the myriad species that nested there. And every mature tree cut down was one more that would never *become* twisted and hollowed and aged, a shelter for the birds and animals to come ... if there were still homes for them, food for them, land that had not been taken for the hungry beast called war.

Three years ago all this area had been woodland, despite her grandmother grandly referring to it as 'the Park'. Now it resembled the parkland she had wished it to be, though she would have shuddered at the tree stumps and lack of stately avenues.

The surplus branches, however, were a welcome source of firewood. She and Sam and the girls had hauled them home, and Sam and Deanna chopped them with the crosscut saw into lengths that would fit the fireplace or the wood stove when they dried in a year's time.

By December 1941 nightly Blitzkrieg bombing had ended. Bombs continued to fall, though now usually only on strategic targets, aerodromes, factories and the port cities. But far away an air strike by Japan destroyed the US fleet stationed at Hawaii.

President Roosevelt finally had the popular backing he and his wife had campaigned for to declare war, not just on Japan but on the entire German–Italian–Japanese Axis.

At the Women's Institute, in the Reverend Goodword's sermons, in the grocer's shop, people no longer spoke of 'keeping on', but of winning.

It felt immoral to be glad of the devastation of the American fleet, but for the first time, as her family sat with Sam and the

Thrippses in church on Christmas Day, Deanna felt that it was possible to pray for 'the end of the war'. One day, though years away, there would be the peace of victory instead of the subjugation of defeat.

Half a year later, Hitler invaded Russia, making his major ally an enemy.

The British people rejoiced. Men shouted each other pints of weak war beer in pubs. The invasion of Britain was postponed until the Russian campaign had been won. Russia, after all, was Hitler's chief fear and hatred, after the Jews.

The war staggered on. A deeper than usual midsummer haze softened the twilight this year, the float-fine debris of bombing, of shattered concrete that crumbled even more as the months went by, of land freshly ploughed that blew to dust, as well as of the usual wheat pollen.

Deanna switched from potatoes to peas to rest the land a little, though stringing up the vines and picking the pods was as back-breaking as digging up potatoes.

She still woke to the alarm clock in the mornings, in almost dark, misty midsummer dawns, swearing under her breath at the 'Double Summer Time' that gave much longer evenings to townies planting turnips in their gardens and allotments, but for her meant continuing to get up before the sun, even at this time of year, as well as feeling the duty to keep working later. She was tired. Everyone was tired now.

She resented leaving sleep even more this morning. She'd had the dream again.

She lit the lamp, then glanced at the painting Sam had given her. Yes, those were exactly the same cliffs. But the dream hadn't told her what lay beyond them. Would Sam tell her if she confessed just how often she had seen those cliffs?

There was no time to dwell on it. The girls were already dressing. Dusty deigned to jump down from Anna's bed just as the smell of breakfast drifted up and made his way downstairs. Omelettes for everyone, Dusty too — the hens were laying again now the days were longer — and toast with rhubarb stewed with the last of the Sturmer Pippin apples. Deanna preferred porridge, but porridge brought back too many orphanage memories for her daughters: porridge for breakfast, bread and margarine for lunch, cabbage and potato stew for tea and, twice a week, a dessert of tapioca and prunes.

She finally got all three girls out the door, and then dashed in again when Rosa remembered her homework. She waved them off down the lane.

And she had a morning off. Even the vegetable weeding and woodpile were up to date, thanks to Sam and his colleagues from the base, who claimed they enjoyed sawing logs, splitting them and stacking them, especially when thanked with sponge cake topped with strawberries and cream.

She spent the time checking her rabbit snares.

She was striding down the headland, two fat rabbits in hand, already gutted — the eagles would scorn such small fare but the stoats and foxes might enjoy it — when she saw Sam's bicycle pull up at the shed. She waved, the day no longer grey despite the clouds, and held up the rabbits in triumph, the gas mask bumping at her hip. A chlorine gas raid was almost impossible here, especially with the wind from the sea, but 'Lady Deanna' must set an example.

'How are you at skinning rabbits?' she called.

He made a face. 'Are you joking? Deb and I used to trap them by the hundred. We got good money for the fur.'

She looked at him enquiringly. It was bad form to discuss money, but she had assumed that as he'd competed in European air races his family must be comfortably off. He understood her glance. 'Dad believes kids need to learn hard yakka.'

'Yakka?'

'Work.' He grinned. 'I need to teach you some dinkum Aussie. Come on, I'll help you skin them, but to be honest, I won't miss your stewed bunny when I'm on duty tonight. I'll have a gift for you next week,' he added lightly.

'More dripping?'

'That's up to Deb. No, one of my mates put me onto a Pig Club. Porky's for the chop. The farmer gets the hindquarter and I get a forequarter.'

Pig Clubs were encouraged by the government as a way of turning scraps into meat, though half of each animal had to be surrendered to the Ministry of Food.

'What would you like done with it?' she asked.

'I wouldn't mind an invitation to dinner.'

'Ha. You've got your legs under our table when you're off duty anyway. I meant how would you like it cooked?'

'No idea. Roast pork?'

'Roast it is, and I'll pickle the rest. No,' she added, as he made a face. 'You'll love pickled pork. It's like juicier ham. I can smoke it if you'd rather, but that takes months.'

And 'months' was what they might not have. Every time they parted, she wondered if she'd see him again. Training roles were relatively safe, but nothing and no one had true security in war.

As if to emphasise her thought the air-raid siren echoed from the church tower. The siren had been heard more often lately, as the German bombers scouted the land before proceeding to their intended targets. She glanced up at the sky, still empty apart from swallows industriously darting after flies.

'Nothing to worry about,' he assured her. 'They'll be passing through to one of the ports.'

She nodded, vaguely uneasy. The only local target, the airfield, must already have spotted the intruder and prepared to attack if they came closer.

Nonetheless, they made for the cellar, leaving the rabbit carcasses in the refrigerator and collecting a lantern, which Deanna lit, in case the electricity went off.

Dusty followed, both for the biscuit he knew Deanna kept in her pocket when she wanted his obedience, and also because, despite the awkwardness of steep stairs for lanky canine legs, the cellar had interesting smells including a flitch of bacon, a Christmas gift from the Higginses' own Pig Club, sadly hung too high for even Dusty's lankiness to reach.

'Tea?' She gestured to the gas ring. 'Or there's whisky, port, Miss Enid's sherry, a fifty-year-old collection of Bordeaux and Burgundies — my grandfather wouldn't have a white wine served at his table. Homemade cherry cordial or water?'

'Better stick to the cherry cordial. I'll be flying again in ten hours.' He lowered himself into an armchair, looking exhausted.

'Sam? What's wrong?'

He forced himself to smile. 'Nothing but the usual.' He settled back in the armchair. 'Looks like this raid will be longer than we thought. Mind if I have forty winks before I get back to pretending to young men that they may survive long enough to use what I teach them?'

'Of course. Use one of the mattresses — they're made up fresh. I'll read till ...' She stopped as the cellar vibrated. 'What was that?'

He stood, suddenly alert, then ran to the top of the stairs and pushed the door ajar. 'Bombs. Dee, stay where you are.'

She could hear the sound more clearly now, thunder upon thunder. 'That's coming from the village!'

'More than one bomber too,' he said grimly. 'I'll have a look. Stay downstairs till I'm back.'

'Don't be ridiculous.' She ran after him, out through the library, the kitchen, then the back door.

The explosions had stopped. Instead, a vast pall of dust and smoke rose above the trees below them. Already the enemy planes were a black-dotted star retreating across the ocean. A single British Spitfire headed back to the aerodrome, clearly launched too late to have stopped the invaders.

'The school,' Deanna whispered. She darted indoors, grabbed the car keys, shut Dusty inside and wrenched the garage doors open. Sam automatically reached to take the keys from her, then opened the passenger seat when it was obvious she intended to drive.

The All Clear sounded. But it is not all clear, thought Deanna: ambulance and police car bells sounded as they neared the village. She could hear screams, now, too, and people shouting orders.

She turned another corner. The library was rubble, the butcher's shop a strangely bare block as if the shop had simply been lifted away, and where the school had been there was a single crumbling wall and flames that caught and flared higher as they ate the timber.

Twenty-Nine

A child's doll, blankly smiling with wide eyes ...
He holds it, puzzled; wondering, where is she
The small mother
Whose pleasure was to clothe it and caress,
Who hugged it with a motherhood foreknown ...
No one replies.

Extract from 'The Burning of the Leaves'
by Laurence Binyon
The Atlantic Magazine

'I saw Miss Hannaford's hand,' Rosa whispered, clutching Deanna on the sofa at Eagle's Rest, a blanket wrapped round her, Dusty at her feet. Anna was snuggled on Deanna's other side.

'She might be just knocked unconscious.' Deanna and the other villagers had ignored the danger and run to the school. They'd shepherded the children away from the burning debris to the pub and wrapped them in blankets, while Ted Bones, the publican, offered lemonade. The pub's cellars were the deepest shelters in the village, except for those at Eagle's Rest, which was too far away to be useful.

Rosa shook her head. 'Her body wasn't there. Just her hand.' She began to sob. 'It should have been bleeding, but it wasn't. I love Miss Hannaford. She's dead, isn't she? No one could lose a hand and be alive?'

'I don't know, darling.' Deanna held her more closely. Dusty whined, then stood and stretched to lick their hands.

Sam had driven the three of them back here, then swiftly taken her car back to the village to help ferry the injured to hospital, the dead to the morgue, and the pieces of bodies that would need to be identified as those still alive were counted.

Deanna had rung the base to ask if he could be replaced tonight, and then Magda's school to let her know her sisters were safe.

It is ironic, she thought in anguish, that the school held evacuees sent away from the death that dropped from the smog-filled city skies, only to have it find them among the fields and cottages of Claverton Minor.

Was Mrs Thripps safe? And Arnold? Sometimes the heat detonated unexploded bombs. Had all the children reached the trenches in time? Almost certainly not, if Miss Hannaford had run back despite the bullets spitting across the ground.

What cruelty could make the enemy attack a school, a library and Mr Filmer's butcher's shop? We will weep for this tragedy, and be angry, not wish to surrender, thought Deanna. War was more contagious than influenza. Once infected by it, if you survived it, recovery was slow.

'They bombed my coat,' said Anna in a small voice. 'My red coat with the fish buttons. I didn't have time to grab it.'

'It's all right, darling. We'll make new coats.'

'But it had fish buttons!' Anna suddenly burst into sobs.

'She can't remember getting new clothes with Mama and Papa,' Rosa said softly. 'Only the gingham and the secondhand ones in the orphanage. She really loved that coat ...'

Deanna would not cry. She must pretend that normal life — or at least a good life — would return. 'We're safe, and together, and nothing really matters except for that, and we'll make new coats — there are plenty of blankets in storage. We can give blankets to the Women's Institute to make coats for all the other children too. I even have a store of the most wonderful buttons.'

Rosa nodded. Anna cried small hiccupping sobs, her head pressed against Deanna. Dusty licked the small girl's face, then jumped off the sofa. He padded out.

Deanna wanted to ask questions. But questions would bring the horror close again.

Something brushed her knee. She looked down. Dusty had brought his lamb-shank bone — his most prized possession — and laid it on Anna's lap. He trotted back to give Rosa the old blanket he slept on by the stove, then settled himself on guard against sadness and other enemies by the foot of the sofa.

How could you not love a dog who gave all he owned for those he loved?

Deanna held her daughters closer.

Hawthorne's headmistress drove Magda home — a white-faced Magda, who clasped her sisters and began to cry the tears she had obviously refused to shed before. The three girls slept together that night for the first time since each had moved to her own room.

Deanna watched them from the doorway, lantern in hand — the electricity was still off. The barn owl hooted from the apple tree. She couldn't sleep, didn't know if she would ever sleep.

What had happened was impossible. Flames and shattered buildings belonged in London, or Dover, or Liverpool, not Claverton Minor.

And yet her mind kept seeing the bodies on the grass, the men and women with Red Cross armbands moving with quiet deliberation from person to person, marking who was dead, or needed immediate help, or who was injured but for whom treatment could wait. The fire brigade pumping valiantly — old men in faded uniforms, with a fire pump at least thirty years old, holding the hose, a grey-haired man with a limp ducking under a hole in a wall to search for survivors.

She should be there, helping. She had to be here, with her daughters.

The sound of the car woke her from her daze. She hurried downstairs to shade the kitchen lamp as Sam pushed the blackout curtain aside to come in. He looked filthy, exhausted. He nodded to her, clearly too tired even for greetings.

'You're all right? Is that blood?'

'What?' He looked down vaguely. 'Oh. Yes. Not mine.'

She desperately needed to ask how things were in the village, who was safe, or hurt or dead, but he looked too shocked and weary to answer.

'Have a bath while I put on some eggs and bacon,' she said gently. 'The hot water's from the stove, so there's still plenty.'

'Thank you. The girls?'

'Shocked. Asleep now, finally.'

He almost collapsed into a kitchen chair, ignoring the offer of a bath. 'The girls must have been low down in the far end of the dugout, thank goodness. They were lucky.'

'Others weren't …?' she asked in trepidation.

'Four kids were hit by bullets or debris at the end of the trench nearest the school. The ambulance drivers think that three just need stitches, but one will need surgery — Dickie someone?'

'Dickie Murtagh.' His parents owned the grocery store.

'One little girl killed — Kitty, one of the evacuees staying with Doris from the telephone exchange. Don't know how she died — no sign of injury. The teacher was killed too — someone said she couldn't see the groundsman in the trench, and so she ran back to get him. Apparently, he's deaf. She must have been caught in the blast. There's no sign of her body. It must have burned.'

Except a hand, thought Deanna.

'The groundsman's fine — he'd already left to help the fire brigade. Dee, those old men held the hoses and bashed with wet sacks for hours, though all of them must have been worried about their families. The women ... the women were wonderful, no uniforms, just aprons or pinnies, helping people, sorting body parts as if they were preparing vegetables for a stew. Not one of them even cried. They just ... kept going.'

Now he had begun it seemed he couldn't stop. 'Mr Filmer's safe — he'd stepped out into the lane to guide the delivery van. The van driver's face and hands were cut by flying glass. It missed his eyes, thank goodness. About half the butchery customers managed to get to the pub shelter and most of the people in the library too. The librarian ... white hair in a fringe?'

Deanna nodded.

'She just sat in the road while the library burned, crying, refusing to move. The firemen kept telling her there'd be no books left in that blaze, and even if there were the water would have ruined them.'

He shut his eyes for a moment. 'They didn't try to move her, even though she was in the way. They just let her grieve.'

'The WI meeting room can be the library for now. The village can have the castle's library — it's in storage in one of the sheds. We can supplement it with some more modern ones, and I'm sure others will contribute too. I'll sort it out tomorrow.'

Or rather, she would call Mrs Goodword, and tell her the solution, and about the blankets, because every other child would have lost their coat too, and their schoolbag. She'd let Mrs Goodword sort out the details. The girls needed Deanna at home tomorrow.

She'd need to ring the hospital to see how Dickie was — his family would expect to be told that 'Lady Deanna rang'. She'd contact every family who had been directly affected, taking them flowers or fruit, but not for a few days, till the shock had worn off, when she would be the unofficial 'someone' who showed that those of the castle still cared.

Magda, Rosa and Anna needed to help too. Helping others was the best way to recover from shock and grief. That and watching the eagle balancing on the wind, the river tumbling over stones then sinking to deep pools, the badger cleaning out the old bracken from her sett now that the weather was warming — the world's beauty so different from the savagery of humans. Eagles preyed, but only for food, and nothing else. Few animals struck blindly at their own species like humanity.

'Why?' she demanded fiercely, though of all people Sam didn't deserve the question, and especially not now. 'Why bomb a school? There were bullets too, so it wasn't just a single plane unloading because they were running out of fuel.'

'No, the school was the target,' Sam said, fondling Dusty's ears as the grey dog laid his head on Sam's filthy lap. 'There were four bombers, so they must have thought it was something major. The school's in an old cider factory, isn't it? I think that was it. Someone in a crew passing above and seeing lots of activity must have assumed it was still a factory — it's near the train line too.'

'But surely once they were closer they realised it was a school ...'

'They probably did realise,' he said quietly. 'There was only one run of bullets. Somewhere back in Germany there are men like me who know they bombed a school and killed children. I'll have that bath now, Dee, love.'

She went to him, and held him, just as she had held the girls. His arms went around her too. It was entirely passionless, and yet she felt closer to him, mind and body, than she had dreamed was possible.

At last she stepped back. 'Bath,' she said. 'Then something to eat.'

He began to comply, then looked back. 'Dee ... are you all right?'

'Yes,' she said, because it was true. Tomorrow she had daughters to care for, and people to organise. She had been born and trained for nights like this. But she had needed Sam to wake her up so she could see what she had to do.

Thirty

Over there, over there
Send the word, send the word over there
That the Yanks are coming
The Yanks are coming
The drums rum-tumming everywhere
Lyrics from 'Over There' by George M Cohan,
a popular Allied song of World War II

By Monday the school had been moved into the village theatre, after the more lurid posters were hurriedly removed. The theatre would still be available at night and on weekends and school holidays for the few troupes not in uniform or making munitions.

The theatre had no playground, but the lane behind would be closed at morning tea and lunch so the children could play, with a movable see-saw, and ropes for skipping, climbing and a flying fox installed by the Home Guard.

Two weeks later the new library was opened with tea, fish paste and mock chicken sandwiches, and great acclaim for the speech of Lady Deanna Claverton, representing the duke — no one asked where a soldier might be in wartime — though much of the acclaim might have been due to the effects of the honey and elderberry 'champagne', made by Miss Primley to her mother's recipe, its ingredients so healthful that it could not possibly be intoxicating.

It was followed by a game of Bobbing for Apples where, after much discussion, it was agreed that false teeth could be worn either in or outside the mouth. The winning apple was captured by Arnold Thripps, teeth out.

'We are carrying on as if nothing happened,' Deanna said to Sam one night as she washed up the pan in which he'd fried their fish-and-chips dinner — Deb was still diligently sending cans of mutton dripping. 'Or rather as if we'd triumphed over the enemy with a makeshift school and library. But we know nowhere is safe now.'

Her daughters still had not gone back to their separate rooms, and there had been sheets to wash two mornings in the past week. The girls even walked hand in hand to take Magda to the train each morning now, as if to make sure each knew where the others were in case the air-raid siren shrieked again.

He was so silent that Deanna thought he wanted to change the subject. At last, he said, 'I take the trainees over London, Dover, Portsmouth, Liverpool. At first I saw forests and woodland and grasslands. Now, there are tree stumps and crops and rubble and Nissen huts. Every month the land has been further transformed for war.' He smiled at her wryly. 'People can recover, but I doubt that all the country we've used up ever will.'

She put the plates back in the cupboard, thoughtful.

Surely land recovered. The fields of Waterloo and the Somme were green now, famously fed by the blood of men. But Sam wasn't talking about battlefields, or paddocks of grass or beets. She'd learned in school that most of England's forests had been felled for Henry VIII's war fleet, never to return; the Great War and now this one had taken much of the remaining forest as pit props and fuel for factories.

What of the animals that had lived there? Had golden eagles become so nearly extinct from the lost forests of some other war? The cities being destroyed must be replaced.

We're in the belly of the beast, she thought, all of us: those who wanted war, those who tried to stop it, those who simply followed where others led. There is no way out, nothing anyone can do to mitigate the horror, until the beast is dead.

There were no more direct raids on Claverton's village, the castle or the land nearby. Planes passed to the south or north, but on their way to other targets, though the air-raid siren sounded every time. No bomber dropped the load it no longer had fuel to carry; no damaged plane crashed to earth into their fields.

But in Singapore, to the north of Australia, Japanese General Tomoyuki Yamashita achieved the unthinkable: the capture not just of Malaya but of Singapore, a city of over a million people, and over a hundred and thirty thousand Allied troops, among them Sam's brother-in-law, Deb's husband, Ron.

Sam cycled through the Claverton woods to Eagle's Rest when the cable arrived. The family were collecting wood, sawing branches fallen in the last blizzard in the small forest Miss Enid had owned that adjoined the Claverton lands.

The air had the tinny smell of just melted snow, and all were bundled in whatever was warm from the attic trunks, from a moth-eaten mink coat for Magda to a 1920s black and white–striped pony-skin cloak for Rosa, and for the Amazing Anna a bearskin jacket that came down to her knees. Dusty, sensible hound, had stayed home, guarding the stove and its precious rooster casserole.

Deanna noticed the set of Sam's face. She dumped her branches and ran to meet him. 'What's wrong?'

He held the yellow telegram paper out to her. On it she read four names, then the words ALL MISSING BELIEVED CAPTURED, then, DAD HOLDING UP AND ME TOO STOP LOVE DEB.

'Ron. Oh no! Who are the other names?'

'Ron's brother. Two cousins on Mum's side.'

'I ... I don't know what to say.'

'Nothing. I'd like to kick the Pommy bastard who surrendered our troops from a supposedly impregnable fortress, but I can't.' He took a deep breath. 'Can I collect wood with you?'

'We would love you to collect wood with us,' she said with feeling. She hugged him, quickly, then stepped back as the girls approached.

Sam hesitated, then held the telegram out to them. The three read it together. Each girl, by now, knew exactly what it meant: the possibility, near certainty, of never seeing loved ones again.

Suddenly he was being hugged by all three of them. 'I want to collect wood,' he repeated, over their heads.

'That sounds good,' said Magda. Anna held out one of her mittened hands for him to take. Rosa offered him her gardening-gloved one. 'We need to take some wood to the Thrippses, and to old Mr Jones and Mrs Froggins,' Deanna informed him.

'And there's rooster and apple casserole and baked potatoes and pear pudding for dinner,' added Rosa.

'Best dinner ever,' said Sam.

Months of waiting, plodding, celebrating where they could, until a midsummer sun hung over England; the air was hazy again from pollen, from construction of the new American air bases, and from the dust of bomb damage carried by the winds.

War news was sketchy and unreliable; Deanna knew too well anything that might shake precarious morale would be labelled top secret. But the Japanese progress down through New Guinea could not be hidden, nor the attack on Sydney Harbour by Japanese submarines.

Sam spent whatever free time he had at Eagle's Rest now.

Deanna was not sure if the other men on the base were given so much freedom, or if this was another case of higher-ups wishing to please the aristocrat with whom they might have to negotiate the use of the castle and its grounds.

Village gossip spoke of Sam and her as a couple now, according to Mrs Thripps. 'The only question now, dearie, is when he's goin' to pop the question, an' will you say yes.'

Mrs Thripps looked up from the hand-crank of the mangle she was turning as she fed the washing in to remove as much water as possible, while Deanna pulled out each garment at the other end and put it in a basket to be hung up. 'I says to them that you wouldn't be havin' him hangin' around if you were goin' to give him the bum's rush.'

'He hasn't asked me,' said Deanna shortly.

Mrs Thripps looked at her shrewdly. 'Mebbe he don't think a commoner should ask a lady for her hand. Or mebbe he don't want you to be a widow instead of a wife, though there's plenty that gets spliced with more dangerous jobs than his.'

'He hasn't even hinted at marriage,' said Deanna.

'What I'm hinting is mebbe you should ask him yourself,' said Mrs Thripps flatly.

Deanna was silent, pulling a sheet through the mangle. She loved Sam Murray; she was sure he loved her too, and not as a sister. She also desired him, a sensation similar to influenza — flushing, aching — the poets who called love a fever were not wrong. It had taken her twenty seconds to realise that her feelings were directed at the man sitting on the hearthrug, playing a game of Pull the Rope with Anna and Dusty.

Many Englishwomen were marrying foreigners serving in Britain, planning to return home with them when the war ended, which would not be this year, nor even the next; though it finally seemed possible that Germany would be defeated.

But Japan, and the war in the Pacific? That war could still be lost, and soon. No one had defeated the Japanese advance on land yet, though the Australians had held back their thrust into New Guinea, and the US had inflicted major damage on the Japanese fleet at the recent Battle of Midway.

What would the world be like by the end of the war? What would her daughters be doing? She longed to have the certainty of marriage now, the warmth of Sam against her, whether it was for days, weeks, months or for life, however long that might be ...

'Speakin' of his lordship: here he comes,' said Mrs Thripps, peering out the laundry door as Sam bicycled up the lane. 'Off you go, lovie. I'll handle this then make myself scarce. You take my advice and tell him he's got to make an honest woman of you.'

'Are people really gossiping?'

Mrs Thripps laughed. 'They've been gossiping about your family for generations. Ooh, you should've heard the talk about your ma. But they *like* you, dearie. They like Sam too. You ain't got nothin' to worry about — toffs don't keep to the same rules as other folks, anyway. Now you go and see to your gentleman.'

'Her gentleman' was propping his bike up in the shed. It held a large green canvas bag. For once he didn't walk towards her but waited for her to join him, his body slumped. His face was drained of all emotion.

'Sam, what is it? News of your family?'

'Just a letter from Deb. No real news. I'll show it to you later ...' He hesitated, then said, 'I'm being transferred.'

'What! Why? Everyone says you're the best trainer they've ever had!' *Everyone* was via the pub, courtesy of Arnold, though she didn't say so.

'I don't know why they're moving me,' he said frankly.

'Can you tell me where?'

'No. So I'm not telling you this, and you can't tell anyone, even the girls.'

'I understand,' she said quietly.

'I'm off to a new unit called the Pathfinders, headquartered in Buckinghamshire. I'll be flying a new craft nicknamed a Mosquito. It's made of plywood, small, fast, and can be used day or night; but we'll be primarily leading the bombers to their targets.' His mouth twisted. 'Churchill has finally accepted that four out of five bombing missions miss. It's our job to make sure the bombs get where they're supposed to go.'

Her heart squeezed in her chest. 'Impossible! Flying ahead of everyone else? In daylight?'

'Sometimes in daylight. The Mosquito is the fastest craft around, and the most manoeuvrable — pretty much like the crate I used to race: only room for two of us, or three at a pinch. If I fly fast enough and keep the sun in their eyes with it directly behind me, or use clouds or fog, I have a chance.'

A chance. He was being realistic, and doing her the honour of being honest too. He had a chance.

'The Mosquitoes are unarmed,' he added quietly. 'The Air Ministry tried to get the manufacturers to put a machine gun on them, but it's too heavy.' He attempted a smile. 'At least I won't have to decide whether to kill some poor bastard or not.'

'When?' she said hoarsely.

'In a week's time. I've got leave till then.' He gestured at the canvas bag. 'May I stay here, if Mrs Thripps will chaperone us?'

'You are staying here, and I'm not inviting Mrs Thripps.'

A week, she thought. This might be the only week she ever spent with him, the last week she ever saw him. She didn't care if people talked. They would be a family, just for a week. Her, Sam and the girls. The housework, the pea crop, the glasshouses could all be left.

This time was for Sam. She might even use the diaphragm that still lay unused in her underwear drawer. She would need to practise inserting it again.

They spent their seven days like misers counting every second. The girls were allowed the first and last days of Sam's leave as holidays from school. They spent the weekend with him too.

Deanna and Sam had three days alone together, as well as the evenings after the girls went to bed. For the first time, this week, Dusty didn't follow Anna to sleep on her bed, but stayed by Sam's side, as if he sensed whose need was greatest.

Rain filled the first day. They played Shove Ha'penny on the kitchen table with Dusty snoring on Sam's feet. The girls performed charades, rummaging in the attic chests and the smell of mothballs for costumes.

On fine days when the girls were home they fished, roasting their catch on sticks by what Sam called a 'swaggie's fire' of twigs and leaves, and 'billy tea' in an old tin to which he'd attached a wire handle. He swung it seven times to brew the tea without spilling a drop, a skill the girls demanded to learn, though he only let them try with cold water from the stream.

After the girls were reluctantly herded upstairs, Dee and Sam and a snoring Dusty spent clear nights lying on blankets in the last midsummer dusk to watch the eagles, two adults and another juvenile, emerging every evening as if they knew Sam watched for them, swooping down to snatch a rabbit or a hare.

The twilit peace on the grass seemed too fragile to break by going indoors. Mostly they stayed till true darkness, watching the stars' great wheel circle the sky. Sam knew them well enough to orient himself in this new hemisphere, but not the ancient myths Deanna knew, of Venus and the warrior Mars, or Jupiter or Pluto.

Aircraft shared the sky too, unwelcome daggers of reality: pilots practised night training; and once two enemy bombers headed south. Deanna tensed, waiting for the siren if the enemies appeared to be coming closer, but they finally vanished.

Several times on those nights, Sam reached for her hand across the blankets. His warmth spread to hers. But he made no move to kiss her.

It would have been so easy to laughingly roll over him and offer her face for a kiss. She couldn't. He had erected a wall between them that only hands were allowed to cross, though love and longing flowed between their fingers.

Mornings with Sam when the girls went to school meant cup after cup of tea, talking, Sam shelling peas or peeling carrots while she cooked everything he might enjoy: sponge cake with cream and strawberries; rock cakes with the last of her dried fruit; a young hen sacrificed and stuffed with herbs and lemon and breadcrumbs.

It was only days later that Deanna realised they had shared all that was most precious to them both — her daughters, dog and knowledge of her land — instead of spending that week lunching at Claverton Major or visiting a movie theatre. Seven precious nights talking together after the girls had gone to bed, sipping her grandfather's scotch by a fireplace filled with a giant vase of roses instead of flames.

Sam did not come to her bedroom or take their intimacy further. Each evening he sat in an armchair, not on the sofa, as if creating a barrier to bodies drifting closer — once again a barrier she reluctantly respected. She presumed he needed focus. She must not distract him.

And yet they talked: of her grandfather and Sam's parents; of shearing sheds and royal garden parties; of the Snowy Mountains that only bore snow half the year; of deer hunts in the Scottish highlands; of the blue distances of gum trees, the trees that shed bark instead of leaves; of how old-woman kurrajongs hoarded water and annual tucker for droughts when it was needed most; and of floods so strong they tossed cows and tree trunks in their swirls.

Strange that poor, silly David Windsor could be a governor, while Sam was a pilot ordered to probable death by ...

Who ultimately gave his orders? She neither knew nor could ask. Was the RAF command more intelligent than many who ran this war? She hoped so. And no, she thought fiercely, Sam would not be killed. Some couples superstitiously married, thinking 'the candle in the window' would bring the soldier home. Others just as superstitiously wouldn't even become engaged. She didn't think Sam was superstitious. She did know he trusted her, walked hand in hand with her, shared the intimacy of firelight, without feeling he must explain why he offered no more. She dared not crack his confidence that she would accept the role of beloved friend, not lover.

His last afternoon they spent picnicking in sunlight on the headland, lapping waves below and eagles peering down, as if Eagle's Rest had brushed its hair and shined its shoes to look its best for him.

Deanna lay back on the grass, chewing a daisy stem, watching the clouds like newly shampooed sheep laze across the sky. Sam lay on his stomach on the blanket, watching her, and smiling. 'You belong here, don't you?'

'I suppose I do.'

'You never thought of moving away?'

'I assumed I'd have to,' she said frankly. 'Donnie was the heir, not me. I'd planned to get an apprenticeship at a good couturier, and then eventually find a cottage on a farm or even in a wood, and work for a few select clients.'

'But it wouldn't have been home.'

She turned to meet his eyes. Brown eyes, eagle eyes. 'I'd have made it home, learned the animals, the local mushrooms or cob nuts or hawthorns, where the squirrels hoarded nuts and the owls roosted. I'd have missed the eagles, but I'd have been happy.'

'Are you sure about that? Land you know as well as love isn't easily replaced.'

Was this a veiled query about her possible life in Australia? 'I'd learn it, and then love it, or maybe the other way around. What about your family place?'

He glanced at his watch. 'Not today. The girls will be home from school soon.'

He stood and brushed the dead bracken from his trousers, then held out his hand to help her up. Her daughters had kept their own backgrounds secret. A niggling whisper said that Sam kept secrets too. What? And why from her?

He said farewell to Dusty first on the last morning, kneeling by his kitbag, offering a crust of toast and raspberry jam saved from breakfast, which Dusty accepted. He hugged the big hound, then looked at him sternly. 'You look after the family, you hear?'

'*Woof*,' said Dusty agreeably, sniffing Sam's fingers for toast crumbs, or even a lick of butter.

'You bark if any strangers come.'

'*Woof*.' Dusty snuffed in a pocket which might once have held a bar of chocolate.

Sam stood. 'You're useless, aren't you?'

'*Woof*,' said Dusty complacently.

'And the most lovable dog in the world?'

Dusty didn't bother to reply.

Deanna and Magda were trying not to cry. Tears ran down Rosa's cheeks. Anna let out a sob.

Sam kneeled again and hugged her. 'You are the Amazing Anna who has found a good life despite all that has happened to you. You understand? Whatever happens now, you know you can find happiness again.'

Anna nodded, and clutched his neck, then let it go to present him with a knitted face washer with his initials on it. He kissed her cheek. 'I love it. I'll use it every day.'

Rosa handed him a handkerchief. 'It's got our names embroidered on it, and yours too, so you won't forget us.'

'I never could,' he said gently, kissing the top of her hair.

Magda put out her hand to shake his, then clasped him in a hug instead. 'It's not fair!'

'Magda, love, none of this is fair,' he said gently. 'All that happened to you isn't fair either. We just get through the bad bits, and remember the joy, and find good where we can.' He managed a smile. 'I bet you know a hundred arguments why we shouldn't expect life to be fair.'

Magda met his eyes. 'Yes. But none of them are good ones. Here.' She handed him a beanie. 'I know it's not regulation, but caps are stupid, and a wool beanie doesn't burn. Wear it under your cap.'

He sketched her a salute. 'Yes, Sergeant Magda!'

He turned to Deanna. She'd managed to scrub her eyes free of tears. 'I knitted you gloves. Magda's right. Can you wear them under your flying gloves? Though I suppose yours are wool lined …'

She had never asked a question about his uniform or duties before. Suddenly arms were around her, his body pressed to hers, his hands pressing her buttocks, his mouth open on hers so firmly, so melding, it seemed they must eventually become one.

At last he pulled away, his hands shaking. She trembled too. 'I must report in by ten,' he said, and she knew that was why he had finally let control slip, as all the officialdom of Britain would be after him if he was even ten minutes late.

'I love you,' she said, aware the girls were watching, listening. She was glad. They needed to know love was still possible and worth hunting for among the matter-of-fact 'must marry someone fast' wartime alliances, worth even the knowledge of loss to come when you knew your time together might be short.

He met her eyes — her brown eyes, like his and her grandfather's. 'I love you too. One day ... one day we can talk more about love.'

She managed another smile. 'I'd like that.'

He nodded, as if he didn't trust himself to say more. She kept the smile until he gave his final wave and turned into the lane, then ran upstairs to her bedroom, with Dusty loping after her, and sobbed. Five minutes later her daughters joined her.

Thirty-One

What are they burning, what are they burning ...
Truth, justice, love, beauty, the human smile,
All flung to the flames!

Extract from 'The Burning of the Leaves'
by Laurence Binyon
The Atlantic Magazine

She had hoped he'd get leave. He didn't, or not long enough to reach them at Eagle's Rest. But letters arrived every few days, addressed to all of them, for one man couldn't take time from the war to write letters and postcards to his family and friends back in Australia as well as three girls and a woman who wrote to him every day in England, sitting at the kitchen table, with Anna adding portraits to her compositions: *This is Dusty finding a dead rat. It smelled. This is Mum taking the honey from the bees with lots of smoke. This is Rosa when she fell off her bicycle.*

Eagle's Rest echoed with his absence. He had been with them every few days for over two years, laughing with them, catching fish or cutting wood for them or frying fish and chips, sharing a land beyond the war, or at least a domestic haven beyond the crumpled cities and hungry bellies.

He hadn't been a brother or an uncle or a husband. He had been Sam. Which may have been part of why she loved him, Deanna thought. She had known Sam Murray for over two years, and he had never expected her to be wife-like, to subjugate her life to his.

Sometimes at two am she wondered if that was why he had not asked to make love with her. Respectable men did not ask nice women to sleep with them without an offer of marriage. Surely she had shown she could be a partner in his farming life: could keep a house, milk a cow, skin a rabbit, use a cross-saw. True, she had never coped with a thousand sheep, but she had every confidence she could.

And with that thought came the knowledge that she would leave this house, her eagles and her land, to share his, if it meant they could be together. Not abandon them — keep them cared for, visit often, especially if her daughters chose to stay in England, or if they returned here. But she would move her life's centre for Sam.

Did he know that? Mrs Thripps was right, she thought. I need to tell him. I *will* tell him, the next time he has leave.

Meanwhile they had his letters: he was learning all about his new aircraft, which was 'a beauty', though he gave no other details.

Deb had had a postcard from her husband in a prison camp at Changi in Singapore. She sent Eagle's Rest not just dripping but a whole bag of sultanas too, made from grapes that had been dried by the three Italian prisoners-of-war working on Sam's farm, living in the house with his father.

Other than brief praise of the plane itself, Sam wrote nothing else about his own work, whether he had begun flying missions or who he flew with, though there were several references to a 'Pete', who told the worst jokes in the world: *A penguin comes to enlist. He asks the recruiting officer, 'Has my brother been here yet?' And the recruiting officer says, 'What does he look like?'*

Anna had loved that one. Rosa had preferred: *How do you know if there's an elephant in your plane? There's a trunk behind the pilot's seat.*

There were tantalising glimpses of the other men he worked with, too, most of them Poles who had escaped to Britain to keep fighting when their country was captured.

> *Bonza blokes,* Sam had written. *Though it took almost six months for the Colonel Blimps [REDACTED] to realise.*
>
> *England seems to have accepted the Poles now, though. One chap escaping the Nazis parachuted down in the middle of a tennis party when he ran out of fuel. He was invited to make up the four in a set of doubles as one of the players hadn't turned up. He accepted and they won, and he stayed for afternoon tea before informing the base he needed to be collected.*
>
> *Another landed in a family's back garden. They invited him to Sunday dinner and two months later he and the eldest daughter were married.*
>
> *But my favourite story is when Jan parachuted down to [REDACTED]. The farm workers assumed he was a Jerry and approached with pitchforks, and a carving knife attached to a broom handle. He yelled 'F* off' at them. They stopped and yelled, 'It's all right! He's one of us.'*

Magda rarely laughed at any of the jokes. 'Jokes make cruel things acceptable,' she said.

'Sometimes they are just funny,' said Deanna.

Magda shrugged. 'The butt of jokes is too often an outsider.'

Dee wrote to Sam almost daily, not knowing if her letters were a burden to be read and answered when he was exhausted and preoccupied, or if, as he hinted, they were a treasured glimpse of the family and place he had come to love.

> *Dear Sam,*
>
> *Such a ruckus you never have heard! An American colonel called on the mayor yesterday to demand that the local council forbid American 'coloured' troops from using the pub and be served out the back door. Our mayor, Mr Septimus Filmer, who is also our butcher, took what might have been a suggestion to be an order, and from a Yankee colonel who arrived late to the war, too. While there have indeed been some murmurings about the number of coloured men in the village, according to Mrs Thripps, who had it from Mrs Filmer herself, Mr Filmer made it quite clear that England is a sovereign nation, and neither England, nor Claverton Minor, nor its public house are under American control, and if the colonel didn't like it his men could find another public house and stop drinking the beer that all good Englishmen deserved, as <u>they</u> do not have American PXs to shop at, with endless chocolate, canned ham, and nylon stockings with which to bribe good English girls to walk out with them.*
>
> *It seems Mr Filmer was particularly vehement about the canned ham, which has appeared on many local tables since villagers have followed the government's suggestions and invited Yankees far from home to tea. It's been years since Mr Filmer had ham to sell.*
>
> *It is to be hoped that the colonel has more luck in the battles to come with Herr Hitler than he did with Mr Filmer. The colonel apparently also made a visit to the Vixen Tea House, only to find each table occupied by coloured troops. Miss Vixen regretfully told the colonel that she was far too busy to serve him but 'Do come back another day'.*
>
> *We assume that was a set-up, hurriedly arranged by Mrs Filmer. It might have backfired: no coloured troops have been*

seen in the village since, so it may have been made out of bounds for the poor men, which is terribly unfair. I've talked with Mrs Goodword about a dance with special invitations for the coloured troops.

There is no other startling news. Anna made a much more successful batch of scones this afternoon, and we congratulated her by eating them all with raspberry jam. I am sending you a jar and hope it gets to you safely as it will be far superior to the air force's canned plum jam, even if it won't keep as long. In fact try to eat it in a week, in case it ferments when opened.

We plan to pick hawthorn berries or 'haws' to make jelly for winter and then go fishing this weekend, and will make billy tea in your honour, and, as always, wish you were here.

With love from us all,
Dee

Work was an even more necessary distraction now. She taught Rosa more bee lore — Anna was nervous of the stings. Magda preferred to spend any spare time reading books of ancient history and philosophy, as if she was trying to make sense of the present, Deanna thought, by looking at the past.

Magda did not discuss her reading though, or not with Deanna at least. Did she think her adopted mother too ignorant to discuss the fall of the Roman Empire, or were Magda's conclusions too depressing to be shared?

Hawthorn berries and red currants set into jelly without sugar. Sugarless jam didn't keep well, but it was welcomed by the elderly, the injured, and those too busy to pick wild fruits as a welcome gleam among the grey turnip, cabbage and Spam diet of war.

Deanna refused to add turnips to their diet. She hated the smell, and they reminded her daughters of the orphanage, but she was well aware of her privilege in refusing to eat what was becoming the national vegetable, closely followed by the parsnip, which was delicious if you had enough Australian dripping to crisp it in the oven.

Christmas 1942 was ... empty, though the Thrippses joined them once again, and they played the same games and sang the same songs. Sam, it seemed, could not get leave; nor had he time to procure gifts, and phone calls were limited to official purposes. Deanna had wondered if she could ask Uncle Jasper to wangle him some time off, then rejected the thought. Sam would not thank her if he found out men had died because a Pathfinder had been given leave.

But according to his letter he loved the socks Magda had knitted, the shirt Rosa had altered to fit him, the scones that Anna insisted, contrary to all evidence, would still be edible when he received them, as well as the small bronze eagle Deanna knew her grandfather had given Miss Enid for Christmas, fifteen years earlier, and which had sat, wings unfurled, in the library ever since.

An eagle in full flight seemed a good gift for a man who must fly with wings built and maintained by others, dodging missiles and bullets across enemy territory, then finding his way home.

Deanna explained to the girls that Sam would have had little time to shop, and possibly nowhere he *could* shop. But he had asked Deb to send the girls books he had enjoyed as a teenager, and Deanna a bunch of dried flowers he called 'Everlastings': bright gold and starlike, and carefully wrapped in used tissue paper.

Deanna suspected they would not last forever, but she placed them in a small vase on the kitchen table — they had no need of water. Now and then she sat with them and drank a cup of tea, Dusty at her side, imagining Sam was there, and the silence companionable instead of empty.

★★★

The new year oozed in with no bells ringing but a dance at the new American base nearby. The Women's Institute put on an afternoon tea for American servicemen, with Lady Deanna Claverton of Claverton Castle to welcome them, on the condition that coloured men be invited too.

A white major with a southern accent had invited her to the dance. She smiled, refused, and introduced him to a more willing partner. She wondered vaguely if the Americans allowed coloured troops at their dances. She supposed not, but it did not seem tactful to ask.

'Did you hear about Daisy?' Mrs Thripps asked breathlessly one morning, placing her string bag on the kitchen table and unpacking the rations she had collected the day before: a white roll of paper that contained two lamb chops meant to make a stew for a whole family. Mrs Thripps would keep the other rations, the small packet of sugar, the twist of tea. The string bag would also be full of potatoes, beetroot and onions going home.

'What about her?' Deanna scrubbed her hands in the sink. She'd been checking the sacks of potatoes for rotted ones — rot spread — and though she had found only one, her hands still stank of it.

'She hanged herself from the hall rafters last night!'

Deanna gasped. 'No! Poor girl — she was walking out with someone, wasn't she? Was he killed?'

'No, he's hale and hearty but mad as a hornet. Seems Daisy was up the duff. Her young man was more than happy to marry her, and him being a motor mechanic like her pa, her family welcomed him with open arms, especially as he said he'd come back to England to join the family firm. That's how they met — he saw Daisy's dad's legs out under a car and offered to help, and spent all his spare time with them after that. But it seems a Yankee soldier has to get his commander's permission and the commander wouldn't give it.'

'Why on earth not?' There had already been two marriages between village women and members of the American forces, even though the brides could not travel to their new homes till the war and threats to shipping were over.

'He were black, weren't he? That commander won't give no permission to no black soldier to marry a white girl. He even had him transferred so he couldn't even meet her.'

'That's ... that's horrible. I must send a note to her mother. Falling in love is natural in wartime, even if they jumped the gun a bit.'

'I'd like to kick that commander in the you-know-where. I wouldn't be surprised if her brother does it next time he's on leave.' Mrs Thripps shook her head. 'The baby would have been coloured too, of course. I seen a coloured baby once, such a pretty little thing. We played a whole season with the Jolly Jazzateers, black as the ace of spades and my word they could sing. And that trumpet player! Jericho Smith, they called him. Like all the saints were marching in. Mrs Smith — she was the mum, an Irish girl from the Sligo Songstresses — had a baby halfway through the season, relying on tight lacing and ruffles. She even made it to the end of the performance before the baby came half an hour later and we made him a cradle in a costume box.'

She sighed. 'Me and Arnold would have liked a couple of our own, but it wasn't to be.'

Letters became a lifeline. Deb and Deanna wrote to each other often now, a correspondence begun to thank Deb for the dripping.

Dear Dee,
 I don't think I have ever met anyone who's made a snowman before. There's snow each winter in the mountains about a hundred miles from us. I've ridden up there a few times. I love the way snow sits on the snow gum trees, and once we saw a

wombat toboggan down a slope then scramble up and slide back down again.

Come to think of it I've never met anyone with a title before, either. Trust Sam to pick a good 'un.

There is so much I'd like to tell you, and so much I'd like to ask, but the censor would black out anything useful we had to tell each other, so I'll save her the trouble and be discreet. Did you know the censors are mostly women? Women write the letters of condolence too, even though men sign them. Let's see if the censor keeps that bit in. Come on, censor — I dare you!

I hope you have enough firewood to keep you warm. I wish I could send you a parcel of our heat, as well as dripping, and maybe you could send us a package of cold too. I'd forgotten how hot it gets working in the top paddock in summer. I've got soft, living in town. I wish we'd managed a baby on his last leave. I wish ... well, I wish so many things, and you must too.

With even more of my best wishes,
Deb Hanrahan

Dear Dee, Magda, Rosa and Dusty. Oh, and the Amazing Anna! I nearly forgot! (Just joking.)

Well, we've had our football match to celebrate the season. One problem — no one could decide what game we'd play.

About a quarter of the Aussies wanted Victorian rules, and there was much support for Rugby League with a minority wanting Rugby Union, from the poms. There was considerable support for soccer, and the USA nearly outvoted everyone for gridiron.

In the end we all played whatever code we wanted. No one is sure who won, but a good time was had by all, not to mention six black eyes, a sprained wrist and a small punch-up which was voted to be 'half time'.

I miss you all. Give Dusty a hug from me and tell him I miss him too. My feet are never so warm in England as when he is sleeping on them. I'd like to commandeer him for the RAF as a footwarmer but am sure he'd rather be with you.

Love to all of you,
Sam

Rosa joined Magda at Hawthorne Grammar, with Anna at the junior school. Both girls had seemed unhappy at the village school since the bombing and Miss Hannaford's death. And in February Uncle Jasper invited Deanna to morning tea.

His office had moved to an upmarket Mayfair flat this time. A one-legged man operated the lift, who tipped his cap and said, 'Good morning, ma'am,' and undoubtedly had a pistol in his jacket and two throwing knives in his socks, as well as training in unarmed combat.

Uncle Jasper's face had become puffy; it was soft, rather than fat. His eyes had lost expression. Yet once tea had been served, with a stale bun each, he took her hand. 'I wanted to tell you personally. Robyn was killed last week.'

Deanna blinked back tears. She and Rob had managed to exchange a few letters, with plans to meet on Rob's next leave 'How did she die?'

'Executed. There is no possibility of mistake.'

'Thank you.' There were other questions she could have asked, but he would not have told her the answers, and nor did she need them. Rob was gone. She did have one request, however.

'The last time I was here you warned me that Flight Lieutenant Murray's loyalty might be in question. Was that why he was moved to a unit with so little chance of survival?'

'He seems to have survived surprisingly well.'

'Do you still doubt his loyalty?' Deanna insisted.

'As it happens, no.'

She took the first full breath she'd tasted since Sam left. It smelled of burst sewer line and dust, like all of London, even probably the palace. 'Will you transfer him back to the training unit then?'

'No.' Uncle Jasper held up his hand. 'Firstly, it isn't in my power to do so. Flight Lieutenant Murray has proved brilliant in a difficult job, and I am sure his superiors will refuse to let him go. Secondly, while I personally no longer doubt him, others still may.'

'Can you at least tell me why?'

'I'm sorry. No.'

'I have never known anyone with so much courage and integrity as Flight Lieutenant Murray,' Deanna said quietly.

Uncle Jasper gave a wry smile. 'That is the trouble, isn't it? War is not always a good time for integrity. The car will take you back.'

'Thank you, but I'll take the late train.'

'Your invaluable Mrs Thripps is staying with your daughters?'

For a moment Deanna considered telling him that Mrs Thripps had joined an ENSA team as an exotic snake dancer. But that would be childish, and besides, Uncle Jasper knew exactly what Mrs Thripps was doing and had let her know it.

She stopped at Vonderfleet's before she took the train back home; the cab halted often, changing lanes and routes, passing through one patch of recent damage where women in aprons and wielding trolleys kneeled on the shattered ground, trying to piece together bodies from last night to identify them. The most shocking aspect was not the bodies, nor the still guttering fires, but the matter-of-factness. This is the world now, she thought, and so we deal with it the best we can.

Mr Vonderfleet changed her second diamond for what seemed an inordinate amount of money. The remaining diamonds must be kept aside, for now, at least, to provide her daughters' security, but this diamond would help those in need.

She took the train to Claverton Minor, accepting the seat a young lieutenant offered her, though she felt he deserved it far more than she did. Her bicycle was where she'd left it, dusted with snow.

She wiped it off, wound her scarf around her face, and cycled home to an excellent egg and spinach pie, made by her daughters and left in the warming tray for her, with the ingredients for cocoa thoughtfully lined up on the bench.

She ate, though she wasn't hungry, and drank because her daughters had been kind, and took the time for tears, for Sam and herself and for dear Rob, with the egg and spinach pie and cocoa to comfort her.

Thirty-Two

Mock Cream

INGREDIENTS
four tablespoons margarine
one tablespoon fine granulated sugar
one tablespoon dried milk powder
two tablespoons milk

METHOD
Mix well.

Dusty heard it first: a stutter not a roar. He rose from where he'd been sleeping away the midsummer day under the oak tree and gave one sharp, alarmed bark.

Deanna made out the sound then. It came from the sky, but the air-raid siren hadn't sounded. She ran from the glasshouse and looked up, shading her eyes from the sun, in time to see the last balloon top of a parachute drop far beyond the bulk of the castle.

The buzzing grew louder, like a horsefly ... or mosquito. A small black object swayed near a tuft of cloud, almost above the castle now.

A Mosquito, she thought. The aircraft that Sam flew. But now it was above her she could see it was hardly a plane at all — one side shattered, part of a wing gone, and suddenly, a trickle of black smoke that billowed into flame.

The aircraft only just missed the southern turret. It dropped to tree level, then floated across the bare headland, the flames eating the craft so swiftly that, by the time it reached the beach, all she could see was fire.

A crash, and it was down in the shallows beyond the shingle, the flames now dancing on the water.

She ran, stumbling across tussocks, snagging her overalls on gorse bushes. Dusty was faster. She had never known the dog to bound before: down the path and over the bridge, across the headland and down to the sickle of stones that was the beach at low tide.

The wreckage was perhaps ten yards from the shore — oil, flame, blackened struts.

It didn't hit us, she thought, panting. It kept going over paddocks, castle, headland. Nowhere it might have landed on a person.

Dusty leaped into the waves, jumping over ripples until the water was too deep, then furiously dog paddling. Her heart screamed as she dodged rolls of barbed wire.

Something moved near the fallen craft, a face lifting into the oily flame that still burned, even with the waves around. The red-black flesh gasped, then sank.

Dusty grasped something in his teeth, pulling, straining. A lump of rag moved slowly to the shore till the big dog found his footing in the shallows, and Deanna saw the rag was a man.

She waded in, shoes slipping on the shingle. She turned the pilot till his burned face was bobbing up out of the water for brief seconds so he could gulp the air, finally hauling him beyond the waves.

She bent her head and found he was still breathing, in faint gasps, choking now and then. She rolled him onto his side. He vomited seawater, weakly. One arm hung at a strange angle. One eye was puffed burned flesh: indeed that whole side of his face was black except where it was blistered red.

It was Sam. She only truly recognised him now she could see his face, but had known it from that first dark speck in the sky, seeing him search for the castle, straining to reach the water so no one would be hurt by a falling plane.

Bells sounded, ambulance and fire brigade and probably the Home Guard, Red Cross, Mothers' Guild, WI, the Ladies' Guild and the cast of *Charley's Aunt*.

She looked around for Dusty and found him next to her, stretched out on the stones, panting, shaking. 'Good dog,' she managed. 'Oh, good dog!'

Dusty stared at her. His eyes twitched to look at Sam, then back at Deanna again. His long hairy body gave a convulsive heave, and then lay still.

Thirty-Three

When a silver aeroplane flies over, it's American. When it's green, it's British. When there are no aircraft, that's the Luftwaffe.

German joke from the last years of World War II

They took Sam to the castle hospital. She knew there'd be no news for an hour at least. The girls would be home soon.

The fire brigade and Home Guard stayed after the ambulance had left. She found Arnold by her side as she huddled on the shingle, cradling Dusty's body.

'Lady Dee? That were Sam, weren't it?'

'Yes,' she said.

'Did the plane hit the dog?'

'No. The dog ... Dusty heard the plane's engine before I did; he must have worked out which direction it was going in because he began to run — he dragged Sam to the shore where I could reach him, and then he ... he died.' Please, God, she thought, don't let Sam die. Dusty gave his life. Sam has to live!

'He was an old dog,' said Arnold gently. 'Such a good old boy.'

'He didn't obey anyone,' said Deanna blankly, 'and sniffed for food in the rudest places ...'

'He did what a dog ought to do. He was loved. That's a dog's real duty. I remember when the old duke got him as a puppy, that Bill Martins saying in the pub that the rest of the litter looked proper lurcher like, but this one were to be drowned if no one would take him, so the old duke did.'

Dusty didn't drown, thought Deanna. He lived a full life and then he died, with me and Sam. He died knowing he was loved, and a good dog, the best of dogs ...

'How about me and the boys wrap him in a blanket and give the two of you a lift back to the house? We can dig a grave for him under the oak tree,' Arnold coaxed. 'The girls would like that.'

She had to tell the girls. She could tell them about Dusty but would probably have no news of Sam. *What should I tell them?* she thought desperately. All she knew for sure was that he was alive, or had been.

She let Arnold help her into the back seat of the truck and held Dusty's blanket-covered head on her lap. She sat below the oak branches, still holding the old dog, his body stiffening now, while the men dug deep into the soil — two hundred years of decomposed oak leaves — then lowered him into the grave as Mrs Thripps arrived on her bicycle. Arnold met her at the gate, obviously to explain what had happened, as the men filled in the grave, leaving the soil piled on top, properly grave-like.

'I'll go bring some stones up to cover it,' said Arnold. 'And old Frogget will engrave a stone if you give him a bottle of the old duke's whisky in exchange.'

Deanna nodded. 'Thank you.'

'A cup of tea,' said Mrs Thripps, as Anna's bicycle sped through the puddles in the lane, the other girls not long behind her. Anna looked at the chaos of the garden cautiously.

Sam, thought Deanna. Sam ...

Thirty-Four

Chocolate Patty Cakes

INGREDIENTS

a quarter cup apple, stewed
a carrot, very finely grated
half a cup raw beetroot, very finely grated
a quarter cup dripping, butter, cooking oil or margarine
a quarter cup walnuts, rolled as finely as you can make them
a quarter cup maple syrup or honey
one and a half cups self-raising flour
three tablespoons cocoa
half a teaspoon ground cinnamon

METHOD

Mix all ingredients. Place into patty cake shells. Bake in a moderate oven for about fifteen minutes till risen, firm and beginning to brown. They may grow mould after two to three days.

Recipe by Lady Deanna Claverton,
not the Ministry of Food

★★★

Mrs Thripps made cocoa for them all. The firemen left, except for Arnold, so there was nothing to be seen of the accident except the Home Guard hauling the wreckage of the plane down on the beach. And the new grave.

Her mind seemed dulled, but Deanna managed to explain to the girls that Dusty had known who was in the aircraft, had saved Sam, then had died next to her, happy and triumphant and in no pain (she prayed that last was true), and that Sam was in the hospital.

The phone rang in the library. Deanna rose to answer it and found the world spinning. She waited till it passed. Mrs Thripps was already speaking into the mouthpiece, the girls crowding around her. 'Lady Deanna's phone, Mrs Thripps speaking … Yes, Her Ladyship is here. It's the hospital, Dee love,' she said.

'Hello?'

'Lady Deanna?' It was the matron, whom Deanna had met on her dutiful visits to the different waves of men who'd inhabited the makeshift wards in her old home, bearing flowers and bars of soap that weren't carbolic. 'I thought you might like to know that Flight Lieutenant Murray is out of surgery and should recover. He has a broken arm and some nasty burns and a concussion.'

She breathed deeply. 'Thank you. His eye?'

'It's too early to tell yet. The swelling needs to subside. He's not regained consciousness, but the doctor says his vital signs are good.'

'Can I visit him?'

A pause. Visitors were only for visiting hours, and even then, only family members. Except, of course, for the Lady of the Castle.

'I think it would do him good if he could hear your voice,' said the matron, suddenly sounding human. 'Come to the front desk and ask for me. I'll get the orderly to put an armchair by the bed for you.'

'Thank you,' Deanna managed.

'He's going to be all right?' cried Anna, as Deanna put the receiver down.

'Yes. Yes, he will be all right. It will take a while, though. But I can go and see him now.'

'Us too?' demanded Rosa.

Deanna shook her head. 'They're making an exception just for me. I'll send you a message as soon as I know more, I promise.'

'But we're his family!' Anna broke into sobs. 'They wouldn't let us see Papa, and he died …'

'Sam's not going to die! I'll make sure you can see him tomorrow. Mrs Thripps?'

'I'll stay here tonight, and as long as you need me. I'll call Doris to get a message to Arnold to bring me things up, and his too.'

She looked at the white faces of the girls and said exactly the right thing. 'Now, how about we go outside and say a prayer for Dusty, to give thanks for his life and for being with us, and to thank him for saving Sam?'

'Do dogs go to Heaven?' asked Anna in a small voice. 'The vicar said they don't.'

'The vicar's wrong,' said Mrs Thripps with certainty. 'What does he know about dogs? We played a whole season with Percy and his Performing Poodles and sure as eggs they're performing up in Heaven right now, and getting all the dog biscuits and bones they want. Dusty's there among the angels. An' I bet he's already got a whole roast beef just for him, and angels scratching his belly. Come on, lovies. Let's say goodbye to him proper.'

With Christian prayers, thought Deanna, as she hurried up the stairs to wash and change out of wet and filthy overalls, and she took the girls to church each Sunday. Even Magda had expressed no wish to practise the religion of her ancestors. Their parents had taken them to an Anglican church in Oxford, but was this born of fear, in case the antisemitism always bubbling in Britain suddenly grew to the devastating levels they knew existed on the continent?

She grabbed a dress Sam had once admired, made from flowered curtains that had covered a guest-room window, and a coat in case the weather changed.

Should she take the car? No — the precious coupons must be saved in case Sam was given permission to spend medical leave with her. It was only ten minutes up to the castle on her bike.

The girls and Mrs Thripps knelt by Dusty's grave as she passed.

They had put Sam in her old bedchamber, or at least in part of it, now partitioned into several small wards. But she took comfort that his narrow metal bed sat where her seventeenth-century wooden one had rested, its bed curtains long faded and consigned to the rag bin, not the attics.

Matron herself escorted her to the door, then checked his pulse, lifting his right eyelid. She smiled reassuringly at Deanna. 'His pulse is strong and steady, Your Ladyship, and Doctor says there is no sign of any brain damage. Ring the bell if there's any change.'

'I will.' Deanna sat and took Sam's cold hand in hers. 'Sam? It's me. You're in my bedroom, my old one at the castle. Magda and Rosa and Anna send their love and Mrs Thripps her best wishes ...'

She kept talking, saying nothings, in case her voice anchored him and brought him back. Minutes passed, or hours.

He didn't move. A VAD brought her a cup of tea and an elderly bun, with an awkward curtsey. Deanna would have liked to make it clear she expected neither formal address nor curtsey, but it was 'Lady Deanna of Claverton Castle' who had been allowed here, and she could not risk losing the privilege.

Trolleys clattered. Patients were fed. Matron appeared again, carrying a flask of beef broth. 'I'll just see if he'll swallow ... Ah, excellent, he still has his swallowing reflex. That's a good sign. Would you like to feed him, Your Ladyship? Just a spoonful every minute or so. Check that he swallows — if he doesn't, or coughs, stop at once, and call for the nurse or a VAD.'

'Thank you, Matron.'

'You're freeing up a nurse,' said the matron matter-of-factly. 'I'll see they bring you some dinner later. You'll not go home tonight?'

Deanna shook her head. The matron left them alone.

She spooned up broth into Sam's mouth. He swallowed it. A VAD took the flask and brought her another. He was dehydrated, it appeared, but equipment was in too short supply to put a man who could swallow on a drip.

Instead of dinner another VAD brought what Deanna recognised as her own picnic basket from home, filled with cheese, egg and tomato pies, a flask of real coffee made with milk and fresh scones — Magda's scones, not Anna's — with a jar of the stewed raspberries that were as good as jam.

Some time, long after darkness fell, she must have slept, because she woke to find herself wrapped in a blanket, her head propped on a pillow, and a VAD washing Sam. She'd replaced what looked like a vast baby napkin. The VAD informed Deanna that the one in the bucket was reassuringly wet.

She drank the rest of the coffee, scribbled a note and asked a VAD to phone and read it out to Mrs Thripps at Eagle's Rest, saying Sam was still unconscious but doing well. She hoped it was true.

She found a rudimentary new bathroom in what had been the Green Guest Room, washed as well as she could and returned to find a young man in RAF uniform feeding the still unconscious Sam what looked like thin custard.

He stood on her arrival, though he looked as if he should be in bed too: pale, a wound on his cheek recently stitched, and hollowed eyes.

'Lady Deanna? I'm Pete Martin.' His accent was English. 'I was in the plane with Sam. They ... they say he's going to be all right.' He looked at the man on the bed doubtfully. 'He saved my life, you know.'

'What happened?' She sank into the armchair so he would at least sit down.

'We were heading back over the Channel. A Messerschmitt got us, took out the radio and I don't know what else. Sam managed to get us up into a cloud — we were faster, even if we didn't have firepower — but we couldn't see where we were, or contact anyone, and the engine kept hiccupping. I looked out and part of the wing was gone, but somehow Sam kept her up there, balanced on the wind with what we had left ...'

He shut his eyes for a moment. 'Lady Deanna, I don't know how he did it, but Sam knew where we were in that cloud and kept us in the sky. We came out near a beach. He followed the beach till he saw the castle in the distance — and then he found an updraft somehow and took her higher. That's when he told me our landing gear was bust. He ordered me to jump. She was bucking all over the place by then. I could smell smoke, too. I told him he had to jump after me, but he just said, "Get the hell out of here." Then, "Tell them at Eagle's Rest I love them. Tell them I was an eagle at the end, watching out for them. Now get out! I can't hold her up much longer."

'And so I jumped,' Pete said simply. 'And the 'chute opened just in time, and I landed in a clear paddock with the Home Guard racing towards me.'

'You look like you should be in hospital too.' She slipped another spoonful of the runny custard into Sam's mouth and watched him swallow.

'I am, on the floor below, with eleven other men. They're giving Sam the royal treatment.'

The Claverton respect, she thought, glad of it.

'Mind if I stay here a while?'

'No. I … I like the company. Sam used to tell us your jokes.'

'I bet he only told the clean ones. You've three daughters, haven't you?'

She nodded.

'You look too young, I mean, I beg your pardon …'

'I adopted them. Or they adopted me. Sam sort of adopted us, too, though he has his own family, of course, in Australia. They've been told?'

'His father has. He's listed, along with you, as next of kin.'

For a moment, she took it as almost a declaration, then realised Sam's father was far away. It made sense to have someone nearby who could make … arrangements.

'Why didn't Sam jump too?'

'He said the plane was so light the wind might blow it off course onto someone's house or a school. He had to get it out to sea. I saw the flames after I landed. I thought he had no chance …'

'He landed near the beach.' She couldn't bear to repeat the details. 'Tell me a joke.' Maybe Sam would hear it, and smile.

'There's one I heard the other day. It's a bit rude.'

'I'm unshockable.'

'All right then. This pilot goes to give a talk at a school about their recent exploits. "We were over France," he says. "A great horde of Fokkers came behind us, then suddenly another lot were to the left of us, too —" The teacher breaks in and says, "The Fokkers are a Dutch aircraft, I believe." And the pilot says, "Yeah, but these Fokkers were Messerschmitts."'

She found herself laughing, slightly hysterically. A nurse looked in. She was of the face-as-starched-as-her-uniform variety. 'Mr Martin, you should be in bed!' She gazed at Deanna. 'I'm sorry, miss, but no visitors are permitted. I'll show you out.'

'I'm Lady Deanna Claverton, and this is my castle — this was in fact my bedroom — and if you want me to move you had better check with Matron first.'

'Well!' The nurse stared, as if force of personality would win. Hers lost. She took revenge by leading Pete Martin back to his bed, holding him around the waist, an imposition he clearly found embarrassing.

Which left Deanna with Sam.

He had been washed, changed, fed. And the door even had its old lock on it, the one without a key — just a snib that could shut it from inside. She peered down the corridor, shut the door, then locked it.

She slipped off her shoes and slid into bed with Sam, checking his bandaged arm and making sure his head was kept straight by the pillows on either side, and curled herself around the edge of his body, one arm over his chest, feeling it rise and fall, the other up on the pillow so she could stroke his cheek.

She must have slept again, for when she woke someone was banging on the door, and Sam was awake and smiling at her.

Thirty-Five

Baked Apple

Take two firm apples for each person. Remove the cores, then slash the peel six times so it doesn't burst with baking. Stuff it with whatever you have that is sweet: jam mixed with crushed nuts, or dates, or apricot jam mixed with stale macaroons.

Dot with butter if you have any. Bake in a moderate oven for about forty minutes, till the apples are soft and almost bursting. Good hot or cold. They are excellent eaten with custard, if available.

Warming wartime recipe by
Lady Deanna Claverton

He had only moved his head slightly, and only one red-rimmed eye looked at her from the unbandaged side of his face, but he was conscious, and knew her, and was alive.

'Coming,' she called to whoever was banging on the door. The sound stopped. She gazed at Sam. 'I love you,' she said.

'I love you too.' His lips were cracked, the sound barely audible. She reached over and kissed him gently, then quickly slid out of bed, put on her shoes, tried to uncrumple her dress and untangle her hair, then gave up the effort and opened the door.

'I'm sorry,' she said. 'It sticks sometimes. There's a trick to opening it.'

The starched nurse from the day before glared at her. She held a tray with cloths and dishes. 'It's never stuck before. Why didn't you notify someone?'

'I only just became aware of it.'

'I need to check the patient. Would you mind waiting outside?'

Deanna wouldn't try to fight this battle. 'He's conscious,' she said.

She slipped outside and walked down to the window at the end of the corridor. It, at least, hadn't changed: stained glass on top with St George fighting the dragon, and clear glass below. She looked down at the now mown lawn, the men in pyjamas sitting on benches. She glanced at her wristwatch. Ten past nine — she felt vague indignation that no one had checked on Sam before. But they had known she was with him, and Matron trusted her …

A doctor appeared and vanished into Sam's room, then exited before she could make up her mind about whether to join him and hear his diagnosis firsthand.

She waited another ten minutes, then walked back towards the room just as the breakfast trolley rolled along the corridor.

The VAD she had seen the day before stopped and held out a dish for her. 'Custard for Flight Lieutenant Murray.' She smiled shyly at Deanna. 'He gets a cup of tea now too. You'll feed him again?'

'Yes, thank you. You're doing a magnificent job here.'

The young woman flushed. 'Thank you, my lady.' She bobbed again.

'Call me Lady Dee, if you must, and no curtsey needed,' said Deanna.

The starched-face nurse glanced up as Deanna entered and began to gather up the cloths. She said, reluctantly polite, 'The doctor says there's no sign of brain damage. He thinks the burn will heal well, and his eye too. The arm has a clean break, so he doesn't need any more surgery. You're a lucky young man,' she informed Sam.

'Very lucky,' he whispered, gazing at Deanna. He was propped up on pillows now and looked most reassuringly alive.

'Can he have visitors?'

'At visiting time this afternoon,' said the nurse, holding her ground. She left, holding the soiled towels like armour before her.

Deanna sat back in the armchair. 'Hello,' she said, strangely shy despite spending the night in his bed.

He smiled again. 'I could hear you this morning,' he murmured, only one side of his mouth moving. 'Felt you too,' he added.

'I wanted to be near you. Here.' She held the tea up to his lips and he sipped half of it slowly. 'My word that's good.'

'This won't be,' she said, picking up the bowl of yellow gloop. 'It'll be powdered milk and custard powder. They'd make the water powdered too if they could work out how to do it.' She shrugged. 'Maybe they already have. They just add water.' She held out a spoonful of custard. He ate it, making a face.

'Do you feel up to the girls visiting this afternoon?'

'Of course. I've missed you so much. All of you.'

'We've missed you too. I'm going to ask Matron if you can convalesce with us. I suspect it will be a while before you can fly again.'

'I won't fly again,' he whispered.

'But the doctor said you'd recover ...'

'I'll be able to see with my left eye, but it won't ever be as clear as before. He said I might not even notice it, but the RAF will. A pilot needs perfect eyesight.'

'Do ... do you mind very much?'

'No. I'm glad. Don't think me a coward.'

'You could never be a coward!'

'I'm free of all the killing at last. The choice has been made for me. That dunking in the sea washed me free of blood, and I can be myself again.'

She nodded, understanding. 'You'll come to Eagle's Rest?'

'There's nothing I'd like more.'

She held his good hand with hers and used her other to feed him custard and the rest of the tea. His unbandaged eye was drooping by the time he'd eaten.

'Sleep,' she said. 'I need to get changed, then I'll bring the girls back with me.'

She looked at her dress, then touched her tangled hair again. She had not even thought to bring her handbag, much less a comb. 'I look a mess.'

'You look beautiful.'

'Sam ...' She should not be asking this now, but the compulsion was too strong. 'You said you love me. Did you mean it?'

'I mean it. Dee ... I assumed I wouldn't survive the war. Now it looks as if I might. There are things you need to know ... important things.' He was obviously struggling to stay awake.

'They can wait till you're home with us. I love you too.' She bent to kiss him once again.

Thirty-Six

Fruit Jelly Cake

Serves four to six unless you're greedy.

INGREDIENTS
one cup strawberries, peaches or other soft fruit
one cup raspberries
one cup mulberries, stems removed
one cup white wine
one cup castor sugar or half a cup of honey
juice of two lemons if available, or half a cup of the juice of green grapes or green apples
half a cup water
two sachets gelatine

METHOD
Grease a cake tin well. Place sliced strawberries or peaches in an attractive pattern on the bottom; empty in the other fruit. Heat all other ingredients except the gelatine till nearly boiling; take off the heat; add gelatine. (Mix

a little with some of the liquid first so you don't get lumps.) Pour liquid into the cake tin. Leave till set, which will take several hours. Turn it out onto a plate. If it won't come out easily, dip the base of the tin in hot water in the sink for about thirty seconds — make sure no liquid gets into the tin though! This will loosen the jelly enough for it to slide out. Serve in slices with cream if you have it.

Note: if that amount of gelatine doesn't form a well-set jelly, the whole thing can be slightly warmed and more gelatine (mixed with a little of the warmed liquid first) can be added. For some reason sometimes more is needed — it depends on the ripeness and juiciness of the berries.

Recipe by Lady Deanna Claverton

The Amazing Anna had already stitched two soft cotton cushions together to rest his arm on. Magda had found some Wodehouse books she didn't think he had read. Trust Magda, Deanna thought with pride, to notice which type of books Sam had borrowed from the library and which volumes he hadn't yet read. Wodehouse was a perfect choice: silly and hilarious with no trace of war or trauma.

Rosa and Mrs Thripps had disposed of a rooster and made clear chicken soup, flavoured with herbs and vegetables, totally unlike the brown 'broth', smelling of salt and elderly cabbage, Deanna had fed him last night.

The Amazing Anna met her at the door. 'She's back!' she yelled to the other inhabitants.

'Yelling isn't polite,' said Deanna automatically.

The Amazing Anna just grinned. 'He's all right, isn't he?' Rosa and Magda galloped down the stairs to them. Mrs Thripps appeared from the scullery.

'A broken arm and some cuts, and one side of his face is burned, but it will all mend.'

She didn't mention he would no longer fly. 'I'm going to ask Matron if he can recuperate here.' And if Matron refuses, I'll pull rank, and get Uncle Jasper to have a word, she thought. He can't possibly doubt Sam's loyalty after this.

Mrs Thripps grinned. 'Tell the lad I'll be in tomorrow, when my beauty won't overwhelm him. A man needs strength to cope with the belle of the music hall.'

'I'll tell him,' said Deanna gratefully. 'Thank you. You've been an utter brick.'

'I'll be off then — you need at least three hours in the queue to get the meat ration these days, and I've got the fishmonger's and the grocer's to get to as well. But you tell your young man his room is waiting for him, and the bedroom fire ready to light too.'

She gave the Amazing Anna a light slap on the head. 'Missy here insisted so we did it last night.'

'I *knew* he'd be all right,' said the Amazing Anna.

'Thank you,' said Deanna again. Money couldn't compensate for kindness. 'I'm just going to have a bath and get changed. Why don't you pick some flowers?' she added to the girls.

'There's chicken and salad sandwiches wrapped in a napkin in the refrigerator,' said Mrs Thripps. 'You get those into you while you bathe, lovie. Don't want you dropping out of hunger.'

The bath was wonderful. She used a careful spoonful of her diminishing violet-scented bath salts, soaking away the aches from sleeping in a chair as well as pulling Sam's body up the beach.

She noticed some scorches she had ignored yesterday, but all were minor. She ate the sandwiches slowly, enjoying every mouthful. She washed her hair too, dank with salt water, then pulled it up in a high ponytail, suitable for wet hair but where it would also curl naturally down to her shoulders as it dried.

Some of her precious lipstick, the dress with blue cornflowers he had once admired on her hat, the high heels she hadn't worn since the last Christmas with him …

She could imagine his convalescence here. The girls would help him outside and surround him with cushions. There'd be good soups — thankfully, a number of young roosters had hatched in spring and were ready for the chop. Orange juice, and early peaches that were ready in the glasshouse, and her share of the next Pig Club was due in a month — surely he'd need more than a month to convalesce.

He could watch the eagles with binoculars, then slowly begin to walk, to the river first, maybe with a fishing line ... She hoped the beach didn't haunt his memories. But that was where he'd headed for safety.

She hadn't told him about Dusty, she realised. He'd expect to see the big dog welcome him. Did he even know Dusty's role in saving his life? I'll play it by ear, she thought, and tell him what I told the girls, that Dusty died saving someone he loved. Dusty's love would be with them always.

The girls were waiting for her, with enough roses for the entire ward, and a basket of other provisions.

They walked up to the castle, the girls chattering, Deanna enjoying the glow of loving and being loved, and having Sam safe from further missions in the war, too.

They climbed the front steps — she had a flash of memory of Perkins the butler descending those very steps to open the door of her grandmother's car — then into the partitioned-off reception area.

Deanna smiled at the VAD, one she hadn't seen before. 'I'm Lady Deanna Claverton. We're here to see Flight Lieutenant Murray. Matron gave us permission.'

The woman stared at her. 'I'm sorry, Lady Deanna, but Flight Lieutenant Murray was taken by ambulance over an hour ago.'

Thirty-Seven

Vegetable and Oatmeal Goulash

INGREDIENTS
500 grams to one kilogram turnips, parsnips, swedes, potatoes
a knob of dripping
60 grams coarse oatmeal
475 millilitres vegetable stock
one teaspoon meat extract
mixed herbs, salt and pepper

METHOD
Prepare and dice the vegetables and fry in dripping until slightly cooked. Add the oatmeal and keep stirring until fat is absorbed. Fill with vegetable stock until covered and simmer until vegetables are soft and mixture is really thick (about forty-five minutes). Mix in meat extract when cooking, then mix in herbs, salt and pepper to taste.

A Ministry of Food recipe. Do not try it.

It took half an hour to see Matron, who was visibly restraining her impatience at dealing with visitors — even a titled one — instead of the injured and ill.

'He's been taken to another hospital — I'm sorry, Lady Deanna, I don't know where. Yes, it was very sudden. I gather,' she said carefully, 'that there is a hospital ship due to leave for Australia soon. Of course its departure date is top secret, so I'm sure you won't mention that to anyone ...'

'They are taking him to *Australia!*' exclaimed the Amazing Anna.

'He is Australian,' the matron reminded her.

'But how can we see him? We haven't even said goodbye!' protested Rosa.

Matron looked uncomfortable. 'I'm afraid I'm unable to give you any more information. There is a war on, you know. Loose lips sink ships.'

Deanna said nothing, as the girls tried to coax more from the increasingly taciturn matron. Sam probably was fit to be moved today, though several more days would have been safer after concussion and all he had gone through. But she couldn't believe there was a more suitable hospital. Claverton Castle had empty beds, and even empty rooms, with no major casualties expected from cities nearby. It frequently filled in for the overflow from city hospitals. Sam wasn't even taking up staff time — she had been here to feed him and keep watch, and Matron would surely expect him to convalesce at Eagle's Rest.

What had changed in the few hours she'd been away?

Evidence that he'd been a traitor, using his position to make sure the bombing attacks went astray? Yes, he'd been unequivocal about the valuelessness and cruelty of attacks on civilian targets, but Uncle Jasper had said he had proved so useful leading attacks that he wouldn't be sent back to training.

What had changed?

The crash wasn't his fault — his achievement of getting back safely must be extraordinary. He was a hero, not just saving Pete's life and making sure no one was hurt by the wreckage, but bringing back parts of the craft that might possibly be used, and extinguishing the fire in the sea.

Sam was not a fascist. She had never asked what his ancestry was, but it was obvious his identification with Australia was total. Uncle Jasper would have mentioned any German connection. Sam didn't need money, for by all indications the wartime price of wool had made his family wealthy, if they hadn't been before.

He had travelled in Italy to race, but she could not believe he had admired Mussolini, nor would mere admiration have led him to betray his country. Besides, if he was suspect, why keep him in an area of operations when he had information to give away?

She stood. 'Come on,' she said to her daughters. 'We must leave Matron to her work.'

'But —' began Anna.

Deanna took a deep breath. 'Darlings, I don't know what is happening. But Matron is right — now Sam can't rejoin the RAF he will be sent home on a hospital ship to Australia. It just seems ... hurried.'

'But Dusty saved him for us!' wailed Anna.

Deanna shook her head. 'Sam will be safe at home with his family.' If the hospital ship wasn't sunk by U-boats, if the Japanese didn't invade or bomb Australia, if his burns did not get infected ...

He is safer this week than he was last week, she told herself. I must cling to that.

Meanwhile, she was going to send a letter to Uncle Jasper.

Thirty-Eight

Under the level winter sky
I saw a thousand Christs go by.
They sang an idle song and free
As they went up to Calvary.
Careless of eye and coarse of lip,
They marched in holiest fellowship.
That heaven might heal the world, they gave
Their earth-born dreams to deck the grave.
With souls unpurged and steadfast breath
They supped the sacrament of death.
And for each one, far off, apart,
Seven swords have rent a woman's heart.

'Marching Men' by Marjorie Pickthall

Dear Uncle Jasper,
We have had some terrible news — a dear friend of ours crashed nearby. We hoped he could recuperate with us, but he was taken away to a far-off hospital the next afternoon. I am

sure it is a mistake — we are the closest thing to family he has in England — and badly wish we could do something about it.

I do hope to hear from you soon.

Your loving niece,

Dee

She read it four times before she posted it. If anyone was checking her mail surely it would be natural to mention something as momentous as Sam's disappearance.

Is he really being sent to Australia? she wondered suddenly. Had he been imprisoned as a fifth columnist, a spy, a saboteur, or whatever accusation they might level at the hidden enemies of Britain? Perhaps even now he was in a lightless cell like Kurt's ...

She walked briskly down to the post office in time to slip the letter in the box for the mail collection. She was surprised, though, to find an answer poked through the letterbox in the front door the next morning by the postman on his rounds. It couldn't possibly have been through the censor and the sorting office by now. Someone, somehow, had taken her letter directly to Uncle Jasper and slipped this one into the postbag for Claverton.

My dear niece,

I can imagine how upsetting the last few days have been for you. I know how fond you were of the young man. Will you take the advice of an old one? Whatever has happened to him will be for the best; he is going where he will be well cared for, with qualified staff for his injuries and rehabilitation. Let those who know best take care of him.

Your aunt sends her love, as I do. She was also going to send a pot of her mock chicken paste, but it grew a most interesting set of green whiskers. I was prepared to see how long they grew as an experiment, but Fogger's pig bin got them instead. I devoutly hope his pigs are none the worse for it.

   Your devoted uncle,
   Jasper

Deanna put the letter down. This was as firm a confirmation as could be put in a letter, and it had been sent as quickly as possible, with no telegram or phone call that Doris at the exchange could gossip about.

She must pretend what had happened was normal — casually remind the girls that despite their anguish at not even seeing Sam, they must not mention him or his destination to anyone.

'He'll be on a ship,' she could say, 'and we can't afford any hint to enemy agents that a ship may be leaving for Australia.'

Please, she prayed, let him be safe. Let him be on his ship and reach the safety of home.

She did not pray, *Let him not be an enemy agent or even a sympathiser,* for she could not believe either.

A postcard from Sam arrived a week later, one of the ubiquitous war-themed ones showing an elderly man virtuously tending cabbages, which told nothing of wherever he might be.

Deanna read it before she took it from the front hall to show to the girls. It seemed genuine, the wording so much like Sam, with no hint that he was imprisoned.

But would he risk those he loved by hinting that?

'A card from Sam,' she announced.

The girls looked up from their poached eggs, toast with cherry jam, and glasses of milk from the Higginses' cows, except Magda, who had quietly promoted herself to milky tea a few months before, using Deanna's four-times-dried-out tea ration so as not to deprive her mother.

'What does it say!?' demanded Anna.

'Is he all right?' worried Rosa.

'Let her read it,' said Magda calmly. Too calmly. Deanna glanced at her. Magda was frightened, but intelligent, and far too experienced for her years. She, too, was worried about the suddenness of Sam's departure, and was determined not to show her fear to her sisters or adopted mother.

The writing was so tiny she had to squint to read it.

Dear Dee, Magda, Rosa, Amazing Anna, and Dusty,

'He doesn't know about Dusty,' whispered Anna.

'Maybe he should never know,' offered Rosa sombrely.

Magda shook her head. 'Dusty deserves that he should know. And Sam needs to know that Dusty loved him so much he gave all he had to save him.'

'But not just yet, perhaps,' said Deanna quietly. She began to read the postcard out again, deciphering its tiny spidery writing: Sam had fit as many words as possible onto the card, and any spare space at the front.

> *As you will know by now, I was gathered up, bag and baggage, into an ambulance, except I had no bag to gather, and shipped to a hospital at a place I am sure the censor will delete, so I'll save her the trouble. I now have a bag, complete with pyjamas, shaving kit and blue convalescent uniform. I'm bound for civvie street — I'm more use dagging sheep back home. I'll write again when I get a chance to send a letter.*
>
> *I'm healing well, and the doc says my sight will be almost unaffected — 'almost' is not good enough to be a pilot. You all saved my life, you know. I was in that mist over the Channel but somehow I knew where you were. I just had to keep her airborne till I saw the castle towers. All I could think of was that I was coming home to you.*

I wish with all my heart I could be with you now.
Love to you all,
Sam

Love to us all, thought Deanna. So many kinds of love. The love of a soldier far from home in wartime might be very different from what he felt after six months back in his own world, with the women who'd known him all his life. If only he had been permitted to convalesce here, she was sure she'd have been wearing an engagement ring at the end of it. The diaphragm would no longer be tucked away in the drawer under her knickers but kept handy in its discreet box.

She and Sam were helpless, caught in the threads of war. Some might snap forever; others knot eternally, with no way to speak feelings clearly without the censor reading the words.

She did not even have an address to write to him, except, perhaps, through Deb.

Another letter arrived six weeks later, a proper letter.

Dear Eagles,

I can see blue sea! And more blue sea, and beyond that even more. It is very blue, and very boring, but better than the green and white storm sea we had last night. I was seasick, as were two of my ward mates, and there were not enough buckets handy. I'll spare you the rest, but for the first time I was glad I was a patient and told firmly to stay in bed, and not given a mop, scrubbing brush and carbolic.

We are being stuffed with 'wholesome' food six times a day, porridge and what I am sure are nourishing stews, and a mix of cheese, onion and powdered egg that I am told is an omelette. It looks ashamed of itself every time it sits on the plate, just like Dusty when he does a particularly big fart. Come to think of it, the omelette smells a bit like Dusty's farts.

We have exercises twice a day, suited to our respective injuries, but apart from that we are ignored, surplus to war requirements. I'll be glad to be home again and should be fully healed by then too. I wish they would at least let us peel the potatoes, but then we might find out what goes into the stews. Stu (no relation to the meals) says the meat is probably rat, which are always abundant on ships, and swears he can hear the skins and innards being thrown over the side each night.

Love to you all,
Sam

She was sure the letter was genuine this time. Sam *was* going home, presumably not just because of his injury but possibly because, from his remote farm, at some distance from a small town, there would be nothing he could divulge to the enemy, nor sabotage ...

A sudden thought struck her. Had he crashed deliberately, unable to keep doing a job that created so much death and loss, with Pete ordered to parachute to safety so Sam could die at the place in England he loved best?

No. Impossible.

Spies carried cyanide capsules to use when they could bear no more torture, but Sam loved life too much. Nor would he need to have killed himself to escape the Pathfinders and the bombing raids when a far smaller injury could have forced him from the RAF, just as had indeed happened.

She must accept that the crash had been an accident, even if the choice to place Sam Murray in the almost invariably fatal Mosquitoes had not been. She still had no inkling why he might be considered a danger, or why he had been permitted to fly despite those suspicions.

The fear for him began to fade, which just left longing.

Thirty-Nine

Lay the paper the butter was wrapped in on your dish of boiled peas or new potatoes. The buttery scent will flavour them!
Helpful Hints from the Ministry of Food, World War II

No one, these days, discussed the future, except as a 'when the war is over' hypothetical.

It was 'When will we win?' too, not 'Can we survive?'

Magda was weighing up physics or medicine; and Anna currently wanted to be a circus performer, if only Mr Higgins would let her practise on his draught horses. Meanwhile she juggled, managing two and sometimes three apples in the air at once. Rosa always answered, 'Vet science, maybe,' if asked, though she spent hours designing frocks, evening trousers and flamboyant hats neither she nor Deanna had time to make. The war ate time as well as energy.

And herself? Deanna had no idea. If there had been no war, she might never have even considered the question, content to spend her life here, like Miss Enid, tending bees and watching birds, visiting the old schoolfriends she had now lost touch with, admiring their babies, enjoying a Friday-to-Monday or a garden party or even a debutante ball as their children grew older, but glad to come back to the peace of home. If there had been no war, she would never have met Sam.

His first letter from home was sent the week Italy surrendered to the Allies and arrived six weeks later.

> *Dear English Eagles,*
>
> *I've finally seen a wedgetail again! I'd like to say it swooped down to welcome me home just as Dad's truck pulled up, but there also happened to be a fat wonga pigeon trotting down the track — wonga pigeons prefer to walk, not fly. That pigeon is now a pigeon dinner for the wedgetail.*
>
> *I've thrown away my walking stick — though actually it's thriftily left in the hall cupboard in case anyone needs one again.*
>
> *The RAF and RAAF still insist I can't fly and Dad sold my own craft for me to put the money into war bonds in '39. But I'd rather live with the eagles above me now than try to fly like them, and I hardly notice any problem in my eye, just cloudiness if I look to the left, and I've learned to turn my head to compensate.*
>
> *It is so good to be home, to be in a familiar bed and know I won't be woken up by nurses or roll calls. I am a civilian and a farmer again, though as yet I have done no farming, just eaten vast amounts of mutton grilled and roasted by Mrs Hobbins, who's been coming in to care for the house since I was a kid. She correctly believes it has been far too long since I had a good stuffed shoulder of mutton with roast pumpkin. I wish I could send a side of mutton to you.*
>
> *Dad is frailer, and Deb has still had no word from Ron. One of our workmen, Irish Ken, escaped Singapore in a dinghy and managed to get home via New Guinea, but lost some toes on the way, so the army kicked him out, just like they got rid of me. He's back here rounding up sheep again now.*

The Italian prisoners of war who worked here for a while have been replaced by four very efficient land girls boarding with two of the families whose men are away. One of them, Susan, was even studying zoology before the war, and has been noting when the eagles breed, as well as the wombats, rock wallabies, swamp wallabies, roos and possibly the humans too. She reminds me a bit of you, Amazing Anna: full of questions.

I'll gird myself up to dag some fly-struck sheep tomorrow. I'll only explain dagging and fly strike if you really want to know and ask in your next letter. Let us just say it is hot, smelly, and unpleasant for both the sheep and the human, but needs to be done. I'll really know I'm home when I've dagged some sheep.

Love to all of you, including the eagles.

Sam

They each wrote to him: Magda sporadically, now she was seriously studying for her final exams. Deanna suspected she was hoping for a scholarship to Oxford and wondered how to tell her that she only need gain enough marks to enter one of the Women's Colleges — admittedly still high marks, but ones she could easily achieve. Her daughters probably assumed she grew the vegetables and glasshouse crops because she needed the money, not to help feed Britain.

She had told them how Miss Enid had left her the property — they loved stories about Miss Enid and the animals she had cared for, like the squirrel that fed from her hand, and the fox that hid in the shed from the fox hunt, which was now thankfully suspended for the war. She hadn't mentioned money, because one didn't mention money — not 'people like us'. But that was as silly as assuming a 'gel' would have a debutante season and a man like Arnold Thripps who cooled his tea in his saucer wasn't worthy to be a friend.

Magda, Rosa and Anna probably assumed they lived simply but comfortably because that was all that Deanna could afford. She would have to find a way to tell them there were enough funds for them to do essentially anything they wished, from university to climbing Mt Everest, if — when — the war should end, and pursuits such as that were possible again.

Some of Sam's replies were to them all; some were in reply to their individual letters. Deanna wrote weekly, but mail was so disrupted it was impossible to know if he replied weekly too.

He and Mrs Thripps were the only two people she could talk to about the girls. Arnold and Mrs Thripps could, at least, stay for birthday dinners and come to watch the girls perform in the school plays, with Arnold yelling 'encore' when one of the three wise men began to juggle his conveniently round gifts of gold.

Each time a letter arrived from Sam for her alone she kept it till she could read it by herself, then re-read it, hoping for whatever perfume gum leaves had, and the scent of Sam, too. But inevitably all she smelled was canvas, from the bag it had been stored in, and sometimes gasoline or engine oil.

A letter arrived two days after D Day, 6 June 1944, as Allied troops poured into France again, despite the rain and fog, and this time forging ahead, despite enormous losses if the lists of dead in the newspapers were a guide. But here at Eagle's Rest the sun shone on land girls weeding the potatoes. Deanna opened Sam's letter up on the hills, listening to the slap of waves, the scream of gulls, and hoping that, just possibly, an eagle might come to watch over her.

Dear Dee,

She bit her lip at the salutation. They had known each other for almost four years now, even if more than two of those had been by letter. They had slept together, even if no intercourse had taken place. Surely by now he might have begun his letters with 'Darling Dee', at least?

> *For the first time I was glad you weren't here last week — a dry thunderstorm, a bad one, and several lightning strikes. Luckily the wind blew the fires down to the river, as half the bushfire brigade are overseas and the other half average over ninety-four on a good day, but we spent more than ten hours keeping the flames from the house and sheds. We've lost the grass from four paddocks, but it rained the day after, like it often does, so there's green already through the trees.*
>
> *The fire is my fault, or no one's fault, or maybe Mr Hitler's. We usually do a low patch burn every winter, so that by the seventh year the whole place has been cleared of too much tinder, but there've been no burns since '39. I need to get onto it again, even if it means training the land girls how to follow a fire line. I'm sure they can do it though — no one would ever know that four years ago they'd never mended a fence or fed a mob of poddy lambs.*
>
> *It's brilliant Magda has done so well in her exams — she didn't even mention them when she last wrote. I know you don't read the girls' letters to me, so let me share this with you.*
>
> *'I haven't told Mum about the American soldier who kept meeting me at the train station after school and asking me out, because she might peck his eyes out for trying to date a schoolgirl. I finally got rid of him by asking if he thought that Hitler's ideas had been influenced by Nietzsche or Charles Darwin. He looked just like a hooked trout with his mouth open. I am DEFINITELY going to study philosophy when I get to university.'*
>
> *I had to admit I have never read anything about Nietzsche, and only vaguely know about the theory of evolution, so I hope*

she doesn't decide I am unworthy of more letters. I love hearing from the girls, and of course from you.

Give my best regards to Mr and Mrs Thripps,

Yours always,

Sam

His always, she thought, dismayed. She signed her letters to him 'with love'. He had sent his love too until the last few months. It was as if the more possible it became for them to be together, the more distant he became.

True, the war in the Pacific still raged, but war brides across England were putting their names down to cross oceans to be with husbands in America, Canada and Australia.

Was the problem their allegiances to different countries? That could be overcome, as a man who had already flown to Europe and back several times would know. The pre-war commercial flights to Australia would begin again. The distance could be covered in less than a week. If he had been here, Deanna decided, she would have damn well asked him to marry her instead of waiting, as per Mrs Thripps' suggestion.

But Sam wasn't here. It was all too possible that a lonely man had imagined that friendship and sexual desire were love, and that now he was home only that friendship remained.

Dearest Sam,

Now D-Day is finally over I can write about this without the censor blacking it out or even a knock on my door by the police, but I have been longing to tell someone. I was invited to accompany Her Majesty on one of her visits to a factory where we 'happened' to pass an army camp for the BBC to film in the background, but secretly the tanks and aircraft were all balloons, there to fool the enemy into thinking the troops were massing to the north, not in the south.

So there I was, in my best tweed suit — a bit moth-eaten because I'd forgotten to replenish the mothballs and lavender, but Rosa and I mended it artfully — and a most respectable hat and pearls, riding in one of the cars behind Her Majesty ... and a wind suddenly gusted from nowhere and one of the tanks began to float away. Men dashed from everywhere to hold down the ropes. The BBC people must have known the footage was meant to mislead so would have been careful where they aimed the cameras, but it was so funny. I had a vision of a tank flying over the Isle of Man. Now <u>that</u> would have been impossible to explain away.

Her Majesty was wonderful, greeting all the 'factory workers' who were really government officials playing different roles each time. I wonder what they are doing now that the pretence is no longer needed and we are forging towards Berlin?

I enjoyed myself enormously, though it's not a world I want to go back to except for a rare visit. But when I finally got home — on a train, as it seemed I was only due a limousine while actually accompanying Her Majesty — I found that Anna had missed school again.

She wouldn't even give me an excuse this time, just said she didn't want to go, then yelled at me to mind my own business. I am more worried about that than her missing school. She's always been a bit of a monkey but also almost angelically helpful and polite.

I didn't know what to say, so I said nothing. Mrs Thripps would have recommended a spanking — she's told me how her father used to give them all a belting every Saturday night on principle, because he was sure they deserved it for something, even if he didn't know what. But whatever is wrong with Anna, I don't think it would be solved so simply.

I did ask Magda if she knew what was wrong. She could see I was upset, and made me cocoa, which made me tear up for some reason, remembering all the times we've drunk cocoa. Magda said just to 'leave her and she'll get over it' which I'm doing. But Sam, she didn't even want to come fishing with us last Saturday.

We fished at the pool by the cliffs, but only caught one trout. You'd have caught half a dozen. I missed you and not just for the fish.

Love,
Dee

By some intricacy of wartime mail the reply came five months later, along with eight other letters written at various times, and his Christmas presents to all of them — his sister's usual can of dripping, accompanied by a massive fruitcake, and, from Sam, a giant sofa rug of the softest fur Deanna had ever touched, more so even than mink, which he said was possum fur, and opal pendants for all of them, each one exactly the same, except for the varied colours of the stones.

She opened hers and tried to seem delighted in front of her daughters and the Thrippses.

She had hoped her gift would be as personal as hers to him had been: one of Miss Enid's paintings of a golden eagle by the artist Cecile Walton, moderately famous, despite being a woman, so the work might possibly be valuable.

The response to her letter after D Day left her equally dispirited.

Dear Dee,
I had to read out your account of the queen and the floating tank to everyone — they thought it hilarious and were also impressed, and impressed by me knowing someone who accompanied the queen too.

I asked Susan's advice about Anna — she has two younger sisters. She laughed and said all girls were like that at her age, then when I explained the background bit, said very sensibly that maybe Anna is making sure that you will love her even if she's not angelic. I hope all has settled now.

Our main news is that Deb has had a postcard from Ron — it really just said he's still in Changi, but at least we know he's alive and presumably safe. The only other event of note has been the annual Budgie Creek races. By common agreement there is no starting gate, as breaking into a gallop a few seconds before the starting gun goes off is meant to be part of the skill — anything short of actually knocking off another rider.

I used to take part ... I was going to say 'when I was young' then realised the last was only eight years ago but seems a lifetime. I didn't this year, but we all crammed into the car, Susan, Harriet, Mary, Marg, Ken, Dad and me, which was a squash, but we have petrol rationing too, though it's not nearly as severe as in Britain.

Irish Ken came third in the wood-chopping, and Susan and I came second in the three-legged dash and Harriet and Marg won! Not just that, but Harriet won the egg and spoon race too, so we felt Eagle Mountain had sufficient glory.

It seemed a world away from England, and the war. Well it IS a world away from England, but I wish the war were further away, though we seem to have the Japanese on the hop at last. I miss you all, but it is so very good to be home.

Love to you all,
Sam

It was a hint, she thought, or, rather, one of many hints that he'd sent which she finally needed to accept. Sam had been a friend who had believed he loved her when he thought that as a pilot his life might be short. Now, he was back in his world while she was in England indefinitely, the war with Japan parting them for years more, perhaps.

It was a truth often acknowledged that men needed wives. Men with farms or estates, especially, needed wives. The world pretends that the London Season and making one's debut is all about a young woman catching a husband, Deanna thought, but it is really for the benefit of the men, so they can assess who would make the most suitable companion to organise the domestic side of their lives, as well as be a companion in bed and at breakfast, arranging the social life, producing and rearing the children so the farm or estate can continue ...

Sam, too, must hope for children to pass his farm to, as well as for the daily companionship it seemed he had now found with Susan.

And why not? she told herself firmly. He had a right to a family. With so many men away, and a large and obviously wealthy farm, he was undoubtedly the area's most eligible bachelor.

Susan sounded ... suitable. Sensible. She had even been right about Anna, whose rebellion, after two months, had stopped as suddenly as it had begun, and who was now enjoying school with her sisters again, and practising the high-wire act, with coaching from Mrs Thripps, on a very low rope tied between two posts in the barn.

And it was the festive season, when it was her duty to be happy, especially when it seemed — finally — that in the year to come the war truly might be over by Christmas.

Forty

April 1945

How can a German soldier coming back from leave know his comrades on the Eastern Front are pleased to see him? They run two hundred yards to meet him.

Joke from late in World War II

Even in a wartime spring, Deanna decided — especially in wartime, and even more when the end of the war seemed possible — there should sometimes be a Saturday afternoon for a spinster of this parish to devote purely to delight, as the daffodils unfurled, the brown oak tree branches suddenly greened overnight, and the land was dappled with shadows after the starkness of winter.

She settled herself with a cup of pale tea — the provisions in the cellar were finally depleted now — on the old cane lounge against the cottage wall, with the Parson's Blush rosebuds showing the faintest hint of pink. The girls had departed on a major adventure: taking the train by themselves to a matinee at Claverton Major's picture theatre, with money for fish and chips to eat on the way back, and a string bag of mock-cheese sandwiches.

There were no marrow-growing competitions to judge today, no Girl Guides to present with honour badges. She had yesterday's war-thin newspaper to read, as well as the good, thick *Jane Eyre* she revisited every few years, and a letter from Sam to read in private, so she would have no need to mask her misery and show delight if — when — he announced his engagement.

True, there had been no more mentions of Susan in the letters she'd received from him in the four months since Christmas, but why should a man tell a woman he had once been close to the details of his courtship of another?

The very absence of any reference was significant.

She glanced at the postmark. Budgie Creek, and three months ago. Wartime mail was so erratic she had to keep checking the dates when the lambs arrived six weeks before the rams had been let into the ewes.

Dear Dee,

She skimmed the letter quickly, in case it had a major revelation, but it seemed to be more about eagles and sheep than the humans who shared his life. She began to read again.

'Mum?' She looked up. Her daughters stood in front of her, hand in hand, their faces blank with shock, curiously like the trio she had first seen five years back. She hadn't even heard their bicycles.

'What is it? I didn't expect you for hours yet!' Not a bomb, she thought, not now and not in Claverton Major. Another car crash ...

'We only saw the newsreel,' said Rosa, her voice as expressionless as her face. 'The British army has liberated another concentration camp, at Bergen-Belsen this time. The British army filmed it ...'

And they put it in a newsreel that children might see! thought Deanna, horrified. There had been reports in the newspapers about the horrors Russian troops had found at Auschwitz and Majdanek, and a few photos, but the camps had been mostly empty.

'Thousands of bodies piled up,' whispered Magda. 'And people like skeletons, just sitting, staring. The commentator said there are sixty thousand in the barracks, but most will die, have died, hundreds of thousands, millions ... Mum, that would have been us.'

She stood up. 'No, my loves. You had parents who made their home in England long before—'

'You don't understand!' cried Rosa. 'England *wasn't* safe! If Hitler had taken England, or if there had been an alliance, we'd have been gassed too!'

And even being Lady Deanna Claverton with an Uncle Jasper could not have stopped it, thought Deanna, stricken. Kurt had intended her daughters to join their 'relatives' in an internment camp. England had rounded up most of the German Jewish people to hand to the Nazis on a plate, she thought. Had Kurt known that?

'I want to machine-gun them,' said Anna fiercely. 'I want to kill them all from a plane, like the one who shot our village. I want to kill as many as I can!'

'No!' Deanna ran to them, gathered them in her arms, felt them tremble as they had that first night, but not from cold now. 'If we kill them for being German, we have become the Nazis too.'

Magda broke away and stared at her. 'So we do nothing?'

Let other people sort it out, thought Deanna, for surely there'd be horror spreading across the world at this. But that was exactly what had caused the tragedy — people knowing or suspecting and doing nothing, letting others sort it out. 'I don't know. I have only lived in a country that fights its way to territory, kills its enemies and mostly wins, so it sees battles as the best solution. I don't think there is one answer. Maybe … maybe if you study philosophy, you'll find a way.'

Rosa looked up at her. 'There is a way. We hear it in church every Sunday. The vicar says "thou shalt not kill" and "forgive your enemies" — but then he prays for victory.'

'Mr Reverend Goodword is …' She wanted to say, 'not very bright.' Instead she said, 'I think Mr Goodword is like many people — he doesn't think of enemies as people like us, the ones the Commandments apply to.'

'People in all those countries Germany conquered didn't think people like me and Anna and Rosa were human like them. They had camps to murder people like us too. The Nazis built the camps, but the nations they conquered across Europe hated people like us enough to fill them. How can something like that change?' asked Magda.

Deanna felt unbearably weary. 'Sam said those who fight a bushfire together put away their quarrels. Maybe the whole world should fight a bushfire together and feel we are one? I just don't know.'

'Cocoa,' said Anna, her voice still muffled. 'When we came here you gave us cocoa.'

'You'd like cocoa now?'

Two nods against her shoulder, and a 'Yes please,' from Magda, who was no longer looking blank and helpless but as she did when engaged with a particularly interesting problem in her homework.

Magda is working out how to save the world, thought Deanna desperately. But, for now, there would be cocoa.

Forty-One

Here dead we lie because we did not choose
To live and shame the land from which we sprung.
Life, to be sure, is nothing much to lose,
But young men think it is, and we were young.
'Here Dead We Lie' by AE Housman

Germany surrendered on 8 May 1945.

People crowded like ants at the base of the Victoria Memorial, while in the ballroom of Windsor Castle the king awarded military medals including the Distinguished Service Medal and the Military Medal to nearly three hundred recipients.

At two forty pm, following lunch, Churchill returned to 10 Downing Street. The route to Whitehall was held open to enable him to deliver his victory speech in a live broadcast at three pm: 'God bless you all. This is your victory!'

The crowd roared back, 'No — it is yours.'

The church bells rang; the wireless pealed an endless chatter of cheering and dancing in the streets. Mrs Thripps did not appear for work. Presumably she and Arnold celebrated too.

'... and a dance on Saturday night at the village hall,' said Mrs Goodword. 'I'm sure we can count on your contribution, Lady Deanna. Perhaps you would care to lead the first dance and make a speech?'

Deanna glanced at the three children sitting behind her at the kitchen table. The news of Bergen-Belsen, and all the horror still unfolding, had brought back their personal trauma too: the loss of their parents; their own injuries, alone in hospital; the savagery and racism of the orphanage; the final nightmare train ride, so much like one that might have taken children to a concentration camp, but instead had brought them here to her.

There had been too much. Even overwhelming good was too much to easily cope with now.

'I don't think we'll attend,' said Deanna quietly. She tried a smile, and truth. 'We are just tired, Mrs Goodword. I'll make a giant celebration cake.' It would need cardboard icing, even though she had sugar left, for iced cakes were still illegal. War might have ended. Rationing had not. 'You can announce it comes from me. Perhaps you could read out a small speech given in my name.'

'We are all tired,' said Mrs Goodword, and for once she seemed to have heard what Deanna said and understood. 'But one must carry on.'

'We'll carry on. Just not dance just yet. War hasn't ended in the Pacific.' Nor had the suffering across Europe stopped just because the bells had rung.

'Ah, your Australian pilot. How is he?' The bright eyes were looking for tradable gossip now. The postmaster had undoubtedly made it known throughout Claverton Minor how much correspondence with Australia arrived at and was sent from Eagle's Rest.

'He's very well, thank you, though worried about members of his family still fighting the Japanese, or in prison camps. There seems no chance of a quick ending to the fighting in the Pacific.'

Mrs Goodword moved outside slightly, so she no longer stood in the back door, but out of earshot of the girls at the table. Deanna followed her automatically. 'My dear, if you will forgive me,' said the older woman quietly, 'there might be … gossip … if you and your daughters didn't appear.'

'I don't understand.'

Mrs Goodword looked at her incredulously. 'Your daughters are German, Lady Deanna. Of course they are English too,' she added hurriedly. 'And legally your daughters. But still, it would be … tactful … if you all appeared.'

Deanna shut her eyes briefly.

Her daughters had been accepted only because she was Lady Deanna of the Castle. No school friend had ever been asked to join their badger spotting or afternoons up on the headland sharing the binoculars. No school friend had ever asked one of her daughters to tea. They only had each other, and now her.

And she had never admitted it before.

'We'll bring the cake,' she said wearily. 'I will make a speech, and the girls will stand with me, and we will all sing "God Save the King". Will that be enough?'

Mrs Goodword nodded. 'I'm sorry,' she said simply. 'I … I do understand.'

'Do you? I don't,' said Deanna. She watched the vicar's wife vanish down the lane, then turned back to make a rabbit casserole for dinner.

Forty-Two

How to 'ice' a cake in Britain, 1945

Take a sheet of white cardboard. Make four slits to form a box to fit over the cake and glue with a flour and water paste. Decorate with rings of a mix of salt, flour and water, gaily painted. Remove before the cake is sliced, and put away carefully to use again.

Lady Deanna Claverton opened the Victory Ball with a waltz with the mayor of Claverton Minor, Mr Septimus Filmer, butcher. She stayed to dance with each of the aldermen, as well as Arnold Thripps.

The first of the bride ships sailed to the US and Canada — Australian waters were not yet deemed safe for civilians. The size of the National Loaf was reduced.

The queue at the grocer was forty-six women at nine am, according to Mrs Thripps, and it took a full day's queuing at the various shops just to get the rations for one family.

The Allies faced not only the problems of their own lands, but administering a Germany reduced to rubble and starvation, with hundreds of thousands of concentration camp victims needing urgent medical care, and few Germans prepared to give it, even if paid, and perhaps a third of civilians homeless, with soldiers demobilised not knowing where their families were, or even if they were alive.

This was peace, of a kind.

The phone call came at nine pm with the twilight gathering at the centre of the sky, slowly dropping its curtains over the mid-summer light. They were already in bed, exhausted from picking peas. She had to run downstairs to answer, though Doris at the switchboard knew she was in, and so would keep ringing until she answered.

'London calling!' exclaimed Doris. 'Oh Lady Dee, you'll never guess who! Putting you through now,' she added in her professional voice.

'Dee, honey? It's me, Donnie. Free at last and up in London.' Deanna could hear laughter, voices in the background, and the pop of a bottle of champagne, but the voice on the other end of the phone had a forced jollity.

She swallowed her first exclamation, which was, 'You're alive.' She had expected to be told if Donnie had been found alive in a prison camp, or if his death was finally confirmed, but of course she wasn't his next of kin — merely a second cousin, and his agent.

'How wonderful,' she managed. 'When are you coming down?'

'Never.' The voice lowered to an almost whisper. 'I'm sorry, Dee. No one will ever know what they did to me because I was the Duke of Claverton. I want nothing to do with Claverton or the title ever again.'

Deanna felt her hairs rise as if faced with endless cold. Kurt's story of an unsuspecting Donnie in the next bed had been lies too.

'You're well?' He didn't wait for an answer. The forced jollity returned. 'Dee, I've seen old Truscott, so you no longer have to bother with the estate. Neither of us does. The army will hand it back officially as soon as they can organise the paperwork, which might be next century, but meantime I've sold all rights in it to a man called McIntosh. He's in property development and plans to make the place into a high-class golf resort, members only, so you won't be bothered with oiks next door. I've made him promise to give you an honorary membership for life.'

'I ... I ... thank you.' Golf means mown grass, she thought. No rabbit warrens or bluebell woods, no woods at all but stands of ornamental trees. 'I'm so glad you're back, and ... and safe at last.'

'One day I may even believe it. In a minute, Clarinda darling,' he added to an insistent voice in the background. 'Goodbye, Dee. I'll write when I get home.'

Home. The USA, not Claverton. She had been so eager to believe Kurt's lies that Donnie had loved Claverton. Perhaps before they tortured him for information, he had.

She put the receiver down. Doris would spread the news, of course.

The loss of Claverton's dukedom struck her first. The title might survive somehow, but there'd be no duke in residence, tactfully remitting the rent for a widow, or a man who'd injured his arm in the threshing machine; and no duchess or other female relative taking port wine jelly and roast chicken to the ill or elderly, or making sure talented children had a chance at scholarships, and adding a little to make sure those scholarships were enough.

The castle itself meant little. Its transformation would mean local employment, possibly film stars visiting. She thought there would be few in the village who would object to the golf club. No one would ask squirrels, field mice, owls, badgers or eagles for their opinions. But rabbits, perhaps, might eat the grass, and eagles eat the rabbits. Humans would be inside partying at night, leaving the world to animals.

Kurt had lied to her even at the end. Even if his aim had truly been peace between their countries, he must also have known about Dachau, at least.

Could enough alliances with more moderate countries have been enough to stop the worst of Hitler's atrocities? Could Hitler slowly have changed his views, as one did, when working with good people instead of sycophants?

No, she thought. He killed any good people who opposed him. There would have been camps here, too.

What if England had kept the promise she had made in World War I to hand over Palestine as a Jewish homeland? Would that have just created another war? What if Sam's Australia and so many other nations had not refused to take in those Hitler would exterminate — not just those with a Jewish heritage but gypsies, the blind, the homosexuals, the communists, those who followed the teachings of their church and not the Führer?

I never saw Kurt as he truly was, she thought. I made a fantasy of Donnie too, one who would love Claverton, and care for it, a man who didn't even bother to see it on his last leave. Nor did I know Sam, a lonely pilot who found a temporary family and a wartime romance. She must admit that now.

Sam's letters had grown shorter, no longer the long yarns of neighbours' eccentricities or boxing matches with kangaroos. Sam was fading from her world, but every breath she'd felt him exhale upon her skin was still as warm as the summer days he had spent with her.

Sam might find another mate. But like the eagles she loved — and Miss Enid too — Deanna felt the first man she had both loved and desired would be the only one. Was this what the Duke of

Windsor had felt, perhaps still did feel: a passion he knew would last his whole life? Had he known Mrs Simpson had other lovers and would never reciprocate the devotion he felt for her?

The Duke of York had made an acceptable king before the war, despite his stammer. The conflict had made him a hero to his people: a leader who refused advice to evacuate with his family to safety in Canada so the royal line might continue even if England was lost to the enemy. His wife and daughters were heroic too. The short reign of Edward VIII was already almost forgotten. He would be remembered for his abdication, and ironically for a love affair that existed only in his imagination and his lover's calculations.

Deanna had been foolish too.

Maybe, as life slowly became normal, she would forget the feel of Sam, the smell of him, the comfort of his presence. She would meet another man ...

She did not believe it.

But it was time to write a letter.

Dear Frau Schmidt,

Please forgive my writing to you in English, and without introduction. The brother of an old friend of mine is going to try to have this delivered to you so it is not censored.

In 1940 I knew a man who said his name was Kurt. He was tall, blond, possibly thirty.

I'm afraid I must tell you that he died. I can't tell you more, only that he lived and died bravely in the knowledge he had done his duty with all he was capable of, and was proud to have done so. He gave this address to me just before he died, so I believe his last thoughts must have been of you. He asked me to tell you that before he died he had happy days, picnicking by a river.

Yours most sincerely,
Deanna Claverton

There was no reply. Nor did that street exist in Dresden any longer, for most of Dresden had been destroyed in the firebombing that made no difference to the outcome of the war. Instead, the land had been taken, mile by mile, by Americans or Russians, the civilians still staunch despite the destruction, till Germany was no longer its own.

The brother of Deanna's friend, Alice, however, did not give in. He contacted the Red Cross and found a woman who had lived at that address, though her name had not been Schmidt. He assured Deanna the letter had finally reached her.

Did it matter after all these years? Or did it just extinguish someone's hope that 'Kurt' had been tending beetroot and parsnips on some English farm, and one day, kitbag in hand, would come limping or striding home?

She would never know. But she had done her duty.

Forty-Three

Mock Duck

INGREDIENTS
a can of Spam, sliced
230 grams onions, grated
230 grams apples, peeled and grated
one to two teaspoons fresh sage or half a teaspoon dried sage

METHOD
Spread half the Spam into a flat layer in a well-greased baking tin or dish. Top with a layer of grated onion, apples and the sage. Cover with the rest of the Spam and form into a duck breast shape. Cover with greased paper and bake in a moderate oven for forty minutes.

World War II recipe

The family at Eagle's Rest didn't see the film footage of the devastation of Hiroshima and Nagasaki. After the trauma of the Bergen-Belsen newsreel, Deanna carefully suggested they not attend a movie theatre until she deemed it safe. Some things must be known, but without seeing the full horror: the burning children with peeling skin, the flattened cities, the hospital wards of wide-eyed people who simply grew sicker every day until they died.

But Anna studied the photos in the newspaper, then looked up at Deanna and said, 'We did that.'

'We have become the Nazis,' murmured Magda. 'If the Americans just obliterated a small island the Japanese would have surrendered.'

Deanna gazed at the photo of a dying child with weeping skin. 'The Japanese leaders might have kept the destruction of an island secret. They had already ordered everyone to commit suicide as soon as enemy troops landed.'

'Sam said that bombing civilians just made them long to destroy the enemy even more,' said Anna.

'How can we change things like this?' demanded Rosa.

Magda lifted her chin. 'Nietzsche said to look for role models and educators, friends, family, public figures and ancient philosophers, whose way of looking at the world means they do good, not wrong.'

'Like Mum,' said Anna confidently. 'And Mrs Thripps. And Dusty. And Sam too.'

Cleaning houses and entertaining audiences were good things, Deanna supposed, as were 'encouraging the villagers', the phrase she had grown up with, providing vegetables, fruit, firewood and eggs to those in need, as well as judging the humorous vegetable collection while avoiding the too obviously obscene winner.

Dusty had done his duty even more heroically, though he had a narrow view of what his duty might entail. His duty had been to love and be loved, and he had given his life to do it.

And Sam? He'd been wrong, she thought. Bombs *could* lead to peace. They just had to be big enough. Large enough, perhaps, one day, as wars grew bigger, to finally destroy the world, so the cockroaches and microbes who might be left would have serenity.

Forty-Four

Apple and Date Spread

Peel and core twenty Granny Smith apples. Chop. Add a cup of chopped dates and enough water to cover. Simmer, stirring all the while, till very thick. Bottle and keep in a cool place for up to a week.

Australian World War II recipe

Sam wrote briefly now Australia's war was over too. Deb's husband had returned, thin as a rusty nail, needing long rehabilitation in Sydney for injuries and tropical diseases, and silent about what he'd seen and experienced. Deb was staying with a friend to be near him.

Ron's brother had not survived; nor would Ron give any details about his death. Sam's cousins had survived a prisoner-of-war camp in Malaya, but died on a forced march towards the end of the war as the Japanese tried to keep their prisoners from testifying about their imprisonment.

The land army girls had left. A brief mention told them that Susan was marrying a zoology professor she'd met again when she volunteered at the Repatriation Hospital, and that Sam and his father had sent her a painting of the farm as a wedding present.

Was it like the one he gave me, Deanna wondered. It hung above her desk in the library.

Sam was still single. Deanna did not have the courage to ask why, afraid the answer might shadow the happiness of the years she had known him. Nor was there any point asking Uncle Jasper again why they had considered Sam potentially disloyal. A man who was unreliable in one war might be equally untrustworthy in the next one.

For although the war in the Pacific had ended, with even more bells ringing and yet another dance, smelling of mothballs and making do with a meagre rationed supper, no dove of peace had yet found a safe branch to land on. Germany's occupation of Europe had been replaced by an admittedly more benign and hopefully temporary American one, and by the annexation into the Soviet Union of other countries by Russia, including, ironically, Poland.

We began the war to free Poland, she thought. We end it by accepting that Poland will not be free.

Everything was supposed to change. Little had. Rationing was more severe; life was still an unrelenting labour of growing food and making do.

Only the blackout curtains could be put away, the gas masks handed in. Deanna told the village poachers holding firearms quietly 'liberated' from their time in the armed forces to turn their attention to the castle estate now the air force had abandoned it. No one had arrived even to mow its grass, except for rabbits.

'Should we get another dog?' she asked brightly at breakfast one morning. Dogs were still scarce, but one of the friends from school bred bloodhounds and had a gamekeeper who bred lurchers, who might well resemble Dusty, in looks at any rate.

Once more the girls met each other's eyes in an unspoken agreement.

'No, thank you,' said Magda. She produced a smile. 'I mightn't be here long enough to get to know it.'

The other two just shook their heads.

Something was wrong. Her daughters should be joyously planning a future. Instead, like most of England, they still plodded day to day.

The true end of the war — Dee's war, and all she loved — arrived by plane in November in a grey suit worn by a small grey man who looked as if he had huddled underground with his paperwork for the last seven years and was unable to see the world above now the sirens had ceased, except as lines on a map.

His name was Mr Gardener and he carried plans and a draft contract, which of course she must ask her lawyer to check, though it was equally obvious that as a ministry had drawn it up, no lawyer of hers would be given permission to change it, except perhaps the amount of money offered (the least important clause of all).

'I'm sorry, Lady Deanna,' said Mr Gardener, his map of her land showing the boundaries of the area the government was resuming, marked in roads and house blocks laid upon her kitchen table as she politely served him tea from the dusty remnants in the cellar, her own weekly ration drunk, and jam drops made with dripping and fresh raspberries instead of jam. 'But you must understand that there really is no other suitable land. It will take years to clear the bomb damage from the cities, and families need houses now. They're being called the "new towns". We estimate at least sixty bungalows in this estate, and another forty semi-detached. You will keep your house of course,' he added quickly. 'And the cliffs and the upper portion of the river, and the farmland under cultivation. Britain needs to eat, too.'

She stared at him blankly. Badgers needed homes and food. So did eagles. The eagles might keep their cliffs, but the territory they need to survive would be under streets and houses.

I cannot bear it, she thought, as she numbly saw him to the door. She didn't even take a scarf or cardigan, running up the headland, the river snaking blue below her, bees humming as they took a final autumn harvest in the wildflowers that would soon be straight lines of zinnias and petunias.

She tried to drink in every inch and breath ...

Mr Gardener's plane rose from behind the castle, as so many had through the war, just as an eagle swooped out from the cleft in the cliffs, heading down the river.

She screamed, waving. The eagle swerved, but too late. Wing crashed into wing. She watched the bird tumble and hit the ground and ran to it as the plane sped on.

A broken wing could mend. But she knew even from twenty yards away by the crooked angle of the neck that the fall had killed it if it hadn't been dead before.

She kneeled and cradled it. It was the older male, not the female she had banded, nor the juvenile.

A shadow crossed her. She looked up. The female circled once, twice, then flapped her wings, no longer resting on the earth's warm air, moving deliberately now, flying not back to the hills by the sea but due north. A shadow rose from behind the hills and followed her: the juvenile.

Deanna knew beyond all doubt she would not see them again. The last of the golden eagles had left England, searching for a home beyond humanity and their deadly engines in the sky.

Forty-Five

Mock Chicken

INGREDIENTS
dripping
two onions, chopped
six potatoes, chopped
six ripe tomatoes, peeled
one teaspoon fresh thyme
one sage leaf, chopped
six eggs
parsley
salt and pepper to taste

METHOD
Fry the onions and potatoes on low in dripping till soft and not coloured. Add the tomatoes and herbs and cook till thick. Mix in the eggs and place in a baking dish. Bake till firm. Serve with parsley and carve like chicken.

Australian World War II dish when backyard hens and their eggs were common, but meat rationed

★★★

You do not bury an eagle. You carry it to its hills and leave it on a ledge, to become one with the scavengers of the area, as it too had eaten the dead of its land.

She saw Anna's and Rosa's bicycles in the shed as she walked down the headland, then Magda arrived, stowing her bicycle away too, hefting her books. Magda, who had won a scholarship to Oxford, despite missing a year of school while in hospital and in the orphanage. It's a sign, she thought. I can't stay here. I can't sell the house — not yet, at any rate. But I can rent it, making sure the passage to the cellars is securely fastened so it can only be opened by removing part of the wall.

For the first time in years she thought of the diamonds stitched into the brassiere upstairs. The money for her land would make her truly wealthy, but might not be paid for months or even years. Slugs were racehorses compared to the speed of government departments. I could buy a cottage down near Oxford, she thought. One with a woodland, not farmland. The eagles had flown north. She would go south to Oxford.

She walked slowly to the kitchen. It smelled of tonight's stewed rabbit. Dusty had loved rabbit hearts, livers, leftovers and whatever else he could reach. Everything has gone, or is going, she thought. But I have a family.

The girls had already spread their homework over the table and were eating bread and raspberry jam. They stared at her. 'What's wrong?' demanded Magda.

She could not, would not, tell them about the eagle. 'The land,' said Deanna numbly. 'The Minister of Works wants to build a hundred houses on all our land, except the farm and house and garden and the cliffs.'

'But he can't!' cried Rosa. 'What about the badgers? The otters?'

'I don't know.' Though she did know. This was the death of the badgers. Dogs would eventually hunt the otters.

'What would you think about all of us moving to Oxford?' she asked with desperate gaiety.

The girls sat silently. It was almost like those long moments when they had first come to Eagle's Rest and had communed with no words spoken between them.

Magda met Deanna's eyes. 'I'm not going to Oxford next year. I couldn't bring myself to tell you when it seemed to mean so much to you. All Papa's colleagues, Mama's friends — they are probably still there. In all these years none has even looked for us, to see that we are all right.'

'Cambridge then ...'

'No. I love Eagle's Rest. I loved it even while I wondered what would happen if the Nazis invaded. Would Mrs Goodword have helped round us up for the gas chambers as efficiently as she settled us as evacuees? I want to go far away. We all do.' Magda glanced at her sisters. 'I don't have to go to university straight away. We ... we want to go to somewhere there has been no war. Somewhere with sunlight, and eagles ...'

'Australia,' stated Anna.

'Sydney University is excellent,' said Magda. 'They'll accept my finals results and teacher recommendations.'

Dee realised her jaw had dropped and she was gaping most inelegantly. 'You've written to them?'

'Last year,' admitted Magda. 'Just ... just to see if it was possible. But we couldn't leave you. You love this place so much ...'

'Mum?' said Rosa gently. 'Who do you want to be now?'

'I ... I don't know.' She tried to smile. 'I spent half my adult life caring for my grandfather, and the other half in war.'

'Nietzsche says we already have who we are within us. We need to carve out our ideal selves. It's both discovery and creation.'

Deanna looked at her brilliant daughter, torn between exasperation, pride and a wish to tear up everything Nietzsche had ever written. 'And that means?'

'You're already your ideal person. You just need to get rid of the other bits and associate with people who'll help you find and keep your ideal.'

That actually made sense. Sometimes the girl's insight startled her, this waif she'd found on a railway station. 'I ... I think I am who I've always been. Someone who needs to live with animals and birds and trees. Someone who is part of a community — a figurehead for good things, because figureheads help keep an organisation together, especially if they help make the metaphorical marmalade. It's what I've been bred for,' she added apologetically. 'As for people to help me keep my ideal — I've got you three.'

'You've got Sam, too,' said Anna firmly.

'Anna, darling, I don't have Sam. I wish I did. I was a close friend at a bad time. He has made very sure, both then and in his letters now, that there is nothing more than that.'

'Show her the letter,' Rosa ordered Magda.

'What letter?' asked Deanna.

'Magda wrote to Sam when the Japanese surrendered,' said Rosa, as Magda slipped upstairs and back again. 'Sam wrote back.'

'It came last month,' said Anna. 'I *wanted* to show it to you then, but Magda and Rosa ...' she looked at them resentfully '... said we needed to think about it first.'

'We thought maybe Sam didn't want to make you choose between here and Australia,' explained Rosa.

'We didn't want to make you choose either. But now Australia might be where you can find your ideal self,' said Magda simply. 'It's got trees and animals, and enough space to make sanctuaries for them that won't be taken for houses or golf clubs. And it's far away from Europe,' she added, her voice breaking a little. 'I think we all need to be far away from Europe.'

Anna handed her the envelope; its sheets of paper were smudged with jam and crumpled with much reading.

Deanna sat automatically, staring at the page.

> *Dear Magda, Rosa and Amazing Anna,*
>
> *I hope you are well. Yes, you deserve the truth, but I trust you not to tell your mother. You had a secret when I first met you. I had a secret too. I ask you to keep it.*
>
> *I couldn't ask your mother to marry me because I am a quarter Aboriginal, which here just means 'Aboriginal'. Your mum would have said it doesn't matter, but it does. I love your mother very much. I love you three too, and always will.*
>
> *Love,*
> *Sam*

She put the letter down. He loved her. She was lovable. Not as Lady Deanna, but for herself.

Aboriginal. I've never even met an Australian Aboriginal, she thought.

The Prince of Wales had met Aboriginal people when he went to Australia. He'd talked to her about them, laughing as they danced. What had he called them? 'The lowest form of human life.'

But she *did* know an Australian Aboriginal. She knew Sam, and knew his family from Deb's letters, too.

'Mum?' said Magda gently, handing her a cup of sweet tea. She sipped as her eldest sat and took her hand. 'I read as much as I could after we got the letter. I'd never even thought about Australian Aboriginal people before. I think these days it's not as bad as being Jewish in Germany was, though people tried to exterminate them last century. But many are still imprisoned on reserves, unable to leave without permission.'

'But Sam is wealthy!'

Magda sat forwards, ready to talk through her research. 'Probably his grandmother was Aboriginal, and Sam's dad inherited the farm from his white father. Sam can vote. His father probably can't — the laws are different in the various states.'

'Mum?' asked Rosa anxiously. 'Was it wrong to show it to you? Do you mind? I mean we understand, because people hated us as Germans, and Jewish, even if we aren't, or only sort of are. We know who we are, even if other people don't. We know who Sam is too.'

'We love him,' said Magda simply.

'And I want to kick anyone who says he—' began Anna.

'Shh,' said Magda. 'Mum, shouldn't we have shown you the letter? Does it matter to you that he's Aboriginal?'

'Yes, it matters. It matters because it stopped him, stopped us ...' Because if people don't take a stand against evil, then evil wins, she thought. I fought the Nazis in a cave and won. I will not let this stop me now, or ever.

She met their eyes. 'I am going to phone my Uncle Jasper.'

Forty-Six

Scones

INGREDIENTS AND METHOD

One-and-a-half cups of flour, small piece of butter, small pinch of salt, small pinch of sugar. Mix together well with a knife. Add one cup of milk with a wee pinch of baking soda, dissolved. Roll lightly, bake at once, fifteen minutes. A little cream will improve scones. Use self-raising flour.

Verbatim recipe from a World War II Australian
personal recipe collection

This time the man she had known as Uncle Jasper invited her to his home in Essex: two changes of train through miles of quickly erected small plywood boxes — flimsy homes for those who had lost them, the men and women who had returned from war to find no other accommodation than a damp spare room in a half-burned house.

Uncle Jasper's home, however, was a small manor house, ivy-covered, with a rose garden that had survived the edict to turn all gardens over to cabbages and beets.

They drank tea on the terrace — weak stewed tea, for it seemed the man who still preferred he use his wartime name did not patronise the black market either. She realised he trusted her enough to find out his true name. It would be simple to ask in the next village about who lived here with a wife named Deirdre. She was a small brown finch of a woman with intelligent eyes.

The end of the war, it seemed, had not meant a change of Uncle Jasper's career. He smiled at her knowingly. 'Have you come to ask me for a job? I thought you might be bored with peace and reconstruction.'

She frowned over her tea. 'I don't understand.'

'We have another enemy now. With your daughters growing up you might be interested in another intelligence role. A Deanna Claverton, whose ancestral home will be turned into a luxury hotel with American capital, might well decide to join the Communist Party. They'd find you extremely useful, which would be useful for us, too.'

'No. Let me be frank.' I should not say this, she thought, not if I want favours, but it needed to be said. 'I do not accept this "Cold War" of yours. I believe that too many people promote war for obscene profits and almost limitless personal power.'

'My dear, that is extremely naive. Communism and the Soviet Union are real threats, no matter who profits.'

'It's a simple viewpoint, I admit, but simple can also be accurate. Do we put even a thousandth of what we put into armaments into negotiating?'

'Armaments cost more than negotiating.'

'Then why don't we spend more time working out more effective methods of international cooperation?'

'Because they don't work.'

'Really? Gandhi and his non-aggression seems remarkably successful in India. I'm backing him to win against all the weaponry of the British Empire. I am not your dear, either.'

He lifted an eyebrow again. 'So you came here for weak tea?'

'I came to ask three questions and a favour. Did the Duke of Windsor really plan to come to England in 1940?'

'No, of course not.'

A large Labrador came bounding up. Uncle Jasper fondled its ears while he added, 'Several men lost their lives just before the occupation of Germany and the surrender, making sure history cannot record that any such thing could ever have happened. I hope you do not say anything that will mean they gave their lives for nothing. Royalty is a symbol of unity. It matters.'

So David *had* planned to be 'the King Over the Water', welcomed home to save his country. She presumed the men had been lost trying to retrieve David's letters to Hitler. But his American magazine interviews could not be retracted. Uncle Jasper must know this, too.

'Your next question?'

'Why did you warn me Flight Lieutenant Murray might be a security threat?'

'Ah, I hoped you'd have long forgotten him. Sam Murray is an Aboriginal Australian. That didn't matter while the war was a European one. It did matter when Japan entered the conflict, with Australia as a target for the raw materials, like iron, which they lacked.'

'I don't understand.'

'Japanese and Australian intelligence believed the Aboriginal Australians would side with the Japanese after they invaded Australia from New Guinea if they promised self-government.' He shrugged. 'The intelligence services were wrong. Aboriginal Australians resolutely fought the Japanese, but we could only act on the advice we had at the time. It was reasonable to think that a previously loyal pilot would give his allegiance to his people, not to Britain, once we were fighting on different sides. But there was another reason, a personal one.'

He put his teacup down. 'Dee, my dear — and I am not patronising you by calling you that. Your grandfather spoke of you so often I care what happens to you, for his sake and yours. You were alone, and lonely, and a handsome, dashing pilot came into your life. Flight Lieutenant Murray was a cad and a bounder not to have let you know his background before you even invited him into your home, much less let the relationship run so long on a false footing.'

His mouth tightened. 'You are a Claverton, not to be wasted on a colony at the end of the world, peopled by the descendants of convicts, gold miners, and the poor who had nowhere else to go.'

Deanna stiffened. 'Those apparently unworthy descendants helped save this country. How many Australian pilots volunteered or were convinced to fight for Britain? How many died?'

'About six thousand Australian pilots died,' he said quietly. 'And about ten thousand volunteer Australian ground crew — that is in our own air force, of course, not Australia's.'

'Australia had the leftovers when their own country was in need, after you had picked out the best flyers?'

'Britain's defence was more urgent. The empire could afford to lose Australia. It could not lose Britain or India.'

It was her turn to raise an eyebrow. 'It looks like the empire is going to lose India anyway.'

Uncle Jasper suddenly looked as tired as any of the tattered, hungry homeless in the crumbled streets of London. 'I don't have the power to stop wars. My job is to do the best we can when our leaders — backed by our people — enter those wars. I was not even in a position to object when I could see ... when anyone who actually evaluated the situation *must* have seen that the last war was being fought stupidly, with a waste of men and resources. Some people,' he added softly, '*did* do very well from the war. But I will never say that publicly.'

'So you played Follow the Leader with all the rest?'

'Not quite. I did my best. I still do my best. Would it make any difference to you if I said that I hope Gandhi wins independence for his country, and that I admire his methods of non-violence, even if I do not have the courage or expertise to follow them?'

He does care for me, Deanna realised. He has asked far less of me than he demands of himself.

'I'm sorry,' she said quietly. 'I don't suppose I'll ever know how much you and others like you helped us survive in those months when it seemed inevitable that evil would cross the Channel.'

He smiled at that. 'I doubt I'll ever know either. But all I couldn't do still wakes me at four am. You also wanted a favour?'

'I came to ask you to arrange passage for myself and my daughters to Australia.'

He stared. 'To go to Murray? Has he told you what life would be like married to a native? Deanna, you think you know what his life is like because he has a large farming station, and money. You can have no idea what natives face in Australia. Ostracism is the least of it. They are not equal under the law. Full-bloods and half-bloods aren't even included in the census. Many are imprisoned in reserves, with almost no education, fed on starvation rations, their only hope of release a menial job working on the roads or as domestic servants.'

'Sam doesn't know we are coming.'

'Dee ...' For the first time she saw the man who was her grandfather's friend. 'I am sorry about your land. There is nothing I can do, especially with the Claverton Estate to become a commercial operation. But running after a man you hardly know in a strange country is not the answer.'

'I'm not entering this naively. I don't know if I will want to marry Sam the farmer, when he is no longer Sam the pilot, fitting in with English ways. My daughters and I can settle anywhere in the British empire, but I need to see Sam first.' She met his eyes. 'You owe me that, as well.'

'You won't last ten seconds out there.'

She smiled. 'Then you needn't worry.'

'The sooner you get rid of this crazy impulse and find a life you do want, the better.' He looked at her over steepled fingers. 'Most civilian ship berths are kept for war brides. How do you feel about flying?'

'To Australia? I didn't know it was possible unless you could hire an aircraft and pilot.'

He smiled at her. She realised he had not been offended by her speech about the Cold War. Perhaps, in part, he even agreed with it. But he was a man who would fulfil the duty his country's rulers had arranged for him.

'A company called Trans Australia Airlines is attempting to organise passenger flights to Australia, but theirs will be a small craft, and uncomfortable. Coincidentally, a luxury aircraft passenger service has just applied for permission to fly a trial run to Sydney in a fortnight. So far, they have only twenty or so official passengers for only part of the journey. It would be good, perhaps, to add more, so we can observe their level of service.' The smile became a grin. 'Could Lady Deanna Claverton and her daughters be ready to leave in a fortnight?'

No. Of course not. Yes, she thought. She'd sell the farm to Mr and Mrs Higgins and their son James at a pittance — she could sign the papers, even if the transfer would take longer.

And Mrs Thripps would love to live at Eagle's Rest, looking after the place with caretaker wages and all expenses paid, so their pension would stretch to comforts. Arnold would tend the gardens and the glasshouses as caretaker and doze under the big oak. The cliffs and river not suitable for housing could go to the National Trust, to keep them safe, at least — the lawyers could handle that.

And Sam?

Sam had been family. Was that an illusion?

She had a sudden memory of the cliffs in her dream, and in the painting. Perhaps she must walk between those cliffs to find out.

London was ... crumpled. Grey-faced people in faded clothes, weary people who had not starved but faced gnawing hunger on margarine and boiled cabbage for seven years, walked with eyes downcast to avoid the rubble or broken glass. Perhaps they merely avoided looking at the city, dusty, dreary, with the life almost sucked from it.

The most dangerous of the bomb damage had been removed, but eyeless houses still stood with only three walls. People lived in the lower floors, sweeping brick dust into the street, where rats scuttled in the gutters, unafraid now they no longer had to worry about explosions, only humans, who they vastly outnumbered.

The pale-faced people walked slowly, with none of the determination, stoicism and compassion she'd seen in them during the war. Only the price of the National Loaf seemed to raise passion in the newspapers.

Mr Vonderfleet — his shop miraculously intact, even if his windows had suffered — arranged matters too. Deanna was here for advice this time, not to sell a diamond. British citizens were only permitted to take a small amount of money and valuables out of the country, but no one would dare to do a body search of Lady Deanna Claverton, especially on a private aircraft.

Mr Vonderfleet gave her the name of a cousin in Australia who he would write to, and who she could trust to give her the true value for any stones she took to him.

They farewelled Dusty on their last morning with Arnold and Mrs Thripps, under the oak tree, with scones and sponge cake and sandwiches, and imagined him snuffling all the crumbs, then waiting, tail wagging, for the leftovers.

Deanna said goodbye to the headland that afternoon, sitting with the wind in her face, knowing she was right to leave now, before the housing estate foundations went in, before the transformation of the castle and its grounds.

This was who she had been: Deanna of Claverton. And Claverton would be gone, so she must be someone else. She couldn't clothe her daughters in the rags of her pre-war life when they longed for Australia, or at least their vision of what Australia might be. Without them she might have worn the shreds of her old life. Now, for their sake, and her own, she must create a new one.

Australia was far from a peaceful Eden, or even a land of equality and justice. It had accepted few Jewish refugees before the war, and still accepted only those sponsored by Australians, other than single men who must work in remote areas where most white Australians didn't want to labour. Australia had rationing too, though not as strictly as in the UK.

But there might be Sam, and eagles.

It was over two years since they had seen each other. The girls had promised not to let him know they were coming. If he had formed a relationship with another woman in the last few months, one he hadn't mentioned, she didn't want him to feel any obligation to or even awkwardness with her.

This might be a visit.

It might be marriage and a lifetime.

She turned to look down at Eagle's Rest. It would probably hardly change in the next few decades, its paddocks and acres of gardens and glasshouses protecting it from the drabness of the post-war houses around. She didn't know if she could bear to visit again, but her daughters might, or their children.

Forty-Seven

Chicken Mayonnaise with Grapes

INGREDIENTS
four chicken breasts
white wine stock
two cups seedless grapes
one onion, chopped finely
two tablespoons olive oil
half a teaspoon your choice of curry paste
one cup mayonnaise
juice of half a lemon or lime

METHOD
Sauté the chicken in a white wine stock with half the grapes. Sauté the onion in the olive oil until soft. Add the curry paste and cook for one minute, stirring well so it doesn't stick. Stir in the reserved grapes. Take off the heat and leave until cool. When cool, stir in the chicken, mayonnaise and lemon juice. Serve chilled, with hot rice or a green salad.

A recipe that would be impossible under
World War II rationing

★★★

The aeroplane was enormous, two storeys high. Deanna and her family sat in what would be First Class, in the middle of the top floor, the butter-soft leather seats arranged like small cabins, with polished wooden folding doors between them that could make areas of the plane entirely private.

Deanna stared down at the runway. It was impossible that such a monster could fly, but the craft lumbered along the tarmac, bumped three times, then finally wobbled into the air in a way any eagle would have scorned.

Champagne was served, with sparkling lemonade for Anna and Rosa, and, after a discreet nod from Deanna, both the lemonade *and* a half glass of champagne were offered to Magda.

The girls giggled at the bubbles. Rosa and Magda remembered bubbled pre-war drinks, but Anna did not.

'Mum, why are there bubbles?'

'It makes the drink more fun.'

'How do they get them in the bottle?'

To Deanna's relief Magda answered this one.

The plane descended almost as soon as it had risen to an airfield in France, possibly to pick up supplies unavailable under British rationing, as well as a small party of English and Americans, by their accents, who were escorted by hostesses to the plane's front seats, where the cabin walls kept them invisible.

More champagne was offered, with citron pressé now, which Deanna accepted as well as the girls. Oysters on the half shell …

'Snot,' Anna decided, and oysters Kilpatrick, heavy on the bacon, which all enjoyed. Small cheese puffs, caviar with tiny boiled potatoes, and out-of-season asparagus wrapped in Spanish ham, though Deanna reminded herself they were heading to a land where it was now late spring, and asparagus would almost certainly be available.

It seemed they were to eat and drink their way to Australia.

'Mum, why is the asparagus green?'

'We mulch ours with straw to keep it soft and white, and farmers in some other countries don't.'

'Ours tastes better. Can I have another lemon drink?'

They were offered a choice of peach Melba, with a wafer stuck in the top of the ice cream, or chocolate mousse.

'Ice cream!' Even Magda suddenly seemed ten years old. Deanna had attempted homemade ice cream in the tiny freezer of her fridge, but it had not been a success.

'May I have another, please?' Anna asked the air hostess politely.

Seconds were quite possible, it seemed, as were thirds.

Champagne rather than peach Melba flowed in an unceasing tide to the party in the front. Cigarette smoke floated back. A familiar brand pre-war, though Deanna couldn't remember where she had smelled it before.

A woman stood: slim, tanned, exquisitely if plainly dressed in dark blue linen, diamonds at her neck and arms and a smile painted on with lipstick. She wavered her way towards the lavatory at the rear of the plane. Deanna's hand unknowingly crushed the meringue it was holding.

'Mum! You've made a mess.' Rosa bent to sweep it up with her hands.

'Leave it,' said Deanna automatically, her eyes on the woman in the aisle walking towards their seats. Her daughters had never had servants cleaning up after them. The airline hostess would need to sweep the smaller crumbs anyway.

The woman passed without a glance of recognition, stubbing out her cigarette in the ashtray next to them with no apology. Why should the Duchess of Windsor recognise a woman she had met only twice, both times in evening dress?

The Deanna of today was 'just a mum', upper crust of course, or she would not be sitting here, but negligible, a woman who had not relegated her children to a governess elsewhere on the plane, who was dressed in a wool suit that was far out of fashion, for in the last years she'd had no time to do more than keep her daughters, herself and any villager in need clothed, her only decoration the pearl necklace her grandfather had given her. Her daughters each had books open on their side tables, just as she had, to compound their insignificance. Who of social importance ever read books for pleasure?

The hostess passed towards the front of the plane with two more bottles of champagne for the party at the front, and a glance of apology at Deanna and her family for leaving them for fifteen minutes without nourishment. She returned with a brush and dustpan to clean up the mess, more meringues, a plate of chocolate eclairs oozing cream and lavished with the chocolate almost unobtainable for seven years, and a menu for luncheon that ran to seven courses.

'Smoked salmon pâté, mousse de artichoke, quail's eggs on brioche,' sang Anna to the tune of 'The Twelve Days of Christmas'. 'Mum, what's an artichoke mouse? Do we have to eat it?'

'It's mousse, like a cold soufflé.'

'Why don't they say soufflé then?'

'Shhh,' said the family in unison.

'It's unfair! Why do people on this plane get all this to eat …'

'Because it's a plane,' said Deanna absentmindedly. 'It stops at places where there are no shortages.'

The duchess made her way back. Deanna heard a familiarly light, querulous voice say something to her, and then her husband made his way towards them, to reach the lavatories in his turn.

Magda leaned over Rosa to speak to Deanna. 'Is that the Duke of Windsor?' she asked quietly. 'The woman looked just like a photo of the duchess.'

'The one who was going to sneak into England from our home?' demanded Anna, too loudly.

'Shh. We'll talk about that later, then never mention it again. *Ever.*' She should have known the girls would have eavesdropped that night so long ago, despite them never asking her a single question since. 'Order lunch for me if I'm not back. Please — don't talk about the duke, and don't come after me.'

Magda caught her arm. 'Mum, you're not going to do anything dangerous?'

'Not for me,' said Deanna.

She followed the duke down to the back of the aircraft.

He had vanished into the men's lavatory at the tail of the plane. She waited, sitting on one of the sofas that furnished the small sitting room outside the women's and men's lavatories. The hostess passed, with two more bowls of peach Melba, presumably for Anna.

The door to the men's room opened.

'David!' Deanna smiled at him laughingly as he emerged. She stood and curtseyed, relieved she could still do so with grace after so much potato digging. 'Or, rather, Your Royal Highness,' she added.

He blinked at her, obviously pleased at the salutation, and just as obviously not recognising her. 'I say ...'

'Lady Deanna Claverton,' she reminded him. 'How splendid to see you again! On an aeroplane, of all places.'

'Of course! Dee, old girl. Simply super to see you again,' he said vaguely. 'Splendid little jaunt, isn't it? We're off to do a spot of tiger hunting with a maharaja. Jolly good fellow for a darkie.'

Drunk already, she thought.

'How is ...' he obviously fumbled for her connections, and then smiled, relieved, as he recollected them '... the duke?'

'My grandfather is dead. The new duke is an American who has sold the estate for a golf course and hotel.'

'Bad luck, old girl, though the Yanks can be jolly good fun. Tell you what, move to France. Better food, more sunlight, and dashed good parties. I'll make sure you get invitations. Just mention my name.' He made to move back to his seat.

She spoke quietly as he came close to her. 'David, tell me, when you agreed to go yachting with your Swedish friend in the Bahamas, did you know he would deliver you to a German submarine to take you to England?'

He froze. 'What? Haven't the foggiest idea what you're talking about, old girl.'

'I met the men preparing the way for you to arrive in Britain and announce you had arranged an alliance with Germany and would take the throne again. Had you agreed? Or were they still trying to convince you?'

'How dare you speak to me like this?'

'Because I was involuntarily involved.'

'I could have you imprisoned—'

'Could you? Perhaps. But the world has changed. It's easier for information to spread now. Perhaps I've left a tape or a film, not with the BBC, with the British government able to stop transmission, but with an American or European company, one neither you nor British agents could find. There might even be more than one.'

He stared at her like a rabbit caught in the headlights.

She smiled at him. 'So if anything happened to me, or my family ... what would be on the tape, David? What would the film show? Or the letters. You really shouldn't have sent those letters ...'

A more intelligent man would not have fallen for the bluff. An innocent man would have no reason to be afraid.

He seemed to shrink, becoming simply a perfectly tailored grey suit, a starched shirt and cufflinks just a bit too large for good taste: a gift, presumably, from his duchess.

'What do you want? Money?'

'Just the truth. But I have that now. Did anyone ever tell you how men died trying to help you claim your throne or hide the fact you tried to reclaim it? At least four I know of, but almost certainly far more. Not as many as at Culloden, of course ...'

'Culloden?' he said, puzzled and scared.

'The battle to bring back Bonnie Prince Charlie to the thrones of England and Scotland, when tens of thousands of those who fought for him were killed. Tell me, and I promise I will never breathe a word. Would you really have taken back the throne if it were offered to you by Hitler? Was it all just for that?'

For long seconds he seemed to hardly breathe. 'I don't know ...' The words were torn out of him.

'Darling, there you are! Here's Dinky. Dinky, darling, take our little Peter Pan back to his seat before he flies in quite the wrong direction ...'

The axe-faced duchess glared at Deanna. 'I don't know who you are, or who has put you here, but you will be put off this plane at the first stop.'

The duchess left, linen swishing, her jewelled arms as bony as chicken legs, her high heels tapping despite the carpet on the floor.

Magda, Anna and Rosa craned their necks to see what was going on. Anna's face looked vaguely green as the duchess reached them.

Too much ice cream, Deanna thought, just as Anna leaned forwards, stuck her finger down her throat and vomited a mess of white and yellow over the duchess's shoes.

The duchess screamed in incredulity as much as shock and anger. The duke stared. Vomiting children were apparently outside his experience.

A hostess hurried up, miraculously ready with wet towels.

'Get these people out. Now,' hissed the duchess, stepping out of her shoes and away from the puddle of vomit.

'Yes, Your Grace. At once, Your Grace.' The stewardess kneeled to wipe the splash of vomit from the duchess's ankles. The duke gaped, helpless.

A steward appeared. 'Would you mind moving to the back of the plane, Lady Deanna?' The polite phrase was a demand. 'We need to clean the area.'

Anna looked at the Duke of Windsor. 'You didn't care that people like us would be killed in concentration camps. You just wanted to be king.'

'Anna, no more,' said Magda quietly. 'We promised, remember.' She met the duchess's cold eyes. 'People know. Not just us. But we won't talk. We won't even speculate what might have been.' She bent to wipe Anna's face.

The duchess strode towards the front of the plane without looking back. The duke followed, puppy-like, his expression both horrified and confused.

What might have been? wondered Deanna. If the Duke of Windsor had remained king, or regained his throne before 1939, possibly, probably, there would have been no war with Germany — or not for the British Empire. But forty million would still have died in concentration camps — probably more, without the Allies curtailing the expanse of the Reich — people like her daughters, and like the Russian prisoners told to dig their graves before being shot, pushed into the dirt and buried, some still alive. The Soviet Union might not exist if Germany hadn't had to fight Great Britain too.

Perhaps Hitler would be rampaging in Africa by now, exterminating the dark-skinned people he felt were subhuman too.

'Sometimes the price of peace is too high,' she muttered.

'No, it isn't,' said Magda. Deanna must have spoken more loudly than she had thought. 'When psychopaths seize power, we have to stop them. Our only choice is how.'

They moved to the back of the plane. Deanna noted with relief that none of their books, clothes or games had been touched by the vomit. Anna had aimed well.

She realised that Uncle Jasper didn't know her daughters knew the significance of the events at Eagle's Rest. Now, presumably, he would find out, as the duke would demand they be silenced. Secrecy was taken for granted in wartime. It would be harder to enforce silence now, especially as the only reason was to spare the royal family embarrassment.

Those who broke the code of 'Top Secret' also broke the law, and she and her daughters would be the ones who suffered for it. That, she realised, would almost certainly be reason enough for her daughters to be discreet — at least for the next few decades.

Meanwhile, she had to think what to do next.

The scent of vomit, undisguised by the lavender lavishly sprinkled on the damp carpet, filled the plane.

The aircraft's next stop was Tripoli, for which they had no visas, nor appropriate currency, nor even a guidebook, and where they might be stranded for who knew how long.

How could she have so impulsively endangered her daughters? Why hadn't she even recognised the danger? She had always been Lady Deanna Claverton, her position protecting her. She had never faced an enemy with more social power than her own.

And for what? Did David's guilt or innocence really matter now? She already knew how ruthless the British government could be for no more reason than to save ministers, military dignitaries or the royal family embarrassment.

'Madam?' It was the co-pilot, come to make the demand formal. 'Madam, I am sorry, but I have to ask you to leave the plane at our next fuel stop. I will call the embassy to assist you, of course.'

Courtesy and following proper procedure wouldn't work here. She thought suddenly of Mrs Thripps, belting out songs to a cheering theatre. She had no theatre, but she could pretend she had one.

'No,' said Deanna loudly. 'We are not getting off this plane.' She raised her voice further, so it could be heard well beyond their seats. 'If you attempt to move us, I will tell the world — beginning with every passenger in this plane — how the Duke of Windsor planned to leave the Bahamas.'

Suddenly a man in a sombre suit — not drunk, and almost certainly not a friend of the duke's but presumably there for his protection — strode to the back of the plane.

'Lady Deanna.' His voice was calm and sure. 'His Royal Highness has decided that he no longer desires this little ... holiday. He and his party will be the ones who will leave the plane at Tripoli. We will call ahead and make sure he and the duchess have some other means by which to return to Paris.'

'Don't forget the champagne,' said Deanna bitterly.

He met her eyes. 'We never forget the champagne. Would you and your daughters mind staying in these seats until Tripoli?'

The roomy six rows of empty seats they were to occupy for the time being proved a delight for Anna, who dashed from one side of the plane to the other to enjoy the view, and with room in between the rows for her to sprawl on the floor in her favourite reading position.

They stayed at the rear of the plane for the entire flight to Tripoli, tactfully silent behind screens while the duke's party left the plane.

The next stop was Cairo, where they slept overnight at a hotel with long fans and cane chairs and a vast dinner of spiced chicken and rice, a parsley salad and flatbreads once Deanna had slipped a pound note to the waiter, along with a request that they be given the local not the English menu.

The girls slept at last. Deanna did not. The duke had said, 'I don't know.' What would the next words have been? She suspected he wouldn't have said, 'I don't know what you are talking about.' Perhaps, taken by surprise, he would have blurted out the entire truth. He truly did not know what he would have done, torn between ambition and a wish for revenge, his fascist beliefs, versus fear for his person and genuine loyalty to his country.

He had threatened to call for revolution before, the morning after the abdication, to restore him to the throne, but had been easily dissuaded. David, Duke of Windsor, believed in the monarchy, an establishment that had no more basis for existence these days than Father Christmas or the Easter Bunny. But it suited most people to enjoy the trappings and gossip of royalty, as well as the glamour of being a kingdom, owning an empire (if not for very much longer), not merely a nation, just as they hung up empty stockings on Christmas Eve.

A true royalist would surely obey his king, even if that king was his younger brother.

But his wife?

Had the duchess seen a chance to rule a kingdom and liaised with Germany to seize it, knowing she could persuade her husband to follow her orders?

I do not know, she thought. I will never know and must accept that.

She tried to think of Sam instead, and a possible life ahead, and to fall asleep to pleasant thoughts, but instead visions of the armies of the dead filled her night, the broken cities and dead eagles, a thousand million dying eagles, so that she was glad of the muezzin's cry that woke her from the nightmare, and drank thick coffee till she could face her daughters and the aeroplane again.

The pyramids passed below them the next morning: deserts and sky and clouds, all the same red-dust colour, but sadly no camel trains or brigands with swords between their teeth like in the moving pictures. They had the entire top floor of the plane now, refuelling at Karachi, then Calcutta, passing over slums just below them bursting with more colour and movement than she had ever seen, the girls glued to their windows, then too tired from doing nothing to venture out from the overnight and morning stay in Singapore, not at the Raffles, presently used as a hospital for prisoners of war too weak to transfer to hospital ships, but in a house hired for their use.

Next morning's flight was over wisped clouds, turquoise seas and green vegetation upon serried cliffs until Darwin, which seemed composed entirely of tin shacks and bomb damage and army huts.

They refuelled, then flew across more greenery, then grey desert, endless dry gullies and odd-shaped trees.

If this was Australia, Deanna didn't think much of it.

The novelty of flying and watching new scenery had worn off. Magda had her books — as the plane was almost empty they had been allowed as many trunks of luggage as they wished. Rosa stitched at a 'new' blouse, the top of an 1880s walking dress with its embroidered panels removed, replaced by more modern strips of piping and double-stitched edges to collar and cuffs.

Deanna had her own book, or at least held it in her lap. Mostly she remembered: watching a fox play with her cubs with Grandpa, climbing one of the towers with Donnie, strictly forbidden. Playing mahjong with Miss Enid — she had never played it with anyone else; watching plovers guard their nests through binoculars; Sam's first true kiss with her; the last sight of him in the hospital bed.

She looked back down at the channelled grey brown of Australia, seemingly endless. Had the bond melted in the years they'd been apart? Was that bond enough to reconcile her to the drab endlessness of Australia?

So much had been lost — trees older than Julius Caesar, rock walls held together by time, foxes' dens and brambles — all gone as surely as if Hitler's bombs had shattered them. Hitler had not destroyed the animals and their homes. English people had done that, and believed they were doing good.

Perhaps, if the war had not eaten so much of Britain's land and wealth and people, Eagle's Rest might have been saved. If fools on either side of the conflict hadn't spent so much time, money and life on bombs, the war would have finished sooner, or at least with less loss.

Perhaps.

'Mum? Mummy?'

'Anna, what is it?'

'I've invented a game. It's called World Peace.'

'That sounds ... interesting,' Deanna said.

'All the leaders who want war meet. No one can see their own problems clearly enough, so they solve each other's. Ireland and England decide what happens in the Greek civil war, and the Greeks and South Africa could decide about China and Taiwan; and China and North Korea would decide about Ireland and England.'

Deanna shook her head, smiling. 'You still need each country to keep their word.'

'We could hypnotise the leaders!'

'And have the populations of each country so angry, if they didn't like the solutions, that another leader would emerge, even angrier and more war-like?'

'Oh.' Anna looked sadly out the window. 'It's not easy, is it?'

'I don't suppose it ever has been,' said Deanna. Shutting your eyes to evil meant supporting it.

We need a vast movement of individuals, she thought, like Gandhi is rallying his people. Peaceful resistance. But going 'bang' was so much easier for men in power to organise, like playing cricket between Eton and Harrow. If you lost one game you trained until the next time so you might win. Making machines that went 'bang' and supplying armies made men and companies wealthy. No one made money from a peaceful crowd simply sitting in a road. And what was to stop bombs being dropped on them?

Forty-Eight

Peach and Caramel Baked Custard

INGREDIENTS
two cups yellow peaches, chopped
one cup orange juice
ground nutmeg or powdered ginger
two cups cream
four eggs
eight tablespoons brown sugar

METHOD
Place peaches in an ovenproof dish with the juice and spices. Beat the cream, eggs and sugar together. Pour over the peach mix. Bake in a moderately hot oven for half an hour or till firm.

Australian hotel recipe from World War II

Brisbane was a country town of tin-roofed wooden bungalows, dirt roads and a tiny stretch of grand English-style stone buildings upriver from a bay of green water and flat inlands surrounded by black mud.

The family drank tepid lemonade or water and wiped off the sweat from the humidity for three hours in the hot tin hut that Brisbane regarded as an airport while the aircraft was cleaned and refuelled.

To Deanna's relief, the final leg of the flight took them over different greenery: lush forests with the treetops twined in vines under mountains of thin twisted rock that gleamed in the sunlight, curving valleys and wide slow rivers and miles and miles of impossibly white sand with rolling surf in gaudy blue and green topped with froth, the waves so large she could even make them out from the plane.

The luxury of the meals had declined. Lunch was simply sandwiches served on damask napkins, with cups of tea and lemonade and plain biscuits, but food was irrelevant. This was a land she didn't understand but could possibly love.

Sydney's cliffs, harbour, the lavishness of its beaches and the blazing sunlight was almost too much beauty. They landed, and, as at all the other ports of call, they were ferried through customs with diplomatic passports as well as their own. Uncle Jasper had worked swiftly and thoroughly.

He had even arranged a car to meet them.

The city just outside the airport seemed designed to depress visitors and send them quickly back again: thin harbour inlets, more floating oil and sodden rubbish than water, sandy soil dappled with half-hearted weeds; rutted narrow roads through slums of terrace houses, where bare-bummed babies in tattered singlets stared at the passing cars and dark-skinned men gazed at them from the shabby steps.

The streets changed to feature seedy nightclubs, then more respectable terrace houses. Suddenly they topped a hill and found buildings of a somewhat imposing grandeur below them, and parks with ancient trees that offered vast, dense shade, and then a hotel above the harbour, glinting a blue that Édouard Manet could never have imagined, and sailboats playing in the salt breeze.

The Wentworth Hotel was not the Ritz, but was magnificent nonetheless. 'The Prince of Wales himself danced here, madam,' the porter boasted, taking them to their suite.

Deanna noticed with relief that Anna had not filled her pockets nor her 'new' handbag (circa 1929) with food scavenged from the journey, a habit she had temporarily returned to after the images from the concentration camps.

The hotel was fully booked, but Uncle Jasper's connections (of course) had found them a suite with adjoining bedrooms. Magda and Rosa were on single beds and Anna a trundle in one room, and Deanna had the double bed next door.

The sitting room looked out onto the glittering harbour. Khaki still dappled the footpaths, and miliary vehicles dominated the road, but the crowd below seemed well fed; women wore bright florals and sandals, even here in what was presumably the centre of town, moving briskly and with laughter.

Australia had suffered too, but Sydney had an air of life beginning again instead of each day being a burden you must get through via duty and perseverance.

They bathed away the travel as soon as they arrived in porcelain baths with gold taps, drying themselves with thick, sheet-like towels.

Fresh again, they emerged to order room-service dinner: rump steak with chips and an ice-cream sundae — foods Rosa and Magda only vaguely remembered and Anna not at all.

Australia might still have rationing, but not at the Wentworth. They stared as the waitress removed the silver covers. Each vast steak was perhaps a month's meat ration back in England, almost covering the entire plate, topped with parsley butter that oozed into the juices. Even the old duke's second cellar could not provide luxury like this. Separate dishes held crisp roast potatoes, glazed carrots with parsley, beans tied up with chives in bunches, with a silver jug of red wine sauce.

'Can anyone eat so much meat?' whispered Magda in awe.

The fruit salad served with the ice-cream sundae contained bananas — Anna discovered that she loved them — as well as chopped melon, pineapple, passionfruit and papaya, which in Australia was called 'pawpaw': fruits that had been luxuries in England even pre-war and which the girls tasted warily, then with delight.

They drank fresh orange juice. So much local wood had been depleted back at Eagle's Rest that the fires that had warmed the glasshouses had been allowed to go out the past two winters. The orange trees survived but hadn't fruited. The scarcity of wood had also meant more frugal heating and hot-water use.

These rooms were warm, the sheets starched — when had Deanna or Mrs Thripps last had energy to heat the old iron on the stove to iron starched sheets?

Exhausted and with a weird sense that it was really early morning, they did not explore the town that evening, but gazed out the window at the lights on the ships in the harbour, the squat ferries busily circling from dock to dock till late at night.

Deanna had booked the suite for three weeks. Their world had vanished too quickly and they needed time to find themselves again, to adjust not only to the new time zone but to the shattered blue and gold light from the harbour, spring instead of autumn, and to absorb their new surroundings.

Deanna appointed Magda in charge of the other two girls the next morning on one of the scurrying ferries with its puffs of steam to visit the zoo, where they might meet their first kangaroo and koala, and eat as much ice cream as they wanted.

Meanwhile she had a cautious conversation with the concierge, unproductive until she produced a twenty-pound note and quietly slid it over the desk to him. Miraculously, the three- or four-year waiting list for a car became, 'My cousin has a secondhand Holden, 1939, reconditioned engine, new tyres.'

The price was far higher than the car had cost new, but a car was essential if they were to get to Budgie Creek. She also wanted to arrive in a way that made it clear that they were exploring and could easily leave.

She enquired about a house or flat to buy near Sydney University, but this even the concierge could not supply. No homes had been built during the war, and few during the Great Depression. Many families shared one house; verandas had been enclosed for whole families to sleep in.

He did, however, procure her an estate agent, and by midday she had visited Mr Vonderfleet's cousin then put down a deposit on two dilapidated shopfronts with a double-storey apartment above them at Vaucluse, though Magda would need two trams — or a car of her own — to get to the university. The shops would bring in at least some small income.

It would be ... discreet ... to have an Australian source of income.

I am a criminal, she thought. But that, too, was a family tradition. Clavertons had always done what they thought best — which was often simply what they wanted — and mostly got away with it.

The estate agent promised to advertise for tenants for the two shops, and to arrange their renovation. Both shops and the apartment above had been acquired by the American army, who had seen no need to repair the wreckage when they left. One of the walls was partly burned; two doors were hanging off their hinges; and broken bottles filled the fireplace.

A possible tenant — and business partner — appeared unexpectedly: a thin, bent woman with white hair but unlined skin and a tattoo of seemingly random numbers on her wrist, who the concierge arranged to visit the hotel to fit them all for clothes more suitable for country life.

Uncle Jasper had provided Australian ration coupons, far more generous than those in Britain, but while they would be enough to buy boots, fresh undergarments, sun hats and the kind of creamy brown moleskin trousers worn by memsahibs on safari, the coupons would not stretch to blouses or dresses for hot weather.

Mrs Goldfarb took Deanna's lack of coupons in her stride. 'My husband buys old clothes, old curtains, any old schmatte, and I transform them. See?' She showed them a small book of photos with two women in evening and afternoon styles. 'Those I can make for you.'

'You were a dressmaker?' The designs were excellent, based on recent Paris models but also original, perfectly tailored, with exquisite patterns of beading.

'I made dresses for the best families in Vienna, then I made uniforms in a factory near the camp, and so I lived. My daughter, she came here in '31, and so could sponsor us after the war, me and my second husband.'

Deanna asked no more, merely commenting, 'I make my own clothes from old material too. My middle daughter loves sewing and creating patterns. Thankfully my ancestors threw away almost nothing but kept it in trunks in the attic. I've brought four trunks of my favourites with us. The rest are being shipped out later.'

Mrs Goldfarb fingered the cloth of Deanna's jacket and nodded. 'It is good cloth — far better than is made today. Your designs are good too. You have talent, even if no training.'

'I must show you some of my other clothes. I made an evening dress once out of a ball gown an ancestor wore in the time of Queen Anne, and cocktail dresses from French designs of the 1890s.'

She found Mrs Goldfarb staring at her. 'You cut up fine old clothes? Dresses from hundreds of years ago? Masterpieces lost so you could play with them!'

'I didn't have enough money to buy suitable clothes ...'

'But ... but such garments should be preserved!'

It had never occurred to her. 'I ... don't think I have destroyed much. I mostly adapted my mother's clothes, and then used curtains and other fabrics. I'm sorry ... I never thought ...'

'And the garments will come here? May I look at them? I can help you preserve them, repair them, but they should be displayed.'

The plan evolved that moment, as quickly as Deanna's decision to come to Australia, almost as if a jigsaw was ready to complete.

'Mrs Goldfarb, I have just bought a shop — two shops, which might be made into one shop — in Vaucluse.'

The sharp eyes assessed her. 'A good area.'

'I see now that the heritage clothes must be preserved, but there are enough bed curtains, embroidered tablecloths and much more cloth to make many more garments. If you had those materials, and two adjoining shops, and an investor to back you, would you be interested in a partnership in a dressmaking business?'

Mrs Goldfarb assessed the luxury of the suite, Deanna's pearl earrings, her linen dress and jacket of such quality that it hadn't creased. 'I would be ... intrigued. But I must consult with my husband.' She raised an eyebrow. 'And a lawyer.'

'How do you think your husband might react?'

Mrs Goldfarb laughed. 'Gerard worked for Madame Chanel before the Boche put him on a train to his death. Instead he found me, and then a life here.'

Deanna hoped frantically she hadn't destroyed any of Mr Goldfarb's creations her mother might have left her.

'I think, perhaps, my husband would be most pleased with a double shop. The fashions of the past could, perhaps, become a background for our new creations. There would be much to decide.' The sharp eyes looked at her. 'And Gerard and I would be the ones qualified for the artistic decisions.'

'Agreed.'

'You would not mind the name Goldfarb upon your business, instead of perhaps Smith or de Vere?'

'Perhaps Claverton and Goldfarb? My title might bring in customers, especially with signed invitations to each new collection. Mrs Goldfarb, my daughters' surname by birth is Grunberg. I adopted them after their parents died. It was wartime, and they were young, and their parents' friends had abandoned them.'

'They were lucky to be rescued,' said Mrs Goldfarb, without emotion.

'I was the lucky one, to find daughters. Their parents were not observant Jews, but one day my daughters may want to explore their heritage. I would be grateful indeed to know they had guidance.'

The woman in front of her made no reply for a minute, perhaps; merely sketched on her pad. At last she held up the outline of a dress, her face wet, with no move to wipe the tears. 'You see — cotton, for coolness, and a slim silhouette but with the pleats so the dress will swirl; cap sleeves, and stiffening here and here, so the bodice will not need a brassiere, which will help with coolness, and not confine the beauty of the female form. I have the fabrics already, two matching shades of blue and a border of another blue, with flowers. You like it?'

'I adore it. You are a genius.'

'I am well trained, and so now are my daughter, nieces and granddaughter. Four dresses of similar design will be ready the day after tomorrow, and there will be more by the day after. Lady Claverton, God is very good.'

Forty-Nine

Peach Champagne Granita

INGREDIENTS
one and a half cups champagne
half a cup chopped very ripe white peaches
one tablespoon castor sugar, or to taste — depends on sweetness of peaches
two splashes bitters

METHOD
Blend all ingredients. Freeze in a shallow tray for at least two hours. Chill two wineglasses. Blend again; spoon it quickly into the glasses and eat at once.

Hotel recipe of the 1940s

They took the train to Katoomba for a day of gazing at endless blue-green valleys and rocks that looked like the petrified droppings of a monstrous bird. They ate excellent roast lamb and even better chocolates and more ice cream at the Paragon Cafe.

Another day, Deanna tried out her new car and maps for a picnic by the Hawkesbury, the food packed by the hotel. This was a river of character and serenity, with white-trunked hills that stretched into blue distance. Deanna had seen enough to know she would stay somewhere on this vast continent where humanity clung mostly to the sea edge, and the beaches were clad in gold. Even the rivers felt old — far more ancient than they did in England, despite that country's claim to greater history.

Magda seemed to find Sydney University a home within a week. Rosa had announced, as expected, that she wanted an immediate apprenticeship with Mrs Goldfarb, but was told by her mother and prospective employer that she must finish school. Anna visited the elephants of Taronga yet again.

Deanna had hoped to see a wedgetail eagle in the Blue Mountains, or even a sea eagle nearer the coast, but hadn't yet.

There will be eagles soon, she promised herself, and somewhere they would find a home.

Fifty

Pumpkin Scones

INGREDIENTS
one tablespoon honey
one teaspoon grated orange zest
two tablespoons butter
one cup mashed cold pumpkin — as orange and sweet as you can get it
half a cup cold milk
juice of a lemon
two cups cold self-raising flour
one well-beaten egg

METHOD
Quickly mix all except the egg. Cut into thin rounds. Brush with the beaten egg and bake in a hot oven for ten to fifteen minutes.

They left the Hotel Canberra — a capital city still with no city — before dawn. By the time the sun rose, the road was dust, the sheep a darker dust, the rocks low and grey and the paddocks endless unlike the almost English green of their first day's travel from Sydney. A crumpled bloody lump lay ahead of them on the side of the road. Black crows pecked.

'A dead kangaroo,' said Anna in a small voice as they passed it and the crows flew off to sit in the single gum tree visible, deceased as well, though the branches still provided good roosting for the carrion birds.

Erosion gullies wandered deep orange through paddocks divided by rusted barbed wire. More crows gathered at the carcass of another dead roo. They rose, protesting, but settled back as soon as the car had passed.

How could people live in such desolation? But they did. People had ringbarked those hills so the trunks shone white and lifeless. People had built those square fibro cottages in faded shades of mauve, yellow and even pink, with flashes of geraniums in old tin cans or oleander hedges up to the backyard outhouse the only brightness.

The sheep stared at the passing car as if they already knew their fates: to be roast dinners, and probably overcooked at that. Life clung as precariously to this land as its soil.

The road slowly rose as Deanna edged the car around the potholes. She had already changed one flat tyre and hadn't another spare. They crested a low hill and suddenly they seemed to be in another country: cream and orange-splotched fat-trunked trees, a creek of clear water wandering snakelike around tall ferns and between rocks, and then an actual snake, black and shiny, darting across the road to escape the car's vibration, reaching the other side just as they approached it.

'Snakes kill people here,' said Anna uncertainly.

'So do adders in England,' said Rosa.

'Snakes do it better in Australia,' said Anna. 'And spiders and crocodiles ...'

'The crocodiles are far to the north ...'

'And bushfires and dust storms ...'

'Instead of blizzards and war,' said Magda firmly. 'Look, there are more kangaroos!'

The mob gazed at them from a small clearing in the trees, very much alive, a giant square-jawed male, females with joeys in furry pouches or at foot, in small groups as if gossiping. They looked annoyed at the intrusion.

Another fence, another paddock, this one bare and cut by another deep erosion gully, but, from now on, the treed land, some of which had sheep, predominated.

A smudge on their left became hills and then mountains with hills leading up to them. The road turned and there was a river, calm and bordered with white-gold sand, the kind of river that pretended to be unchanging through the aeons, though Deanna could see debris from its floods high up the white-armed trees that bordered it.

This was not the lushness below the flight to Sydney, despite the vines thick as wrists that clambered to the treetops then fell in thick bunches of cream flowers. Nonetheless it felt comfortable: a land that had accepted humans and come to an accommodation with them, instead of eroding under their neglect.

'Should we stop and have lunch?' asked Magda. 'We could even swim — look, you can see the bottom of the river, so it must be safe.'

'Or there might be quicksand, water snakes, water spiders, jellyfish and freshwater sharks,' said Deanna, 'plus crocodiles who have decided to explore south, and an Australian version of piranhas. We'll be at Budgie Creek in half an hour and can have a proper meal at the hotel. Pass me a sandwich, please.'

She had booked rooms for three nights. It had belatedly occurred to her that even if Sam welcomed her, he might not have beds ready for four guests, or even enough bedrooms.

He had described his home as rambling. She had assumed it was similar to the mansions she was accustomed to, but some of the fibro squares had enclosed verandas and sheds around them that might be also described that way.

Sam had his own aircraft before the war ... but a good mechanic could make the small plywood craft he'd described reasonably cheaply if you could afford the time to do so. He flew in competitions in Europe. He had said his father was happy with the price of wool, and that they'd all be blinkin' millionaires if the war continued, which must be an exaggeration, but ...

But Sam had also never told her the most vital part of his identity. Sam Murray might not lie, but how much had he carefully not told, Sam Murray who was now a farmer, not a Flight Lieutenant. I do know him, she thought. He kept writing for years to three girls across the world, and he told Magda the truth when asked.

She kept driving.

Budgie Creek announced itself with a sign and a faded claim that the population was 620, which it must have been when the sign was painted but might be one or two thousand now, or possibly twenty-four people and a ghost town.

A two-storey stone house with a remarkably English garden reassured her; two fibro cottages — the fibro in both was cracked — depressed her; but the bungalows on either side that looked as if they belonged at the seaside, with fruit trees behind and cabbages and pumpkins growing in the front, as well as many well-staked bushes of tomatoes dug for victory, were the same pre-war designs she was familiar with in England.

She turned down what must be the main street, for the roads branching off featured only houses, not shops. A saddlery, a funeral parlour — how welcoming — a Bank of New South Wales, a large sign advising The Budgie Creek Hotel and an even larger sign advertising beer. She pulled into the kerb and the four of them examined the hotel.

There seemed to be no front or back door into this establishment, just a choice of doors, none more prominent than any other, though through one of them she could see men — and only men, in several shades of blue shirts, singlets, moleskins or jeans, boots and sweat-stained hats — drinking at a bar.

Another man sat alone on a bench outside one door while the other men drank inside. His hat was dusty and pulled down over his eyes. His face and skin were dark from heritage, tan and dust, his shirt was blue check, his moleskins stained with dust and his boots mostly dust as well. He was drinking a small bottle of beer, regarding it thoughtfully before he took another swig.

She leaned out the window. 'Excuse me, could you tell me which is the front door?'

He put the bottle down and stared at her, pushing his hat up.

It was Sam.

Fifty-One

Pickled Eggs

Traditionally served in large jars at pubs, along with jars of pickled onions.

INGREDIENTS
three whole cloves
one teaspoon whole peppercorns
one bay leaf
one teaspoon coriander seeds
a chilli (optional)
one tablespoon brown sugar
one litre white or red wine cider vinegar
twelve hard-boiled eggs, shelled

METHOD
Boil the spices, sugar and vinegar together for five minutes, then pour it, while hot, over the eggs in a jar. Seal. Leave for at least three weeks before eating.

***

Whatever reunion she had imagined had not included dust, beer and a man who looked exactly as he had described himself to Anna: native. Nor had she expected the smell of manure, though admittedly they had met when she'd exuded a similar scent.

His skin must have paled in England, she thought, and darkened when working in the sun again, and indeed as he automatically pulled back his shirtsleeve, she saw his skin was paler there.

He stared. 'Dee.'

'And me!' yelled Anna. 'All of us!' She scrambled from the car and into his arms.

He hugged her automatically, waking from his daze, unable not to grin. 'You've grown!'

'Of course I've grown! Do you think that I am beautiful? Mrs Goldfarb said I was beautiful in this dress, but she might have meant the dress, not me.'

Sam reached out to hug Rosa, and then a more tentative Magda. He looked up at Deanna. 'What in blue blazes are you doing here?' His voice was two-thirds fury, the rest incredulity and what might possibly be joy.

'Visiting you,' she said lightly. 'I was tired of grey skies and had a chance to fly here.'

'We read her your letter,' said Anna scornfully. 'She loves you too, so we came here.'

He shook his head, helpless.

'I've booked rooms here for three nights,' said Deanna, to clarify he was expected to neither embrace her nor marry her within the month.

He straightened, one arm still around Anna, the other on Rosa's shoulders. 'Dee, I'd offer to carry in your suitcase, but I'm not permitted in the pub, except to buy beer from the side counter if I drink it outside. We can go to the Magpie Cafe if you like,' he added stiffly. 'They allow natives inside.'

'Does it have milkshakes?' asked Rosa.

'Probably, but I wouldn't drink them. They don't have a fridge. Don't try the scones either, or you'll chip a tooth.'

Deanna shut her eyes, hoping for another piece of serendipitous jigsaw to fall. Amazingly, it did. 'Does the hotel have a ladies' lounge?'

She had been introduced to the concept at the Wentworth, which might treat its guests with elegance, but still had a public bar with a six o'clock swill where, apart from the harried barmaids, only men were permitted, drinking as much as possible before the law closed the bar at six pm.

'Yes,' Sam said cautiously.

'Then we can all have a cool drink there.'

'Dee, I told you ... it will embarrass the girls if they order me to leave.'

'No, it won't,' said Rosa. 'It will make us angry.' Again they were the threesome Deanna had first met: inseparable, tortured but indomitable.

They are even stronger now, she thought with pride.

'We might embarrass you though,' said Magda perceptively.

He smiled at her. 'If you're up for it, so am I. It might also make your mum see sense,' he added grimly. He had not even offered her his hand, nor kissed her cheek. 'It's this door here.'

Deanna surveyed the room he indicated. The ladies' lounge did not seem a place that expected ladies, unless the cockroach scuttling under a table and the four thousand flies were all female.

The cane chairs were worn, and placed so exactly by the small round tables that they possibly hadn't been moved even to sweep the floor. Apart from the flies and the single cockroach, the room was immaculately clean and impeccably soulless.

Deanna moved to a table near the door, where there was the ghost of a breeze. A woman's face peered in from a window into what must be the bar, started, then vanished.

A man appeared at the inner door; he was in his late fifties, with a beer belly he must have spent several decades accumulating, and a shirt his wife had bought when he was two sizes smaller.

'Look, Sam, I'm sorry, but you know the rules,' he began.

Deanna stood and held out her hand. He shook it automatically. 'How do you do? My name is Lady Deanna Claverton — I have booked rooms here for three nights while we visit Flight Lieutenant Murray, who became our close friend in England during his heroic war service there. His aerodrome happened to be next to Claverton Castle.'

She smiled at Sam. 'Flight Lieutenant Murray left before the queen could give him this medal, awarded only a fortnight ago. She gave me the honour of presenting it informally instead.'

She reached into her pocket and opened the case. The publican stared at it. So did Sam. Deanna grinned. Uncle Jasper had worked miracles to get the medal most definitely due to Sam in time.

'Blood— blimey Charlie,' said Sam. 'What's that for?'

'Facing almost certain death to save the life of a fellow officer and an unknown number of civilians, as well as your work guiding bomber patrols. You left before they could award it to you. Your DSO should come through on the next Honours list.'

She turned the full-wattage smile of generations of titled and entitled Clavertons onto the bewildered publican. 'These are my daughters, Lady Magda, Lady Rosa and the Amazing Lady Anna, but please tell your wife not to curtsey. None of that matters among friends and neighbours, does it? Not after all our two countries have been through together?'

'Um. Er. No, Your, um, Grace?'

'I'm just a ladyship. His Grace was my grandfather and Daddy a lord, being only a viscount ... If I decide to settle here you may meet the present duke. He's an American, but, after all, they were our allies so we must be tolerant. I may also be visited by a scatter of honourables and an earl or two. They will simply adore your hotel. It's so ... Australian. What can you offer us that is cold to drink?'

'Lemonade?' he said hesitantly.

The woman's face appeared, with her body below it in the doorway. She had evidently been listening. 'There's lemonade, creaming soda, ginger beer or I could make you a nice cup of tea or fresh orange juice, My Ladyship.'

She pulled at the edges of her floral apron and bent one knee in the obeisance Deanna assumed she made at church.

'Please, no fuss.' Deanna smiled at her and held out her hand again. 'And do call me Dee.'

'I'm Muriel, and this is my husband, Jim Nuttly — Nuttly by name and nutty by nature, so excuse him. Sam, another beer for you?'

She made it sound as if he had been drinking inside the pub since he turned twenty-one, and no question about it.

'Thank you,' said Sam. He took the box with the medal and examined it as Mrs and Mr Nuttly backed away, visibly uncertain as to how one left the presence of an aristocrat.

Sam raised an eyebrow at Dee. 'What strings did you have to pull to get this?'

'A few, but there was already considerable guilt about other medals you deserved to get, but didn't, once the ministry had been informed of your background.'

'Being banned from a pub isn't the worst of it,' he said quietly to them all.

'I know,' said Dee, equally softly.

'We know more than we did,' said Magda. 'I asked about the condition of Aboriginals in Australia at the museum in Sydney and the lady there introduced me to two ladies in the Presbyterian Church who send out a monthly newsletter. It had photos of Aboriginal people in tin shacks and children starving on bread and nothing else. We didn't see a single coloured person the whole time we were in Sydney except near the airport.'

Muriel Nuttly entered with a tray of fruitcake, and her husband followed carrying a tray of varied drinks, one of which was a bottle of beer, with glasses. 'Thought you might fancy a shandy, Your Worship; goes down nice and cold on a day like this. Sandwiches in a couple of minutes,' Muriel added. 'Egg and lettuce, and cheese and salad, and mutton and chutney, and no worries the flies have been into the mutton because I checked.'

They backed out again. Deanna took a lemonade. The girls cautiously poured and sipped the extremely red creaming soda.

'You told me I wasn't a lady, not even an honourable,' Anna pointed out.

'Shush. You are going to be the Amazing Lady Anna here and if you complain I'll make you a countess. In fact, I suspect His Majesty's government might bestow titles on you if I request it, just to ensure my silence.'

She suddenly realised how convenient it would be for His Majesty's government if she stayed in the back blocks of Australia after the embarrassing confrontation on the plane. If she married Sam, Uncle Jasper might even offer to resurrect her father's title of viscount, lost when he died.

Sam, however, did not look as if he was considering a proposal, but more as if he was wondering how to evict her permanently from Budgie Creek. He took another swig of beer and shoved the medal into the greasy pocket of his moleskins.

'I think I'll like being a lady,' said Anna.

'I shan't,' said Rosa. 'Aristocracy is an outmoded concept.'

Deanna wondered what she'd been reading lately. Not that she disagreed: she was simply prepared to use her title as necessary, for as long as people were prepared to be impressed by it.

'It would mean you don't have to be a Miss or Mrs,' said Magda.

'Which has been convenient for me,' said Deanna. 'Not being a Mrs but having three daughters. I don't even have a widow's wedding ring.'

'You've just won a minor skirmish to get some drinks and sandwiches in a pub,' said Sam shortly. 'That's not the same as spending your life fighting a war against prejudice.'

'No, it's not, but it's what you were prepared to do for a cause you believed in.' She held his gaze. 'Anyway, I hope our lives won't only be battles.'

He drank the beer absentmindedly. 'Do you really want to stay here in the pub? Plenty of room at home. And we can talk freely there.'

And out of sight of the gossips, thought Deanna. 'Two questions first — you're not engaged, or seeing anyone?'

'No. What's the second question?'

'Do we need to get some groceries before you have four guests?'

'I reckon we can manage. Mum used to shop in town once a month and get the other supplies sent down from David Jones. We pretty much follow her example.'

'Then we had better eat the sandwiches, and at least a piece of fruitcake, before I cancel my reservation, leaving full payment of course.'

'And the puppies,' said Anna. 'You said in your last letter to me there were puppies!'

'Your father won't mind?'

Sam grinned suddenly. 'He's so bored he'd welcome a gang of bushrangers if one of them could play chess. He'll show Anna how to train a sheepdog and try to beat Magda at chess.'

'He'll lose,' said Magda confidently.

'And he'll take you fishing, once he makes sure you all know how to swim, and none of that dog-paddling stuff you do back in England either ...'

'We're going to Sam's! We're going to Sam's!' chanted Anna.

Sam leaned over and took Deanna's hand in both of his, but he still made no move to kiss her. 'I'm glad you're here. I'm glad you'll visit my home. But that's all it can ever be. You understand?'

She bent and kissed his cheek, and tasted dust and sweat and Sam, and what might possibly be sheep. 'Not yet. Nor do you. We'll have to see.'

Fifty-Two

Potatoes, Eggs and Bacon

INGREDIENTS
one onion, chopped
four tablespoons butter
four rashers bacon, chopped
two cups cooked diced potatoes
six eggs
one tablespoon grated cheese

METHOD
Sauté the onion in the butter until transparent. Add the bacon and cook for five minutes. Add the potato and cook until lightly browned. Break one egg at a time into the pan (don't beat them first). Stir until the eggs are set. If you beat the eggs, the dish will have a heavy feel to it. If you don't beat them, you'll get a much creamier dish, with bits of yolk and white still separate.

1940s country breakfast dish

They followed his long truck down the road, watching blobs of shit bounce out from between the slats of the bed. He had evidently just sold a mob of sheep at the Friday sales he sometimes mentioned in his letters.

Here was the river he had spoken of, far below the road now, the deep pools with the fish called Murray cod, lined by thick-trunked trees, their dappled white and orange arms reaching to the sky.

The same trees stood taller, straighter, to accommodate closer fellows in a forest that rose in low hills. Sheep rested in the shade, or wandered their own paths to waterholes too round to be natural.

It was beautiful, in an alien way. It wasn't home. She missed the sea. To her surprise she even missed the bulwark of the castle, humanity announcing, 'We have built a vast structure and so own this land.'

This land owned itself, though humans might be part of it.

Brown shadows flickered between the trees. For a moment she froze, thinking it a flood — her senses immediately called 'danger' after all the years of war — but this tide flowed downhill in countless bobbings instead of waves.

All at once she realised it was birds, hundreds, maybe a thousand, long-legged and with long necks, in a vast migration to the river.

She braked as Sam had done while small black-feathered, red-legged ducks-that-were-not-ducks ran out of the way of the enormous striding birds, and ducks-that-were-ducks rose in indignation.

'Emus,' breathed Rosa, holding up *A Guidebook to Australian Wildlife*. 'And those small birds are native hens and the others wood ducks. *Emus are known to make vast migrations*,' she read, while Deanna watched, entranced, then looked up to see how far the ducks had flown.

And saw the sea. Not a sea with waves, but a sky so richly blue you felt you could dive into it, round at the horizon like the sea as well, except where mountains blocked the view instead of

...dlands. But this sea was brighter than she had ever known, and truly endless.

The land rose as they drove on, twisting in curves that were more yellow dust than road. Another curve, and suddenly the line of hills in front of them cracked into cliffs, each almost a mile high, shattered in places by scree slopes, or reshaped into lines like rocky organ pipes, ledges, with trees that twisted almost horizontally from crevices.

She'd seen those crevices and cliffs since she was a child. Not dreams, she thought. I just remembered backwards.

A small animal with a long tail and bright orange stomach fur blinked at them, then bounded down a vertical slope and vanished. A shadow crossed the road in front of her, but the bird had vanished by the time she looked up.

This was eagle country.

The truck and her car bounced over a metal grid she supposed would stop sheep wandering, then wound down an avenue between lines of the great white-trunked trees. Another curve and she saw the house.

It was like no house she'd ever seen, except that, like most ancient homes of England, it had grown through generations, but for owners who had more feeling for the land than the Victorian nouveau riche, who had added brick wings to Elizabethan mansions.

This house was as large as a mansion, too, in a sprawling, relaxed way, shabbily painted white, for of course there had been no house paint available in the war years, and nor was there any now.

It was wood, not stone, except the chimneys. The wood was logs in what must be the original portion, and planks in the newer wings, with broad windows so the inhabitants might have a view both of cliffs and river. Only the wing closest to the cliffs was bordered by a veranda, though the front door had a useful porch.

Farm sheds stood to the back of it, and haysheds, with a stone building half-buried in the slope — possibly a dairy or meat house, or both. Two elderly tractors and an extremely new one with an assortment of attachments sat in a proud display in an open shed.

Sam pulled up between two sheds. Deanna parked in a three-sided shed next to two tray-backed trucks, both battered.

The girls spilled out the back door and were joined by a horde of bouncing young dogs that, on second glance, turned out to be merely four, all identically black, except for one, older and slower than the rest. Anna sped to Sam, dancing with joy. 'We saw emus and native hens and wood ducks, and I *think* I saw a koala and a tiny kangaroo.'

'Wallaby,' he said, automatically. 'How is Dusty?'

'He died two years ago,' said Magda briefly.

'He pulled you out of the water,' said Anna, her arms suddenly full of squirming dog, trying to lick her face.

'What?' Sam looked stunned.

'Mum said he wasn't hurt or in pain. She was with him,' said Anna, slinging the delighted dog over her shoulder and patting his shoulders.

'I'm sorry. I ... I loved Dusty. Don't bother with your bags,' he added, obviously trying to ease the emotion-filled moment. 'I'll ask George to bring them in. Come and meet Dad, and Mrs Purdon. She comes in each day to cook,' he added. 'I can cook anything as long as it's fried, but Dad demands gravy and dessert each meal.'

'Even dessert for breakfast?' demanded Anna.

'Yes, if you count yesterday's scones toasted with jam.'

They entered by the back door, while Sam made it clear that this was not a social occasion that included dogs. Deanna gazed around. A small passage led to an old-fashioned scullery with a glimpse of an equally old-fashioned larder on one side, and a large kitchen on the other.

Sam took off his hat, showing a clean line of skin that his hat had protected from dust and wind-blown sheep shit. He placed it on a hallstand already adorned with hats and dull leather coats and jackets, then led them to a kitchen, its front windows gazing out over river and cliffs.

The room had a polished wood floor, with Persian carpets by the table and sofas by a vast stone fireplace at the other end from the stove: the same functional design as at Eagle's Rest, thought Deanna, though larger. A polished table in a dark red oak-like wood near a flyscreened window seemed permanently set for meals for two, with condiments in silver pots.

Wooden kitchen benches matched the table, made by a craftsman; there was a kerosene refrigerator and what looked like electric lights as well as hanging lamps; a wood stove of the modern, well-insulated variety pumped out a gentle heat; she smelled baking peach pie and fresh bread; and by the front windows stood a middle-aged woman almost as round as she was tall, with improbably bright gold hair piled high till she was almost a foot taller.

'And who have you brought home with you today, Sam?' she demanded in a strong Central European accent.

'This is Dee Claverton and her daughters, Magda, Rosa and Anna. This is Mrs Olga Purdon.'

'Ah, the lady he writes to and the girls. At last, you have reached here!'

To Dee's surprise each received a hug smelling of gardenias. 'Almost the pie is ready, and the goulash too. You can heat it up for dinner?' she asked Dee. 'This one and his father are chop men, fried fish and fried potatoes men, who do not know how to stir a goulash, so it burns on the bottom, and I must scrub the pot the next day. I will the beds make up. Sam, get the tea and tell your father we have guests.'

'Come out and meet him,' Sam suggested, his expression impossible to read.

They found Mr Murray Senior dozing on the veranda, a translation of *Thus Spoke Zarathustra* on his lap, a chess set on the table by his side, and a view of the cliffs in front of him. Hens pecked in a run in the yard below.

He stared as they crowded around him. Deanna realised he was slightly deaf and hadn't heard their arrival.

'Dad, this is —'

'Lady Dee!' The old man stood, supporting himself with his left hand. The left side of his face hung crookedly, but the right side grinned in delight. He looked much like his son, but his ancestry was unmistakable.

'I hoped you'd come, the lot of you. Almost invited you myself, except I'd never hear the last of it from Sam, and there are enough arguments already when the young ram takes over the property from the old one. You're Magda, you're Rosa, and you must be the Amazing Anna.'

'I am now Lady Amazing Anna,' decreed Anna. 'Mum says in Australia we get to have titles.'

Mr Murray grinned lopsidedly again. 'Joining the long line of newcomers who suddenly announce their royal connections once they get here. Good on you.'

'*Thus Spoke Zarathustra?*' queried Magda.

'Haven't read Nietzsche for years. Thought I should when Sam read me your letter. I wanted to be a philosopher,' he added. 'I managed to get into Sydney Uni and got a decent degree, but I doubt there's a native academic in the country. Anyway, you can be philosopher enough without a university job. Now Sam here always wanted to be a farmer. Spent his three years at Canterbury Agricultural College in New Zealand and after all that took up flying.'

'Blame it on the Kiwis,' said Sam. He glanced at Deanna. 'But no more flying now I'm back where I ought to be.'

Mr Murray grinned at Magda. 'Bet I'll beat you at chess.'

'Bet you won't,' said Anna. 'What are the puppies' names?' Three of the half-grown animals had gathered about them again on the veranda, two of them rolling over for the convenience of having boots scratch their chests, tongues lolling in doggie grins, the third leaping into Anna's arms again.

'Perce is all black, Cecil has a white toe, and Useless is the one who has decided you're his best friend and will give him a biscuit.'

'That's called "giving a dog a bad name",' said Anna sternly. 'Good dog, Useful.'

The puppy gazed at Anna adoringly.

'See?' said Anna. 'He knows his name already.'

None of which was what Deanna had expected.

Nor were their bedrooms, which Mrs Purdon led them to while Mr Murray and Sam attended to some farm matter.

Blinding white lace curtains hung in front of flyscreens, and the bedcovers were white too. 'White's easier to bleach the dust out from,' Mrs Purdon explained. 'I have been here a year only, and always dust.'

Mrs Purdon had been sponsored to migrate to Australia by a charity who had contributed enough electoral campaign money to the local MP to get permission to sponsor a small group of female refugees just before the war in the Pacific stopped civilian travel. She had seen Mr Murray's advertisement for a domestic worker: Budgie Creek was the furthest place she could find from the war.

'Us too,' said Magda soberly.

'Mrs Hobbins, she showed me what to do, retired a few months ago to small house in town. Is good here. Some Australian towns just flies and football,' said Mrs Purdon. 'The library, it is good, the coffee terrible, but no one calls you reffo in the street. Oh, we had war enough, making the camouflage nets in the town hall; working in the biscuit and wireless factories for the army; and trying to teach land army girls who attempt to milk a bull and scream when they see a snake.' She shrugged. 'But I scream too. The land army girls learned to milk, and not to scream.'

Her first husband, a Hungarian butcher, had died in the invasion. Her second had been home on leave at Budgie Creek. They'd had ten days of marriage. 'He died, in Japan, after Hiroshima. He was one of the first prisoners-of-war to go in from the prison camps to help. They said he took six weeks to die. Yes, I cried for him, but do not cry for me. I have a life, a house, friends, and a pension that might feed a rat, if it was not a hungry rat. I am happy.'

'I'm so sorry,' said Deanna gently.

She shrugged. 'The war was not as far away as I was thinking. But Mr Murray I like, and Sam so kind, and the animals interesting.'

She left at twilight, expertly driving a small cart with a large horse.

They ate the most excellent goulash in the kitchen, but with what was evidently the best crockery and cutlery. All had showered and changed — Deanna into the flowered dress Mrs Goldfarb had made before she left Sydney, her hair permed and curled and her nails manicured as much as work-worn nails could be in the hotel's beauty salon, where she had bought what was probably black-market lipstick: her first black-market purchase and, she told herself, her last.

The girls wore new dresses too.

It was a happy meal, despite Sam's silence and his obvious discomfort with his father's tacit assumption that they all would stay permanently once they had learned about the obvious Budgie Creek delights — the New Year's Day swimming party on the river; the new movie theatre, the ice-skating rink that would soon be up and running again; and the town hall, where theatrical companies performed two or even three times a year. Rosa and Anna would go to school here, and Magda would return in university holidays, bringing friends, thus providing his house with a ready-made — and expanding — family now his daughter lived in town.

He talked, obviously glad of the company, about the time Sam and Deb, now still in Sydney, had decided to collect honey from the native stingless bees for their mother, but when they climbed the rocks to find the nest they found it held paper wasps instead, and the two of them slid down the cliff into the water in a cloud of wasps — thankfully a kind not inclined to sting — landed on a black snake, which was more startled than they were, jumped from the creek, stopped to take off their wasp-covered clothes, and arrived stark naked, yelling, 'It wasn't our fault!' when their mother was hosting her bridge club.

Later he and Magda played chess. Deanna was glad to see Magda's pleasure when the old man clearly floored her, taking her seriously as a player.

Sam washed up and Anna dried, quick-firing questions at him about how many rams were needed for the ewes, how did you know which ram had covered which ewe; were they still feeding the poddies, and her delight that Rocky the Rigg — a male only half castrated, who had escaped during the war — had mated with Houdini the ewe — another escapee, recently recaptured, whose late-season lamb was expected any day now.

Rosa sat on the veranda with Deanna, watching the stars — so many more than in Sydney and so different from home — listening to new frog calls, and crickets, and an almost familiar barn-owl hoot, and another owl that burped 'mopoke, mopoke' from a tree near the house.

'I'd like to make a dress from the sky here,' Rosa said dreamily. 'Black that goes forever and stars that sweep across the skirt.'

Mr Murray kissed their cheeks goodnight. Sam kissed the girls, taciturn again. Deanna showered — a most splendid Australian invention — brushed her hair, and dabbed herself with what had been Chanel No 5 but seemed now to be mostly alcohol.

She dressed herself in an unworn scandalous Parisian peignoir a schoolfriend had sent for her twenty-first birthday, carefully inserted her diaphragm, then crossed the hallway to his room.

The door was not locked, possibly because it had no lock. The lamp was out — Mr Murray had turned off the electric generator for the night — but Sam was not asleep. The moonlight washed a tide of gold into the room, showing his arms behind his head. He was gazing at her.

'No,' he said.

'Don't be so bloody middle class!'

He blinked. 'What do you mean?'

She sat on the end of the bed, the silk pooling around her legs. 'Every man in my life has either treated me like a stud mare for aristocratic breeding or the gracious lady of the manor. You saw me as a woman. I hoped you still did.'

'Of course I see you as a woman,' he said impatiently, 'but that isn't the point. Dee, you're enjoying the novelty. You wouldn't be happy here, not long-term.'

'How about tonight?' She laughed at his expression. 'See, I said you were being middle class. You think sex means marriage. Sam, darling, every debutante ball ends with couples at it in the rose gardens.'

'Were you ... at it ... in the rose gardens?'

'No,' she said simply. 'You're the first man I've ever wanted. Probably the last, though who can tell? I've imagined making love with you so often I deserve the real thing. But I don't expect it to mean we're engaged by breakfast time. I have a diaphragm,' she added, 'so I won't get pregnant.'

She saw him absorb this with a look of slight bafflement and shock. 'Others will assume your being in my bed means marriage.'

She grinned. 'I know. But they'll assume we're having sex anyway, so we may as well enjoy our ruined reputations ... Was there someone else since you've been home?'

'Yes,' he said simply.

'Susan?'

'Yes. Dee ... back in England I didn't think I'd survive the war. I could love you and it wouldn't matter, because sooner or later I'd be gone, and you knew that as well as I did. Then after the accident all I could think of was you and Eagle's Rest, and staying there with you, where who I am didn't matter. I'd have been "Lady Dee's husband". But then they bundled me onto the ship, and as soon as I saw Dad and Eagle Mountain I knew I had to stay here.'

'You could have told me,' she said quietly.

'No, I couldn't. You'd have done just what you've done now, said it didn't matter and come out here without knowing what you were getting into, and no matter how bad it got you wouldn't have given in. It wasn't fair to you, or the girls.'

'Or Susan?'

'Or Susan. I thought if I married it'd make it impossible that we could ever be together.'

'If she could marry you, why not me?'

'She'd been here two years and knew what she'd be getting into. Sue's far happier with a man who truly loves her than living here with no art galleries or Bach concertos except on the radiogram.'

'The last time I went to an art gallery was for a school excursion. The only theatre I've been to in the last ten years is the village Christmas plays. I suspect Budgie Creek matches their standard.'

She undid the ribbons at her throat. 'May I take this off?' She tried not to sound nervous.

For answer he pulled back the sheet that covered him. It was her turn to blink. 'Good grief. You ... you don't look like Michelangelo's David.' His skin shone in the moonlight, the scars on neck and leg pale rather than red.

For the first time since she arrived he grinned. 'That's the only nude male you've seen?'

'And a few paintings.' She was suddenly not sure about this at all. His sagging testicles and erect penis were unexpected. The size and hardness of the penis shocked her, and the reddish head too: how could that possibly fit inside her? His chest also seemed so much larger, more muscled, out of his shirt. His legs were more hairy, but his chest less so than she'd assumed it would be.

He held out his arms to her. She slid under the sheet. 'Sam ... I want this, but I ...'

Suddenly he was the Sam she'd known before, the one she wanted, needed, now. 'Shh. Don't worry, love. We'll go slow.'

'You can do sex at different speeds?'

'Didn't girls at school discuss this stuff?'

'We were kept as chaste as your ewes till breeding time, which in our case was the London Season, but which I didn't attend. My, er, education has been the photos in *Classic Myths of Greece and Rome* and Mrs Thripps' references to giving Arnold a Friday Night Special, which I thought was a dessert till I asked her for the recipe.'

He held her as gently as he had when they shared a bed before, except for his erection. 'What did she say?'

'She laughed so much she nearly fell into the washing machine, and then she told me.'

'So what's the recipe?' He kissed her neck softly.

Mrs Thripps had given her details she hadn't really understood till now, and still wasn't sure she could perform. 'Sam ...'

'Slow means this.' He sat and undressed her gently, touched her breast with his hand, then put his mouth to it, then his fingertips on her other nipple. His mouth moved, to her neck, ear, then to her breasts again ...

'Should I be doing something?' she asked breathlessly.

'Definitely not this time. The next time, maybe.'

'Why not?' she managed to gasp. So there would be a next time.

'Because this is supposed to be slow, and if you touch me at all it won't be.'

'When ... when your father spoke of rams to Rosa ... rams do it more than once a day. Can men?'

'Yes,' he muttered, from somewhere near her stomach.

'Can you?'

'Mmm.' His tongue was doing something she would have thought quite insanitary, but now ...

'Good,' she said, then gasped again.

It rained during the night. Briefly, in between lovemaking — the caress of breast and belly and her own explorations of his body, which, it seemed, were the times when sex grew even slower — she was aware of a strange drumming on the roof.

Rain, she thought. The land is welcoming me. Or maybe I have just accepted that this will be my land, and so I welcome the rain.

She woke again as the moon bounced like a balloon between the clouds outside the window. The sweat on his back from their lovemaking gleamed gold. She found him watching her, his expression impossible to read.

'I love you,' he said quietly.

She sat up and curled herself against him. 'I've known you love me as long as I've loved you. But it hurt tremendously, not knowing why you kept us apart.'

He took her in his arms, wrapping his legs around her. 'I'm sorry. I've bungled it, but I didn't know what else to do. I was about to tell you everything when they snatched me from the hospital. Dee, do you remember back in England, and you asked me for a story of my home?'

She nodded.

'I think it's time you heard the story. The prejudice you've seen so far — it's nothing, Dee, compared to what's happening still around Australia. Thank you, by the way, for not suggesting I move away and pass for white, as I did in England. Here I'm Sam Murray. It's my identity, my land, and I'll be blowed if I'll leave it.'

'You mean you feel Aboriginal here?'

'I have no idea what feeling Aboriginal means. That's part of what being Aboriginal means in 1945. The Murrays are the only Aboriginal family around here, and we got to stay because my grandmother married a man with enough money to hire lawyers to stop the authorities trying to take any of his kids or grandkids. My winning flying prizes before the war was probably my way of showing I was worth something, because I'd never be on the local footy team. Not forbidden — just no place for me on the field.'

'So what's your story?'

He stared out the window. 'My great-great-grandfather squatted on this place. He expected natives to work like his convicts, for bread and tea. When they didn't he had troopers sent down from Sydney. They raided the camp at daybreak, took the men away in chains, and made them carry those chains all the way to Sydney. Half died of thirst or hunger or exhaustion on the way, the others soon after, of illness, locked in cells at night then chained up again to build Sydney's fine roads.

'Some escaped the massacre. Great-Great-Grandpa hunted them for sport. He even invited friends to join in. The women who survived were mostly sent to a mission school down the coast, where they were kept locked up, starved and beaten to learn how to be servants, far away from here, and sent to prison if they left where they were assigned. They were paid — but the government kept the money. Neither they nor their descendants ever saw it.'

'They said at the museum that's still happening.'

'I expect it is. Great-Great-Grandpa had two sons. One died. The other only ever had a daughter, who married a man called Murray — a black stockman she met at the Royal Easter Show in Sydney. She inherited Eagle Mountain. Suddenly Budgie Creek's biggest property was owned by a black man — Dad, when *he* inherited it.'

'That's your story?' she whispered, thinking of the men darkskinned as the rough-barked mountain trees, stumbling, bloody, barefoot, dying of thirst and starvation in the strange flat country by the sea.

'That's just where the story begins. I don't even know what this land was called when my grandfather's people owned it, nor have I any way to find out. They're gone, every one of them. Dee, what you've seen in your life is like first and second class in a train. You think you'll stay in first class, even married to me. That's what Jewish people in Europe thought: I am one of them, I'm safe. But hatred was waiting to grow. The same "not really us" is lurking underneath all the time here.'

She sat silent, still holding him.

'Well?' he said at last.

'What are you going to do about it?'

'Not stand for bloody parliament, if that's what you mean. I'll do what I've always done, try to show I'm as good as any white man, or better.' He hesitated. 'And feel ashamed that I'm glad my kids will probably be whiter than I am, and will escape if some Aussie Hitler tries to kill us all again.'

She put a finger against his lips. 'Who knows who will be the scapegoats next? But if you think that I'll scuttle back to England, where my own ancestors were villains, because I might have to battle here …' She wound her arms around his neck and rolled over so he was on top of her. 'We've just won a war, Sam. You and I were part of it. I hope to live in peace all my life, but if we need to fight prejudice, then I'll face it here, with you.'

He bit her neck, gently. 'You are magnificent,' he said. 'But I'm still not marrying you.'

Sunlight ran in a river between the curtains when they woke again.

'Holy hell.' Sam uncoiled himself from around her body and sat up. 'The whole house will be up soon. You'd better get back to your room.'

She stretched luxuriously, slightly sore in some places and others swollen for quite different reasons. 'Don't want to.'

He kissed her lips gently, but broke off when she lightly bit his lip. 'You're the only aristocrat in this house. The rest of us are middle class and expect you to pretend to have slept in your bed.'

'Shh! Sam,' she said softly. 'Look!'

He followed her gaze out the window. A vast bird dropped to just below the veranda roof, talons down, wings vertical. It grabbed a fat grey pigeon, then flapped twice before it became airborne, the dead pigeon in its talons.

Deanna ran to the window as it soared without flapping, catching a current of air to take it to the cliffs.

'They're nesting again,' said Sam. 'That one's the male.'

She watched till the bird vanished. 'Do you cook breakfast?' she asked at last.

'I will if you go back to your room and sleep for a bit.'

'I couldn't sleep.'

'You need it,' said Sam gently. He padded naked to the door, peered out, gestured to her. She flashed across the corridor. Mrs Purdon had placed her only a yard and a half from Sam's bedroom. Mrs Purdon had expected this. Sam's father possibly had too, and Anna would probably ask them for details at breakfast.

Later, she thought, lying in the fresh sheets of her bed. Later …

Fifty-Three

Traditional Tomato Relish

INGREDIENTS
twelve peeled and chopped brown onions
one cup water
twenty-four very ripe tomatoes, skinned
one cup white vinegar
two tablespoons cornflour
one kilogram brown sugar
six garlic cloves
one tablespoon hot curry powder
one teaspoon ground cinnamon
one teaspoon ground nutmeg
one teaspoon white pepper
one teaspoon ground dried ginger
a quarter teaspoon ground cloves
salt to taste

METHOD

Boil the onions in the water for ten minutes; add tomatoes and vinegar. Boil ten more minutes. Add cornflour mixed with a little more cold vinegar; stir on a low heat till thick, add everything else, then bottle while hot. Will choke a brown dog when fresh but mellow and be delicious in three days.

It was eleven am when she looked at her watch. Would everyone assume she had slept in after being confused in a new time zone?

Not a chance.

She showered, washing her hair, glad that the perm and haircut meant that after a brief towelling it curled again; she dressed in slacks, riding boots and a faded linen shirt: a deliberate point — I am at home here, and so do not wear lipstick or wait for my hair to dry. She investigated the kitchen and found Sam dozing on the sofa by the unlit fire, a newspaper over his face.

'Where is everyone?'

He peered sleepily over the newspaper and sat up. 'Dad's taken the girls in the truck to see the property. Mrs Purdon packed them a picnic to have by the river. Don't worry — it's pretty shallow there, and the water is clear enough to see any snags.'

'They're not bad swimmers. We swam most afternoons in Sydney. We even surfed at Manly.'

'Hope you don't have dysentery. The sewage outlet comes out there,' he said drily.

'Where's Mrs Purdon?'

'Everyone's being tactful so I could have a much-needed forty winks. Mrs Purdon's done the washing and now has gone into town for groceries we don't need.'

'You're sure?'

'It's one reason Eagle's Rest seemed so like home. Mrs Smith does the dairying for the whole property, and we have our own meat and hens, an orchard and vegetables.'

She already knew from his letters that they had six men employed again now the war was over, five of whom had wives and houses, the other boarding with a mate and his wife. Shearers were contracted once a year.

He looked at her boots. 'Planning on riding?' He had also told her they had temporarily retired the motorbikes they'd used for farm work in the '30s because of the fuel shortage and gone back to horses.

'I'd like breakfast first.'

'Another chance to show you my frying skills. I could do with an early lunch.'

Two lamb chops, one 'breakfast steak', two eggs, fried tomatoes, fried leftover baked potato, toast with marmalade and three cups of tea later, she felt she'd need one of Higgins's draught horses to carry her.

'You eat like this every day?'

He grinned. 'Not quite. I used up energy somehow in the night.'

She took the last piece of toast. 'I've changed my mind. I do expect a proposal. I don't have a father with a shotgun, but I suspect yours would do the job if I asked him.'

'Too right he would. I bet he'll have them calling him Grandpa by the time they get back. Dee ... it's not just the native business. I saw you back home. You love that land, every inch of it.'

She carefully spooned out more excellent grapefruit marmalade. 'Not anymore. It's been resumed for houses, all but my house, garden, cliffs and the vegetable fields. One of the castle's turrets has finally fallen down, and no one knows if that's put the kybosh on the golf club plan, but if that's fallen through, the ministry will probably take the estate too. They may anyway, with the exception of the castle; I doubt they'll want that. Maybe it'll be gifted to the National Trust and sell teas and teacups with the Claverton crest to daytrippers.'

He stared, stricken.

'I couldn't stand it,' she said quietly. 'They ... the man from the ministry ... his plane accidentally killed the male eagle. I planned to move somewhere else in England anyway, then found the girls wanted to go as far away from war as they could. Like your Mrs Purdon. They showed me your letter, so I knew I could come here.'

He took her hand, and began to speak, but she kept talking. 'Sam, I'd have come anyway if I'd known why you never asked me to marry you. I made my choice long ago — if it was you or Eagle's Rest, then I chose you. I'd have wanted to go back to England often — it's only a few days by plane and there are commercial flights starting up again — we came on a trial run for one.'

'But the girls ...'

'They really have always wanted to leave England. I just didn't know it. It's not only because of the way they were treated after their parents died. They never made close friends in the village — they always felt like outsiders: German, Jewish. The other end of the world was the perfect solution, they thought. Not to mention dogs, horses, and an abundance of new animals. They also love you.'

'So, you're proposing they join a family of outsiders, in a place where they will also be outsiders?'

'Are you an outsider?'

'To some people. A lot of people. But I have a lot of friends too, and a heck of a lot of relatives. You wouldn't be lonely; I can tell you that much. But there'll be people who'll look down on you. You've never known that before. I want you to be yourself, Dee, not just a farmer's wife.'

'I will use my title like the spears of my ancestors against anyone who tries to look down on me. You may be surprised how few will try it, at least not to my face. And why should I care what they say in my absence? But no, I don't intend to be a farmer's wife; I knew I wasn't suited to that back in England.'

'But then —'

She held her hand gently over his mouth. 'I intend to be a *farmer*. I like growing things. Get used to the idea. Women showed they could farm in the war. Just don't ever ask me to grow another bloody potato. I've also begun a dressmaking business in Sydney with a Mrs Goldfarb — I'll tell you about that later. But I want to live with trees, not houses and roads and cars. Magda has already adopted Sydney University and spoken to some of her potential professors. I hope you can get a driver's licence in Budgie Creek — and someone to give her lessons. Rosa wants to do a dressmaking apprenticeship in Sydney when she finishes school — though I'm not sure I can persuade her to wait that long. Anna may need to be forcibly removed from the farm already. Would you really turn us out?'

'Of course not.' He looked at her wretchedly. 'I'll wait till you come to your senses. Rosa and Anna may love the farm, but they'll be called names at school.'

'Not after they graciously give permission for everyone not to use their titles. I'm joking, of course. I was always Lady Deanna of the Castle in the village. I won't make that mistake here. We'll invite their classmates and their parents out here. Most bigotry survives because of ignorance.' She grinned at him. 'We are extremely likeable.'

'You can't just stare down racism that easily.'

'Not against the whole of Australia, maybe, but in one country town? We faced worse odds in the war and won. And if there are some bigots left, it's their loss.'

She covered their joined hands with her other one. 'If the girls don't find friends here, they will at university, or wherever else they decide to go, as long as it is *not* a London Season. Thank goodness none of them has suggested that.'

'But you'll be stuck here.'

'Exactly. Just as I'd be stuck at Eagle's Rest. But here I'll be with you ...'

She didn't say she had dreamed of the cliffs she had glimpsed yesterday since she was a child, or that she'd felt they meshed like two pieces of a jigsaw puzzle ever since she saw him gaze at a golden eagle, or that he had her grandfather's eyes, and his father's eyes, eagle people all of them, who chose and made their own lives, and their moral decisions too; they were not sheep who blindly followed the next sheep in the line along a well-worn track.

Nor did she say that she'd felt the eagle's acceptance this morning. Not welcome — an eagle didn't welcome. But somehow, deeply, she knew its presence at that time and place was one of the endless strings that held reality together.

How much had Sam been hurt in the past, seen his family abused, so that he failed to realise that, of all the women he might marry, she was the least likely to face discrimination?

Discriminate against a Claverton? Budgie Creek could be only a hundred years or so old. The Clavertons went back, not merely to the establishment of the dukedom, but to the Battle of Hastings, where family tradition had it that a certain remedy for post-battle haemorrhoids had persuaded the victorious king to grant the knighthood that 600 years later became the dukedom. Clavertons discriminated, but were never discriminated against.

The land greened within twenty-four hours of the rain, and then grew greener still.

Deanna continued her nightly visits to Sam's bed. Rosa caught a twenty-two-pound Murray cod, and Magda charmed Constable Heaton into giving her driving lessons and taking her to the pictures.

Deanna managed to find a secondhand Morris Eight for Magda, and Grandpa Murray gave her the petrol ration for a visit to Sydney to formally enrol. Sam had been wrong — it took forty-eight hours for his father to get the girls to call him Grandpa.

Within a fortnight Deanna found her youngest daughter with her arm in a ewe's uterus, with a look of focused bliss as she successfully separated twin lambs.

Useless/Useful became Ulysses. He completed his journey by discovering Anna's bed, from which both refused his being evicted each night.

Somehow the girls were borrowing horses and being taught to ride them by a mob of Sam's cousins once, twice and possibly three times removed before their elders knew anything about it, in the big secure Australian saddles. Sam's mother had four sisters, and his father had two, most with farms, or at least a paddock for horses, and the younger generation was eager to show the exotic newcomers everything from the best dam to catch yabbies to the Saturday afternoon movies at the picture theatre. Constable Heaton bravely faced the competition to take Magda to the Saturday night dance, and lost.

Grandpa Murray enrolled Rosa and Anna in school in time for both to play sheep in the Christmas play, roles they insisted they had earned through their most-accurate portrayal of sheep sounds and mannerisms.

'And the school has a paddock for horses — half the kids ride in, Mum, so can't we too, please? And there's a bring-a-cake stall next Tuesday …'

Once or twice she had scones — appalling — at the Magpie Cafe; she managed an occasional shandy, simply to make the point, at the pub, where she noticed that men with skin decidedly darker than Sam's were now drinking — if they weren't at the bar, they were at least at tables in the same room; there were long phone conversations with Mrs Goldfarb, as well as the painter, carpenters and signwriters who were part of the Vaucluse refurbishment, with a tentative opening date of March next year; and there was the delivery of dresses for her and the girls — 'trial models', to see if Deanna approved.

She did.

The Christmas tree was a gum tree, chosen by 'Grandpa' and the girls he now referred to as his granddaughters. The ornaments were mostly hand carved, and generations old. The mistletoe did not look like mistletoe, but Magda looked it up and assured Deanna that it was.

Deanna and Sam kissed beneath it several times, mostly to stop everyone gazing at them until they did so.

The church they went to each Sunday was a small one, with what Deanna suspected were more dark faces than at other local churches, though men around here were so tanned it was hard to tell.

The service was the familiar one, though it seemed odd to sing snowy Christmas carols in the heat while fat iridescent beetles tumbled off the tin roof.

Gifts for men were always impossible to find, unless you stuck to cigarettes, socks and ashtrays, but Deanna had bribed the help of the Wentworth's concierge in Sydney, who had obviously been asked the question many times for many years.

He'd arranged for custom covers with which to insulate a steering wheel in a car that had been sitting for an hour in the sun, an automatic ashtray on a wooden stand that opened and closed on the ash when you pressed its edges — Sam didn't smoke, but he would have visitors who did — superior shaving soap and razor blades (probably black market), boxes of chocolate (ditto) and tie pins with a discreet ram on each.

The girls' gifts to Deanna were handmade, as they had been by necessity every year. Now it seemed this would continue as tradition: knitted socks for wearing inside boots; a silk scarf cut to shape and hemmed; and a necklace of beetles painted gold from Anna. 'They were dead already,' she assured her.

'Christmas beetles,' Sam explained.

He had given the girls books on various aspects of Australia — Deanna recognised them from the catalogue — as well as Akubra hats in white, bone and brown and a large tin of (catalogue) humbugs each.

Father Christmas, it appeared, also knew the Eagle Mountain chimney, and had left three stockings filled with minute carvings of emus, echidnas and every other animal they had seen, from Murray cod to snake, which made each girl cry as well as smile. Deanna found herself crying too.

Her own presents included a brooch from Mr Murray, a green and mauve opal in a filigree of gold that had belonged to his mother, whose death had come several years after Sam's mother's, so it had never been given to her.

Sam presented her with an opal bracelet, new, but matching. Deanna had also bought (for herself) a selection of underwear nice women did not wear, and which she had had to open a sealed section of the catalogue to peruse. She would show Sam those in private.

Mr Murray's gift to the girls was a horse each, superior to the various ones they had been riding. Magda's would be cared for while she was away.

Deanna glanced at Sam, who was carefully smiling. She guessed his true feelings. This was the epitome of a family scene and he still did not believe such happiness would last. Eventually Deanna and the girls would leave, even if they visited again as friends.

Worse: she might stay, and pretend happiness, for love of him and because she had not let herself find anywhere else to go.

Deb called from Sydney, a three-minute call only, as the lines were so busy on Christmas Day. 'I'm glad you're here,' she said to Deanna. 'Hope we meet soon — Ron and I should be back in a few weeks. Give my brother a kick in the pants for me, will you?'

'Why?'

'For not inviting you here years ago, even if you couldn't get here till now.'

Murrays arrived, and Murrays, and more Murrays, and people who had Murrays somewhere in their family tree or whose great-grandfathers had been mates with some Murrays; and there was noise, laughter and gifts, appropriate or not; three roast turkeys; pumpkin; baked potatoes; baked hams; pickled collar of pork; a giant brawn, slightly melting in the heat; cod; wild ducks; potato salad; more potato salad; green salad dressed with condensed milk and vinegar; pickled beetroot; a bathtub filled with yabbies, served with mayonnaise or just more yabbies; seven plum puddings and many competitive glances by cooks to see which one was preferred; custard; lemon sauce; orange jelly; and a game of cricket that had rules resembling those at no other match in the world (e.g. 'if the ball lands in a cowpat it's a sixer' and 'kids under twelve get three goes before they're out').

Deanna looked at her daughters' joyous faces and knew they mirrored her own. For the first time in their lives, they were with people who understood the illogicality of racism and exclusion, and who accepted them with no thought of race or background, except curiosity — especially about 'their' castle.

Sam still did not propose.

Fifty-Four

January 1946

> *A shabby lad says to a boy in a public-school uniform wheeling a barrow of manure, 'What are you doing with that manure?'*
> *'We put it on our lettuces.'*
> *'Oh really? We prefer salad dressing.'*
>
> World War II joke

Deanna came in on the first Sunday afternoon of the new year and found a strange woman sitting at the table in what she was almost thinking of as her kitchen, as she planned new curtains from the David Jones catalogue, and exactly where her favourite pieces from Eagle's Rest might go. The eagle statue and the painting she had given Sam already had pride of place in the sitting room, perpetually neat because it was seldom used.

She had already put her name on the waiting list for another fridge. The larger family needed one, and if she didn't stay here, she would still need a fridge. The current wait time was at least four years, as it was for all the appliances that had halted production in wartime.

The woman stood, her dark hair in a classic perm, her skin tanned, wearing a dark blue linen dress with white piping and white sandals. 'I'm Deb. You're Dee? 'Scuse me helping myself to tea.'

'Not at all. This is your home! I'm just a visitor.'

'I hope you'll be more than that. My brother's always had a stick up his arse, excuse my French. Don't get me wrong, he's one of the best blokes I know, but he can't see that his kids and mine will be white, and the native part forgotten.'

Deanna grinned. 'Maybe not. I have Norman blood from a thousand years ago, and now and then I make people remember it.'

Deb shrugged. 'Maybe in a thousand years our descendants will be proud, too, and it will be too late as everything will be forgotten.'

'Thank you for all the dripping, by the way. It really did come in handy.'

'A pleasure. Have you finally managed to seduce Sam?'

'Yes,' said Deanna, blinking.

'Thank goodness. I was afraid he'd get a case of dog's balls every time a good-looking sheila walked by. There was Susan, but I don't think there was much testicle relief from that department — not for want of her trying either.' Deb lifted the teapot. 'Cuppa?'

This woman could take over a room even better than the Duchess of Windsor. 'Yes, please.' Deanna sat in the chair opposite. 'May I offer you a date slice?'

'Please.' Deb took a sip of what looked dark, and strong, and milkless. 'Sam won't marry you, you know.'

Deanna met her eyes. 'He will. I'm stubborn too.'

'He is more stubborn. People can pretend I'm white, and that my sons are too, apart from a few dyed-in-the-wool racists, because I married a white man and played the game. I pretended not to notice when they called me "burned toast" when I was five at ballet school. I act white. I also no longer have the name Murray.

'Everyone remembers Old Mr Murray, the best judge of a good ram around. They asked his advice, but never asked him and Gran to dinner, which means they remember that his grandson is part native. Dad looks like his mother, too. Sam could have moved away — though I can't imagine it. Instead, he proved he could outride the entire district, went to agricultural college in New Zealand, and took up flying, making enough prize money to keep him independent.' Deb shrugged. 'You know what came next. He went to war and arrived home on crutches, announced he was a farmer and was never going to leave again. He also had mysterious letters from four English females — gossip's faster than flies around here.'

'It does that back in the village I came from.'

'You're a village girl?'

Deanna laughed. 'Sam only saw me in the war. He seems to think there are royal garden parties and eligible viscounts waiting for me now the war is over.'

'Are there?' Deb asked curiously.

'Probably. I don't want them.'

'Why not?'

'You starve at royal garden parties. Your high heels get stuck in Their Majesties' blasted chamomile lawn and every eligible viscount or honourable has an ageing house in need of a new roof and an even more appalling social life, both of which I'd be expected to devote my life to. I like it here — it's familiar, but different, too. I'll stay in Australia, somewhere, even if I don't marry Sam. But I intend to.'

'Okay then.' Deb held out two sheets of paper to Deanna. Her hands were callused, tanned, but the nails were manicured, presumably from her time in Sydney.

Deanna took it. 'What's this? A test?'

'In a way. You'll know what you're getting into within a month. If you still like Budgie Creek, Sam will have to admit it.'

Deanna read the first page. '*CWA, two pm Tuesday, the pink cottage by the library. Historical Association annual general meeting eight pm, upper-floor library, Wednesday. Offer yourself as treasurer. Three pm Thursday meeting with principal, Central School, to volunteer for tuckshop duty. Four forty pm meeting with me, Ron and the mayor to discuss the new Sam Murray memorial swimming pool, though it won't have an official name ...*' She looked up at Deb, who seemed amused. 'But he's not dead!'

'No, but he's an acknowledged hero — Muriel Nuttly has spread the news of the medal all around town. The council can't stop Aboriginal people swimming in a pool that's been donated by Mrs Murray, which you will be by the time it's built. What exactly did he do that was so heroic?'

Deanna explained. Deb suddenly looked sober. 'Trust my brother not to tell us. That wonderful dog. Er ... I presume you do have enough money for a swimming pool? Dad could pay for it, but he'll say everyone can swim in the river.'

'I'm rich because I lived in a castle and have a title? The castle went to my cousin, who sold it. I have a small income left by an old friend, and will have money from the forced sale of most of my land.' She grinned again. 'Can you keep a secret? I've only told my eldest daughter.'

Deb nodded. 'I won't even tell Ron.'

'I have diamonds sewn into my oldest brassiere. My grandfather accumulated them for me. I have a feeling he broke at least one law in giving them to me, and I broke another by smuggling them into Australia. But I can pay for a swimming pool, and a new home, and whatever life for myself and my daughters we want.'

'Diamonds in your bra!' said Deb dreamily. 'You're exactly the sister I've always wanted. I don't suppose you throttled a Nazi with your bare hands?'

Deanna stared. 'What has Sam told you?'

'Nothing! You mean you *did* throttle a Nazi?'

'No. There was … an incident, and your brother knows about it, but it's top secret and a long time ago.'

'Now I really *have* to know.'

'Ask me on my twentieth wedding anniversary. I doubt they will arrest us for breaking our oath then … Come to think of it, they forgot to make me take it.'

'You're on. Now for the next item in the "get the broomstick out of Sam's arse" campaign. There will be an article about the two of you meeting in the shadow of your family's castle in the next issue of the local newspaper, with a most impressive photo of said castle, though admittedly it's possibly a little dated, as it was taken during the king's visit there in 1919.'

'How do you know?'

'Ron's going back to editing the local paper. Well, what do you think?'

'That Budgie Creek is totally different from the village at Claverton, and entirely the same too. It feels like home.'

'Have dinner with us and Dad and the Lanyons on Saturday night. He's the mayor.'

'I can give you dinner here. I like cooking.'

'Even better. I'll arrange it with Glenys Lanyon. Ron will take photos so the paper can record the event in its social pages, in which you will appear each week until your wedding.'

'You'll decide on the date and we can read when it's going to be in the personals column?' asked Deanna innocently.

Deb laughed. 'I'm not quite that bad. Sam has been unhappy, like a ram who turns his back on all the lovely sheep.' She suddenly looked uncertain. 'Will you really be happy here? England may seem tired and hopeless just now, but that won't last. Australia has its problems too, and Budgie Creek may not be as far away from the next war as we were the last.'

'I don't expect a paradise.'

'And Sam?' Deb broke off as something brown flashed by the window — the wedgetail eagle, rising now, a chicken in its claws. 'I needn't have asked the question,' said Deb quietly. 'The eagle answered it. So did you, when you didn't have hysterics about losing a chook.'

'I don't understand.'

'You will, one day. Eagles matter to you, don't they?'

'Yes. They always have.'

'You'll make a good Murray then.'

She stood. Deanna automatically rose as well, and just as automatically returned Deb's embrace. 'Sam had to go a long way to find himself an eagle,' said Deb. 'And in an English castle, of all places.'

Deanna found she was crying, had been crying perhaps for quite some time. Her handkerchief was wet and she hadn't noticed it till now. Tears for the lost eagles on Eagle's Rest and all of England, tears for so many lives lost, and so much land, and people homeless, and hatred still drifting about the world. Tears for all that was never counted as lost in war: not just eagles but badgers and horses and dogs like Dusty, tears for the house she'd lost ...

'I'm glad he found me too,' she said.

Fifty-Five

Iced Watermelon

Pick melon. Cool. Slice. Eat.

One month later, Lady Deanna Claverton, patron and treasurer of the local Widows and Orphans Fund, treasurer of the local Historical Association, winner of the Sport's Day Ladies' Cowpat-Throwing Competition, Treasurer of the Show Society, sandwich cutter at the school tuckshop, and presenter of winner's cup at the annual Budgie Creek Show Day Ladies' Hammer and Nail race, sat at her kitchen table with a cup of tea, toast and Mrs Purdon's excellent strawberry jam.

Deb had been right that any local club would be overjoyed by a new victim as treasurer. A patron with a title was miraculous.

She was still not Mrs Murray. Nor had Sam asked her. His father had told her, privately, that Sam had already had his grandmother's engagement ring sized for her finger, using one of her own rings as a guide.

Deb was exasperated, but also clueless.

Outside nothing moved, except possibly the world's fattest flies butting between the flyscreens and the windows. The world's stickiest flies, too, capable of crawling into your eyes and nose no matter how often you waved them away: they bashed at the inside of the glass, trying to get out, though why anyone would want to was a mystery. The bare blue sky looked impervious to clouds. The ground was hot enough to bake an egg, a project which Anna had successfully tried last weekend.

Newly shorn sheep and moulting hens stood like statues in the coolest shade possible, lest any movement increase their heat. The native animals had undoubtedly found traditional refuges, too. Mr Murray ('Call me Dad,' he told her blithely while his son glared at him) had taken the girls swimming.

The men were doing the things men did in sheds, especially high-roofed cool ones. 'I'm just going down to the shed for a while,' was possibly the most overused phrase in Australia.

She had got used to it. She had not got used to the flies, but the house was well screened, and Deb had shown her that a hat large enough to shadow her face would keep out the bush flies, while a container of rotten eggs mixed with prawn heads, with small openings that flies could enter but not get out of, could be hung from high tree branches where the smell would rise in the heat and lure in the big blowflies before they spoiled a picnic.

She was not used to red-bellied black snakes, brown snakes, copperhead snakes, tiger snakes, or redback spiders, but was confident that a) no two would attack at once, and b) the house was snake-proof, and so were her daughters' boots and new moleskins.

She had learned to cope with the heat, i.e. remove herself from it; to love lamingtons, but never make them, as they were an invariable gift for that inestimable newcomer, Lady Deanna; that pumpkin scones stayed moist for two hours, whereas English scones became cricket balls in ten minutes; to offer a cup of tea, pikelets, biscuits or cake to every caller, or she'd be thought 'stuck up'; and likewise to accept the offerings at every place she visited, from swaggies' camps to the Lanyons' mock-Tudor house and garden.

The ritual made sense in a land where everyone would be hot in summer or frozen-toed in winter, and guests had travelled what would have been regarded as an expedition into a new country in Britain but here was, 'Just down the road, twenty miles past where Shannon's shearing shed burned down in the big fires of '39, take the second track to the right, go through five gates and you can't miss us.'

This was the place where she could be exactly the person she had always preferred: a semi-recluse but with her family around her, as fond of birds as of people, and the lady of the manor, even if the castle was gone. 'Lady Deanna' was enough for Budgie Creek.

She also knew her daughters expected this to be their new family base, no matter what paths their lives might take. She cherished the sandy river, the tree roots that clasped vertical cliff faces, the melodramatic sky, either pure blue or thunderous, with the kind of love she'd felt when she'd first known Sam, a love she knew would become passion, devotion and, above all, understanding.

The marriage services she had witnessed spoke of 'man and wife as one flesh'. She and Sam shared that nightly. The marriage services neglected the more important vow, to share a life. It had never seemed to occur to the church to say that people and land could be one flesh too, that you should find a land you could love and care for it as deeply as for any marriage partner.

She buttered another slice of toast, added jam far more liberally than she ever had before the war, and opened the weekly mail, delivered that morning by the postie with half a pumpkin, because a whole one went bad before you could use it unless your family was enormous, no matter how many roast dinners — with pumpkin — or pumpkin scones you made.

There was *The Land* magazine for Sam; a machinery catalogue; the new David Jones catalogue; a postcard from an old schoolfriend congratulating Deanna on the marriage that gossip must assume had occurred; invitations to a cocktail party, a Friday-to-Monday and a fox hunt from acquaintances who didn't know she was no longer in England and had never hunted; a thicker letter from Mrs Thripps, who forwarded her English mail; and a thin aerogram with a German postmark.

She opened the aerogram first.

> *Dear Mrs Claverton,*
>
> *Thank you for the letter about my son. His name was not Kurt, as you have probably guessed, and nor did we ever live at the address you sent the letter to, which is why I do not sign my name now. I hope you will excuse it.*
>
> *I am glad my son had no regrets. I myself do, perhaps, but try to put them aside. If he had died in a motor accident it would be different, and my whole being would be grief. But he lived as he chose, and for the cause he chose, which was to try to find peace, even though he must pretend to be a true soldier of the Reich to do it.*
>
> *I hope he found a friend in you. I am glad you were there, if not at the end, at least for him to be sure he would not be just another ghost lost in the tragedies of those years.*
>
> *May Gott keep you, and may your life be happy, and know each night you will be in the prayers of one who signs herself, most truly, as*
>
> *A mother*

She sat with it in her hand for a long time. So 'Kurt' *had* been a man who wanted peace, at least with England, and if with

England, possibly other countries too, despite his lies, his — at best — tolerance of disposing of any but perfect Aryans, and presumably his participation in whatever Donnie had endured. She would also pray for the woman who had sent this.

The Duke of Windsor would party his life away. He had no other role he could be trusted with now. But her new life was just beginning. She would pray that Kurt's mother found happiness and fulfilment in the years to come as well.

She found she was smiling as the screen door clanged, followed by the sound of Sam removing his boots.

'You're back early.'

'It's going to bucket down any moment. Anything good in the mail?'

'Mostly catalogues.' She would tell him about the letter later, when her own feelings were clearer. Perhaps not for years, once his own nightmares faded.

'Surely it can't rain today!' She glanced out the window. 'Oh!' The blue sky now looked like it had two black and purple eyes swelling rapidly from the horizon.

Mr Murray's truck roared up the drive. The girls dashed in just as the first clatter of hail sounded on the roof, followed by Mr Murray and Ulysses, who now went wherever Anna went, including school, even if they made him wait, tied up under the coolest of the buildings, till the bell rang.

'Boots off!' said Deanna automatically.

'The sky is green and purple!'

'Grandpa showed us how the ants cover their nests with sticks and leaves before a big rain.'

'The sheep have all gone to the west paddock under the trees — the bush trees, not the big old ones that might get hit by lightning, except some of the rams. Grandpa says rams often aren't very bright.'

Mr Murray grinned at his son as the girls flung open the door of the fridge and investigated the cake tins.

'Can I have a strawberry milkshake?'

'Mum, did you make any scones? You *said* you were going to make scones ...'

'They're in the green tin ...'

'Anna, Ulysses has my sock. Make him give it back!'

'Who ate the last banana?'

'Mum, I forgot to tell you, I need to have a rose costume for *The Nutcracker* by Friday ...'

'Ulysses, bad dog! We don't chew socks!'

'Can we have peach Melba again tonight? There's still some strawberries ...'

Rosa's voice was silenced as the world split open, the noise louder than Deanna could remember, even more monstrous than the sound of the bomb on the village school. The light in the kitchen turned bright white. The clamour changed to what sounded like shrapnel on the roof.

'Look at the hail! It's as big as oranges!'

'Sam, can you make a hailman, like a snowman?'

'I don't know.' Sam grinned. 'I've never tried.'

'Can we make one now?' The hail was already easing, the storm visibly moving down towards the river.

'If you like. I want to take your mother somewhere.'

Deanna stared. 'Now? The ground is ice.'

'It'll melt by the time you've got your boots on.'

'But dinner's in the oven. It's stuffed shoulder of lamb and I haven't done the vegetables.'

'I'll do them,' said Magda, looking at Sam and her mother, curious.

'I'll pod the peas and make the gravy,' said Rosa.

'And I'll make the peach Melba,' said Anna. 'Except I won't stew the peaches — we can have them cold.'

'In other words just peaches and ice cream with strawberries?' asked Deanna.

Anna nodded. No one seemed to object.

'Ulysses is still hiding under the table,' Magda pointed out.

'Poor baby,' said Anna.

'No, he's not. He's just playing "poor dog" so you give him the shank bone, and I want it for the gravy,' Magda objected.

'Maybe he'd like a scone. Who's seen the apricot jam?'

Mr Murray met his son's eyes. 'We'll be fine till you get back. About bloody time too.'

'Now I know why sons move into their own houses,' said Sam.

Mr Murray laughed.

The melting hail was trickling through the tussocks and the sky was a gaudy dust-free blue. Thunder muttered somewhere towards town.

'Does a storm like that happen often?' asked Deanna as Sam took her hand.

'Sometimes every few weeks, sometimes not for years.'

'Where are we going?'

He gestured towards the cleft in the cliffs.

'Why?'

'To show you something. I had a feeling we were building up to a hailstorm. I've been waiting for it.'

We're going to see whatever was in my dream, she thought. She had never mentioned it to him — the man had enough pressure to propose to her already without her informing him that she had dreamed of this land since she was a child, that whatever decision would rule the rest of her life would be made here.

The ground grew rougher, ridges of rock like solidified waves, and then the way was clear, a new stream of melted hail snaking between two cliff faces.

'We won't be washed away in a flash flood, will we?'

He shook his head. 'Not enough rain for that. Anyway, we'd hear it — it sounds like a hundred helicopters. Here, let me give you a hand up.'

The light changed as they walked between the cliffs, green tinged though there was no greenery, just grey and orange rock, except a few clumps of rock orchids high above them. Suddenly Deanna heard something. 'A waterfall?'

He grinned, calmer and more certain than she'd ever seen him. 'Not yet. If we walk a bit further there's a pool where I swim sometimes when I want to be alone.'

'Why alone?'

'Nowadays it's to wash away the blood,' he said simply. 'It works, too. I'm Sam Murray, farmer. The rest has gone. Sometimes, though, it needs a little help to stay away. No, not that way. Turn around here ...'

She gasped. A hole in the rock about three yards above her head spouted a thin stream of water, harder and fiercer than any hose. It arced above them, and caught the afternoon sun, so the whole cliff face and the roofless cavern to one side of it were drenched in rainbow.

She ran towards it, and found herself bathed in colours — green, red, yellow.

She reached for Sam, and he became a rainbow too. She twirled in the thin spray, letting it drench her hair, her dress. Sam laughed and took off his shirt.

'At least one of us has sense,' he said as he started to unbuckle his trousers.

He slid off his boots and socks, trousers then underpants, putting them on a ledge to stay dry. By then she had removed her own clothes, including her new scandalous mauve French knickers. She hesitated. 'I didn't bring my diaphragm.'

'I didn't bring a condom. But I did bring this.' He reached into his shirt pocket where it lay on the rock ledge, brought out a square jeweller's box, and opened it, then bent on one bare knee. 'Lady Deanna Claverton, will you marry me? And say yes quickly because this rock is as sharp as old bones, and if you say no my entire family and half the town will never speak to me again.'

'Yes.'

'No elegant speeches?'

'Not that I can think of.' She stared at the emerald, set in what might be two folded eagle's wings.

He stood and slipped the ring onto her finger as she drew him close and kissed his lips, and then his neck. He kissed her hair, then held her slightly away. 'Unless one of us is going to go home with a sliced back, would you like to try making love in a waterspout?'

She stepped back, leaning against the water-smooth rock, and he lifted her legs about his waist. Her last coherent thought was that this had never been part of her dream. Her dream, before this moment, had just been an early echo of the moment that would change her life. If she ever dreamed it again, she would remember all of this, even in her sleep.

Fifty-Six

Wedding Almonds

You will have the same number of children as the number of almonds the least hungry guest eats.

INGREDIENTS
one cup sugar
half cup water
red food colouring
four cups peeled raw almonds

METHOD
Boil a cup of sugar with half a cup of water till thick and bubbling hard. Divide into two. Add two drops red food colouring into one lot, and then two cups of peeled raw almonds. Stir to combine. Place another two cups in the plain mixture. Stir. Leave for ten minutes, then spread out to dry, turning two or three times till the covering is even. You will have sugary pink almonds and pure white ones.

★★★

It was growing dark by the time they left the cliffs, hand in hand.

'Sam? Why did you wait so long before you proposed? Did you want to make sure I knew what I was getting myself into?'

'I admit I had a few weeks of fear that you'd kiss me kindly, pack your car and drive away. Then I wanted to be sure you were happy here after the adventure had worn away.'

'You're sure now?'

He laughed. 'No. There'll be bushfires, locust plagues, dust storms, clouds of flies that crawl all over you, and maybe a snake that decides to live in the bonnet of your car. You'll wish you were a thousand miles away. But you fit here, just like I do.' He kissed her gently again. 'We'll be happy ninety per cent of the time, which is pretty good going for the human race. Our children will be happy too.'

'Does it bother you their skins will be paler than yours?'

'No. They can choose whatever parts of their heritage they want.'

Something moved uphill ... Sam strode up to have a look just as an eagle spread its wings. Four great flaps and it was airborne, something white and bloodied dangling from its talons.

'Dead lamb,' said Sam.

'I thought you said back in England the eagles don't attack the lambs.'

He shook his head. 'Not live ones. That one would have been dead already or we'd have heard its cry. No sign of its mum either. Maybe it was struck by lightning, if it strayed out here in the open.' He took her hand and smiled at her. 'I'm glad the eagle found it before the goannas.'

'You don't like goannas?'

He shrugged. 'I like them well enough. But eagles ...' He stopped and met her eyes. 'I used to feel like an eagle sometimes, when I flew. You don't see borders from the air. But you can see where overgrazed land is eroding into a river, or too much water has been taken and the river's a green trickle. Maybe the world needs more eagles, who can see what's wrong and help clean up the dead stuff.'

'Back in the hospital, Pete said you'd asked him to tell me you'd been an eagle at the end. I'm so very glad it wasn't then.'

'Me, too.'

They began to walk again. She wondered if teaching the world to have eagle sight might help to finally bring peace to the world. Or would people still refuse to see anything that challenged their world view?

'Do you miss flying?' she asked at last.

'No. The war took that.' He lifted her hand and kissed it. 'But it gave me you, and daughters.'

It was dark when they reached home, Sam leading the way by star- and moonlight. The lamps gleamed; the generator was off. Rosa was stirring the gravy as they came up to the house and opened the door. It still felt strange not to worry about blackout curtains.

The room smelled of roasting lamb with rosemary. Anna was setting the table with the good cutlery and plates, and champagne glasses, with the champagne in an ice bucket.

'Took a lot for granted,' said Sam, glancing at the bottle as he took off his boots.

'Humph. I had your mother wedded and bedded in six months.' The old man's voice was gruff as the girls crowded around, exclaiming about the ring, Deanna's wet hair, and the dress, which thankfully had dried a little on the walk back.

'Welcome home, girl,' Mr Murray added, and for a moment Deanna heard her grandfather's voice. It was almost as if he had provided this for her too.

Fifty-Seven

August 1947

Apple Crumble

Half fill a casserole dish with stewed apple. Mix two cups self-raising flour with half a cup brown sugar and rub in three tablespoons butter. Sprinkle loosely on top of the apple. Bake in a moderate oven till just browning on top: about twenty minutes.

'Mum! I've brought the mail! Rosa's new dress has come from Mrs Goldfarb, and there's this week's newspaper too.' Anna looked at it critically. 'The photo on the front makes you look like you're going to have an elephant, not a baby.'

'Sometimes I feel like an elephant. There's apple teacake in the tin.'

'Good-o.' Anna was quickly adopting Australian phrases too.

Deanna smiled, put her pen down and blotted the last lines of another invitation to the launch of the First Annual Claverton and Goldfarb Fashion Show, written in her most aristocratic handwriting, and put it on the growing pile, hoping to get them all done before the baby's birth.

The more exclusive the school, the more illegible the handwriting. Sydney Society would know just by looking at the envelope — even without the Claverton crest on one corner — that they had aristocracy among them.

Lady Deanna Claverton and Esther von Goldfarb request the pleasure of your attendance ...

Uncle Jasper had called in favours from Government House. The cream of New South Wales Society — and some of the wealthy 'plain milk' too — would receive their embossed invitations in four months' time.

The event should be the social and fashion highlight of the year and discussed for decades.

Rosa had even been allowed to cut out one of the patterns, and to contribute a design of beads to a dress so as to give sufficient weight to its fabric to hold pockets and hem in place.

These garments had also been made of antique material of less historic value — including Deanna's grandfather's tweed suits, now delicately re-tailored into tweed jackets over lightly pleated skirts; and her mother's valuable, if to Deanna's eye tasteless, finery, including her cloak of alternating white and black–striped cow hide that made it look like zebra skin. The cloak would now be the skirt of a dress topped with plain black silk and worn with pearls. It would be the most exquisite collection Sydney had seen in decades.

The first evening was by invitation only, each garment never to be duplicated — a useful sales technique, but also not a choice, as there were no similar materials.

By then 'The Bulge', as Sam called it, would be in her arms, and she would be able to fit into the vaguely medieval garment created for the event, cloaked front and back, disguising any post-baby tummy, the narrow underskirt and jersey sleeves showing off her slimness, the gold embroidery subtly reminding the buyers that, hundreds of years ago, Deanna Claverton's ancestor had an intimate encounter with royalty's haemorrhoids.

Her own more recent encounters with a man who had been king had never been mentioned, not from secrecy, but simply because it was irrelevant to their lives. Maybe, in decades to come, sitting with well-iced homemade lemon cordial on the veranda, someone would say, 'Do you remember when ...?'

Today and tomorrow had absorbed those fading days of war and tragedy. Magda was driving her friend Thomas back for the weekend. Thomas was not her boyfriend, because Magda hadn't yet noticed he adored her, but Deanna suspected that one day she would look up from her Descartes and find the world held more than philosophy.

Rosa and Joshua Goldfarb would occupy the back seat. They were most definitely a couple and had been from a month after Rosa had begun to work full-time at Claverton and Goldfarb.

Joshua's parents had perished, not in the concentration camps but the refugee camps that followed, saved by his aunt and uncle sponsoring him and the Australian Government's decision to allow in a certain number of single skilled male refugees. Married refugees, and their families, were still forbidden entry.

Joshua had trained as a tailor and was now training further as a designer. Deanna wasn't sure what his parents would have made of Rosa, technically Jewish but brought up in a Christian household. Joshua's aunt and uncle, however, were delighted. Rosa boarded with them in Sydney and attended synagogue with them and was learning the laws of Jewish Reform housekeeping.

Magda had declared her complete lack of interest in religion. Anna had finally taken study seriously and decided to do veterinary science, but unless it had four legs, feathers, scales or fur she was currently not interested either. She was excited about the birth of a new brother or sister, though Deanna was not sure if her interest was more scientific than sisterly. She certainly intended to be present at the birth, and Deanna doubted any matron could prevent her.

Deanna glanced at the rest of the mail: a machinery catalogue; a postcard from an old schoolfriend, with a belated congratulations on her wedding — yet another cut-glass vase wedding gift would undoubtedly arrive in time; a thick letter in Mrs Thripps' copperplate, and the monthly letter from Uncle Jasper.

She did not know if he wrote from affection, or a belief that one day she might choose to Be Of Use to British or Australian intelligence. These days, however, the news of his family and Britain were truthful, or so she assumed.

She skimmed it — Britain held little interest now, as did any further work in whispers. She stopped suddenly, laughing, at the final paragraph.

'His Majesty agreed that as a wedding gift and thanks for services, he will restore the title to your present family in the next King's honour's list ...'

'What's so funny?' Anna plonked herself down beside her, a hunk of cake in hand, Ulysses at her feet, watching for crumbs. 'I really have found the answer to world peace, Mum!' she added, not waiting for a reply.

Deanna put the letter down. This was not the time to tell the girls they would be 'Honourables' or even 'Ladies', depending on which title 'Chummy' meant. 'Excellent. What is it?'

'It can be called Anna's Law,' announced Anna. 'No one can own anything that has been gained by violence.'

Deanna considered it. 'Seems fair. How about you go and tell your father? He's mending the tractor.' Eagle Mountain had been well-stocked with machinery at the beginning of the war but finding parts to keep the machinery going even now the war was over was a challenge.

Would Sam be a duke, or viscount? She smothered a grin. He'd ignore it either way, and just have to endure the town's fuss. It would cause even more publicity if she and Sam were to refuse it.

'Okay!' Anna bounced towards the door.

'Okay is an Americanism, and bad manners.'

Anna grinned at her. 'Okay! I want to see Lochinvar's sore hoof, too. Bulls are badly designed: all that weight on just four thin legs. Come on, Ulysses!'

She and the dog galloped out, leaving Anna's schoolbag, school blazer and school shoes on the floor by the door.

Deanna watched her go, a happy, strong, fulfilled young woman, truly as amazing as Mrs Thripps had named her. Deanna could hear her yell 'Dad!' as she bounded up the path to the machinery shed, where the soon-to-be duke or viscount would undoubtedly praise the new Anna's Law and tactfully ask how it might be enforced and by whom, as well as when the law would be held to have started.

Sam's Aboriginal, Irish, Welsh and Scottish ancestors had all been robbed of most of their estates. The Claverton ancestor of 1066 had almost certainly robbed someone of his estate.

Which was not to say it wasn't a good law; it was the best, in fact, that Deanna had heard. It would just need a band of impartial Martians, perhaps, to implement it.

She made a cup of tea before sitting down on the sofa with her legs up to enjoy the letter from Mrs Thripps. Good, strong tea, and the apple cake was Mrs Purdon's mother's recipe. Another smaller envelope fell out, but Deanna read Mrs Thripps' missive first.

> *Dear Lady Dee,*
> *I hopes this finds you and your good husband and daughters as well as it leaves me and my Arnold. Well, there's been a right*

to-do and no mistake. Another of the castle turrets fell down and squashed the butcher's van but Mr Filmer weren't in it and no one knows who to blame, either the Army or His New Grace or the fellow he sold it to, but it's barricaded off now so no one can get in the castle grounds except for those who has always gone round the back, so to speak, for a fine night's poaching.

A fellow from the ministry knocked on the door to show me the design of the new houses for up the hills. All the same they is except some have two windows on one side, and others have two windows on the other. Quite nice they looked, but this house is bigger and far finer than any of them so Arnold and I will be sitting pretty. 'I can't help you, my good man,' I told the fellow, 'as I am only caretaker-in-residence for Lady Deanna, so you have to write to her,' but I don't think he'll get round to it; he just wanted to say he'd met a Lady and scrounge a cup of tea. Well, he didn't get tea from me.

This came for you, and I thought I better send it airmail not sea mail. Give my love to Anna and Rosa and Magda, and tell them I miss their laughter and I'm sorry not to answer their letters more regular but I don't write as quick as them, and tell Anna I love her photos of kangaroos and them emus! I doubt you could fit one of them in an oven though and I'd bet good money that they are as tough as shoe leather. Give me a good young Indian game rooster for flavour and tenderness any day.

My love to you and Sam. Arnold would send his love too but men don't do that much, do they, dearie?

I remain

Yours most sincerely,

Eleanor Thripps, Mrs

Deanna smiled. She had never known Mrs Thripps' first name till they had begun corresponding.

Sam had scrounged secondhand Kodak Brownies for the girls to share, as anything new was still almost impossible to find. The local chemist developed their snaps of the land they were discovering: their friends at school and university and work; Grandpa Sam; Big Cousin Sam, who was six, and Little Cousin Sam who was eighteen, but shorter than his uncle; Cousins Andy Three and Four, and the war memorial with the names of Andy 'One' and 'Two' Murray. There were also photos of a multitude of other cousins, aunts, aunties, uncles, dogs; horses; the river; the platypus who objected to swimming lessons; the brown snake, which had not bitten them; the caged cockatoo who had; the damper Sam had shown them how to make; the hundred and twenty-seven bottles of peach chutney made for the Friday street stall by the local CWA; and the arches of Sydney University, where Magda seemed to have found a home that fulfilled her in quite different ways from her home here.

Deanna had taped some to the fridge and many to the kitchen door, but rarely looked at them, for they were moments past. Tomorrow's would be richer still.

She looked more closely at the enclosed letter, a drab post-war envelope, postmarked from Argyll in Scotland. Who could be writing to her from there?

Miss Jennifer McDonald
Cliff House
ARGYLL
PA34
United Kingdom
14 June 1947

Dear Lady Deanna,
Please excuse my writing to you without introduction. I am Jennifer McDonald, President of the Argyll Ornithological

Society. I am writing to inform you one of our members has spotted a female golden eagle nesting on a local cliff with the leg band you were kind enough to report to the Royal Ornithological Society.

The nest in question has been observed for forty-seven years by members of our society: a sturdy construction of twigs and branches, and well-lined with moss and fur, though it was briefly abandoned four years ago. You may be interested to know that the banded female has most unusually successfully reared two juveniles this year, which have been spotted flying independently on a local grouse moor.

Luckily the land in question is owned by a Mr Roberts, one of our members, who values eagles above grouse.

You would be most welcome to attend one of our monthly meetings. We can guarantee good Highland hospitality. Mr Roberts would be delighted to show you the nesting site from the hide he has built nearby.

Yours faithfully,
Miss Jennifer McDonald,
President, Argyll Ornithological Society

She put the letter down, tears cold on her face again. She cried easily these days, and not just from pregnancy hormones. So many tears were due.

'Dee, love, what's wrong?' Sam strode into the kitchen without even taking off his boots, leaving crescents of manure on the floorboards.

'I'm happy.' Definitely not the time to tell him about the title. She waved the letter at him. Eagles mated for life, but it seemed that, like some humans, they seized the chance for a new life too. 'There are two new golden eagles in the world, up in Scotland.' And may the Cold War never touch them, or us, she thought.

An impossible hope, she knew, as Sam's arms surrounded her with the scent of fresh sweat, machine oil and Sam, unless Martians arrived to put Anna's Law in place. Like her grandfather, she could not shut her eyes and pretend that prejudice and greed would not spark war again. Perhaps humanity could never live in harmony, unless faced with a bushfire they must fight together to survive.

There was no eternal safety, not for humans or for eagles, even now that her family was free of the world of whispers. But like the young female she had tended all those years before, Deanna Claverton had found a solid cliff on which to build her nest.

Author's Note

This book is fiction, except where it isn't.

Despite the many romantic stories to the contrary, King Edward VIII did not abdicate for love. He was tricked by his government and his own family, who realised he was incapable of the duties of a king.

The Duke of Windsor did not give up hope, however. Letters retrieved after the war show that he was in communication with Hitler, and even urged worse degrees of The Blitz to soften Britain up so it would surrender. Hitler certainly hoped the duke would return and take the throne. Operation Willi, to convince him to do so, was begun when the duke and duchess were in Portugal, but they were transported by the Allies to neutral Spain before they could be caught and 'persuaded'.

This is usually where accounts of Operation Willi end. Operation Willi continued, however, with a plan for the duke to take a cruise from the Bahamas on his Swedish friend's yacht, where he could be transferred to a German vessel and returned to England. American intelligence discovered the plot, and the yachting expedition didn't happen.

There is no doubt the duke admired Hitler, was strongly antisemitic, admired the policy of exterminating any 'defectives' and hoped for an alliance between Britain and Germany. It was no secret that he wished to regain the throne. Hitler appears to have assumed that the Duke of Windsor would seize any opportunity to do so, including as a puppet king under German rule. There is no evidence that this was the case. Hitler was certainly capable of fooling himself — the Russian campaign is one example of this. The duke was fascist, and admired Hitler and Germany, but he also seemed loyal to his country and his family, though given he urged even more deadly bombing of Britain, and wanted the return to the British throne that Hitler promised him, it's impossible to say what else he would have regarded as the best actions for a loyal man to take.

There is, however, evidence that telegrams, letters, photos and other material involving the duke, Hitler and other prominent Nazis were seized in daring raids in advance of Germany's occupation and that much more information than eventually came to light in the infamous Marburg Files was destroyed or has been kept top secret. I'd give both readings of the matter equal probability. 'No conclusive evidence' means that neither his innocence nor his guilt can be proved. In this book, unlike many of my others, I do not have sufficient proof to say the scenario I described is likely. For this, I owe him and his family an apology for being carried away by a 'what if' scenario.

Others

'Uncle Jasper', his work, his grass snake and his associates are based on fact, as are Mrs Purdon, Mrs Goldfarb, The Women's Institute, Mr Vonderfleet, Doris at the exchange, the Mosquitoes, the likely result of any bombing of civilians, the Intelligence belief that Indigenous Australians would fight for the Japanese instead of staunchly and courageously against the would-be invaders, Queen Elizabeth (later The Queen Mother) and her encounter with floating tanks, and the luxury aircraft flight which brought the Clavertons to Australia, though as far as I can tell no more flights were made by that company between Britain and Australia. Background historical events are accurate. I would also endorse Magda and Anna's solution to preventing warmongers like Hitler from invading other countries. We need to use history to find the turning point, sometimes long before the guns begin. We also need those trained in conflict resolution. Going 'bang' is simpler, but has rarely been effective in the long term.

I have kept the location of Castle Claverton deliberately vague.

The Men Who Saved Britain

Winston Churchill stated in August 1940: 'Never in the field of human conflict was so much owed by so many to so few', paying tribute to the airmen who saved Britain at its most vulnerable. The public and film assumption that most of those pilots and aircrew were British, however, is not accurate. A British pilot or crew early in the war was rare. Britain simply did not have enough pilots or crew or ground staff with sufficient experience. They looted the colonies of men and aircraft in 1939 and 1940, thus leaving Australia almost undefendable against Japanese attack, forced to accept eighteen-year-olds, like my father, with almost no training or weapons to fight the Japanese advance in New Guinea. Many Danes, Swedes, Americans and a large number of Poles who had escaped invaded Poland also volunteered as pilots and crew. Some crews were mixed, others of one nationality.

The Pathfinders and Mosquitoes

The crews of the Pathfinders were both heroic and brilliant. Surveys of bombing photographs and other sources in 1941 showed that fewer than one in ten bombs fell within five miles of their targets. The Pathfinders were elite, specially trained and experienced crews who flew ahead and marked the targets with flares and special marker bombs.

The Mosquito was, at that time, the fastest craft in the world. The wings of the craft were made of laminated lengths of various types of wood, with inbuilt fire extinguishers that would have allowed Sam to fly with the plane partially burning for so long.

Racial Discrimination in this Book

In the 1940s, Indigenous living conditions and laws varied from state to state, but were uniformly appalling. It would take till the 1970s for an openly Indigenous man, Charles Perkins, to become a public servant. Sam's reluctance to reveal his background may seem excessive now, and his lack of knowledge or even curiosity about his heritage a major failing, but in the 1940s his and his sister's position was eminently reasonable, especially as his Indigenous grandfather was not a local of Budgie Creek, and so would not have known the local language and history.

War

Humanity spends between a third and forty-five per cent of its resources on war or preparing for it. With the global climate crisis we have the equivalent of a planet-wide bushfire. If we work together we can survive it. If we ignore it, we may not.

Acknowledgements

Dear Reader,

If you've read *The Sea Captain's Wife* or *Becoming Mrs Mulberry*, you can skip this bit. Those who gave so much to those books have given even more to this one, too.

First, always, to Lisa Berryman, who is part of the creation of every book I write, from its conception to colour shades of the cover: I would need the entire book to thank you. Julia Knapman now oversees my books for adults, and it's a wonder and a joy to work with her.

Kate O'Donnell and Lisa scrutinise every word, as good editors do. Brilliant editors are captured by the story. I am blessed with two editors who freely admit their emotions as they read, and then re-read, for the sheer pleasure of the book, before lifting their metaphorically red pens to tell me where I'm wrong.

Brady Meyers wrangled a messy ms with many typos into shape; Pam Dunne not just proofread the ms superbly, but once again saved me from a major error. My dyslexia sometimes means I 'see' only the first and last letters of a word, and fill in the rest by context. This means I can speed read, and 999,999 times out of 1,000,000 get the words correct. In this book, and the last, an important word was misread, and only Pam picked it up.

Cover designer, Louisa Maggio, created a cover we all fell in love with as soon as we saw it. Gemma Fahey used it to create the best email banner possible. The marketing team at HarperCollins also used it for their superb banners for social media.

I'd also like to thank all the staff at Mossvale responsible for distributing my books: they do a wonderful job, sending me copies by post instead of the usual courier, as our area doesn't have a reliable courier service. I am grateful every time I open a package from them. Thank you to all bookshop staff and librarians who display my book covers outwards, or post them as 'book of the month' or 'recommended read'. It's still a thrill to find my books promoted in a catalogue or when a friend takes a photo in a shop or library and says, 'Look what I found!'

It's also a joy to hear from readers, especially those who say, 'I usually don't read much but couldn't stop' or who ask for special dedications for family or friends. Once writers send books out into the world we rarely know who reads them, and if they enjoyed the book or left it to the silverfish.

Profound thanks go to Peter Marshall, friend, neighbour and mentor, who not only showed me how to blow up a steamship in *The Sea Captain's Wife* (no steamships were harmed in the writing of the book) and stabilise my road when it turned to quicksand in the flood, but gave me sources for the seldom-acknowledged fact that the air crews who saved Britain in the desperate early war years rarely had even one British crew member, and even fewer English pilots, but were Poles, Danes, Canadians, Americans — even though the USA was neutral at that stage — and many, many Australians, one of whom I knew, and who told me his stories. The 'valiant young British pilot' myth may have been essential for morale, to get British crew and pilots trained as speedily as possible, but it is long past time for the books and movies to not perpetuate the myth.

Peter is also familiar with the unarmed plywood 'Mosquitoes', piloted with such courage and brilliant flying. The desperation that led to the deployment of those flimsy craft also could not be revealed back then. The heroes who so brilliantly flew them, and died in them, deserve recognition now.

The memoirs of British Prime Minister Stanley Baldwin first led me to the beloved myth that the man who would become the Duke of Windsor resigned to 'be with the woman I love' instead of accidentally signing his throne and property away in the belief that he would be made King Regent. Other sources include the East German archives, accessible when the Berlin Wall came down. British authorities had made valiant efforts that cost men their lives to eradicate all incriminating letters written by the Duke of Windsor to Adolf Hitler, but East Berlin was not under their control, nor were the US newspapers and magazines who interviewed the duke.

'No book is an island' to paraphrase John Donne, and nor is this one. It comes from a thousand sources, and from much loved family, friends and colleagues.